The Beauty Trap

Here, at last, is the sensational story of the modeling business—the beautiful faces, the fabulous bodies, and how they are used by their agents, their clients, and their lovers.

Theirs are the faces you see on magazine covers and in TV commercials. In townhouses, discotheques, and boutiques ...through career "arrangements," love affairs, marriages, and divorces...their stories make blistering, nonstop reading.

Jeanne Rejaunier knows it all. A beautiful and successful model herself, she exposes the glamorous world of modeling for what it really is—a cynical business.

THE BEAUTY TRAP

was originally published by Trident Press.

THE
BEAUTY
TRAP

JEANNE REJAUNIER

A POCKET BOOK EDITION published by
Simon & Schuster of Canada, Ltd. • Richmond Hill, Ontario, Canada
Registered User of the Trademark

THE BEAUTY TRAP

Trident edition published July, 1969

A *Pocket Book* edition
1st printing........November, 1969
2nd printing.......January, 1970

Standard Book Number: 671—78026—3.
Library of Congress Catalog Card Number: 69—15568.
Copyright, ©, 1969, by Jeanne Rejaunier. All rights reserved.

Printed in Canada

To my parents
Harriet and Edward Rejaunier

Part

$\sim\!\sim\!\sim\!\sim\!\sim\!\sim$

One

Chapter 1

Miss Eve Petroangeli
191 Carnation Avenue
Floral Park, Long Island
New York 11001

Dear Eve,

We have received your snapshots and inquiry concerning a career in modeling. It is the policy of the Ryan-Davy Agency to hold interviews with prospective new material on Mondays and Tuesdays between three and six P.M. If you will phone us for an appointment, we will know when to expect you. Looking forward to meeting you soon, we are,

> Sincerely,
> Charlene Davy and
> Rex Ryan

Eve Petroangeli's hands trembled as she read the letter. "Thank you," she whispered. "Thank you, St. Jude."

"Was that the mailman, honey?" her mother called from the kitchen.

"Mom, I got it! I got it!"

Maria Petroangeli dropped the load of dirty clothes she was about to place in the washing machine and reached toward her daughter. "Show me!"

"They want to see me."

"Come in the living room. I left my glasses there. Oh, Evie!" Her breath coming in rapid gasps, bosom heaving, Mrs. Petroangeli finished reading and burst into tears.

"Mom, it's nothing to cry about."

"I can't help it. I'm just so overcome—it's everything I could have dreamed for you coming true."

"My novena to St. Jude worked."

"Honey, I told you, ever since you lost all the weight, there's no one can beat you in looks. Oh, Nonna and Uncle Nappi will be thrilled!"

Eve's eyes traveled to the worn furniture of the living room. She wished her mother hadn't mentioned her grandmother and uncle. They both worked so hard, and what had they ever had in life? Nothing but dullness and drabness— just like her mother and father. It made her feel guilty to think her family was not better off financially, guilty she wanted more out of life than they had given her.

Her mother wiped her eyes as a nostalgic smile came over her.

"I wanted to be a model when I was your age . . . or a movie star."

"Why didn't you do it, Mom?"

"I married your father."

"What do you think he'll have to say about this?"

Mrs. Petroangeli hesitated. "Let me talk to him, Evie. I can handle him."

"Oh, Mom, I just want everything to work out."

"We'll see it does. It *has* to." The tears flowed once more and her mother wiped them with the back of her hand. "You're growing up, Evie. My little girl is growing up, and you're all we have."

"Mom. . . ."

Eve wished she could express the mingled feelings she had seeing her mother's head and arms resting on the crocheted doilies of the old wing chair that had needed to be recovered for so long now. Her mother was a young woman, not yet forty, but she looked so tired. It was as though the life had gone out of her, or been driven out by the humdrum of living in Floral Park, married to a grocer.

"Mom. . . ."

"Never mind, honey, I'll handle your father. Everything will work out. I want you to have everything I didn't have. Go call the agency now and make an appointment. This is a Monday. You can go right from school. You look adorable today. Perfect for modeling. Go."

She rose, and while Eve went to the phone, began straightening up the room.

"They weren't in yet, Mom," Eve said, returning. "The answering service said to call back after ten. I guess I better get to school and call from there."

"Here, Evie, let me give you some money for the city." Mrs. Petroangeli reached into her everyday black purse, the one with the cracked leather Eve had seen her use for the past ten years. "Is five dollars enough?"

"Sure, Mom. Gosh, thanks—"

"Hurry, honey; you'll be late. Good luck, and God bless you."

"Mom, you're an angel, and I love you." Eve kissed her mother goodbye and left for school.

* * *

When Carrie Richards awoke, the sun was coming in through a crack under the drawn shades. She rubbed her eyes, turned, curled up, and drew the sheet over her head. But the sound of a buzzer was ringing in her ears. With a start, Carrie popped up to a sitting position. Had she overslept?

The buzzing persisted. Her eyes traveled to the alarm clock. No, it was only seven. She hadn't overslept. But someone was at the front door.

"Who is it?" she called, pulling on a robe as she hurried toward the door.

"Western Union."

She opened the door a crack, leaving the chain on. You couldn't be too careful in New York City, particularly when it was your first week in town.

"Caroline Richards?"

"Yes."

"Telegram."

Carrie released the chain and opened the door.

BEST OF LUCK ON NEW CAREER STOP KNOW PLANS ARE FOR THE BEST STOP KEEP ME POSTED LOVE AND BLESSINGS
MOTHER

5

How sweet of Mother to send the wire. Yes, her new life was beginning and everything was happening so fast she almost couldn't believe it.

From outside the shutters she heard the rumble of trucks, the muted taxi horns of New York City—her adopted home from now on. Her apartment, small and bare as it was, seemed a haven. A whole new life lay just ahead. Less than a week in town, and already she was booked, starting tomorrow, for three whole days on a television commercial for a national product. How lucky could you get?

If only Father had lived to see her graduate from college and begin her own life. Her sisters had both married by the time they were twenty-one, but Father would have been proud to see her strike out on her own and start a promising career. He'd always said she had what it took to be somebody in life.

There were a million things to do today. For the hundredth time, she reread her list: "Agency at 10—take along new contact sheets. J. Walter Thompson at 11. Buy book with acetate pages. See more photogs for new test shots; see about blow-ups. Buy shoes. Write Mother." She knew the list by heart. She set it down, and then once again, as she'd done so many times over the weekend, picked up the manila envelope that lay by her bedside.

Was that really hers, the face in the photos—that compelling beauty with the windblown good looks, sultry in one shot, pixyish in another? She hadn't known she could look that way—so interesting and arresting . . . and, yes, exciting and sexy.

Carrie let her bathrobe drop and studied herself in the mirror. She had always hated her mouth and thought her lips too full. She'd thought of her figure as too lean and bordering on the boyish. Now these were precisely the qualities everyone was praising her for.

Once again her eyes returned to the new photographs. She guessed they were right, that the Ryan-Davy Agency and the Zest soap people knew what they were talking about, that she did belong in modeling.

Yes, she was beautiful, and beauty was the key, the key that would open doors and make the new life ahead for her exciting and worthwhile. She moved into the bathroom, started the tub running, and smiled at herself in the mirror. "Carrie Richards," she told her naked reflection, "your life is just beginning."

* * *

"Room service? This is Miss Haynes speaking from 1606. Will you send me up some breakfast, please?" Dolores Haynes dragged deeply and thoughtfully on her mentholated filter-tip cigarette. "Bacon and eggs, toast, coffee, orange juice. I hope that won't take too long; my time is very precious."

She put the phone down, and lazily inspected the décor of her room—the violin-shaped sconces and the gilt-framed Renoir reproductions, the smoked mirrors that she'd love to have on the walls of her own home.

She'd been wise to check into the Sherry-Netherland; it would provide her with the perfect address in order to create the right impression while starting her modeling career. But within a couple of days she'd either have to find other quarters, or a guy to pick up the tab.

Her image greeted her in the bathroom mirror. Lovely. There was no one who looked like her, had her quality and mystique, her particular beauty. She smiled.

Her unique face would propel her wherever she chose in life. Yes, her face was unsurpassingly beautiful.

But that new herbal masque would provide just the lift it needed this morning; it was never too early to think in terms of preserving one's beauty. She smoothed on the pinkish paste, being careful to treat the skin with delicate strokes. Then she slipped her nightgown off her shoulders to contemplate her naked breasts in the mirror, and massaged them gently.

She went to the phone once more. "Philippe and Jean-Claude of the Rue de la Paix? This is Miss Haynes speaking. Miss *Dolores* Haynes. I'm calling from the Sherry-Netherland. I'm just in from the Coast, and I'd like to make an appointment for a shampoo and set this morning. Well, try to squeeze me in, won't you, darling, because it's *vitally* important."

The air conditioner hummed softly in the window. Outside, Dolores could see the Plaza fountain splashing and watch the buses moving along Fifth Avenue. Once more she picked up the telephone. "What happened to my call to the Ryan-Davy Agency?" she demanded of the operator.

"All right, well, keep trying, and in the meantime get me the cleaning establishment, please." She lit a fresh cigarette.

"Hello, this is Miss Haynes in 1606. Will you send my cleaning to my quarters immediately. . . . What? What do you mean, it isn't ready? I have business conferences scheduled, and this is urgent. I only plan to be at this hotel a short time, and since I have important business to conduct, I can't afford to be inconvenienced. . . . Yes. Yes, I will wait. But kindly make it clear to the manager that my time *is* precious."

Absently she picked up a mirror and regarded her image. Damn! the stupid clerk had made her frown, and the masque had cracked in two spots on her forehead.

"Hello," she said sharply as a voice came over the phone. "I wonder if you have any idea whom you're talking to? This is *Dolores Haynes*. . . . That dress is absolutely essential to my business affairs, and I must have it. . . ."

Impatiently Dolores crushed her cigarette in the ashtray next to the phone. Just then there was a knock at the door.

"Who is it?"

"Room service."

"Just a minute, room service. Goddamn it, I want that dress up here within the hour or this hotel comes up against the biggest lawsuit anybody ever heard of." She slammed the receiver down angrily.

Damn room service for being early! Hurriedly, she returned to the bathroom and washed the herbal masque away. Then, under her nightgown, she donned a black lace bra she'd gotten at Juel Parke in Beverly Hills for $85. Every time she put it on she thought with a shudder of the greasy old octopus who'd bought it for her. The damned bra hurt, but it pushed her breasts up into two neat mounds, exposing an expanse of cleavage. You had to suffer to be sexy.

She gave herself a final approving glance in the mirror, noting with satisfaction that the outline of her legs and pudenda

8

was clearly observable underneath the lace of the negligee and strode toward the door.

The white-coated waiter snapped to attention beside his cart. "Good morning," he said.

Dolores leaned against the doorjamb, and in her most carefully practiced, provocative tones, said, "Won't you come in?"

* * *

Autumn, winter, spring, or summer, Charlene Davy's two salukis, Warren and Kurt, had the habit of stopping at every perpendicular along the route down Madison Avenue from Charlene's apartment on 62nd near Fifth to the Ryan-Davy office in the fifties between Park and Lex. Charlene and the two dogs attracted their usual stares this morning, Charlene in chartreuse, magenta, and purples, long Isadora Duncan scarves blowing a trail several feet behind her, the dogs, on smart matching lizard-skin leashes, regally marching at her side.

Unseasonably hot weather gave promise of another sizzling New York summer, but the temperature wouldn't dissuade the yearly crop of new young beauties from knocking on the doors of Ryan-Davy, leading agency for television commercials in town.

It was beginning again now: all the girls were graduating and swarming to the city, ready to begin their descent upon the Madison Avenue advertising world. By mid-June the Migration would be nearly complete. How eager the young ones always were in their search for success, fame, riches —the same things Charlene herself had long ago fought so hard for.

The dogs eyed another fire hydrant.

"That's enough pissing for one morning," Charlene reprimanded, pulling them from their target in hopes of making the traffic signal.

"Heel, you bastards," she commanded, but the dogs lunged ahead, tugging their mistress faster than she could walk. Just as they stepped off the curb, a taxi screeched around the corner, missing them by inches.

"What're ya tryin' ta do, get yerself killed, lady?" the cabbie yelled.

"Why don't you look where you're going, you bloody idiot!"

"Old dames like you oughta be kept off the streets!" The driver made an obscene gesture before his cab was carried along on the stream of traffic.

Such rudeness! But the city was full of crude people. Charlene would be glad to reach the safety of the office, where she could soothe her nerves with a medicinal snort from one of the bottles in her filing cabinet.

She raised her head haughtily. "Heel, you two," she ordered. "Heel!"

Chapter 2

The dogs' nails clicked on the hall floor. The two animals waited while Charlene unlocked the door to the outer office of Ryan-Davy. Then they followed their mistress into her inner sanctum.

The silence was oppressive this morning. No calls yet. Most of the Madison Avenue people didn't start business with talent agencies till after ten, but Charlene always liked to be in the office early.

Behind her large oak desk stood the filing cabinet. Her eyes went to the liquor drawer. She certainly needed something this morning, after that terrible scene with the cabdriver. A quick nip brought relief.

The sun was blazing through the window. Charlene switched on the electric lights (she'd had the building's fluorescent fixtures removed and replaced by specially designed soft-hued lighting that showed her off at her best); then she closed the blind, so that the rays wouldn't shine on her unflatteringly. Later on, when the sun was in a better position, she would open the blind again.

Her gaze wandered to the wall opposite her desk where ten impressive photographic studies of herself, taken some forty-odd years ago, hung. During the twenties and thirties she'd been one of the great beauties of New York, and the photos attested to it: limpid, expressive eyes (she'd often been told she had the eyes of an Abyssinian cat), straight nose, softly marcelled hair framing a perfect oval face. Her favorite was a full view in which the light from a string of pearls (given her by a French marquis) picked up the light in her eyes and gave her face an ephemeral softness.

*   *   *

The phone rang, and the new week was inaugurated.

"Come off it, Chuck, for Guild minimum you're not getting our Ryan-Davy people to advertise girdles by jumping on a trampoline in a lion's cage," Charlene's husky voice boomed. "In the first place, you know very well bras, girdles—any kind of lingerie—means *double scale* automatically. In the second place, you know you'd have to give stunt pay if any of our girls were crazy enough to do a thing like you're asking. I don't care how tame the fool lions are."

She heard the elevator doors part, and there was a sound in the outer office. The dogs' ears pricked up.

"Charlene?"

Shuffling of feet brought a feminine voice closer. "I'm early." The tones were liquid and soft, and the words were spoken in the faint almost-drawl of someone who had originally come from the South. "I'm supposed to be here at ten."

"Oh, Carrie. Carrie, honey, hello."

Caroline Richards stood in full view, her well-proportioned body framed in the doorway. Her expressive, softly molded face was set off by a long, silky mane of honey and amber; hazel eyes flecked with jade reflected a high degree of intelligence. So accustomed had Charlene become to the hundreds of New York models who all looked as if they had been manufactured from one mold she'd almost forgotten the effect singularity such as Carrie Richards' natural beauty caused.

Off guard for an instant, she envied Carrie's youth, and her eyes flicked to her own pictures on the wall. Then she

11

caught herself and looked away. "These agency people," she mumbled, shifting a pile of papers in an effort to look busy.

"Did I come at a bad time?"

"Not at all, luv, come right in. You'll have to get used to my drivel. I'm always sounding off about something or other."

"I have my tests to show you."

Charlene gave the photos a quick glance. "Well, I told you the minute I set eyes on you you'd go places in this business! I knew you'd photograph as sensational as you look."

She got out a magnifying glass and red marker pencil and began to examine the photos closely.

A moment later Rex Ryan arrived and called a cheery good morning. "Hi, everybody—Charlene, Carrie, dogs; hello, world." He saluted. His tall figure was dressed casually this morning in tight beige linen pants belled at the bottoms, and an expensive Nile green batiste shirt from the latest *nouvelle rage* homosexual tailor. His head, topped by long artificially colored bronze hair, spilling on his forehead and down his neck, reached nearly to the top of the doorframe. Rex's Italian sandal-clad feet struck a languid pose.

"I know Carrie's pictures are going to be simply something *extra*," he said. Then, after beaming for a moment, he strode to the desk to peer over Charlene's shoulder.

Rex Ryan himself had once tried to make it as an actor, but had never gotten much beyond walk-ons and bit parts. Then, eight years ago, Charlene, a lifelong friend of his late mother, had helped him snowball his modest inheritance into the Ryan-Davy Agency. Rex was thirty-four now, and a success. Facially provocative, with a sensual mouth and slack jaw, Rex had nostrils which quivered whenever they picked up the scent of an attractive male model; nevertheless, he applied himself with sincere interest to developing the agency's female as well as its male talent.

"Carrie's doing just great; I knew she would," Charlene said. "A week in town—no composite yet—and already she's the new Zest soap girl and everyone in the business wants to see her." She turned to Carrie. "We're going to get you out all over this city in the next two weeks, honey. So be ready for it."

"What did I tell you?" Rex exclaimed. "These photos are *something else*, Carrie!" He sat down in one of Charlene's wicker chairs and took the contact sheets one by one from the desk. "These pictures are the bitchinest, honey. You're going to be around for years and make this agency a million dollars!"

The phone rang, and Charlene picked it up. "Hi, Valerie darling. . . . Rex? Hold, honey, will you? I'll see if he's come in." She pressed a button. "Rex, it's Valerie du Charme."

Rex made a face. "At this hour of the morning?"

Charlene took the phone off hold. "He's not in yet, luv. Sorry."

"How are you getting along in New York?" Rex asked Carrie.

"Just wonderful, I love it."

"Did you manage to keep busy over the weekend?"

"Oh, yes. I did all kinds of things—went to the Bronx Zoo—"

"How divinely campy!" Rex exclaimed.

"You have brave friends," Charlene observed. "The zoo!"

"I went alone."

"Why, I should think," Rex said, "that just having graduated from—where was it?"

"Sarah Lawrence."

"Yes, Sarah Lawrence. I used to know a teacher up there, in the art department. He was only there for a year, and they asked him to leave. He was too *outré* for them. . . . Hmmmmmm, yes, well, I should think that would have given you lots of New York contacts and friends—

"You're from Virginia. That's what you said, isn't it? How long has your family lived there?"

"Two hundred years."

Charlene roared. "Don't tell me that makes you a D.A.R.? Oh, God, not that!"

"No," Carrie said, smiling reassurance. "Since we're Quakers, my ancestors never fought in the Revolution."

"You're a *Quaker?*" Rex said, his mouth hanging slack. "How simply uniquely marvelous. I've always wanted to meet a Quaker. They don't turn up much in this business." Hand on hip, cocking his head, he studied Carrie closely. Then, with his arm gesticulating broadly, he said, "I knew there was *something* different about you. Still, you're hardly what I'd have expected a Quaker to be."

13

The phone rang again, and Charlene answered.

"What?" she said. "On the Coast they'd pay a thousand dollars to have an actor jump out of a moving car."

She jotted something down on a scratch sheet and hung up. "It's unbelievable, the first thing Monday morning, all these crazy calls coming in from the agencies. Well, thank God Carrie's commercial is an ordinary job and all she has to do is look plain old-fashioned beautiful and wash her face with Zest. With Madison Avenue getting farther and farther out, at least Benton and Bowles is staying sane."

"Oh," Rex said, "it's usually not as bad as the agencies lead you to think. Vince August sweated it out one whole night. He absolutely couldn't sleep one blessed wink because he thought he was going to have to go up in a balloon and glide down with a pack of Viceroys. Let me tell you, he was really *nervous*. But it turned out he didn't have to; they faked the whole thing. They usually find a way around these things. Well, I've finished checking the shots I like."

"You did join the Screen Actors Guild last week, didn't you, sweetheart?" Charlene asked Carrie.

"Two hundred and fifteen dollars; yes."

"Well, don't worry; you'll make five thousand dollars in residuals on the Zest. It's a big payer."

"Soon she'll be joining AFTRA too," Rex said.

"What's AFTRA?" Carrie asked.

"SAG is for filmed work; AFTRA for tape and live shows."

"I don't understand about residuals," Carrie said.

"That's one of the most complicated things about this business," Charlene replied. "To begin with, SAG minimum for daily shooting is a hundred and twenty dollars. That's your basic session fee. You'll be getting three times that on the Zest, since you're booked for three days' shooting."

"That part I understand. . . ."

"If they use it, you get paid in thirteen-week cycles according to how many *units* are involved—units representing major cities."

"You see, honey," Rex said, "a commercial has several categories, or classes—double A, triple A, program, spot, wild spot, dealer spot—"

"It *is* complicated," Charlene said. "For instance, a commercial will have the category of spot if it's aired between shows or late at night, on a minor network—that type of thing."

"A program commercial is the best payer," Rex said, "that's shown on prime time, major network, on a major telecast."

"Correction," Charlene said. "The best-paying commercial is one that runs on program *and* spot—simultaneously in several classes."

"The payment schedule varies," Rex said, "and they have a certain amount of time in which to pay you. You might get the money in dribbles—ninety, seventy-five, fifty dollars or so each separate check, depending. Or it may come as a buyout—seven hundred twenty-seven dollars in advance."

"I can see it's beyond me," Carrie said.

"It's beyond all of us," Charlene said. "We have to trust the advertising agencies' accounting departments. In the meantime, Carrie, you're going to be a busy girl this week. I have another interview for you, luv. Take this down."

Carrie reached into her satchel and took out a pen and a large book bearing scrawls in various colored inks.

"What kind of appointment book is that?" Charlene asked. "Is that one of your college notebooks you're using?"

"No, it's my writing notebook—my journal. I take it all over with me."

"You write?" Rex asked.

"Try to."

"Enjoying it's one thing; earning your living at it's another," Charlene said. "Since one of my husbands was a writer, I can tell you from experience, luv. You're better off being a model. You'll make yourself a pile of money and then retire. The new interview's over at Compton at two-ten. It's for a Mr. Clean. Look fresh and cool."

"Got it," Carrie said, writing.

"Not a trace of the commonplace in this girl, Rex," Charlene said. "She's got class, distinction—the lady-in-the-parlor-bitch-in-bed type. And that's very salable."

Carrie blushed.

"All right, angel," Charlene said, "ready, set, go. Your big career's beginning. Get a move on it; J. Walter's expecting you at eleven."

As Carrie, excited, gathered up her belongings, Charlene picked up the phone.

"Eve Petroangeli? . . . Oh, yes, honey. . . . Fine. Rex and I will be expecting you at five. . . . Bye-bye, luv."

Chapter 3

Rex Ryan had spent most of the day on the phone. In mid-afternoon the rain had started, and most of the Madison Avenue people had ducked out of their offices early to beat the rush hour traffic, which bad weather always complicated. The office was quiet now; from the room next door Rex could hear Charlene drilling her dogs—"Sit. . . . Stay. . . . Come. . . . Down. . . . Give me your paw"—as she was prone to do when the phones stopped ringing.

Rex closed his door so that Charlene wouldn't overhear a personal phone call he was about to make. He dialed the number and waited until he heard a melodious male "Hello."

"Darling," Rex said, "it's me again. I just called to tell you I can't get you out of my mind. It's wild."

The voice at the other end of the line came from a young actor, Tom Calder. Tom was gentle, sensitive, and talented, and Rex was certain he could become a great star. "Rex, sweetheart, I just can't tell you . . . it was beautiful, baby, just beautiful."

"Beautiful . . . yes. That's how it is when two boys find each other. It makes up for so much ugliness, doesn't it?" Rex thought of all the rough trade he'd been exposed to, and of how long he had waited for someone like Tom, who had magic and gentleness coupled with violence and bestiality, and who did things just right. Rex found himself aroused and was about to confess his heightened state when the intercom buzzed. "I'll see you at seven," Rex

16

said, his voice low and husky. "And promise me one thing. . . ?"

"Yes, luv?"

"Wear those luscious tight jockey shorts when you open the door for me, will you, dearest?"

"I will! Oooh, darling, hurry over, I can hardly wait for it."

Rex drew in his breath. "Me either."

He hung up smiling and buzzed Charlene, who said, "Rex, luv, we have a four-thirty with new talent. She's here."

"Oh, I forgot. Who is she?"

"Dolores Haynes. Very good type. From the Coast. Shall I send her in or do you want to come to my office?"

"Send her in here."

A second later Dolores Haynes appeared. Rex knew immediately the agency could make money with her. She had the ingredients: tall, with dark hair, she knew how to dress, she moved well, she had style, poise, and assurance.

"Aren't you brave to come out on such a *miserable* day?" Rex said, and rose to shake hands.

"Oh, I don't mind at all—not when it's for a worthy cause," Dolores Haynes replied.

Rex appraised the slender body, the carefully done face with its small mouth painted into a glossy, pearlized, and unmistakably avaricious *moue,* and the well-madeup deep-set eyes bordered by a fringe of dark, thick, fake lashes.

Someone less expert than Rex Ryan probably wouldn't have noticed the duality of Dolores Haynes' face. But Rex couldn't miss the hard, determined expression behind all the artifice. He immediately penetrated the façade and measured the features that kept Dolores from being a genuine beauty—the too-pointed chin and nose, and the pinched nostrils. But he noted with approval that Dolores' clothes and accessories were exactly right, a perfect complement to her slim elegance. There was no doubt about it: Dolores Haynes knew how to turn herself out.

"So you're from the Coast?" he said, sitting and motioning Dolores to a chair. "Well, we're in the middle of our annual shift. All our New York people are dying to go to Hollywood, and since spring, the California people have been wandering in here in droves."

Dolores laughed studiedly, yet with charm. "Yes, it's the quiet season there now. And the *busy* season in New York, so I'm told. I hope the reports are accurate."

"It's been *very* busy," Rex said. "I see you brought some pictures. May I take a look?"

Dolores handed him a book of eight-by-tens, proving she photographed well and could register several interesting expressions in front of a camera.

"These are excellent. You photograph beautifully," Rex said. "There's only one thing: in the commercial business in New York we use eleven-by-fourteen photographs. You'll have to get some new pictures. But don't throw these out; you can have some of them copied and use them on your composite."

"Fine," Dolores said. "Can you suggest where I should go for new pictures?"

"I'll give you our client list of photographers. But now, tell me about yourself, Dolores, what you've done, and so forth."

Dolores settled back in her chair. "Originally, I came from near Chicago. I modeled there for a while and then went on to Hollywood."

"And what did you do on the Coast?"

"I was under contract to one of the major studios, but I asked for my release."

"How long were you under contract?"

"A year. When my option came up and the studio didn't have a feature for me, I said this is it, I have to make the break now if I ever expect to get anywhere as an actress. The Hollywood system can defeat you. I've seen it happen to so many talented people, but I was determined not to have it happen to me."

"They let you out?"

"No trouble. They'd gotten their money's worth out of me. They wished me the best of luck and said that they hoped the next time we met they'd have to pay me a hundred thousand a picture."

"So your main interest is acting then?"

"Yes, and now that I'm here in New York my goal is to

get a Broadway show. In the meantime I'm going to support myself at modeling and commercials."

"How old are you?" Rex asked.

"Twenty-one."

Rex knew she was lying. But it really didn't matter. Dolores Haynes would fit nicely into the middle category of talent occupied by females who photograph an amorphous, indeterminate age, showing up on TV as the girls who laugh on sailboats and at picnics and in open cars, who wave cigarettes casually in front of streams, who suds their faces and then let the water drip off, who kiss the man who uses the right deodorant, after-shave lotion, or mouthwash, and whose dishes and laundry as new brides are never clean enough until a mother-in-law or neighbor clues them in and saves their marriages. No one knew or cared about the exact ages of these girls; the important thing was audience identification. Dolores Haynes, with her poise and photogenic quality, would be able to cover a lot of ground.

"I'm glad you came to see us," Rex said, "because I think we can get you started soon . . . and make lots of money together."

"Good!"

"I suppose you'll be looking for an apartment?"

"Yes. And I dread that."

Suddenly a name came to Rex's mind. "Well, if you want to room with another girl, I can give you somebody to call," he said. "Carrie Richards."

"Carrie Richards? Who is she?"

"I'm sure you two would get along well. She has an apartment already, so it would save you the problem of having to look. Let's see—it's Plaza 2–3838. The apartment's in a wonderful location."

"It sounds too good to be true," Dolores said. "I'll give her a call."

Rex, standing to shake her hand again, said he would be in touch with her soon; then he sent her back to Charlene, who would take care of further preliminaries and introduce her to the other three agents in the Ryan-Davy office.

Rex busied himself tidying up his desk and making plans for the following day. Which casting people was he due to call for a friendly chat, just to keep in touch? While he was trying to decide, his thoughts drifted back to Tom Calder and the previous night's activities. It was crazy how he couldn't keep his mind off sex. He was about to call Tom again and tell him he just might be able to get away sooner than he'd thought when Charlene buzzed him on the intercom.

"Well?" she asked. "Dolores Haynes?"

"We're going to make some money with that girl," Rex answered. "She's determined, and she's not going to let anything stand in her way."

"I had the exact same feeling, darling," Charlene said. "This girl will make it, no matter how many throats she has to cut."

Chapter 4

During the train ride from Floral Park Eve Petroangeli suffered from jitters and uncertainty. She felt guilty about telling Sister Joanita she had cramps so she'd be excused from after-school sports and not be late for her appointment at the Ryan-Davy office. But mostly she was just frightened at the prospect of meeting the agency people and at the thought of all the meeting meant.

Trying to compose herself, she stared at the dreary hodgepodge of ancient houses bordering the Long Island Railroad —and was conscious of how sweaty her hands were, how nervous she was, how her stomach jumped. Suppose the agency people saw right through her and knew she'd once weighed close to two hundred pounds? If they knew she'd been fat, what would they say?

At length the train passed Jamaica and went into the tunnel. The city, lying only minutes away, beckoned. Soon the train would pull into Penn Station! Eve closed her eyes. Help me, God, she thought. St. Jude, help me during this interview and I'll light a candle on your altar every day.

When she walked out into the rain-washed sunlight on Seventh Avenue, she felt better for having prayed to St. Jude.

The commonplace appearance of the small building in which the Ryan-Davy offices were located surprised Eve. The offices themselves were equally unanticipated, starkly white, with plain modern furniture. The walls, however, were covered with photographs, many of them of models Eve recognized as having appeared in magazine and newspaper ads as well as on television commercials.

A male voice said, "Goodbye, Carrie," and a ravishing tawny-haired girl walked through the outer office, calling after her, "Bye, Rex. Thanks." The girl had a magnetism that was startling. My God, Eve thought, if this is a model, if they all look like that, do I stand a chance?

A tall man in tight beige trousers and a thin green shirt came to the threshold of the nearest door.

"Eve?"

"Yes," Eve replied in a voice she hoped didn't sound too timid and childish.

"Hi"—the man strode toward her with an outstretched hand—"I'm Rex Ryan. I recognized you from your pictures. We've been looking forward to meeting you. Won't you come in?"

Rubbery-legged, she followed Mr. Ryan into his small private office. She was surprised he looked so young. Probably only about thirty, she decided; and so handsome too.

His desk was piled with papers and photos. More photos, a galaxy of faces, peered down from all four walls of the room. Eve found herself so envying the cool sophistication and style of the models she almost didn't hear Mr. Ryan tell her to sit down.

"Now then . . ." Mr. Ryan began, rubbing his palms together. "You're completely new to the business?"

"Yes, but I've always wanted to be a model."

"And you live—where was it?"

"In Floral Park, Long Island."

"Can you get into the city at any time?"

"Yes! I mean, as soon as I graduate, I'll be able to. In two weeks."

"Where are you graduating from?"

"Our Lady of Victory High."

"I see."

There was a buzz and, without looking, he picked up the phone. "Yes, Connie, how are you, darling? . . . No, still no word on Pepsi, but I spoke to Nan at BBD&O, and she says they're going to make a decision by tomorrow morning. I'll call you as soon as we hear. . . . Good, then. See you soon." He put down the phone. "Sorry," he apologized. "Now, let's get back to you, Eve."

For what seemed like several minutes, he was silent, scrutinizing her. Finally he said, "You're a good commercial type."

"You mean—I can be a good model?"

"Absolutely. You've got great potential."

It was as if all the uncertainty and doubt had been removed in one clean stroke by his words, and Eve nearly burst into tears.

Rex Ryan didn't seem to notice. "The major task at hand," he continued in a businesslike manner, "is getting you a book."

"A book?"

"That's what a model's portfolio is called. She carries it on her rounds. It's filled with a variety of eleven-by-fourteen poses. Fashion, windblown outdoorsy, housewife type, glamor; young, romantic boy–girl stuff; maybe a shot in a bikini or shorts; hair up, hair down—and so forth."

"Why do you have to have so many different kinds of pictures?"

"The competition is fierce in this business, and you've got to prove you're just what *everybody* is looking for. Clients will flip through your book, and if they don't see exactly what they want, someone else will be in and you out. You have to be all things to all people."

Eve said, "I—I didn't realize. It sounds like it'll cost a lot of money."

"Don't worry, honey, we know photographers who'll test for nothing. We'll get you your whole book free of charge. The only cost will be the portfolio itself—a little over twenty dollars."

"You mean a photographer would just give the model pictures for nothing?" Eve asked.

"That's right. Of course there has to be a reason. Some

studios—Underwood and Underwood, for instance—want to build up their files of stock photos. They use you in various situations—graduation, maybe, or outdoors; you sign a release entitling them to sell the photos anywhere they want—to suburban weeklies, European magazines, wherever; and in exchange for your time, you get copies of the pictures."

"That's wonderful."

"Then there are new young photographers, just starting out, and darkroom assistants to established photographers, who need to build up their own portfolios. It's an even exchange: the model gives her time, the photographer gives his pictures—everyone's happy."

"And the agency will tell me how to go about all this?" Eve asked.

"That's right. Now I want you to meet Charlene, who'll orient you and give you a list of photographers who do test shots. The very next thing we have to see about is your name —too Italian. Good thing you don't look Italian."

"Well, I'm northern Italian. . . ."

"Oh, they're blond, right? Still, some of the agencies will only hire WPAs."

"WPAs?"

"White Protestant Americans. WPA is a business code. Myself, I'm not prejudiced, but some of the Madison Avenue people and the sponsors seem to think it's a better image for the product. So don't tell them you're Italian. You'll get more jobs that way." Rex Ryan smiled wryly. "Charlene?" He had pressed a buzzer and was talking into the intercom box.

"Yes?"

"Eve Petrangeli is here, luv, and she's a great type. Want to get her started as soon as possible. I'm sending her in now."

Rex shut off the intercom and looked at Eve closely. "Don't expect work right away," he said. "For the time being, we'll try to get you pictures, and you can make the rounds of the photographers and get to know them." He hesitated. "We'll have to do something about your hair and makeup. But we'll talk about that later. Charlene can help you. By the way, how much do you weigh? No, don't tell me. You're five, five and weigh a hundred and twenty-two."

"Why, yes, how——"

"It's my business, honey. You'll have to lose at least five pounds, Eve. I like your first name. It suits you."

"Thank you."

"Eve is perfect. Sensual and primary. Innocent, earthy. It's *you*, and that's how we're going to sell you. But, first things first: the next door down, this side of the hall——Charlene's expecting you."

"You——you mean that's all?"

"Right." He clasped her hand. "Give me a blast later. Glad to have you with us, Eve."

Dazed by her good fortune, Eve moved down the hall to Charlene's office, where two huge, exotic-looking dogs rose from the floor and stood side by side, nostrils quivering, tails wagging.

"Meet my boys," came a husky voice from a vivid fuchsia, almost vulgar-looking painted mouth. "Warren and Kurt, named for two of my many ex-husbands——a Kraut and a Jew. Hi, dear! I'm Charlene Davy. You're Eve, I know; Rex told me all about you. Step around the mutts and come sit down."

"Thank you," Eve said timidly.

As she approached, the dogs retreated toward their mistress, and Warren eased a large paw onto Charlene's lap.

"Down, Warren!" Charlene ordered. The dog slunk obediently under the desk.

Eve stared at the sight before her. Charlene Davy was a bizarre specimen of a woman, oozing energy from the tips of her long, gold-tinted nails, and indeed, from all that was visible of her erect, firm body. She must be over sixty, Eve thought, noting the facial wrinkles that layers of careful makeup couldn't hide. But Eve's glance didn't rest for long on the wrinkles, for Charlene's eyes, large and emerald green, commanded attention. The color of the eyes was matched perfectly by eye shadow and complemented by a thick black liner. Eve was sure Charlene must once have been a great beauty; she handled herself as if she were used to being catered to——and as if she were oblivious to the effects time and dissipation had created.

"My boys are quite well behaved," Charlene said. "They

24

should be, after the months I spent with them in obedience school. But let's talk about you."

As Eve replied to questions about her age and background, Charlene listened attentively, her eyes penetrating, seeming to bore into her.

"You have a thing or two to learn about clothes, posture, makeup, and poise," Charlene said finally. "But all in all, Rex is right about you. And you've got the greatest commodity going for you—youth." Charlene paused. "Did anyone explain who does what around here? . . . No? Well, I happen to be head of talent. That means I'm the one who grooms our people. I spot what needs to be changed in terms of looks, personality, attitude, whatever—to say nothing of guiding and developing ability. Now, with you, Eve, we'll have a few minor physical corrections. I'll have to teach you how to have more style."

She rose and extracted some cosmetic items from a filing cabinet drawer that Eve noticed also contained some liquor bottles. "Why don't we have makeup as your first lesson." Moving to where Eve sat, Charlene began to apply liquid base to Eve's skin. "This business is a constant experience with self-improvement. Since it's yourself you have to sell, you can never know enough about yourself. You'll hear lots of criticism from here on in, and you'll have to learn not to take everything personally."

Charlene stood back a bit. "I'm not used to your face, but you'll be able to do the whole job very swiftly yourself once you get some practice. Always keep experimenting with makeup. You can never learn enough."

Powdering now, Charlene discussed photographic makeup, how to apply it, and how to modify it for street wear. Eve's face was a bit too round, she said, the ideal shape for modeling being nearly an oval. By careful shadowing, however, and especially by using a darker base around the jaws, Eve was given the desired oval effect, which, Charlene assured her, would be even more so in photographs.

Next, Charlene applied rouge, at an angle, explaining that this would bring out the cheekbones to better advantage. Then, with a wet sponge she moistened the entire surface in order to set the makeup and give it translucence.

"You should never make the tip of the brow go down,

like you've been doing," she warned. "It closes in your face and brings your eyes too close together."

After applying gray eye shadow, she took a bottle of liquid liner and painstakingly went over the upper part of Eve's eyelids while Eve blinked from the strain of trying to keep them half shut.

"You can do the mascara yourself," Charlene said. "And better buy several pairs of false lashes, because they give out quickly. False lashes are an absolute must! No girl can ever afford to be without them!"

The mouth was created by using a lipstick brush. Then, Eve's transformation completed, Charlene took a mirror from her desk. "There you are," she said. "How do you like it?"

So heightened were Eve's strong points that her face now commanded instant attention. Happily, she stared at it.

"Well?" Charlene asked.

"I love it—it's fantastic!"

"Good. Makeup does wonders for you, and I'm glad you see it. Now—if you can take your eyes off yourself long enough—here's something else." Charlene put the mirror back on the desk and picked up a sheet of paper, which she held out to Eve. "The client list. Stop in and see everyone you can. Just introduce yourself so they can meet you."

Eve took the list from Charlene and glanced at it.

"Some of the names are of catalog houses," Charlene explained. "But most are of independent photographers, many of whom test. They're the people you want to see first to get your book together. Then you'll have to have a composite made."

"What's that?"

"A group of pictures showing you in various poses. You have it multilithed and drop off copies at the studios and ad agencies as you make rounds. Here"—Charlene drew some papers out of the filing cabinet—"eight by ten. They fold in the middle, making four pages. One beauty shot, one full length, one fashion, one commercial shot."

"I see."

"You can use these for commercials and photography both. Actually, you're a better type for commercials, though we can probably get you some catalog work. You're much too round and wholesome to do high fashion, and not tall enough either. It requires a particular type of look. Now one more thing—"

"Yes?"

"Something important: your voice. You have a trace of New Yorkese—we'll have to work on it. We can't send you out to read for commercials until you lose the regionalism."

"I see." Eve hadn't realized there was anything wrong with the way she spoke.

"When I find someone who has a quality," Charlene said, "I go all out for that person. In your case, Eve, I see great potential. But you're going to need a lot of work. I'm willing to devote the time and effort to improve you—if you're willing to work like holy hell. Are you?"

"Oh, yes, Miss Davy," Eve said. "I want to improve."

"Good. And don't call me Miss Davy. The name is Charlene. And Rex is Rex, not Mr. Ryan. No titles around here. We're an informal family. Eve, I'm glad you're willing to accept criticism and help. It's the first step. Now then, I'd like to hear you read. But not today."

Selecting some Samuel French paperbound play editions from a shelf full of books, Charlene said, "Go home and work on these—the scenes that are marked. Then come back in about a week. That should give you enough time to study them. I just want to get an idea. You may never do any acting, but nowadays models have to be able to handle lines for commercials."

Eve accepted the scripts, then shook Charlene's extended hand.

It all seems so easy! Eve thought, starting toward the door.

"Warren, stay!" As Eve was leaving, Warren, anticipating a walk, rose to follow her. At Charlene's command, he obediently returned to his place under the desk, tail between his legs.

"Thank you; oh, thank you, St. Jude," Eve said to herself as soon as she was out in the hallway.

Charlene reached for one of the bottles in her filing cabinet, poured herself a shot of bourbon, and felt its warming caress. Christ, her nerves were shot, what with the weight of the whole agency on her shoulders—and trying to keep Rex on the ball. There was that one dangerous weakness of his—whenever he drank too much he carried the fag bit too far and went into one of his spells.

Her eyes wandered to the photos on the wall opposite her desk, and forgetting Rex, she drifted back in time. What a stunning beauty I was, she thought. There was no one like me. God, I was ravishing. There's no one, even today, who can compare with me. . . . Oh, yes, Carrie Richards. But Carrie's the only one, the only genuine beauty in the whole agency.

She thought of Carrie's eagerness, her naturalness, her ardor, and it made her want to warn her, watch out, they'll ruin you like they did me. The thing is no one can stand for you being special, so they have to tear you down to their level, make you just as ordinary, just as corrupt as they are. People can't stand beauty, can't stand not having it themselves. They despise the ones who do have it. It's an obsession that they all want to ruin beauty, drag it in the mud. Beauty exists first and foremost as a target for others' hatreds and aggressions. There are playboys and perverts in this town, some operating for forty years, with new ones coming along every year, and all of them know how to wreck a woman's life. Why? Why? All the pain of being beautiful, and you just end up being used.

Don't let it happen, Carrie, Charlene thought fiercely. Don't let them get you the way they got me. Don't let them tear you apart limb by limb. She poured herself another comforting slug of Jack Daniels.

"Yes, Rex," she said at the sound of the intercom buzzer. "That young dish who just left, that's who you're calling about, right?"

"Mind reader."

"She's completely without polish, of course. But she's eager to learn, luv."

"Good. I wanted to get your opinion."

"She's got a quality."

"I felt that immediately myself."

"I've got ideas for this girl, Rex. She's rough, but that's the best time to get them, before they've had a chance to form bad habits. The voice is the first thing I'm going to fix."

"Wonderful, sweetheart. I couldn't be more pleased. This has been our season for new material. First Carrie Richards, then Dolores Haynes, and now Eve. We're really going to move upward with those three, Charlene."

Chapter 5

Only twenty-four hours in New York and already things were starting to swing. Walking back to the hotel, Dolores scarcely noticed anything along the way, so elated was she by her meeting at the Ryan-Davy Agency. She felt her steps coordinate perfectly with the tempo of the city, and she knew she belonged here on these rain-washed pavements. The towering structures above her pointed in the direction of her ambitions. There was no limit to what she could achieve.

Back in her room, Dolores peered at her image with satisfaction. For more years than she admitted to, she had been carrying on a love affair with her mirror. I don't look a day over eighteen, she told herself. No one will ever know I'm really twenty-five, or suspect the studio fired me. That faggot Rex Ryan believed the story I told him. From now on, things are really going to happen!

Soon she would satisfy her ambitions, her craving for fame and glory, footlights, applause; she would become an actress, a fashion figure, a recognized beauty luxuriating in fine surroundings; she would travel, have exciting friends, and give widely publicized parties. And there would be the appropriate man to complement her. A rare gem needs a setting to enhance its sparkle.

The main problem at present was that paying for the hotel room was financially burdensome. Of course she could always find a man to foot the bill, but it seemed a better idea to remain free of ties until she was able to get an adequate picture of the New York social scene. Therefore it was important to find an apartment as soon as possible.

She picked up the phone to call Carrie Richards.

* * *

Working in front of thirty technicians on her first professional assignment hadn't been half as difficult as Carrie had anticipated. The director, a cuddly, funny man who was always cracking jokes, teasing people, and calling everyone "Thweedie"—a part of his "fag bit" (it was amusing to the crew, his pretending to be a homosexual)—had been enormously helpful. Knowing it was the first commercial she'd done, he'd taken her aside before each shot and demonstrated exactly what he wanted her to do and convey. When there were problems, they'd worked on them privately, to save her any embarrassment in front of the crew.

As she was leaving Thursday afternoon he told her she'd done a fine job, and that he hoped to work with her again soon. "You're going to be one of the biggest commercial girls in the business, honey. I can tell talent when I see it, and have you ever got looks!"

He gave her a cute gay-boy wave, and Carrie walked out of the studio exuberant. It was as if New York had settled around her like a golden cloud. No longer did she feel the gnawing unease, the sense of uprootedness, that had been so often present since her father's death the past winter.

In the softness of the late spring dusk, there was a hush to the air. She stopped at a newsstand near her new apartment and bought an afternoon paper.

The flat and its sparse furnishings were still unfamiliar. As she closed the door after her, Carrie thought about giving the place a feeling of home, buying some pillows for the couch, maybe a few knickknacks, something for the walls—just as soon as she had the money.

Checking her answering service, she found another message from Dolores Haynes, the girl the agency had recommended as a roommate. She called the hotel for the tenth time in the last few days. But Dolores was out again.

Settling down on one of the twin beds, she began a letter to her mother.

Dear Mother,

I'm sorry I waited to tell thee of my decision to take an apartment and live the coming year in New York, but with so many hectic things at graduation I had no definite plans until almost the last minute.

This is the way I feel: I know I'm pretty. The point is, why not use my extra advantage? Other girls have to take nine-to-five office jobs to make a living, but I don't. Oh, Mother, join that dreary parade of thousands of girls who arrive in Manhattan every June?

This life is different and exciting. It moves! I can feel myself alive here, accomplishing things. I'd like to do commercials three to six months, and after that, won't it be marvelous to live off residuals!! To have the money to travel. To go to Europe and write.

I want to write. The question is, what do I want to write about? I need experience, time to grow into my material, time to discover. So I'm keeping on with the notebooks. Perhaps out of them will come my material for the future, the same as it did for Henry James, André Gide, *et al.*

Thee knows my main goal is a family of my own, and this business ought to help me get around and meet people. If it happened this year I'd be happy, but, of course, it may not be so easy, what with wanting no less than what Father and thee had together—maturity and wisdom, honesty and true caring.

By the way, I went to meeting here, but the people were all quite old. I was sorry about that; I would have liked to meet some people my own age, of like mind.

I'll keep thee posted on my activities and will hope to see thee at Thanksgiving.

Don't worry!

Love,
Carrie

It was twilight now, and the street outside was rose-colored and mistily incandescent. Carrie sealed the letter into an envelope, moved to the living room, and switched on a light. Feeling elated, she found her satchel and took out the notebook, which she carried to the couch. The

31

pen with which she had written to her mother was still in her hand. She sat on the couch, opened the notebook on her knees, and made an entry:

* * *

June 10. *Only days in Manhattan, and I'm meeting all kinds of people. Everywhere I go, the red carpet is laid out; everyone is so friendly and encouraging, and acts like I'm the greatest thing they've ever met. It's not just in work, but socially as well. The Sarah Lawrence contacts have helped, of course. One or two phone calls to a friend of a friend and the ball is rolling—on a major circuit! My latest prime connection is Geoffrey Gripsholm, considered by society columnists to be one of the ten top "catches" in town. Worth a conservative eighty million, he's a renowned art collector and part-time stockbroker. Though as a date, he leaves much to be desired, still New York social life revolves about him. I doubt I hold much attraction for him; I'm sure that he's a closet queen, for when he drinks, his stylized panache becomes awfully swishy.*

* * *

"Caroline, *mon ange!*"

It was Geoffrey Gripsholm himself. His voice was stuffy with an impossible Harvard accent when he spoke English; most of the time he preferred to speak French, however, since he fancied himself a linguist.

His interest in her, Carrie estimated, might possibly stem from the fact that she'd had twelve years of French in school. Someone to practice on.

"*Comment ça va, ma belle?*" Geoffrey asked in the abominable French he was so proud of, and barely waiting for an answer, he began to quote Baudelaire:

> *Mon enfant, ma soeur, songe à la douceur*
> *D'aller là-bas vivre ensemble!*
> *Aimer à loisir*
> *Aimer et mourir,*
> *Au pays qui te ressemble;*

Là, tout n'est qu'ordre et beauté,
Luxe, calme, et volupté

He made his tones as sonorous, dramatic, and pear-shaped as possible, which was not easy, handicapped as he was with his Harvard accent, which always made it seem as if there were marbles in his mouth. "I have just quoted a Baudelaire poem—the title of which I defy you to give me," he challenged.

" '*L'Invitation au Voyage*,' " Carrie replied.

"My God, you're incredible! Everyone naturally assumes the title is '*Luxe, Calme, et Volupté*,' because of the Matisse painting, *naturellemente*."

"Matisse took the title from Baudelaire."

Geoffrey blew a kiss into the phone. "I shall toast you, Mademoiselle Richards, unto eternity, as the *arbiter elegantiarum* par excellence, and a cynosure of all eyes. My, but you *are* dishy. Come out with me this evening, ducky, and I promise you far more than a Barmecide feast—with plenty of Attic salt, cups that cheer but not inebriate, the company of a belted earl, and redoubtable protection from certain lewd fellows of the baser sort. Ahem!" He cleared his throat.

"Well."

"This English peer . . ." Geoffrey went on, "undoubtedly you've read in the tabloids that I have a distinguished house guest. Well, to tell you the truth, I had considered him humbug in the Pickwickian point of view. But it turns out he's quite unbogus. Definitely not British phlegm, but rather an *enfant terrible*—an Admirable Crichton, really; amusing, witty; he looks slightly tubercular, of course, but don't they all? It's *la nouvelle rage*. . . . But *revenons à nos moutons*—what was I saying?"

"Something about a lord."

"Yes, well, Tony spotted you discothequing just last night, and immediately began quoting Wordsworth: 'Earth has not anything to show more fair,' he said. The poor fellow's been tormenting me all day to have you dine with us. And when better for you to warm the cockles of our hearts than this evening—with *un repas intime à trois* at Lutece? . . . Eightish, then?"

Eve worked on the scenes for Charlene in front of a full-length mirror in her bedroom. Once she had learned the lines, she was amazed at her ability to emote. Could it be she had an aptitude she'd never known about?

Confidently she set out for the city Monday afternoon. But the minute she entered the Ryan-Davy offices, fear and dread replaced the original positive feeling. Her whole body seemed to be shaking. She hoped Charlene, who greeted her warmly, wouldn't notice.

She began to read, attempting to give the lines brightness and a sharp comic touch. But her voice seemed not only drab, but all the words came out flat. She was conscious of the fact that she was neither funny nor convincing.

She swallowed hard after finishing the last lines on the page. If she could only have taken a deep breath! In the next scene, she stumbled on important lines and found herself so out of breath that she wasn't sure she could reach the end of her sentences. Her tongue, a fuzzy weight, refused to coordinate with her lips. She couldn't convey any of the emotion she had given to the lines in the privacy of her own room, and when she'd spoken the last of them for Charlene, she wanted to cry with humiliation. She'd done everything wrong. Everything! She stared at her feet, too embarrassed to look Charlene in the eye.

Charlene lit a cigarette and leaned back in her chair. "You have a lot of work to do, Eve," she said, and Eve felt her heart coast a mile. She knew she ought to say something, but no words would come out of her dry, sick-tasting mouth.

Charlene inhaled thoughtfully. "I know you were nervous, and I never take much stock in first readings anyway. The important thing you've shown me is that you have an intense desire to be good, and that's the most valuable asset for anyone in the business to have. With work, you can do things. You have a definite quality, Eve."

Relieved, Eve smiled at the compliment.

"Now that you're over the initial fright, why don't we tackle it again?"

Eve picked up her script. Most of the tension and fright were gone now, and the lines came more easily. At intervals Charlene interrupted the reading to explain a point or to ask, "Why do you think she says that?" or, "To what is she referring here?" or, "What do you suppose there is in her background to make her feel this way?" Occasionally she suggested, "Try it like this," and demonstrated a gesture or an intonation for Eve, who was now able to forget about her voice and concentrate on the feelings and action of the character.

"I think you can make it, Eve," Charlene said when the scene was finished. "You take directions beautifully. You're intelligent and a quick learner."

"Oh, thank you, Charlene."

"It will be awhile yet before we'll be sending you out for commercials, but when we do, you're going to turn out to be one of our top girls. And mark my words; I know this business."

* * *

Monday evening Dolores was at last on her way to meet Carrie Richards. From what Carrie had said on the phone, she was certain that the apartment was quite suitable. She was also certain that Carrie herself could be useful, for Carrie obviously had many acquaintances who would be worth cultivating. Dolores, however, was completely unprepared for the girl who opened the door.

She was used to contrivance, not to beauty like Carrie's, which had no need for gimmicks. Since she could not admit to being outshone, she was forced to reject the truth of Carrie's superior basic endowments.

After she had seen and expressed her satisfaction with the apartment, she took a seat opposite Carrie in the living room and immediately began to talk about her Hollywood career, the stars she knew, the parts she had played, and her dedication to the acting craft.

"I'm not a model, you know; I'm an actress," she said, but soon realized her superior tone was having little effect on Carrie. And as she droned on she became aware that, despite herself, she was compelled and drawn to Carrie's looks. She's pure, Dolores thought. I hate her for being

35

pure and unspoiled, for coming from a different world than I do.

By the next day, when she checked out of the Sherry-Netherland and moved in with Carrie Richards, Dolores had determined that she could—and would—achieve mental, physical, emotional, moral, psychic, and spiritual triumph, and whatever other kinds of triumph there might be, over her new roommate

Chapter 6

June moved swiftly for Eve. She had been rechristened Eve Paradise, and bursting with energy and hope, was busy organizing her new life.

Before school finished, she managed a Saturday session of test shots. Armed with two suitcases full of clothes, she rode to the city on the Long Island Railroad, struggled through Penn Station, and then took a taxi over to a shadowy studio in the east thirties.

A young photographer awaited her. Coffee perked on a table near the camera equipment, and a Beatles record blared from the stereo. Happily she climbed around filing cabinets, over boxes, cables, piles of books and records, a family of cats, and reached the small area in which the lights were set and the camera waited on its tripod.

Eager but nervous, she gratefully devoured the help and advice the young photographer gave her, and returned to Floral Park determined to go on a crash diet and lose ten more pounds. If anyone ever suspected she had once weighed close to two hundred!

After graduation, following Charlene's suggestions of which photographers were testing and might be looking for new faces, Eve began making rounds, which included going up and introducing herself at some of the stock houses and catalog places, Warsaw Studios, Underwood and Underwood, and Pagano among them. Charlene had said that sometimes a newcomer would have luck and be hired, book unseen.

Now, heart beating, she took a deep breath and entered the door marked "Farrow and Tudor, Catalog."

Meg Tudor and Jack Farrow sat side by side at a long table littered with papers and photographs. Four telephones rested near piles of composites, and the walls were papered with photographic ads and agency listings.

Jack Farrow saw Eve first and said, "Come on in, honey, I'm Jack and this is Meg." He was cradling a phone in one slender hand, looking perturbed at having to hang on. Carefully placing his other hand over the mouthpiece, he hissed, "That bitch! I can't abide broads like her. Have a seat, honey. What's your name?"

"Eve Paradise, from the Ryan-Davy Agency."

"Hi, Eve." Meg smiled, extending her hand. "Rex has told us all about you."

"Finished," Jack announced a moment later. He slammed the receiver down. "Left a message with her secretary. Just a sec, Eve, honey—I'll be right back."

He rose, and Eve noticed that his trousers were even tighter than Rex Ryan's. Watching him stride toward the door, she was both fascinated and embarrassed to see almost every muscle of his thighs and buttocks move with the clinging fabric. Jack, like Rex Ryan, showed traces of an effeminate quality.

"While Jack's out peeing," Meg began confidentially, "let's talk about you. You're overweight; your hair should be lightened; you don't use makeup properly. You have a thing or two to learn about clothes, and your posture could stand some attention. But Rex is right about you: you're a good type. There's somebody I want to have test you for us— Franco Gaetano; he does a lot of our stuff. Have you seen him yet?"

"No."

Without so much as a further glance at Eve, Meg reached for a phone and dialed a number. "Franco? . . . Hi, lover, good to hear your sexy voice. Do me a great favor and test a girl for me. She's young, sexy, and adorable, but greener than a spring tadpole, and she needs somebody exactly like you, baby, to initiate her—ha, ha—to push her

37

buttons just right—" Her voice had become low and fog-horny; she winked at Eve. "Good," she said into the phone, "I'll have her call you next week. And Franco, sweetie, any time you get tired of your wife, Meg is *available*."

Jack returned as Meg was hanging up. He held out a box of chocolate cherries.

"How am I ever supposed to keep my figure with him around?" Meg shrieked. She took a piece of the candy, tossed away the paper that had been under it, and missed the wastebasket. "Damn! Let the cleaning lady get it. I'm too beat."

"You'd think she did something other than sit on her fat can all day," Jack said.

"Look who's talking," Meg retorted. Suddenly she looked at Eve and screamed, "God, that hair is terrible!"

Jack put his hands to his ears. "Women!" he exclaimed. "Especially in this business—they're all a bunch of nervous bitches. I think they just don't get enough sex, that's what's the trouble with them."

"What a thing to say around this sweet young innocent." Meg looked at Eve. "Don't pay any attention to him, honey," she said. "Let's get back to you. Soon as we can see some tests on you, we'll go from there."

"I know she'll photograph great," Jack said.

"Thank you," Eve said.

"Oh, don't thank me; thank God."

"Come back and see us as soon as you've got your pic-tures, Eve," Meg said. "We're real anxious to use you, honey."

*   *   *

Maria Petroangeli smiled softly as her daughter entered the house at the end of another day in the city spent mak-ing rounds of the photographers' studios. Sometimes it was difficult for Mrs. Petroangeli to believe this womanly young creature was her own Evalina: the pink and white baby, so docile, so good, who had turned into a child requiring almost no discipline and had then become an adolescent gourmand gorging in maniacal fashion on everything in sight —chocolate pies, a quart of ice cream a day, candy, cake,

38

everything she could lay her hands on—until, in a three-month period, she had gained forty some pounds and reached the hundred ninety-seven she was to maintain for over five years.

Poor Evie, it must have been painful for her. Completely withdrawn, she had no friends at all. She had prayed a lot during her obese period, when she was constantly lighting candles at the altars of the saints. Mrs. Petroangeli had often wondered what her daughter was petitioning for and if her requests were granted. But Eve had never liked to talk about it. Then, just in the past few months, a great change had come over Eve; she had lost over seventy pounds and was now so slender no one recognized her.

"Uncle Nappi sends his love!" Eve called as she went upstairs to wash for dinner.

"Oh, did you stop by his barbershop while you were in the city?" her mother asked.

"He can't wait to see my new pictures."

"Neither can I, honey!"

* * *

But, at dinner, Eve's father was not enthusiastic. "How's the modeling going?" he asked with obvious sarcasm.

"Fine, Pop. I saw six photographers today. Charlene says I ought to have my book by the end of July."

"What are you going to do for money in the meantime?"

"Help you out in the store?"

"Well, I still say you should get a good secretarial job," Joe Petroangeli said. "Hundreds of girls try modeling every year—thousands of them. And most of them fail and end up prostitutes—"

"Joe, please—"

"Models are all tramps. They have no morals. We've raised Eve to be a good Catholic girl. Do you think I like having her go into that environment?"

"Joe, I have faith in Evie. She's always been S., S., and G.—sweet, simple, and girlish—and that's the way she'll stay."

"Uncle Nappi's glad about my modeling too, Pop. He says I'm going to make it."

"How would he know?"

"And the agency says I can be a top model."

"Joe, it's not like you think at all. Everybody says she can be successful. We both want her to make the most out of her life."

"The best way for her to do that is to marry a good Catholic boy and settle down in Floral Park where she belongs."

*   *   *

That night, as Eve lay in bed planning all the things that were going to take place in her life the next day and the next year, her mother came in and sat next to her.

"Don't worry about Pop, honey," she said. "I can handle him. I want this for you, Evie. I want you to have all the things I missed."

"Thanks, Mom," Eve whispered, squeezing her mother's hand.

"Your father's a wonderful man, honey. But he doesn't understand the kind of dreams a young girl has. You're a beautiful girl, and you deserve the best. But we mustn't hurt Pop, Evie; he's done the best he knows how to do, and he loves us both very much."

"Okay, Mom."

"I'll be praying for you, honey," her mother said. She kissed Eve, and walked out.

Chapter 7

Five-thirty, the end of another busy day of trudging around in the heat, a day of go-sees, appointments, business errands, of arranging for more test shots, phoning in every hour to the agency—not a moment to think since early morning.

Carrie was exhausted, with swollen feet, grimy face, sticky clothes, damp hair, aching body.

She checked with her answering service and found a call from someone she could not place, Saul Franklin. She dialed the number.

The raspy voice at the other end of the line said, "I'm a friend of Geoffrey Gripsholm. Did Geoff mention me to you?"

"No."

"I saw you the other night with Geoff at Lutece. Found out who you were. Geoff and I are old friends. I think you have one of the greatest faces of all time."

"Thank you."

"I've been wanting to photograph you since I saw you. Trying to figure out an angle. Now an emergency just came up. This could be something big. I'd want to test you first. Can you come up?"

"What sort of thing is this? I mean, is this a modeling job?"

"Like I say, I'd have to shoot some tests; then we'd see where we were at. Can you come over now?"

"You mean right this minute?"

"Sure."

"It's the end of the day, and I'm awfully tired. What about tomorrow?"

"No. Like I say, this is important. I'll make it worth your while—I'll give you all the eleven-by-fourteens you want."

Carrie wondered if she ought to call the agency and verify with Charlene or Rex.

"How did you get my number? I thought the agency didn't give out home phones."

"Oh—this was different, inasmuch as it's an emergency."

"Oh."

"Come on over. It's not far from where you live. I'd say it could wait till tomorrow, only it can't. Something's got to be done on this situation in the next hour."

"Well . . . all right, then."

*   *   *

Saul Franklin inhabited a large, dark-paneled apartment on Park and 62nd. Carrie followed the maid through the gloomy hush of an apparently unlived-in drawing room, noting the old moire couch and chairs, the yellowed photos from an era long past, and frayed tapestries depicting Jonah and the whale, Moses striking water from the rod, and an apocalyptic vision of the Last Judgment. Down the hall the door to a bedroom stood ajar.

The maid signaled Carrie to go through and scurried off.

The room was musty, dim; a deathlike vibration seemed to permeate it. Carrie stood just inside the entrance looking at the large bed and the sallow, emaciated old man—he must be well past seventy—sitting up in it. The man was wearing rumpled Chinese silk pajamas and a soiled blue serge wrapper. His lips were pale, and open enough to show inflamed gums and defective teeth. His hands, resting on a faded coverlet, were clublike and covered with liver spots. A few thin strands of grayed hair descended from his skull to his forehead, their color just matching that of the shaggy stubble of his beard. From underneath wrinkled, blue-veined lids, his undersized ebony eyes peered at Carrie like two suspicious and malevolent beetles.

On a stand beside the bed were three telephones, each with a series of buttons and lights, several of which were flashing now, an ashtray full of cigarettes, each one-third smoked, a few glasses, spoons, and at least a half a dozen medicine bottles, which Carrie nervously began to count.

Saul Franklin ignored his phone buttons and peered at her. Then, his gravelly crisp-as-celery voice, even raspier than on the phone, said, "You're lucky you got me. At five I stop answering the phone, so you just caught me in time. Come on in."

Carrie entered, feeling uncomfortable with the gloomy sickroom atmosphere and the presence of the old man.

"You can sit over there, deary," Saul Franklin said, and indicated an ugly overstuffed blue chair. "Aren't you lucky I saw you at Lutece the other night." He leaned over the night table and clutched a pack of Gauloises. "My lighter's broken. I'm always either losing lighters . . . or breaking them. Got a match on ya, deary?"

Carrie handed him a pack and returned to the ugly chair. Its upholstery prickled and made her feel itchy.

"You certainly have got looks." Saul Franklin's beetlelike eyes narrowed down to slits.

"Thank you, Mr. Franklin." She was wishing she'd called the agency first.

"Call me Saul. And don't thank me—never say thank you for something you had nothing to do with." He made a couple of abortive attempts to light his cigarette, finally succeeded, took a long drag, and coughed from deep within his chest. "Don't let me scare you, deary," he said. "I haven't been well. Doctor tells me to stop smoking, but Christ—" He took another drag, and this time his body only heaved slightly. "The first pull on a cigarette's always the worst—particularly on a Gauloise. What was I saying?"

Carrie shifted her weight on the prickly chair. "About the doctors not wanting you to smoke. . . ."

"Oh, yeah. Well, it's like I say—there are so few genuine pleasures in life. . . ."

The unanswered phones flashed distractingly. Saul Franklin settled back on the pillows, closed his eyes a moment, and said, "Soon as I start feeling better, deary, I want to do those tests on you. You see," he continued, "I've been ill—have to take injections every day. Yesterday I was feeling fine; tomorrow I'll probably be okay again. In the meantime I just wanted to meet you and talk to you in person." He yawned. "Besides, the lens on my Hasselblat's smashed. But I'm glad we could get together. Is there anything I can get for you, do for you? Do you need anything? Money?"

The suddenness and nonchalance of the question alarmed Carrie, and she wondered how she could leave without a scene.

Saul Franklin looked at her long and hard. Then he said, "I've got instincts about people. I go by first impressions. You didn't have to say a word and I knew all about you—knew from the moment I set eyes on you at Lutece. You're not just another beautiful girl. You've got it inside—got it here." As he tapped his chest his body heaved again.

She should never have come. What could she have been thinking of, to just go up to a strange man's apartment that way?

43

"I'm not like most people, deary," he said. "Most people are takers in life. Well, I'm a giver. And now, I'd like to give you a present."

The itchy upholstery on the chair had made her thighs perspire. If only she could think how to escape gracefully. "Mr.—er—Saul, I mean, I—"

"You're a new girl in town. I like that. I'm always interested in new people. Like I say, I'm a giver. I like to be of *service*. Heh heh!"

He rested his cigarette in the ashtray and bent over, creaking precariously in the process. He opened the bottom drawer of the night table and took out several packets of money. "Know how much is here in this drawer? Two hundred thousand—in cold cash—thousands, five hundreds, and hundreds. Take whatever you like. Only take it in small denominations. The grand notes are all registered."

"No, thank you." Carrie tried not to appear ill at ease.

"Don't be proud, deary, I'm sure you can use it. Buy yourself something nice."

"No, *thank you!*"

"I don't take a fancy to every girl who comes along, you know," Franklin said. "You're special. So"—he threw the money casually on the bed—"anytime you should change your mind you know where to come. All you have to do is open the drawer. I told you, I'm a giver—and a person of instincts. I've seen girls come and go, mostly come—heh heh!—and I can tell you there've been few like you. Almost none, deary. Quality, that's what you are. Real quality; I saw it right away."

He gave her a deep, intimate stare, and she knew he was mentally undressing her. Only now did she notice that when he'd bent over to open the drawer the bedcovers had slid aside and his wrapper had fallen open, revealing through the half-open fly of his rumpled pajamas, a limp, grayish sex organ. Carrie could well imagine what type of photographs he must have had in mind. Alarmed, she knew she had to end the interview with him quickly.

Rising, she bent to pick up her satchel. But Franklin, in a miraculous sudden recovery, had bounded out of bed and was standing over her, hovering like a bird of prey, trying to secure her in his grasp. His voice came in short gasps.

44

"Deary, listen, deary, I'll give you anything you want. Anything—just name your price. A girl with looks like yours could take twenty years off my life."

He grabbed her wrist. "How about a little kiss, just a little one, only a tiny little kiss—that's not asking too much, is it, deary?"

In revulsion she pushed him away and fled.

On the street once more, she was inordinately aware of the warm air on her skin, of the smells of early evening; of the sounds—the rumble underfoot, the distant blare of horns, the soft humming of air conditioners. All around her were deepening shadows. Where the fading light still touched stone and cement, their colors—gray, gold, ocher, saffron, topaz—were eerily muted.

Suddenly she was full of longing, a strange desire for something she could not name, but which if she could only identify she felt sure held the key to her life.

* * *

"Hello, Uncle Nappi," Eve said, standing in the doorway of the shop just off Eighth Avenue in the mid-fifties.

"Evie!"

Napoleone Petroangeli, her favorite uncle, was the oldest male in the Petroangeli family. He stood with a pair of shears in his hand, bending over a customer.

"This here's my nephew's little girl." Uncle Nappi made a broad gesture with the scissors. "Evie's going into modeling. Hey, Evie, when are you going to give your old Uncle Nappi a picture?"

"Just as soon as I get my composite made up, Uncle Nappi." Eve smiled at the sympathetic face, catching Uncle Nappi's eyes in the mirror. He had the softest, brownest eyes in the world. Uncle Nappi was always joking with his customers or singing things like *"O Dio del ciel, che fai fiorir le zucche, fate venire più belle le ragazze,"* a crazy folk-prayer asking the God who makes pumpkins bloom to make girls even more beautiful.

"My little Evie's gonna be a big success!" Uncle Nappi said.

After he finished with his customer, he drew Eve aside.

"You take this," he whispered, and poked something into her hand.

Eve's mouth opened in surprise as she saw the crumpled ten-dollar bill in her palm. "Uncle Nappi, I—"

"Don't say anything to your mamma and papa. They might not understand." The brown eyes twinkled. "But *we* know you're going to be a big model, and in the meantime, you need a little something—"

"But I—"

"Shh. *Zitta!*" the old man insisted.

Eve hated to take money from anyone in the family, knowing how hard they all worked for it. Uncle Nappi understood. "You can pay me back when you make your first killing," he promised, patting her arm. "You got everything it takes, Evie. You gonna be a big, big success."

Eve beamed. "Thank you, Uncle Nappi, thank you for everything."

CARRIE'S NOTEBOOK

June 28. The atmosphere was colorless last night, the people faceless. This was supposed to be a big deal, a shipboard party given by Edmund Astor, one of New York's leading lechers; but it was just another one of the tiresome things Geoffrey has dragged me to. I was bored and wondering why I'd come, when he appeared. Mel Shepherd.

And just as simple as that, the moment I set eyes on him, I knew I could fall in love with this man, and I knew why it was I had come.

What was it about him that drew me? The air of the foreign and the quixotic? I don't know. I'll try to describe him:

Dark sandy hair, wiry and longish, with a suggestion of a wave; a tinge of the sardonic about his mouth, with its arched lines; but he appears deeply engrossed in all he does and says—and watching him rapt in conversation, I knew exactly how it would be with that attention focused on me; arms that are relaxed, yet vital, with an inner tension, an inner dynamic (looking at those arms, I was desperate to have them draw me close, suck in my essence, give me his). There is something about him, a dash and sparkle, coupled with

46

gentleness and strength, and there is something about how he moves his lithe muscular body—and yes, even about how he wears his clothes—something that spoke to me and that had the power to make me feel I would willingly follow him to the ends of the earth and back, any day of the week. And now, writing these words, I know what it is—he so resembles Father! Now I understand.

When we were introduced I found out he's a motion picture producer.

"Have you known Edmund long?" he asked me.

"We just met. And you?"

"Oh"—he made a breezy gesture—"we have mutual friends."

He had come with the head of one of the major Hollywood studios, R. T. Schoenfeld. After the party Dolores and I had a late dinner with them at the Côte Basque, followed by dancing at El Morocco.

I scarcely know what went on at dinner—can't remember what we said, what I ate—for the only thing that mattered was being with Mel. At El Morocco, all sorts of people stopped by our table. Dolores, in her element, went out of her way to charm old, bald R. T.

Mel held me close on the dance floor; our bodies swayed to the lazy, sensuous music. El Morocco is one of the few places you can still dance in, he said. We were in a fog, deliciously so, and the music encouraged us to melt into each other—as if we needed the prodding!

At one point he held me at arm's length. "You're too good to be true," he said. "Every bit of you's for real. You're so beautiful I have to hold you away from me to appreciate you fully." He squeezed me to him, and when he kissed me lightly, close to my ear, I could feel his breath. How happy I was, nuzzling against his strong shoulders!

"I'd give anything not to have to go back to the Coast tomorrow," he said. "In less than a single evening, you're the most important thing I have."

Not since my father's death has anything touched me so deeply.

The first thing this morning he called! He said he had business uptown, and could we have lunch around Yorkville, if that wasn't too out of my way? I canceled two appointments

47

to see him. Am I crazy? Am I in love? The mere sound of his voice sent me soaring.

I was early, of course, and afraid he wouldn't be there. But he arrived only a few minutes late.

We ordered bratwurst, sauerkraut, potato pancakes, and dark beer, stuffed ourselves, talked and laughed.

"I'm a good influence on you," he said. "You're even more beautiful than last night."

"You only met me last night!"

"Yes, but I can tell I'm good for you. You need someone like me."

Yes, that's just it. I do need. Not just someone like him, but him. With him I could be more—more everything. He gives me the sense of belonging, of coming home.

Home! The similarity to Father is so strong it's undeniable; even Mel's hands—strong, and rather squarish—are like Father's were. Perhaps this is why I feel so right with Mel.

He said, "I'd like to make a woman out of you."

"You don't think I am one?"

"No, you're a young girl—a young girl alone. The world you're in is a tough one for a girl to have to fend in. I know how it is." At that moment there was a look of such gentleness about him. His unguarded eyes met mine. My eyes started to fill; my throat swelled. It was awful and wonderful, and I don't understand it. Nothing like this ever happened to me before.

On the street, he squeezed my arm and kissed me ever so lightly on the lips. We left in separate cabs. All day I have been full of him. He seems close even though he's gone now.

I can't believe what's happening. Is he too smooth? Is it all too quick? I hope I'm not being foolish. He said he'd call and let me know when he'd be in town again. Oh, I can hardly wait!!

* * *

"You sure were enthralled with Mel Shepherd," Dolores said as she tugged at her false lashes in front of the bath-

48

room mirror. Carrie was standing near the door; she had just finished the June 28 entry in her notebook and was waiting to take a shower. Dolores turned to look at her. "I thought you didn't like old men."

"Mel's not old. He's in his thirties."

"He's lying in his teeth. You should see what those guys go through. They're vainer than women about their looks. I know for a fact Mel Shepherd takes daily steam baths and has a masseur on his payroll. I'm sure he's had his face lifted. Did you look at the lines in his neck?"

"That's ridiculous!"

"You're blind, kid. I'm telling you to watch out for this guy. He's a notorious Casanova."

Dolores began applying cold cream, carefully massaging in gentle upward strokes so as not to pull the skin. "Hollywood guys are no damned good. I liked being seen with R. T., but do you think for one minute I'd consider having a romance with him? Not unless he hands me a contract on a platter. These guys are so jaded, they've seen so many beautiful girls over the years, one's the same as the next to them. Women are interchangeable parts for guys like R. T. and Mel." Wiping off some of the cream, Dolores got ready to explode her bomb.

She turned to Carrie again; then she said casually, "If I'm not mistaken, Mel Shepherd also happens to be married." She watched Carrie's incredulous reaction, then continued airily, "Oh, sure, Mel is married to some rich bitch. He's a real opportunist. Used her to get where he is, matter of fact. You know, Hollywood's rampant with nepotism."

She pretended not to notice how shaken Carrie was. Then the phone rang and Carrie ran to answer it.

Dolores peered at her face devoid of makeup, at the pores exaggerated from the shiny residue of cream, the grayish cast to her cheeks, and the fine crinkly lines around her small, red-rimmed eyes.

Without artful makeup she was ordinary. Her success lay in self-knowledge and carefully executed plans. You wouldn't catch me making a mistake like Carrie, she thought. That's what spells the difference between getting somewhere in this world and not making it.

Chapter 8

Rex Ryan closed the door of his office and clicked the lock, so no one would barge in on him. Then he sat down at his desk, opened his fly, and examined his troublesome penis. Yes, he was certain: first had come the painful urination, and now the white sticky substance from the urethra. He was sure; he had it again, the Big G, given him by that bastard Tom Calder, whom he had thought of as being so unsoiled, so clean. The prick!

Rex was finished with Tom anyway. The whole affair had been disastrous—and just last night he had indulged himself in some tangy, spicy rough trade that had really been exhilarating. But now this problem. What a nuisance, with business swinging, to have to go to the doctor and get penicillin. What a bloody bore having gonorrhea *again*. Shit!

The intercom buzzed, and Rex answered. "Honey," said Charlene, "it's about Lorna Carroll."

"Yes?"

"Remember the doctor we used in Queens for Nancy Avery and Sue Stoddard? Well, I suppose you heard he died. Now Lorna's in trouble and we'll have to find someone else. Can you help?"

"I'll have to ask around," Rex said.

"We've got to work quickly. Lorna's doing a commercial at the end of the week, and she's booked into the Coliseum for the trade show at the end of the month."

"I'll see what I can do," Rex said.

"And that mobster keeps calling."

"Which mobster?"

"Oh, what's his name? The warlord who's keeping Lois Daniels."

"Oh, him. What does he want?"

"Wants to know why Lois isn't doing more work."

"Tell him just because she's a good lay doesn't mean she's a good type for commercials. In fact, she's—"

"I know, I know. But try to tell *him* that tactfully. I don't want to get my brains blown out some night. By the way, luv, I'm all out of bourbon. Have you got a little something there for me? Something warm? I need a bracer to get through this bloody day."

"I've got something warm and bracing," Rex teased, "but it's not bourbon."

"Oh, shit," Charlene said, and buzzed off.

*   *   *

When she saw her first contact sheets, Eve was disappointed. She looked awkward and tense. The poses seemed all wrong, and the photographer hadn't done a good job in the darkroom. She'd hoped for much better pictures, but the agency told her not to worry.

"This is fine for a first group," Rex said. "Look, these two heads aren't bad at all. In fact, we can use them if he'll crop them right." He marked one of the pictures with a red pencil to illustrate what he meant, and Eve saw that he was right: minus the torso, which had been distorted, the picture was good.

"This is what test shots are for," Rex said. "It's always a pruning-down process. The pictures I've checked will be fine when they're blown up."

"Besides," Charlene said, "the photographer isn't one of the better ones around. I don't know why you picked him."

"She's seeing Franco next week," Rex said. "Then we'll *really* see some results."

*   *   *

"I brought you a sandwich, Uncle Nappi."

"Sandwich?" The old man was lathering a customer. "Sandwich is not what I'm waiting for from you, Evie."

Eve sidled up to her uncle, and they peered at each other affectionately in the mirror. "I've brought you *that* too," she said. "Surprise!"

"A picture? The one you've been promising all this time?"

51

"That's right. It's only a little one, from my contact sheets. Soon I'll give you a blow-up, though."

The old man was ecstatic. "I'm gonna put it up right on the mirror where everybody's gonna see it, they're all gonna see what a beautiful little niece Nappi Petroangeli's got."

How she wished she had a blow-up to give Uncle Nappi. Why was it taking so long? All the other models at the agency had such a collection of pictures. Even the new girls all had their eleven-by-fourteens. It shouldn't be taking her so long to get started.

*   *   *

"I had lunch with Uncle Nappi today," Eve announced at the table that evening.

"What did he have to say about the way you look?" her father asked. "I bet he didn't like having you in the shop wearing all that makeup."

"He didn't say anything at all about it."

"Well, what do you want to bet he doesn't like having you come in looking like that?"

"I look fine!" Eve insisted.

"You look like a clown. Those false eyelashes are ridiculous."

"I told you, Pop, models all wear them."

"Well, is there any reason you can't be different? You look much better without all that junk on your face."

"I have to wear it. The clients expect it."

"Honey, your father and I liked you better before," Mrs. Petroangeli said. "Before you were S., S., and G., sweet, simple, and girlish. This is the way Pop and I like to see you. We don't like you to pretend to be sophisticated, wear those cheap styles, and all that makeup. I'm sure the modeling people would like you better if you'd be your *real* self."

Eve grimaced. She'd never been allowed to be anything but fat and goody-two-shoes. That wasn't her real self—this was. She would do exactly as the agency told her. Charlene and Rex were directing her life now, and they knew best.

She realized how fortunate she was that Ryan-Davy was starting her out, for hundreds of unsatisfactory hopefuls, she knew, were given the brush-off weekly. The choice handling and management she was getting were reserved for what the agencies referred to as "top material." Now if only she'd get her eleven-by-fourteen pictures soon, and start working!

Rex and Charlene had warned her it would be slow at first, that getting a book together took time. But if Carrie Richards and Dolores Haynes, who were also new at the agency, had no trouble in getting their books, and in fact were already working regularly, why were things so slow in *her* case? The question had been eating away at her; she wanted to ask Charlene about it, and that evening she resolved that she would.

* * *

Carrie entered the bathroom in search of a lipstick. She was wearing a new dress, of a deep tangerine shade that particularly suited her hair and skin.

Dolores was in front of the mirror. "Oh, isn't that cute!" she said. "Where did you get it? I want one exactly the same, color and all."

"Bloomingdale's. Aren't you going out tonight? I thought you had a date." Since moving in with Carrie, Dolores had been busy not only with interviews each day but also with dates every night. This was her first free evening in over two weeks.

"Oh, I did, but the prick is in bed with a virus, so I guess I'm stuck home tonight," Dolores said. "Well, I'll use the time to practice poses in front of the mirror and try out new hair styles. By the way, do you think I should cut my bangs?"

"They don't look too long."

"Maybe I'll set them ten minutes. That'd help."

"They look fine. Besides, you're not going anywhere tonight."

"I want to get my hair long," Dolores said, pinning on a twenty-two-inch fall. "I mean, falls look great and all, but it's not your own hair, and I don't like having to disillusion guys. I mean, it's pretty hard to screw with that mess of stuff on top of the crown, and you might wreck the fall and all—a good one's so expensive. I paid four hundred dollars for this one."

Out of the corner of her eye she looked at Carrie's hair, nearly as long as her fall, but natural and so thick. She was glad she'd told Carrie that Mel Shepherd was married. Carrie had seemed subdued ever since.

The door buzzer sounded, and in a moment Carrie was gone. Shit! Dolores thought. She proceeded into the bedroom and sat down at the vanity. Its softly lighted triple mirror enhanced her loveliness. She stared at her varied images. Shit! she thought again. I'll be damned if I'm going to just *sit* here.

She rose, went to the dresser, and took out a small plastic box containing marijuana and some zig-zag papers. She rolled herself a joint, found a match on the dresser, and lit up, then dragged slowly, several times, holding the fumes in her lungs as long as she could, until at length the drug began to take effect. Settling into a comfortable position on the bed—one from which she could view herself in the mirror above the dresser—she took another drag.

My life, she thought, this has to be where it's at. God, I can't stand wanting everything so bad—to be everywhere, go everywhere, be with all the right people, the people who count, to wear Diors and St. Laurents, and to make everyone else look sick next to me. . . .

And to have everyone see me—opening nights, like at the opera and Broadway theaters, and important benefits, and big parties, all over New York in season. And Paris! And in January, skiing in Europe—Saint-Moritz, Klosters, Gstaat . . . I can see myself in the most marvelous ski clothes— maybe I'll learn how to ski . . . but who cares if you can or not, just as long as you look right—and fuck right, and I do, I do. Cocktails after dancing, and *après* ski lounging. Fun! I'll be casual, my hair a little disarrayed, with a band on, maybe, very little makeup—I've got the skin for it. Oh, and February will be the Caribbean—Round Hill, Lyford Cay, Paradise Island, Lucaya, Barbados—sun. The sun! I was made for the sun—my body all bronzed, in Puccis and bikinis and Luigi sandals, riding in a Maserati with all the barons, the gamesmen, the sportsmen, the princes, the rich, rich, really *rich* staring at me. Parties all night long, the gaming rooms, champagne at three A.M.

There he is—tan and rugged, in his two-hundred-dollar-a-day suite. Some count or other, maybe, in a blue blazer with a crest on the pocket, gold buttons, a Cardin ascot, and white trousers made in Rome. What's the name of the tailor?— Battistoni. Oh, yes—and he'll have a Dior flown in from Paris for me. . . .

I'll wear my caftans or my palazzo pyjamas. Damn, why didn't I learn French in high school? Why can't I speak it like Carrie? Damn her. White sand, palms, the blue, blue sea, soft caresses on my skin. And then in March, Acapulco! I'll slay them there. And oh, yes, we'll go on over to Palm Springs and all sorts of people will notice me in my tennis outfit. I'll have to learn to play tennis—no, I can fake it. After Easter, how about Seville, and then to the Costa del Sol, and God, I can just see me there, all those wild Europeans asking about me. And then Madrid, Rome, Paris, London, the thrill of that. It's where I belong, dining at Lassèrre in Paris, going to all the wonderful places *Vogue* and *Town and Country* and *Holiday* write about. And Sardegna—yes! Alghero—everyone's there, absolutely *everyone*, and they'll all see me, and some European producer will want me for a movie. And, of course, I have to go to Capri and Ischia, and Biarritz, and Monte Carlo. . . .

I want to be a star—I want to have everyone want me. God, it's such a shitty world. Women don't really count; it's the *men* who count. They're the doers in life, and the only way to get in is to be important to one of them—even if he's old and unattractive. Hell! Life is what you buy, and so what if he can't cut the mustard in the sack? Kicks a rich bitch can always buy.

The joint was burning her hand now, burning her tongue and lips. Sure, men all want to have me in bed, but I'm not going to be just a ding-a-ling. I count. So the bastards will really have to put out if they want *me* to put out. Shit! Why is it the ugliest schmucks are always the ones with all the money? Oh, shit, shit, I'm tired. I want to curl up and sleep.

Dolores crushed out the joint. Seconds later, her head fell back on the pillow and she fell asleep.

Chapter 9

Eve had had several grooming sessions with Charlene, and already showed the results: her appearance had taken on greater definition; her posture was improved; and she moved more gracefully. The big stumbling block was her voice, but she was a quick learner and faithfully practiced all the exercises Charlene gave her.

They were winding up a lesson when Eve put down the script of the commercial she'd just read, looked at Charlene, and blurted, "Charlene, tell me why Carrie Richards and Dolōres Haynes are working and I'm not? Why do they have books when I don't?"

For a moment, Charlene regarded her with surprise and, Eve feared, even annoyance. Then, still without answering, she opened a drawer and took out a handful of dog biscuits. Warren and Kurt came scampering from under the desk and sat at attention.

"Other paw, Kurt. *Other* paw."

Correcting his mistake, Kurt was rewarded with a tidbit. Then Warren performed—correctly the first time—and gobbled his prize.

Finally Charlene looked at Eve again. "Now what's this all about—comparing yourself to Carrie and Dolores. Come on now, Eve!"

"I can't help it, Charlene. I keep thinking how they came to the business about the same time I did, and . . ."

"And you wonder what they have that you haven't, right?"

"Yes," Eve admitted meekly.

Charlene lit a cigarette and said, "All right, Eve, I'll tell you. Who are you, Eve Paradise–Eve Petroangeli? The daughter of a Long Island grocer, brought up in a nunnery, never been anywhere, seeing the *world* for the first time, imagining that one day you'll belong to it, right?"

Eve nodded slowly.

"The plain fact of the matter is"—Charlene gestured with her cigarette—"that Dolores Haynes has been around this business some time. Had her ground training in Hollywood— a tough school. She knows the score, and how to play her cards. And as for Carrie, the girl has background, education, poise; there's a natural quality there that only superior breeding gives."

"I see," Eve said.

"Now, let's come back to you, Eve. Are you going to eat your heart out with jealousy over something accidental which can't be helped, or are you going to take yourself in tow and work to correct the things that *need* correcting?"

"I'll try," Eve said, not fully convinced.

Crushing her cigarette in annoyance, Charlene said, "I just won't have any more of this, Eve. Did you or did you not hear what I just said? For the love of God, I have to take my valuable time to go through such petty hogwash. Make up your mind, Eve. Do you want this business?"

"You know I do, Charlene. More than anything."

"And you want me to go on coaching you and helping you?"

"Yes. Yes, of course!"

"Then no more comparisons. Do you understand?"

"Yes, Charlene," she smiled in wan agreement.

"You're a unique individual, Eve, and don't you forget it. You have as good a chance as any to make it. But you have a lot to learn before you can acquire confidence, before you *know* you belong. This is what we're trying to accomplish with you."

Eve left the office determined not to make any more unfavorable comparisons. But it was easier said than done. How do you *not* think thoughts that keep returning? Somehow, she couldn't forget Carrie and Dolores, couldn't keep self-doubt away. And it made her sick inside.

I'm Eve Paradise, she told herself as she waited to cross 54th Street. I'll be a top model; my pictures will be all over, and everyone will see how wonderful I am. Charlene says I can make it; she says I have what it takes.

She had just stepped off the curb when the noise of a horn honking forced her to pull back. A shiny expensive English

57

car turned the corner. Through the polished glass, Eve saw a beautiful, poised-looking girl riding next to a handsome man. The girl was probably not much older than she was, but she looked so confident—so sure of herself, as though she belonged. All of a sudden Eve felt like a poor waif trying against impossible odds to sell something that no one would ever, ever, want. How had she ever thought she could compete with Carrie and Dolores?

Her eyes filled, as she stumbled backward on the curb and groped for a lamppost. The tears were streaming down her cheeks.

*   *   *

"Whew! This New York July heat really gets to you!" Dolores kicked off her shoes, unhooked her bra, drew her skirt up to her stomach, and fanned herself.

"I just had a shower. I feel much cooler," Carrie said.

"I think I'll do that too. Then what do you say we make it a girl-girl evening tonight? My date still has his virus. Anyway, I've had enough men in the past few weeks to last me awhile."

"Sure. Where'll we go?"

"How about Gino's? There's a guy going to be there tonight I want to case out. Oh, hey, Carrie, what came in the mail today?"

"Nothing interesting. Nothing but ads."

"Oh. Still no word from that Hollywood prick, huh? You can forget that bastard; cross him off your list." Dolores peeled off her clothes, strewing a path to the bathroom door.

An hour later the two girls sat at Gino's eating manicotti and *osso bucco.*

"I felt like the worst idiot," Carrie said. "I mean, they get you up there in the office, you meet ten people, and then they all line up and watch you *move.* They put on this pop song, and you're supposed to walk in time to it and look switched on and groovy, with all of them staring at you like you were some kind of clod."

"Shit, he isn't here," Dolores mumbled.

"And then, there are so many girls. I never imagined there could be so many models—and all cool. And well dressed too.

The competition in this business is more than I bargained for."

"I wouldn't worry if I were you," Dolores said. "You're just as good if not better. You can hold your own, same as I can. We're both of us unique, each in her own way." She was amazed at her charity and goodwill in conceding as much to Carrie, but the truth of the matter was that she was getting to like Carrie, and to lose the resentment she'd felt at first. Carrie was so genuine you couldn't dislike her for long.

"I have a groovy idea," Dolores said. "Why don't we go over to Twenty One for dessert? It would really be a gas."

*   *   *

"Yes, ladies?" they were greeted at the door to the bar at Twenty One.

"I'm Miss Haynes, from Hollywood, and this is my friend Miss Richards. We're friends of Mel Shepherd and R. T. Schoenfeld from the Coast. The gentlemen told us to mention their names anytime we wanted a table."

"Come this way."

A few minutes later, as they sat sipping coffee, eying the guests, Dolores said, "This is where it's at, Carrie."

"Is it always so noisy?"

"Look at that guy over there; why is he with such a pig? He looks rich, don't you think? I can smell money from here."

"The one standing at the bar's attractive."

"Too clean-cut. Clean-cut guys are bores. Besides, he doesn't look rich."

"Maybe not, but he's the kind you could settle down in the country with."

"Not me. I'm not giving up my career. I'm going places. You could make it too, Carrie. Don't you want to make it?"

"Oh, this is just a lark, a way to make a living."

Dolores pushed her coffee aside. "Well," she said, "we've seen the action. What do you say we get the check?"

*   *   *

"Do you turn on?" Dolores asked as they were heading home.

"Pot?" said Carrie. "No."

"That's too bad. I thought we could get high together. Have you ever tried it?"

"Once, at a Princeton weekend. I didn't like it."

"Too bad." Dolores was pensive for a while. Then she said, "You know, Carrie, you and I are worlds apart, really. We have completely different values, different tastes, we want different things out of life. You're so—I don't know— pure; and I'm . . . well, I'm *me*. Like I want this business, and you don't. I like to blow pot, and I like to fuck—"

Carrie turned, surprised. "I like to fuck too," she said. "What's so unusual about that?"

"You're okay, Carrie." Dolores grinned. "Okay."

*   *   *

Eve arrived at Franco Gaetano's studio at the end of the day, when he'd finished his assignments. She entered the studio timidly. All around were sixteen-by-twenty blow-ups of a blonde model and an infant she later learned were Franco's wife and new baby.

"Hello, there," Franco called out.

At last! Eve had so looked forward to this. And Franco was exactly what she would have expected a third-generation Calabrese to be: bombastic, large boned, and dark, with burning eyes and jet black hair.

"Look, baby," he said soon after the shooting began, "you're awful stiff. You've got to loosen up. Watch me."

He shook his arms, his legs, his head. "Now you do it, honey," he said.

Eve mimicked the series of rapid twitching movements.

"Okay, honey," Franco said, "close your mouth; close your eyes. . . . That's right. Now, every time I get ready to click the shutter, I want you to close your mouth and eyes; that way the expression will be fresher."

A few minutes later Franco demonstrated basic foot positions. "Once the stance is correct," he said, "the whole body will just fall into a smooth flowing line. The arms are more difficult than the legs because at first it seems you have no place to put them."

"I know. I'm all arms."

60

"Don't worry about it, baby! The important thing is to stay relaxed. Just try to be as loose as possible. Think of feathers, think of a cloud; pretend you're a swan with a long, long neck, gliding on a lake."

After they'd finished a series of full-length shots, they proceeded to one of heads. Then Franco asked Eve to lower her dress enough to bare her shoulders. She willingly obliged.

Franco snapped the shutter a few times, then stopped. "It won't do," he said.

"I'm . . . sorry," Eve said. "I . . ."

Franco stared at her thoughtfully; then he said, "Go into the dressing room and take off your blouse and bra. Tie a scarf or towel on your bazooms. I'm only shooting up to here"—he indicated a line on his own chest—"but I want a very long gazelle line."

Eve did as she was told, emerging from the dressing room wearing only a skirt and towel. She was embarrassed, but to her surprise, the embarrassment was mixed with feelings of recklessness.

"I put on some music, kid," Franco said. "It'll get ya in the mood."

Eve took her place under the lights. She couldn't help noticing how Franco's jeans clung to his hips and bulged at the crotch. Funny, she hadn't noticed before. Resisting a sudden impulse to support the towel with her hands—it really didn't need supporting—she wondered what her father would say if he could see her now.

Franco's pelvis swayed in time to the music. He clicked the shutter. "Great!" He clicked again. "Beautiful, honey! Now you're giving me what I want." Click followed click in rapid succession. "Oh yeah, baby, now you're doing it! . . . Now you're really doing it, baby! . . . Great! . . . Wild! . . . Groovy!"

Eve felt like she, too, was swaying. She felt herself burning, surging, felt as if the blood were being driven from her, as if her whole being was emerging out of itself.

Franco's pelvis was gyrating now. "That's it, honey! . . . Crazy! . . . Groovy! . . . Hey, luv, that's kicky! . . . Yeah, baby, now you're really swinging! . . . More! . . . That's it, give it, baby . . . Yeah! Yeah! Yeah!"

Eve marveled at this release, this wild, abandoned feeling she had never before known.

Suddenly Franco stopped and turned away. "Go put your clothes on," he said. "We'll take a cigarette break." All at once he seemed detached, removed.

While she was posing for him the two of them had seemed merged in a mutual love affair. She had felt sensual, soft, and womanly; he'd been aware of it, and responded. Now the spell was broken. Eve got dressed and, fully clothed, returned from the dressing room and sat down next to Franco on the couch, feeling confused and even more naked than before.

Before she knew what was happening, Franco leaned over, lips parted, breath audible, and moved his tongue across her mouth.

"Hey!" Eve exclaimed. "What are you doing?"

His arm had firmly pinned her. "Oh, baby!" he crooned, and his tongue swept behind her hair, into her ear.

Weakly, stupidly, she protested, "I—I don't like that."

He grabbed her roughly.

"That's not fair!" Eve wiggled free.

"I dig you. You're a wild chick." He shrugged. "You can't blame me for wanting to ball you."

*　　*　　*

Later, riding the Long Island Railroad back to Floral Park, Eve turned the experience over in her mind. No man had ever told her he wanted to *ball* her before. In fact, she had never even heard the expression. But its meaning was clear enough. *He wanted to ball me,* Eve kept thinking. He wanted to ball me.

Such an exciting world was opening up for her, so different from Floral Park, from anything she'd ever known. She felt released from chains. At last she was beginning to live, to move, to feel herself and her own aliveness.

Still, she didn't understand the confused feelings Franco Gaetano had roused in her. She wished there were someone she could talk to about it.

*　　*　　*

"Who is this friend of yours—Saul Franklin?" Dolores heard Carrie ask over the telephone.

"Well, Geoffrey," Carrie went on, "I think he's a rather sad, dirty old man—masquerading as a photographer."

It was the phrase "dirty old man" that caught Dolores' attention. "*Sad*, dirty old man" was even better.

"I couldn't help hearing you on the phone," Dolores said.

"That's okay."

"The name Saul Franklin sounds so familiar. I'm sure I've met him, but I can't for the life of me remember where."

"He got my number from information," Carrie said. "Tried to fake being a friend of Geoffrey Gripsholm's. Geoffrey says he scarcely knows him. He offered me two hundred thousand dollars in cash. Does that sound familiar?"

"Two hundred thousand in cash!"

"He just told me to take whatever I wanted. There was two hundred thousand dollars right there; the man didn't even have it in a safe."

"I must be thinking of someone else," Dolores said.

*　　*　　*

The following morning Dolores dropped by the agency with a new set of contacts for Rex to choose from (fags had such good taste about things like that). She then stopped in Charlene's office, made some small talk, then asked offhandedly, "By the way, have you ever heard of a man named Saul Franklin?"

"I used to know him years ago—who didn't?" Charlene guffawed. "And of course I've heard *plenty* about his recent activities. He hasn't changed much over the years. But I don't know if that's a tribute or an insult to the man. Why?"

"Oh, he mentioned he'd like to do some test shots of me."

"I can tell you exactly what to expect, honey. He'll start kosher, using a Rolleiflex. Then he'll switch to a three-D camera, and after a whirl of negligee shots, he'll ask you to do nudes—for which you'll be paid extra, of course.

"The pictures he does with the Rollie won't be of any use to you," Charlene went on, "because despite years of practice, Saul Franklin is still a lousy photographer. The three-D stuff in the negligee is all for him, slides for his private collection. Now this is confidential, Dolores, but the nudes can't do you any *harm*, because no one will ever see them but Saul Franklin. There's a rumor he sits over his pictures for hours . . . and jerks off. He must have a fantastic collection by now. The man's been operating since *I* began as an actress, and that was in the twenties, honey. In one way or another, I guess Saul Franklin's gotten to nearly every girl who's ever come to town. If you need extra money, it's a harmless way of making it—er, I mean, securing it."

"Harmless?"

"Well, sure. First, because he keeps his collection strictly private, as I said—though God knows what kind of a rumpus worried matrons may cause when the old bird croaks off. And second, because"—Charlene's voice fell to a discreet whisper—"well . . . because he can't get it up anymore."

Within the hour, Dolores had looked up Saul Franklin in the Manhattan phone directory and dialed the number.

Chapter 10

"Hi, honey," Rex greeted Eve as she appeared at the door after a day's rounds.

"This girl's looking better every day." Charlene smiled. "Excuse me a moment, Eve. Rex, do you have *any* brainstorms on the twenty-five-year-old for the Allerest commercial?"

"Sorry, not a one. It really is a problem since the FCC started dictating."

"I bet the public would never suspect all the people advertising pharmaceuticals on TV really *do* have a history of the ailment," Charlene said. "Oh, well. Say, did you hear about our little friend here?"

"What?" Rex asked.

"With Franco Gaetano. We'll really be anxious to see

those tests he did. He said the chemistry between them was fantastic."

"Chemistry?" Eve asked. "What did he mean?"

"Honey, that's what either happens or doesn't happen between a model and a photographer."

Eve felt her face redden. What had Franco told the agency?

"It's all sex," Rex said. "Absolutely *every*thing is sex!"

"My goodness," Eve said, feeling weak.

"Don't be embarrassed, honey." Charlene laughed. "You're going to have to get used to it if you're going to be a successful model."

Sex, Eve thought later as she rode home to Floral Park; sex. So *that* explains the funny feeling I had.

* * *

That weekend Eve worked in her father's grocery store, dreaming that the white smock she wore was a glamorous gown and that she was a model in steady demand.

After the store closed, she walked past the adjacent shops on Tulip Avenue and down to Our Lady of Victory Church. Inside, she found the peace she loved in the flicker of candlelight from the altars of the saints and the glow from the crucifix in the nave. Quietly she genuflected and sat in meditation for several minutes. Then she went to the altar of St. Jude, knelt in prayer, lit several candles, and dropped coins into the slot beside the altar.

"Help, help, help me, St. Jude," she begged. "Let this week be the turning point. Please let me get my pictures together and start to work. Please. I promise to spread word of thy benefits, to circulate pamphlets of thy prayers to all the faithful."

She bowed her head low, genuflected, and left the church, feeling immeasurably better. St. Jude had never refused her; she knew she could place her full confidence in him now.

* * *

Carrying a box with two dresses from the Safari Room, Dolores caught a cab from Bonwit's to 62nd Street and

Park Avenue. Saul Franklin was expecting her. He set to work on test shots, beginning, as Charlene had said he would, with a Rolleiflex, then proceeding to the three-D camera.

Dolores was lounging on the moire settee in a black lace peignoir with Jonah and the whale as a backdrop, when Saul said, "You have a beautiful body. I'd like to explore it to fuller advantage—from the photographic standpoint. Heh heh!"

"I've been offered three thousand dollars to be Playmate of the Month," Dolores said. "This is worth more."

"Are you out of your mind?" Saul, wearing chartreuse silk trousers and a brown suede shooting coat, placed the three-D camera on the Steinway.

"Actually, it's worth five thousand."

"Five thousand—that's a pretty stiff fee."

"Stiff, did you say, darling?" Dolores looked at Saul enticingly, giving him her most erotically taunting expression. "Must be a Freudian slip, that word. Saul, come over here, dearest."

A few moments later they were kissing. Dolores moaned and writhed, largely from revulsion. "Oh, Saul darling, you thrill me so. That's good! Baby! More! Yes! Oh, you're fantastic, darling! Oh, you do the most marvelous things!"

Then she pulled away, regarding Saul with feigned shock. "Why, you naughty! *You* are a wild sexy man!"

She allowed him to cup her breasts and jam his damp fingers underneath her bra. He was wheezing with excitement. Out of the corner of her eye, she saw he did not have an erection. She thought of what Charlene had said, and smiled.

Saul was unzipping his fly. "Suck me, suck me!" he begged.

Dolores looked at him forlornly and said, "Darling . . . would that I could."

"What do you mean?"

"I mean—everyone wants the same thing."

"Not me; I'm different. I'm not just interested in you for sex alone." Beads of perspiration had appeared on his forehead, his nose, his neck. "I like you as a person."

"Then *show* it," Dolores said.

"How? I thought I *was* showing it—till you made me stop."

"If you *really* care about me, give me the five thousand I want—for the nudes. Then you'll see how grateful I'll be. Oh, you'll be *so* happy, darling—you'll see. . . ."

Saul was still breathing hard but he paused for a moment and considered. "I'll make a deal with you," he said. "I'll give you three grand—okay? That's for the nudes, and also, we'll go to bed."

Dolores could see he had to fight to wrench out the next statement.

"If you can give me an *erection,* I'll give you a bonus of another grand, okay?"

"No," Dolores was resolute. "It's like I say . . . or not at all. Hard cock or soft cock, my price stands. Three grand buys the nudes and *only* the nudes, Saul. Anything extra's extra—and well worth it, too, I can assure you."

The old relic gave her a sardonic grin. "You come with references?"

"No, that's one of the charming and extraordinary things about me, the fact that I am *not* shopworn. As you well know, most women *are.*"

"Look, how about a fuck for two grand, and forget the nudes?"

She shook her head. "It's a package deal; take it or leave it."

Saul yielded. "Okay, you win," he said. "I don't ordinarily do this, you know. Usually my top price is five hundred. But I respect a girl who's clever; she deserves what she can get. You strike a hard bargain." He went out for a moment, and returned with five thousand dollars in one- and five-hundred-dollar bills.

"Now, let's get down to brass tacks." He grinned. "Or shall I say, let's screw, Sue. Heh, heh!"

"What about the nudes? You want to do them tonight or some other time?"

"I wanna fuck you first, deary," he said, lunging for Dolores. "We can do the nudes tomorrow. I'm horny as hell. Hurry, hurry!"

As she had anticipated, the old goat stayed soft the whole time and had to use a brace. She was surprised, however, at his absolving her from all responsibility in his failure to have an erection. "It's not your fault. You did your best, and it was a ball, deary," he said, referring to the seductive tricks she had used on him.

The next day she paid an early visit to Bergdorf's and ordered a full-length black diamond mink.

*   *   *

Franco Gaetano had done some absolutely sensational photographs of Eve.

To her surprise, he had made six blow-ups of his own choosing without even waiting for the agency to pick, and told her that if Rex and Charlene wanted others from the contacts, he'd make those too.

Trembling with excitement, Eve almost ran to the agency.

"Let me see. I can hardly wait," Charlene said.

"Oh, baby, these are wild!" Rex exclaimed.

"Fantastic, Eve!"

"Honey, you're a gas!"

"This girl's going places. I knew it from the start."

"You really are some broad."

"You've got enough of a book to start work now. Later you'll have twenty or more shots, but for now, this is fine to get you started."

"From here on," Rex said, "you're going to be working; wait and see."

"We'll have to go out and have a drink to celebrate!" Charlene declared. "Our little convent girl's learning fast. Cocktails ought to be her next step."

It won't be long now, Eve thought; I know it won't be long now. Thank you, St. Jude.

*   *   *

It was Thursday evening. "I went to Allen and Cole today," Dolores said. "God, what cute things they've got. I went crazy. I bought belts, scarves, beads, and sunglasses. How do you like this dress for a first date? Damn this frigging wiglet, though. I couldn't get to Philippe today, and he puts my hairpieces on so great."

Carrie was running a bath. She sat on the edge of the tub, clipping her toenails.

"Quit brooding, Carrie."

"I'm not brooding."

"You haven't been the same since you met that schmuck Mel Shepherd. I told you you're better off without him. I told you he's married, and still you can't get him out of your mind."

"I don't believe he's married."

Carrie got into the tub. God, what beautiful breasts she had. Dolores had to pull herself away from the sight of Carrie nude.

She said, "Damn that faggot Philippe. Wouldn't you think with all the business I give that pansy, he could've squeezed me in somewhere? Now this bloody thing looks like shit."

"It looks fine."

"Listen, Carrie, even if I was wrong about his being married, he'd still be bad news. These guys are all the same. Hey, do you think I should wear the black velvet bow or the rhinestone clip? I hate that clip. I wish it were diamonds, and then I'd like it."

"No one will ever know the difference."

"But I'll know, and that's what counts. But maybe if I wear it and this guy Serge sees it, maybe he'll take the hint and give me one just like it in diamonds. Where's my makeup case? I want to put on some more mascara."

Carrie pointed to the case.

"Thanks." Dolores unzipped it. "Do you realize how lucky I am to have a date with old Serge? Every broad in town'll be envying me for getting a crack at him. Hey, Carrie, do you have some white eyeliner?"

"I don't think so."

"I'll use my white lipstick then." She reached into the makeup case, and rubbed the lipstick on her lids, then above it, blended in some brown shadow. The operation took a full fifteen minutes. Then she pirouetted and admired herself from different angles. "You know," she said, "I ought to have a *Vogue* spread. I'm better than all those stupid rich bitches they use all the time."

Carrie, her bronzed body shiny and dripping, stepped to

the floor and reached for a towel. Dolores stared at the curve of her buttocks, then averted her eyes.

"Money," she muttered. "That's all it takes. Do you realize that, Carrie? It's the answer to the whole of life."

Part

~~~~~~~~~~~~~~~~

Two

Chapter 1

Rex could feel every nerve in his body quiver as he waited for his newest love, Sebastian Leonard, to pick up the phone.

"Hell-*o*," Seb answered.

"This is me, luv. Guess what? I've got you up for a Golden Fruit of the Loom underdrawers job."

"How much?"

"What's your hourly rate? Forty?"

"Yes, but I should get double on lingerie."

"Not in this case—"

"Why *not?*"

"It's very *rare* we can get those figures on our male models. Girls, yes, but the boys—"

"I don't know if I should *do* a job like that—"

"What do you mean? Why not?"

"It might be bad for my image, appearing that way, *showing* things—it might tend to *limit* me—after all, I'm an *actor*—"

"You need the work."

"Is it jockey shorts, or what?"

"I don't *know.*" Rex was really irritated now by Seb's ingratitude. He had been trying to do him a favor, after all.

Charlene suddenly appeared in the doorway with her dogs. Rex hung up and said, "What's the matter? You look upset."

"Hold the fort, will you, Rex? I have to rush over to the studio where little Danny Tooey's shooting the baked beans commercial."

"How come?"

"His mother just called. The poor little kid's throwing up on the product. They've put a bucket under him to get sick in, and he keeps having to eat those damned beans. After every take he just upchucks them."

"Oh, no."

"I'm going over there and raise hell. If necessary, I'll call the Health Department."

"Honey, when you get back, what do you say we plan on a meeting? We've got some coordinating to do."

"Let's make it after work."

"Swell. We can grab a bite. I'll even treat you, 'cause you're such a good girl."

"Thanks."

"Know where I'd like to go? Chock Full O'Nuts. They have the best forty-five-cent hamburgers in town."

"I'll be looking forward to it," Charlene said drily.

*　　*　　*

Dolores was now earning a steady income in print work; commercial interviews abounded; and the agency had submitted her for two new Broadway shows. From the social standpoint, her life was bursting with activity: she found herself dining often at Pavillon (chicken champagne was her dish) and at the Colony (Thursdays for *bollito*); the Leopard, Toledo, Le Mistral, Maud Chez Elle, and Quo Vadis became her haunts, as did La Grenouille, Lutece, and the Four Seasons; there was dancing at El Morocco and Le Club, and there were weekend parties in the Hamptons—the Duke Box, Bowden Square, the Westhampton Bath and Tennis Club.

Westhampton was where she went the second weekend in August. She returned to the city late Sunday night. Monday morning, as she and Carrie were dressing for early go-sees, she said, "Guess who I saw in the Hamptons?"

"Who?"

"That creep Edmund Astor. Oh, yes, and I almost forgot. When I was having my hair done Friday I found something in a fan magazine that might interest you. It's about your boy friend."

"Who?"

"Schmuck Shepherd."

"Mel?!"

"Who else?"

"What did it say? Tell me."

74

"I brought it home." Dolores pointed to a chair. "It's over there."

Carrie picked up the magazine, noting that it was eight months old.

"Page twenty-seven," Dolores told her. "It says his wife filed for divorce in Santa Monica. See, I told you he was married."

"But he's *not* married anymore. I told you, Dolores, he would have said something."

"So he's not married. So what? He's still a schmuck, and you're lucky you haven't heard from him. Well, *ciao;* I'm off. Don't do anything I wouldn't do—that should leave you a bit of latitude."

Dolores picked up her book and satchel, leaving Carrie staring at the magazine.

* * *

An interview that morning took Dolores to the garment center, a section of the city she loathed. To recuperate from its effects, she paid a visit to her health club and, detaching herself fully from outside pressures, relaxed in the aquamarine coolness of the pool. She went to the club fairly regularly. But the secret of a well-balanced life was, she knew, more than just unwinding in a gym or pool. You had to unwind in bed too.

Dolores had not yet found the noteworthy—and rich—Manhattanite she wished to concentrate on. It was important, she felt, to remain fresh for the big killing. But in the meantime?

The perfect solution to the problem of her sex life was offered two days later, during an interview for a bug spray commercial. Fred Logan, the paunchy, baby-faced owner of the film house that was making the commercial, greeted her with a sluggish shake of his lily-white hand, produced drinks from the bar in his large maple-paneled office, then said, "There's something I wonder if you'd be interested in."

"Yes?"

Fred Logan's mouth twisted upward. "Every now and then we have clients come in from out of town, and we like to fix them up. It could mean some extra cash."

"I'm always interested in extra cash."

"So we understand one another?"

"Perfectly."

"You'll be paid a hundred dollars to meet and have dinner with them. Anything extra's extra, and up to you."

Dolores smiled.

"Fine," Fred Logan said. "From now on, you're on our special list."

They shook hands again, sealing the deal, and later that afternoon Dolores celebrated her new-found prosperity by going on a buying spree.

* * *

A few weeks later, when Carrie got home from her day's appointments, Dolores stood admiring herself in the mirror. "See what new goody your roomy has bought!" she exclaimed.

"A TV! Now we can watch all those shows you used to do when you were in Hollywood."

"It's in *loving* color," Dolores cooed, sashaying and puckering up her mouth to see the effect she created in a new brocade peau de soie pants suit from Bill Blass.

The phone rang. When Carrie hung up, Dolores asked, "Who was it? Not Mel Shepherd, by any chance?"

"No. It wasn't Mel."

"Still no word. I'm telling you to forget that bastard. Well, who did call?"

"Edmund Astor."

"That creep. What a cheap son of a bitch he is. What'd he want?"

"Wanted to tell me coming within ten feet of me rejuvenates him by twenty years. Says I make him feel thirty again."

"The guy's obviously senile if he thinks twenty years ago he was thirty."

"How old do you suppose he is? Late sixties?"

"Early seventies is being conservative. I'd say more like early eighties."

"Poor Edmund," Carrie said.

"Poor Edmund, my ass. All these ancient Lotharios are deceiving themselves. It's really too much, the way they all

76

tell you youth is an attitude of the mind—talking about *themselves,* of course. Everyone *else* is old. They ought to take a good look in the mirror sometime. Can't admit they're dying on the vine."

It was true, Dolores thought. The only reason for spending time with them was cash. Trouble was, old buzzards like Edmund were too cagey, too cheap.

Dolores was grateful for her deal with Fred Logan. With financial pressures eased, she could relax and enjoy herself on free evenings. Her plans were working beautifully.

She stared with satisfaction at herself. Then she went into the bedroom to try on another newly purchased outfit.

CARRIE'S NOTEBOOK

September 18. I have someone I love! How beautiful that sounds, and is. Everything has happened. Everything?

Yes, Mel!!! I am full and bursting with him, with it, with us. The minute I heard his voice on the phone, Mel was the only thought in my mind.

Where to begin? Maybe just with impressions—fleeting moments. I see us as we entered the theater, crowds around us, yet us alone together. I remember I felt strangely anxious before curtain time, as though I myself were going to perform—or perhaps it was butterflies, being next to Mel again after so long.

We came out of the theater closer than when we had entered. The night was chilly, and I was shivering a little.

"Are you cold?" Mel asked.

When I nodded, he placed a protective arm around me and began rubbing my back in a way that made me laugh. I was giddy. In the taxi, riding to the Electric Circus, he made grrrring noises, like a teddy bear. I was glad I hadn't worn a warmer coat; it was so nice to have him bundling me.

More impressions. There is the picture in my mind's eye of the Electric Circus. Us wedded to the atmosphere; the music exploding in piercing, splitting cadences and suggestive sexual syncopations. There we were in the center. My every nerve and muscle and pore came alive in response to the music and to Mel. Over the noise, talk was limited. You communicated by joining the incantatory ritual, by dancing and abandoning the self, letting the music and the din infect the whole of you.

When we left, about two o'clock, I was glad to return to the relative quiet of the street. "You're really a swinger!" Mel exclaimed, hugging me.

We stayed out late, finally leaving the Brasserie around four. Dawn was beginning to break, and a rooster crowing from someone's apartment made us laugh.

"What kind of a person do you suppose would keep a rooster in Manhattan?" Mel asked.

I wanted him. I wanted him too much. Did anything have a right to be this important?

He put his arm around me, patted me, and said, "Come on, honey."

Riding in the taxi to the hotel, we scarcely exchanged a word. I was aware of the joy of his closeness to me, aware we were going to make love, and there was nothing to be said, for words were not needed now. It seemed I had wanted him for so long, wanted this, wanted to feel this way.

We reached for each other the instant we were in his suite, and just stood there by the closed door, incapable of drawing away from each other, or of ending the long, deep kiss.

At length we gravitated to the bedroom and fell on the bed a unit, tight and strong. It was as if we were enacting an event that had been ordained from the beginning of time. In the sensations of touch, taste, sound, sight, and smell there was infinite tenderness and awe, an intoxication and a holiness which reached to my bones. I wanted to be wrapped in his arms in an eternal embrace, incapable of dissolution— ever, ever, ever.

His intensity washed away all the uncertainties I had felt during the long, long time of waiting for him. All night and all morning we were together. I clung to him in rapture. His fingers and his arms, his mouth, his eyes, his sex, instilled me with the feelings of being cherished.

I had been waiting for something, someone to make me whole. I'd longed for this thing outside myself. And now . . . now there is someone.

Late this evening we kissed goodbye at the airport. Why does Mel always have to be flying off somewhere?

Half of me is dead now he's gone, yet paradoxically I feel whole, whole as I have never been in my life. Yes, and I have a feeling that my life is falling into place, and I am becoming the woman I was destined to be.

Dear Mother,

I really love New York and the business. It is marvelous to be leading such an interesting life. I still want to write and travel, but for now this is really fun.

Oh, yes, Dolores and I have moved. Coming up in the world. Dolores thought we could afford something swankier, since we've been doing well financially. I send my love, and hope thee is well and happy.

Love,
Carrie

Chapter 2

Eve Paradise had begun making money, mostly by hand and leg modeling and by posing for record covers. Then she had been hired for a trade show at the Coliseum, where she'd sat in a booth and handed out folders all day. Now Charlene wanted to submit her for a television commercial.

"Well, who else have we got, Rex?" Charlene said. "Can you think of anyone who's a sexy, voluptuous eighteen-year-old blonde besides Eve Paradise?"

"Every time we get a call for that type I've been sending Ann Young."

"Oh, honey, Ann Young's over the hill. She's been around this business a dozen years. The agencies are getting tired of seeing her. Quit fighting me and send Eve Paradise."

"Charlene, you know I have faith in Eve's *potential;* we're grooming her for big things, but she's not *ready* yet."

"She's coming along fine, Rex. Her new pictures are sensational, and the voice is much better. Besides, there's no dialogue on this commercial."

"She's still unpolished, Charlene; *toujours* the Italian grocer's daughter."

"You think Eve can't handle herself on an interview?"

"I know damned well she can't. Darling, Scope, Fletcher, Ward, Fischer and Reed is a very big account. You know how careful we always are when we send people there."

"Eve has to start interviews for commercials sooner or later."

"Darling, if we start sending her out before she's ready—"

"She's not going to be ready, ever, if we don't let her get some firsthand practice. SFWF&R is just one agency. If they don't buy her, there are plenty of agencies that will."

"Well . . ."

"This is necessary for Eve, Rex. She has to get used to go-sees, and I want to take a chance on her now. If she gets this job, it can mean a lot to her, and to us too. I have faith in Eve. Listen to me on this, Rex: who built this agency? Where would you be without me?"

Rex, knowing she spoke the truth, acquiesced.

*   *   *

"A deodorant?" Eve's mother shook her head in disapproval when Eve excitedly gave her the news that the agency was sending her on her first interview for a commercial.

"I don't like the idea, Eve, appearing on TV in front of the whole nation advertising an objectionable product."

"But, Mother—" Eve's face fell.

"And wearing a *negligee* besides."

"Mother! Please!"

"When you're older you'll understand, Eve. You'll know then, especially when you're a mother and have a daughter of your own. You'll see things differently then. Don't forget, dear, your father and I have always been right."

"But, Mom, I thought you wanted me to be a model—you said—"

"Dear, I'd be thrilled if you got a modeling job where you could be yourself, where you could be S., S., and G.—sweet, simple, and girlish—the way you really are. But this sort of thing, no—it's not you and it's wrong."

"Pop won't mind. He'll be glad when he hears."

But an hour later, when her father came home, he shook his head and said, "I've done my best to be understanding about this whole modeling thing that I never approved of in the first place. Your mother is right; deodorants are an unmentionable product, involved with unpleasant odors from the body—"

"You see, dear," her mother said, "it would be embarrassing to us. Now, just how do you think Pop would feel with everyone coming to the store—they'd all be thinking about his having a daughter like you, dear—advertising an undesirable product—to do with B.O."

"To say nothing of seeing her half exposed in a negligee every night on TV."

"It could mean ten to fifteen thousand dollars," Eve cried. "Do you realize that?"

"I don't care if it's a million," her father said. "The answer is no."

*   *   *

Eve wept all night and most of the next day. Finally her mother said, "All right. I know what it means to you, Eve. Go on the interview."

"What about Pop?"

"I'll take the responsibility. I don't want you hating me for the rest of your life because I stood in your way."

"Oh, Mom, thanks!" Through swollen eyes and a tired mouth Eve grinned in happy relief.

Her mother patted her hand. "I know how you feel, honey," she said with a sigh. "I always felt that way too, when I was young. I wanted things—glamor and excitement. I know Pop and I could never provide you with enough— and if you have this chance, you should take it. Even if it isn't the way we want you to be, maybe it will lead to other things."

Eve hugged her mother with gratitude.

*   *   *

81

"My God, what happened to your eyes?" Charlene exclaimed.

Eve told Charlene about what had been happening at home. Charlene shook her head. "I hate to see anyone stand in your way, Eve," she said. "You have a very unusual quality, and it can take you far. You're quite a woman underneath, but you'll have to discover it for yourself, and I'm afraid you never will if you can't get out from under the influence of what's holding you back."

"Well, they finally let me go on the interview."

"A lot of good that does, when your eyes are all swollen from crying."

"I tried to fix them with makeup."

"As soon as you learn to be independent there'll be no stopping you," Charlene said. "But we've got to get you away from Floral Park. You should think about moving into town. You're going to be getting busier and busier. It'll be the best thing for you."

"But, Charlene, it'll cost money. How can I afford it?"

"Don't worry about money, darling. We'll work things out."

"How? An apartment costs a fortune."

"Just leave that to me," Charlene said.

*   *   *

"Please, Pop, PLEASE."

"You're only eighteen years old, Eve. It's not right."

"Pop, you're living back in the dark ages. This is the last half of the twentieth century. Times have changed."

"I know young people today leave their homes. But not decent youngsters from good Catholic homes like yours. The ones who leave are hippies and all sorts of riffraff."

"That's not true!" Eve cried.

"I gave my permission for you to commute to modeling. I won't give it for you to live alone in Manhattan."

Eve ran off to her room in tears. The next day she begged her uncle, "Uncle Nappi, please talk to Pop. If I have to keep on this way, I don't know what I'll do. It's not fair."

"Evie, you leave everything to me," Uncle Nappi said.

"No more worry, no more crying. I tell you everything is okay. I just talk to your papa and when I talk, he listens."

* * *

Eve's tears and Uncle Nappi's talk with her father finally convinced him to allow her to live in the city on a two months' trial basis, during which time Uncle Nappi promised to keep a close eye on her.

At the end of September she moved into a small room at the Longacre House on West 45th Street, in the heart of the theater district; the rent was a miraculous $17 a week. Charlene was a genius! In addition to finding the room, she had sent Eve on leads that had resulted in her being hired for two part-time jobs, netting her $60 a week. One was an ushering job in a Broadway theater; the other was from nine to one, mornings, wrapping candies in the back room at Barricini. This gave Eve her afternoons for go-sees and rounds. The agency had promised to work around her hours as much as possible for the time being.

"It won't be long," Charlene said. "In another couple of months you won't need these jobs anymore, Eve; you'll be busy with commercials—and the residuals will be pouring in."

Chapter 3

It was nine P.M. and Rex was agitatedly trying to balance the agency books, something he hated to do, but trusted no one else to undertake, with the exception of Charlene. The two of them generally alternated the disagreeable task.

Oh, Jesus! Where was Tor? It was maddening. Toren Lovelace, his new flame, was absolutely *never* on time. All day long Rex had felt horny, anticipating Tor's arrival. Tor was the most thrilling boy Rex had buggered in ages and ages, but it was tormenting, because if they made a date, say, for seven, Rex would be ready for action then, but Tor would keep him hot and panting, straining at the bit, and not come waltzing along until eight or even later. What a sadist!

Sweet pain! The bliss of it. Soon Tor would arrive! They would make it on the office couch, and then go on to a gay bar, and then back to Tor's. Tor had a wild flat, terribly Grecian and phallic. He was so clever with interior decoration.

The phone rang.

"Hello, luv," came Tor's mellifluous reply to Rex's anxious greeting. "Sorry I'm being held up, but—"

"Where *are* you?" Rex demanded, unable to keep the bitch out of his voice.

"Oh, it's been dreadful! I have to tell you when I see you—"

"It's *ten* after *nine!*"

"I know, but it's this *job.* It's kept me late. You know, the booking for the record cover."

Rex, furious, felt even more aroused than he'd been before hearing Tor's voice. "Well, what *hap*pened?" he demanded.

"I'll have to tell you when I get there. Rex, luv, you positively won't believe it—"

"When are you *com*ing? I've given up my *whole* evening waiting for you." If Tor didn't shape up, Rex thought, he'd have to stop getting him bookings.

"I'm leaving right now!" Tor promised.

"Well, *hurry,*" Rex said, the irritation of his genitals mounting in spasms, affecting his voice and making it swishier than ever.

"I'll be *right* over!"

Rex looked at his giant erection and said, "Oooh, baby, hurry! I can't wait!"

CARRIE'S NOTEBOOK

October 10. *Fall—everything is fading now. It brings so many memories. The air at this time of year, the way a pure breath of it can fill your whole being and make you exhilarated and happy to be alive . . . I feel tonight, sitting here in this New York apartment, a longing for the familiar, for my home —for Father—and for Mel.*

Why hasn't Mel called? I can't believe, as Dolores does, he's just a wolf. Too much happened between us for that.

How alive and vivid my last memory of Father is. I can see him carrying his old umbrella, walking over the narrow cobblestoned streets in town past rows of red brick steps and neat shiny painted doors and louvered shutters, the pavement wet with winter rain, leaves sticking to the streets, our feet echoing over the ancient stones. It was mid-term vacation and we were walking side by side to meeting, but then he went ahead of me and I saw him limp. And in that instant I knew how much he had aged.

Remembering that beloved form, his solitary figure below the branches that trembled in the winter wind and beside the young trees that had been planted only last year, I feel a tremendous ache in my heart.

"I am the vine and ye are the branches; he that abideth in me and I in him, the same bringeth forth much fruit, for without me ye can do nothing." His voice, reading what I had heard him read many times before, now sounded out of tune, as though it were already his disembodied spirit addressing us.

I longed to see him as he once was, dressed up as Santa Claus, jolly and laughing, with the long white beard that the child that once was I, tugged off. Now all I could think was, No, Father, don't go; don't leave us; I want to hold you with us forever.

I never saw him again. There is so much that fills me tonight, so much I would like to share with Mel.

It was crazy the way everything happened so fast. It could even have been dangerous, but for one thing: Mel is sterile; he told me not having children of his own has been a big tragedy. I've always wanted a family, but this problem can be surmounted: there is an operation he can have, he said.

Mel could make my life what it was meant to be. It's as though all the answers are with him, and I just have to sit and wait and hope for things to turn out right.

* * *

Charlene stood in the doorway. "*Another* of those hooking in disguise things!" she said.

"What is it this time?" Rex asked.

"Arthur Lane. What a pimp he is; wanted me to send a couple of girls to wear bikinis at a party for some out-of-town clients."

"You'd think he'd know better than to call us."

"I set him straight. Oh, by the way, luv, we have several things to go over together."

"It's nearly time to close up shop. Why don't we go over to Woolworth's for a bite and discuss things there?"

Minutes later the two of them sat at Woolworth's counter, with Warren and Kurt spread-eagled behind Charlene, heads resting on their paws, eyes shut, oblivious to the movement around them. "Isn't it lucky for you I'm never hungry," Charlene said, biting into her slice of apple pie.

"You can bring the dogs here," Rex said.

"Don't give me that crap. You take me here because it's cheap."

Rex looked sheepish. "They have very good food here," he said defensively. "Why pay more? I mean, it's ridiculous to squander money."

Charlene finished her pie and took a sip of coffee. She said, "Remind me to put in a call tomorrow about SOS Soap Pads, and one on Bull Durham tobacco."

"I will, luv."

"I wonder what's going to happen to Gene Jones? I understand Heath, Hayden, Hildreth and Frost know about the racket he was running. Positively outrageous—those phony calls he'd come up with, wasting the girls' time making them read for him and then telling them they could go places in commercials if they only knew how to do lines."

"Then suggesting a school for them to go to—where he's half owner!"

"I always thought Gene Jones was a sly old bastard."

"It'll only be a short time till he gets a pink slip."

"The whole of Madison Avenue walks on eggs," Charlene said. "Especially now—from October to Christmas, when they give out the notices. Poor bastards. There isn't an ounce of security in the advertising business. It's the most vicious business in the world."

"Well, just as long as we keep raking in our ten per cent,"

Rex said, and yawned. He looked at his watch. "I gotta go. I've got a date at the steam bath."

"Have fun," Charlene said, and waved goodbye.

*   *   *

Joy rose in Eve as she left the theater in the Indian summer dark and became a part of the faceless Broadway crowd. She loved to walk home to her room at the Longacre House, passing the jazz joints, ice cream parlors, and film houses that in their garishness were so exciting and alive.

Her favorite shop along the nightly route was a place that sold lingerie: black lace underwear, flouncy crotchless panties ("Sexy Terry Training Bikinis"), European-style chemises, bras with holes cut out for the wearers' nipples to show through, G strings, jeweled pasties, diaphanous harem skirts. The lower half of one manikin, placed upside down, was dressed in transparent black hose. The legs, spread in a slight V, titillated Eve in a strange way she did not understand. She stopped in front of the store to look at it and to read the inscriptions on the photos of the actresses and strippers endorsing the products.

Suddenly she was aware that a dapper elderly gentleman was standing next to her, leaning on a cane.

"These clothes are very interesting, are they not?" he said. Eve nodded. "Yes."

"You find them exciting to the senses?"

"Well, I think they're pretty. . . ."

The man looked so well dressed she supposed it was all right to talk to him. Still, something about him made her uneasy.

"I should be pleased to see you have any item of your choosing." He reached into his pocket, drew out a card, and handed it to her. "If you will call me at my suite in the Pierre, I will arrange to buy your choice for you."

Her discomfort was increasing.

"There is something interesting here," he went on. "I wonder if you have seen that little sign in the corner. Can you read it? 'We make merkins.' I trust a charming young lady such as yourself has no need for such a product, however. But perhaps you have never heard of a merkin?"

"Well, no, I—"

"It's a wig for the pubic hair."

Eve turned and fled, tears forming in her eyes, her heart pounding. All of a sudden, things that had intrigued her revolted her, and the seedy men standing in front of the nudie houses frightened her. She felt so alone and helpless. The whole cornucopia of Broadway raced past the sides of her vision as something in her threatened to burst at the seams and split wide apart. I won't be scared, she thought; I won't. *Oh, Pop.*

Now she understood why her father hadn't wanted her to live alone in the city, and she cried inside, Pop, oh, Pop!

*   *   *

The advertising firm of Garrick, Ford, Ewell, Proctor and Dodson occupied three floors of a new building. After giving her name at the desk in the reception room, Dolores joined three other waiting girls, and without speaking to any of them, began to repair her makeup.

One by one the other girls were called. Then it was Dolores' turn. She was met at the entrance to the conference room by Pris Craig, a thirty-fivish career woman.

"Hi, Dolores," Pris squealed. A forced grin spread over her dried-out face. "It's so good to *see* you again!"

Dolores wondered how long it had been since Pris Craig had been laid, if indeed she'd ever been.

Wesley Ross, a neuter type, sat smugly at the head of the conference table, a pile of papers in front of him. He introduced Dolores to the four men and one woman who were from the client, Fast Fire Frozen Foods, and the agency's account department. Then he asked, "Have you seen a script?"

The president of Fast Fire, a white-haired gentleman with spectacles, was doodling on a clipboard. "Perhaps we should explain what we're looking for," he said.

Everyone turned to him, listening reverently as he explained that Fast Fire was putting out a new line of frozen foreign foods. "The packages have been designed by a top commercial artist," he said, "and will bear a relation to the countries the food represents: there'll be a Chinese coolie for chicken chow mein, the Eiffel Tower for crêpes suzette, Westminster Abbey for London broil, a gondolier and a gondola for pizza pie, a bullring for hot tamales, and so forth."

"It's a very original idea," Dolores said.

"We think so," the president agreed. "We've had it researched and tested. Now, in keeping with our 'far away places' theme we have plotted an intense campaign, and I think at this point I'll let George speak to you."

The account executive took over. Leaning back on his chair until it rocked precariously, he got Dolores far more interested in the chances of his tipping over backwards to the floor than she was in his words. Finally he handed her a script.

She peered at several paragraphs of complicated camera and video directions. In the column marked "Audio" there were only three words other than those to be delivered by a male announcer.

"That's the chow mein script if I'm not mistaken, George," the president said.

"That's right, Ed," George answered. Then he turned to Dolores. "I think I should explain that this is just a general audition script we're using for the time being. Each commercial will be adapted to the product it pitches, but for now you can use the chow mein script; even though we are not, of course, considering you for the part of the Chinese girl. However, the words each girl will have to speak will be the same for each commercial. We'll need a girl to represent each country." As he spoke he held on to the table and extended his arms to their fullest; the chair was two and a half feet away and at a 45-degree angle from the floor. "We've decided to use a product from each country for the first cycle of the TV campaign. Now, suppose we get to the dialogue. We're using three key words in the campaign. As you can see, those words are *far away places.*"

"But how you say those *three little words* is the catch," Pris Craig said, shaking her finger coyly at Dolores.

"Eventually," George said, rocking his chair again, "we'll require a different interpretation for each country. For instance, Spain makes you think of castles, of something mysterious and romantic. And France . . . well, if you were

89

reading the line for crêpes suzette, say, it might go something like this." He stared bug-eyed at the wall as he pronounced the campaign words, "Far Away Places," and one hand, released from the table, floated in evocation of what he imagined was the appropriate aura. "That was just to give you an idea," he said, allowing his chair to bounce back into place.

"I see," said Dolores, not seeing anything at all other than the fact that George was a lousy actor and would never be hired for the job himself.

"So," said Pris Craig brightly, "shall we try it?"

"Do you think you're ready?" asked Wesley Ross with apprehension.

Dolores pronounced the three words, repeating them six times in six different ways. The people around the table nodded solemnly, and a few of them praised her delivery.

"She might do very nicely for the Wiener schnitzel, Ed," George told the president, who agreed, wrote something down on his clipboard, then said, "Well . . ."

The word hung in the air momentarily. George then told Dolores that that would be all for the present.

"We'll be in touch with your agency," Pris Craig assured her as she was on her way out. "Would you tell the next girl to come in, please?" There was a forced bright smile on her lips as she gave a final coquettish wave.

When she got to the street Dolores glanced at her watch. It was still before noon. There was nothing definite she had to do until three o'clock, when she had a booking for a soap ad. She looked at the plodding stream of heavy and noisy vehicles, felt their vibrations deep within her, and looked around, seeing only stone and cement. That's all there is, baby, she told herself. So make it; make it big.

At twenty-five, despite the fact that she looked younger, she didn't have the time that girls who'd begun at eighteen did. Already her mirror at close up revealed tiny crinkly lines about the eyes, and gave evidence of a faint porous quality to the skin, a general fading of youthful glow, as yet unnoticeable to others. In the climb toward stardom, it was important to have that glow. Afterwards, lights would continue the illusion, but to begin a career, youth was the essential ingredient.

Soon! It all must happen soon! This was the critical period in her life, Dolores knew. Money, she needed more money— as much as she could get her hands on—money to create the life she deserved to have.

Chapter 4

During the first two weeks in October three things happened which marked milestones in Eve's life. First, because a Ryan-Davy model, due to shoot a national ad, was sick, Eve was sent as a replacement. The photographer, ad agency, and client, enthusiastic with the results, booked Eve for six more ads. Then the next day she got her first television commercial, a Diet Rite Cola, shot on location in Franconia, New Hampshire; she worked three days on it, earning Guild scale of $120 a day, plus travel time, and $200 in overtime.

She was thrilled. But an even greater thrill came when she met David Rosenberg, a gifted photographer to whose chaotic appearance she was immediately drawn. David's hair was dark, thick, and tousled; his brooding, interesting face had the darkly ruddy color commonly associated with healthy children and tubercular adults; he was tall and wiry, holding himself in a careless stoop, but he grasped her hand firmly when they met, and he instantly said, "I have some exciting ideas for tests. I'd like to do some type-C color."

"I'd love that," Eve said.

"I warn you, luv—no posing. It's an inner essence I want from you, a quality of soul. You'll see."

She arrived for the shooting made up, and wove her way through the littered studio, with its piles of eggshells, the empty soup cans and half-empty tins of sardines, the men's shorts and T-shirts, ties and khaki pants, the old newspapers, the girls' clothing, the plastic flowers, and the books and records strewn everywhere about. David, she decided, was just about the sloppiest man she'd ever met. He needs a woman, she thought, someone to help him organize his mixed-up life.

Donning the various kimonos he provided for her, Eve fell into the required mood. Inspired by the designs and colors and textures of what she wore, and by the records David placed on the stereo—to say nothing of the quixotic and thrilling David himself—Eve became languid and abandoned, absorbed in projecting emotion as he dictated. There was nothing, she decided, this man could not make her do.

Later, David wiped the perspiration from his brow and said, "I've just about had it. You were super, luv—really just fine."

"Thank you, David," Eve said. It was as if a current had suddenly been cut. "I think these will be the best pictures I've ever done. I can feel it."

"We'll have to have a drink to celebrate."

* * *

"I can't wait to see the contacts," Eve said.

She and David were sipping drinks in a dingy neighborhood tavern. He had swiftly downed, almost in one gulp, a double Scotch, followed by a chaser of water, and then repeated the process. Sounds of billiard balls knocking up against each other came from the back room. Now he was sipping a third round—slowly this time. All this had taken place in about fifteen minutes! Eve had never seen anyone consume alcohol so rapidly and she wondered if David might be an alcoholic. If so, this would be another area of his life he could use help with.

"You see," he said, "I had a specific *intent* with you."

"What . . . ?" Eve asked, startled.

"Regarding the pictures, I mean."

"Oh. Yes . . . ?"

"What I was aiming for was eroticism, sensuality, but with a freshness, an innocent enchantment. It's a purely chemical thing—alchemical, if you prefer." He lit a cigarillo, and looked fascinating in the process. "Yes, maybe that's more it."

"I see." Her eyes were riveted to him.

"At any rate, I was aiming for the impossible, the far-fetched, the daring, the absurd, and yet at the same time, the completely *natural* and normal—do you see?"

92

She nodded, though she did not. She lovingly regarded David's uncombed, unruly hair. It was a bit greasy. He probably used the wrong hair tonic. Clearly, he was too busy being artistic to worry about such mundane things as his hair. How dear of him.

"It's an area in which the unexpected seems right," he went on, "the only way it *ought* to be—all within the framework of balance, purity, and serenity."

"Yes," Eve said. She couldn't take her eyes from him.

David tapped the table. "This drink's the last for me," he said. "I have work to do in the darkroom. If you want to come back, you can watch me develop the negatives."

* * *

David's darkroom, with its enlarging machine, its trays of acids, its shelves holding various bottles and all kinds of paper, was somewhat neater than his studio and had, Eve thought, a general atmosphere of mystery. She stood silently by while he developed the negatives and hung them on a wire with clothespins. He said they'd take a while to dry and that he was going to wait until the next day to make contact sheets.

"We've got some beautiful stuff," he said, staring at the negatives with satisfaction.

"How can you tell?" Eve asked, not seeing anything beyond blurs of yellow and green.

"I know how to read negatives," he said. "How about a cigarette outside? Don't want to fog up the negatives."

They sat close on a low, cluttered couch in the studio. At length, after they extinguished their cigarettes, David turned to her, and before she had time to think, took her in his arms and gently kissed her. She felt the soft wetness of his opening lips, then the thrust of his tongue between her teeth, inside her mouth.

Her response came naturally and she found her body wending and winding, weaving and interwining with his, until the two of them were panting and moaning. Then, sharply, she drew away.

"What's wrong?" David muttered hoarsely.

"N-nothing, except—I mean—you don't understand," she stammered, adjusting her sweater. "I—I'm afraid. . . ."

93

He pulled her toward him once more. "Don't be," he said. "It will be fine."

She shook her head. "But it isn't right," she said, her face contorted. "I mean—getting that excited—it might get out of hand."

David looked puzzled.

"I mean," Eve went on, "the thing is, I care about you, David, and I want you to care about me too. . . ."

"I *do* care about you, baby," he said softly. His hair was even more mussed up now, and the expression in his eyes was tender and soft.

"I mean, I want you to have *respect* for me. . . ."

"Well, I do—"

"And the thing is, it's scary for me to get so—aroused. Because I don't know what will happen then."

"What do you mean, you don't know?"

"Well, I mean, I'm afraid I might—commit a mortal sin. You know, break the sixth commandment."

"Huh?" David's frown and gape seemed to indicate he almost thought her insane. "Are you kidding?" he exclaimed.

"So," Eve said, raising herself tall and looking at him regretfully, "much as I am attracted to you, David, and much as my instincts tell me I could—*lose* myself—I'm afraid I have to stop."

David stared at her blankly for a moment. Then he shrugged. "Fine," he said, and rose.

"You're not mad at me, are you?" Eve asked, worried.

He stepped over a few empty cans and kicked some others aside. Then Eve noticed him sort of jiggle himself a bit, presumably to take away his erection. Goodness, had she done *that* to him? In a perverse way, she was quite proud of herself. How she would have liked to have kept on with David. But of course she had to stop things, because sex was a sin in the eyes of the Catholic Church, and also because this way David would have respect for her, and it would mean she would be the kind of girl he'd consider marrying.

"Don't worry about anything, honey," he said, smiling. "I wouldn't want you to do anything you didn't want to do."

She couldn't resist asking, "But if it weren't a sin, would you like to then?"

His eyes bore deep into her. "I would *like* to very much, and it is *not* a sin."

"But in the Catholic faith . . ."

David tucked his shirt in his trousers. "Baby, I want to tell you something," he said in carefully measured tones. "You are the first Catholic virgin I've ever met in my entire life!"

Eve ignored his remark. Her father had warned her men would try to break down her resistance by playing upon her desire to be like everyone else, to be one of the crowd. "I was a boy once myself," Joe Petroangeli had said. "I know how boys are." In the long run, her father said, she would win out by being a good girl; she would win the man's respect, and he would want to marry her.

She sympathized with David. He was only acting like all members of the male sex had to act. Her father had told her it was natural for them to be this way, and that it was an important test for a girl. Eve lauded herself for having passed inspection on the first round.

* * *

That night, in her narrow bed at the Longacre House, Eve imagined how life would be when she and David were married. Mrs. David Rosenberg. Eve Rosenberg. Eve Paradise Rosenberg. Eve Petroangeli Rosenberg.

Mr. and Mrs. David Rosenberg Eve and David Rosenberg. David and Eve Rosenberg. David and Eve, the Rosenbergs.

Mr. and Mrs. Joseph Petroangeli announce the engagement of their daughter Eve to Mr. David Rosenberg, noted New York photographer. Their daughter is Eve Paradise, the famous model.

It was so thrilling she could hardly sleep. Her father would be pleased and proud, she was certain to see her a bride.

But that night, and the next night and the next, and during her daydreams as well, she was startled at how fully she abandoned herself to David, shocked at the things she allowed him to do. And somehow, nothing in her dreams seemed a sin, because she was in love, and giving came naturally. She wondered what her father would think if he could read her mind. Guiltily, she tried to shut out her thoughts, but the thoughts kept on.

Chapter 5

October 20. *Mel said he was going to be spending more time in New York. Even so, I had to wait nearly a month, till last Friday, to see him. The waiting was worth it. But I'm confused, uncertain where we stand. There are strange aspects to it all.*

The world is unreal when I'm with him. There is a sense of exhilaration, where I can never quite get my bearings. All this frantic dashing around he does, the calls, the lunches and dinners that have to be used to transact business deals, and the trips—always taking him away from me.

"You object to my work?" Mel said. "It's part of me, you know." And suddenly I felt guilty and sorry for having said anything in the first place. What a romantic, stupid fool I am to dream of being locked away from the rest of the world, just us. Life is real, and I must live in reality.

I know Mel is a fine person, one with a special integrity, something that very few men have. This quality attracted me to him in the first place, and it's this quality that I long to bring out more. But I remain puzzled by many things about him. For instance, when I asked him what he believed in he said, "I believe in myself."

"No," I said, "I don't mean that."

"Well, what else is there?" he said, perplexed. "Your own self is the only sane thing to have faith in in this world. Everything else is undependable."

"I'm not undependable," I said.

"I know you're not, but you miss the point."

"What point?"

"Never mind, sweetie," Mel said. "We'll talk about it

some other time." Then he excused himself, saying he had to make a phone call.

This is typical of Mel. His behavior is not despicable (as Dolores keeps saying it is), but simply aggravating, elusive. Yes, elusive—that's precisely it; I can never pin him down. I know men complain how terrible it is that women try to set boundaries. But I also know that if women didn't try, men would merely wander from one woman to the next, never finding the deeper joys that are possible in a closer relationship.

In bed, I began trying to put all this into words, but then he reached for me, saying, "Come here, you little nymph. You're the wildest, hottest little bitch I ever fucked."

Later, resting in the crook of his arm, I glanced over and saw him staring at the ceiling. The expression on his face, the way the light from the street struck him, made him seem strange and diabolical.

"Do you believe in God?" My question came suddenly, from nowhere.

After a moment's pause, he said, "I haven't been asked anything like that in years. But if you really want to know, I suppose I believe in some sort of force. How else did we get here? There's something behind it all, but as for God, I don't know. I've often thought we could be the work of devils."

"Don't you think there's too much beauty in life for that?"

He turned to me, kissed me lightly, and said, "You're very good for me, little one."

"I am?"

"You help me in the areas I'm weak in. I need you—I need you to make me more integrated spiritually."

*   *   *

It was as if a prayer were answered when we drove to the country Saturday. A whole day to ourselves! It was beautiful —the fall leaves so many shades of russet and orange and yellow, the air so clean and invigorating. I told Mel about home and how it used to be in autumn, about Father, and about his uncanny resemblance to him. He understood, and there by his side in the car, I felt I'd never belonged as much to anyone, or been more at peace.

"I don't see how you can have any doubts about God," I said.

"Where did that come out of?" he asked.

"It came out of here, everything, the fall flowers, the cleanness of the air—today, the happiness of all this, driving, laughing, sharing, everything. . . ."

"It has been marvelous, darling," Mel said.

"It's as if a button was pressed," I said, "and right here and now things were clarified and made stronger."

"Uh huh." He was engrossed in driving. I tried to discern his reaction, watching him out of the corner of my eye, but he just kept concentrating on the road.

I began feeling uneasy. How terrible it is to be drawn to someone the way I'm drawn to Mel, and then not to feel things progressing to the destiny I feel is right.

I said, "Now that I'm full of all this revelation, the question is, What am I supposed to do next with my life?"

"Have dinner back in town with me," Mel said evenly, his usual wide grin enlarging, revealing the straight row of white teeth. The late afternoon sun gleamed on them in a way as to make them seem unreal, Hollywood products.

I was thinking, life has to be more than dinners here and there. There has to be more than that. And I was thinking about our sex life. It's a knockout. Yet there's another element that enters in, too, and I feel something is not quite right. There's something weird.

When Mel talks of sex, I've noticed he almost leers. It's exciting, but in an odd way. Several times he's talked about our sex life when other people were within earshot; I find this appalling! Why, I wonder, was he so curious about me sexually? Why did he say, "You're not nice to me; you won't tell me about the guys you've fucked." Why is he always talking about my past? What made him ask, "Come on, who was it? Tell me the guy who taught you to suck like that?" Why can't he accept the fact that it comes out of feeling—of feeling the way I do about him? Why is he always trying to bring in other men?

"You're incredible," he said Saturday night. "No one'd ever believe how crazy you are in bed—you look so naïve and refined and ladylike. But why in hell do you play games with

98

me? Why won't you tell me about the other guys you've
fucked?"

"I don't talk about those things."

"It's not fair, you're mean to me."

"Why? You're the one who's not fair. Why do you keep
asking?"

"Because it excites me. When you're sucking on my cock I
like to think of your doing it to other guys, and when you
come it excites me if I can think of your coming with other
guys too. I like to picture you that way."

"Can't you just be excited by the experience itself, what's
happening to us together, now?"

"Yes, but it adds zest to think about you and other guys."

I want to think there's nothing in this, but I keep wondering
if it isn't perverted.

* * *

"Life has to be more than dinner here and there," I said to
him yesterday. We were having dinner at Quo Vadis. "Mel,
how do you really feel about me?"

"You know how I feel."

"No, I don't. I really don't. You've never said. You were
gone for a long time without a word, and now, this time together—well, what after this?"

"I never forget you, honey. I was thinking of you the whole
time, you know that."

"Know that? How do I know that?"

"Because I'm telling you." He touched my arm and stroked
my skin in a way that made me shiver.

"You never called or wrote."

"I did call you a couple of times. You weren't in. And I
told you I'm not much of a correspondent. Dear, you have to
understand my business takes most of my time. Besides, we're
three hours behind you. I wouldn't want to wake you by
calling you in the middle of the night. You need your beauty
rest." His smile was irresistible, and he was convincing me.
"But I thought about you all the time," he continued, "and I
wanted to be with you all the time. I felt as bad as you did,
darling."

"I'm sorry," I said. "It's just that I don't want to be just a way of passing the time."

"You'd never be that."

"What I mean is, Mel, I need a life."

He said, "You have a wonderful life right now, and you know something? You always will have. You're an utterly delightful, exceptionally beautiful and intelligent girl. You'll never have trouble, no matter what. You're young and lovely and"—he leaned in closer and breathed the words in my ear in a way that made me nearly moan—"you have me."

I clasped his hand. "Do I? Do I have you?"

"Of course you do."

I leaned on his shoulder a little, and asked, "How do I have you?"

"You're the wildest little bitch I ever had in bed, I told you—"

"I mean more than that—I mean, in what ways can I depend on you?"

He looked puzzled.

"What do I mean to you? You've never said. Mel, I have to know."

He moved his neck as though his collar were tight. "I don't fare well in this type of discussion. It's tough to put intangibles into words."

"It doesn't have to be intangible. It can be real."

"You and I are real. We're real together."

"I mean more than that. I told you, Mel, I need a life. I need to belong to someone—to make a life together, that's what I mean."

He frowned. "Honey," he said, "as soon as this mess with Margaret is cleared up . . . I don't know—my life is so complicated—you have no idea. You want to put the cart before the horse, and things just don't work that way."

That's the worst thing—his wife. From the clipping Dolores showed me, I was under the impression the divorce was in the works. It's all very strange. After I'd been expecting him to stay a month, he suddenly told me he had to fly to California, problems on his next picture; and then he added, ever so casually, "My wife called. There are problems on the home front in addition. A family thing. . . ."

My wife! he said. *Wife, not* ex-*wife. And the way he'd said it—so easily.*

"I thought you were divorced," I said.

"Not yet."

"I thought I saw it in the papers."

"Oh, well, Margaret did file for divorce, yes; but that action was revoked. We went back together again that time, but now . . ."

"You mean"—I felt numb—"you're still married to her."

"Don't get upset, honey. This is a very long and complicated story. Sometime when we have a few hours together I'll tell you all about it."

"But you're still married!"

"No, dear, the divorce is going to be on again, as of a couple of days from now."

"But you *are* still married. You called her your wife."

Mel laughed as though to brush it all aside; then he kissed me lightly. "The last reconciliation didn't take," he said levelly, staring into my eyes. "This has been going on for some time. We've tried to make it work for the children's sake—I told you we adopted two kids, because of my sterility problem, didn't I? Well, the whole thing between Margaret and me has been dead for some time now; it can't work no matter what, and we both know it. Children or no children, we've definitely decided to split for good this time. Our attorneys are drawing up a property settlement right now, matter of fact." *He flashed me a brilliant smile.* "That's one of the reasons I have to go back to the Coast."

"Oh."

"I love you, honey," he said. "Things will work out, you'll see. You and I will be together. Don't you have any confidence in me?"

"Of course I have."

He looked into my eyes again. "I'm telling you in sincerity I love you," he said. "Business is going to be hectic for the next couple of months, to say nothing of domestic problems, which I hate to even think about—but after I can get all this mess cleared away, we can be together always if you want."

"I do want." *I said it softly, earnestly. But a part of me still feels—lost, unaccepted, as though I had been let down.*

101

Chapter 6

Eve waited impatiently to hear from David. Though she was eager to see the pictures he'd taken, even more than that she wanted to hear his voice, to have him invite her to the studio again. Her thoughts were full of what would happen then.

Finally, after several days, David telephoned. She told him she'd be right over, and within the hour was at his studio, gasping in delight: David had made a half a dozen beautiful color blow-ups, each more staggering than the next.

It was as if something larger than life had been caught and preserved. There in the color, in the light and shadow, was all the joy, the poetry, the tenderness David had seen in her.

Her love for him mounted in paroxysms. She gazed at him with loving eyes, wanting him to know how much he meant to her. Soon he would kiss her again, send her into ecstasy as he had done before. Then they would neck in that wonderful magical way, and again she would have to call a halt, lest things go too far and David lose respect for her. In time, David would desire her so much he would propose and they would get married. Eve sucked in her breath, anticipating the moment he would clasp her in his arms.

"I have to go over to Peerless and pick up some type-C paper," David said.

She couldn't conceal her disappointment. Hadn't he understood she would like to neck with him again? She wanted to say something, but a nice girl couldn't tell a man, I'd like to neck with you. Only a loose woman would ever say a thing like that.

Sadly, she bid David goodbye, and watched his lean and sensual figure until it rounded the corner.

*   *   *

Eve knelt in the dimness of the church. She looked at the beautiful statue of St. Jude, who had helped her so much. She thanked God for all the help and love He offered to man in the inspiring examples and intercession of the saints; then she thought of some of the words of the mass, contained in the Nicene Creed, and meditated on them: "I believe in all things visible and invisible . . . and in Jesus Christ, born of the Father before all ages . . . light of lights . . . true God of true God . . . being of one substance with the Father, by whom all things were made. . . . He will come again with glory to judge the living and the dead, and of His kingdom there will be no end . . . I confess one baptism for the remission of sins, and I wait for the resurrection of the dead, and the life of the world to come."

The spirit of God, peace and joy, flooded her being. Now more than ever before, she understood about Love. All the love man could give or receive or feel or experience in life was a gift of God, and she was the recipient, in her feelings for David, of a force higher and greater than herself.

* * *

The next Sunday at mass, Eve sat in ardent expectation as the priest consecrated the wafers and wine. During the Our Father, she prayed fervently. It seemed as if she had never before heard the words so clearly: "Lord, I am not worthy that thou should come into my room, but say the word and my soul shall be healed."

At that, she rose, went to the railing, and took the wafer. "This is my body, which was given for you. Do this in remembrance of me. This is my blood of the New Testament, which was shed for you and for many for the remission of sins."

As the bread and wine changed into the body and blood of Jesus, Eve experienced it as a living reality. She felt the divine essence, the spirit of God in her heart, felt it surging out from her skin and her being. It was as if her whole body were incandescent, filled with a warm, glowing light.

Thank you, God, she said silently. Thank you for this life, for this knowledge of Thy love, for the spirit of the Blessed Lord flowing in me. Forever and ever, amen.

She made the sign of the cross, and stepping out into the sun, knew she had the strength to make things work out with David.

* * *

Charlene, Carrie, and Dolores sat lingering over Sunday brunch. They had drunk Bloody Marys (Charlene had had four) and Pouilly-Fuissé, ordered *canard à l'orange*, baked Alaska, coffee, and Cointreau. Charlene had merely picked at her food. Kurt and Warren lay in relative peace in the checkroom, their occasional arfs not seeming to disturb the fashionable guests at the Four Seasons.

"Oh, I'm telling you, it's quite an experience running an agency in this business," Charlene said. "I ought to write a book. Between testifying in court cases, trying to cover and beard for half our kids, keeping ex-husbands away, lying to lovers, arranging abortions, pacifying the Mafia—"

"The Mafia!" Carrie exclaimed.

"Oh, sure, honey, one of our girls goes with a top gangster. And I mean a *really* top gangster. If I told you his name, you'd run for cover. Well, between all the activities, all I can say is it sure is nice to come out on a Sunday, relax this way, have a delicious lunch—the delightful company of you two girls, marvelous booze. What more could an old dame ask for?"

"Old, no, Charlene," Dolores protested. "You are one of those rare people who is eternally young."

Charlene grinned and took another mouthful of Cointreau. "I love you, honey. We'll see how young *you* feel after some forty-odd years in the business, four husbands, a hundred or more lovers, the load of the whole agency on your shoulders, the kids and all their problems, watching out for Rex—"

"Can't Rex watch out for himself?" Dolores asked.

"Rex is a lovely boy," Charlene answered. "I suppose over the years he's become like the son I never had. But, I'll tell you—the thing about him is, he can't hold his liquor. Now, I admit I'm an old souse. Can't live without my daily quota. In fact, you might say I drink to keep sober. But Rex is something else. With a few drinks in him he goes crazy. Has these crazy spells."

They ordered another round of Cointreau, and Charlene grew more garrulous. "Everybody's so influenced by television, magazines, films, newspapers, fashion, records. It's as though everything was part of a plot to make us all dying to be part of the world that *matters*. I know how it is for you two. You're just on the edge of the magic circle, the one everybody's clamoring to get into. When can you feel you really belong?" Charlene's eyes were watery and seemed to be looking into the far, far distance. "Is it all worth it?" she said. "I sometimes wonder if life itself is worth it."

"You have to believe life is worth it," Carrie said. Her eyes flashed with missionary zeal. "Otherwise . . . what?"

"Life is worth it when you know exactly where you're going," Dolores said.

"But when you make it, then what?" Charlene said. "I wonder how many of the kids ever consider that? I've often thought in this business it's really the blind leading the blind, and everyone believing youth and looks last forever. Oh, you kids don't realize what you've got, even in the mere fact of youth alone. *These* are the years that count, the years when you've got the chance to put yourselves across. For Christ's sake, use what you've got now." Charlene pounded her fist on the table, shaking the glasses and silver. "Use your looks and your youth. This business gives you an open sesame. Use it to find a rich husband, someone to set you up for life. Don't neglect the personal aspect of your lives. Oh, I wish I had the opportunities you girls have."

"Well, you did all right in your day, Charlene," Dolores pointed out.

"Sure, I did fine. Husbands, lovers, upheavals, cash down the drain, feasts and famines, all kinds of wild scenes. That's all behind me now. I learned a lot. Saw a lot. Did a lot. Now I just wish I could put old heads on young shoulders . . . and maybe in my own case, just the opposite!" She took a warming gulp of her Cointreau and seemed to enter a shadowy half-world of personal dreams.

"Life has a way of turning out other than you expect it to," she said with a bitter-brave smile. "All I live for now is the agency, the kids, the dogs—and this." She held up her glass, inviting Dolores to clink with her.

105

Carrie said, "Charlene, you've got a lot more going for you than most women your age."

"That's for damned sure. Thank God, I keep active."

"It seems to me," Carrie said, "that most of the girls in this business never find anything meaningful. Their only satisfaction comes from having material things."

"Any smart girl who's in the business realizes one important thing, honey," Charlene said, "she's a commodity. Carrie, you are a commodity; Dolores is a commodity. For as long as the two of you are in the business, you *remain* commodities, and don't you ever forget it. It's pretty hard to operate on any other basis."

"Well," Carrie said, "I certainly think of myself as more than a commodity."

"Don't you understand, honey?" Charlene said. "It's the eternal barter. As the old saying goes, women lay, and men pay. Granted, it's true everywhere, but nowhere more so than in this town and in this business. Do you think you're invited to cocktails, to dinner, or for a weekend, because of your mind or your soul . . . or some damned thing? No, honey, it's because of your face and your body. I tell you it's the eternal barter, and you're a commodity."

Carrie shook her head and insisted, "I want more out of life than that."

"You should be grateful for the opportunities," Dolores said, "for all the chances you get. Think how many girls would love to be in your shoes, Carrie, doing commercials, being sought after—having men calling."

"They're nothing but playboys," Carrie said.

"There's one guy she digs though," Dolores said, "and he's the worst playboy of all. Only try and tell her that."

Charlene said, "Do tell."

"Mel Shepherd."

"Oh? The big-shot producer? Who was it he married? Some film tycoon's daughter? Smart man, if I recall correctly. Devastating sort of appeal."

"You've nailed him," Dolores said.

Charlene said, "Just be careful and don't get hurt, honey. I know all about chemistry. There's nothing like it in the world. Enjoy it when it happens to you, but know what to believe and what not to believe."

Dolores said, "Oh, she believes everything. She's been mooning around over him so long now it's been making her sick."

"This is really serious, then," Charlene said. She toyed with her glass, watching the lights from her silver-pink nails shining in the liquid inside. "Well, honey, be wise. Make the most of your opportunities. Don't put all your eggs in one basket. Try to look beyond this business to something else. Because your youth vanishes, and along with it, your opportunities. Do you want to lose out because you were stupid and idealistic? Because you didn't grab your chances while they were at hand?"

"Well," Carrie said impatiently, "I think that at my age, I've got a *few* good years left."

"Sure you have, honey," Charlene said. "You're a baby yet. The thing is to get into good habits, to learn to play the game. It'll stand you in good stead the rest of your life."

"I don't want to play games," Carrie said. "That's what's so maddening about this whole business—so much emphasis on surface values, on face and body and phony charm, on—"

"So who's complaining?" Dolores asked. "You've got no worries on that score."

"No," Carrie said. "But who wants to be judged and appreciated on that basis alone? The people who can hire us, and the people we meet socially, none of them seem to have any other criteria."

Charlene shrugged. "It's a question of direction. A smart girl knows how to play her cards. She sees the opportunities this business offers."

"But that's just my point, Charlene," Carrie said. "*What* opportunities? The social life led by most models in this town is empty; they end up marrying playboys, and all they have is money."

"Money is something I wouldn't underestimate, if I were you," Charlene said.

Dolores said, "I think this business is a wonderful way of gaining attention and social acceptance. It's carte blanche into better worlds . . . everywhere."

"Of course!" Charlene said. "Dolores is right. Carrie, you have no idea of the intoxication, the power, the strength a woman has. You girls have the chance to be what the female

107

deities were to the Greeks! Do you realize what that *means?* You have the opportunity to be a symbol of glory."

Carrie sighed. "I want more than to be a symbol, Charlene. I want ever so much more."

"Well, honey, all the advice I can give you from my more than forty years' experience is this: play it smart. A beautiful woman has problems other women haven't begun to imagine. You've got to take measures, or you'll end up victimized."

"Meaning?"

"Meaning don't ever underestimate the importance of all the men you seem to be spurning all over the place. *Get yourself a live one.* This can be your deliverance."

"To what?"

"The deliverance of your life. To the life you'll be leading for the next forty or fifty years, God willing."

"There's more to life—more than what you describe," Carrie said.

"No," Charlene insisted. She reached for Carrie's untouched glass of Cointreau and took a man-sized swill. For a moment she looked unsteady, then, regaining her balance, she turned her attention once more to Carrie. "If you don't take measures, you'll just end up being used all over the place. Men feed on beauty the way a horse feeds on oats. They make use of a beautiful woman like you, and then throw her aside for a younger dame. And you'd better be careful and not have any illusions about Mel Shepherd."

"I've been trying to tell her that, Charlene," Dolores said.

Carrie said, "Don't either of you two believe in love?"

"Love?" Charlene repeated the word with cynicism. "Sure, I believe in love. I have two loves. The dogs, because they're above human selfishness, and the bottle, because it makes everything bearable."

Chapter 7

Mauve, gray, pink, blue, and violet colors surrounded the Manhattan skyline. It was early evening now. Carrie sifted through the contents of her satchel, extracted her Madison Avenue Handbook, and read the series of scrawly entries from the past week, the last one in the month of October. How time flew. Meeting people, activity, motion, the propulsion of the business were interesting, but it seemed sad, somehow, to be using such a small part of herself.

"What's the matter?" Dolores asked, seeing Carrie silent and pensive.

"I was thinking about our discussion at lunch last Sunday. And about how real and alive some moments are, with some people, and how superficial others are. I mean, when you think of people like Geoffrey Gripsholm and Edmund Astor, and how empty their lives are—"

"Empty? Why empty?" Dolores asked. "I think Geoffrey and his group live very well."

"Yes, they live well in the material sense, but I guess I only want one thing—love. And I miss Mel."

"How long since you've heard from your friend this time?"

"Over a week. He's not much of a correspondent."

"Except in bed," Dolores said, and moved into the bedroom to change clothes for an evening date.

She smiled at herself in the mirror. Beauty, that was the most important raw material in the world. Carrie had that. But what Carrie lacked was power, power to create and enhance the illusion. And beauty without power was nothing, a wasted commodity. Poor Carrie, believing in love.

So what if Carrie was beautiful? Her life was standing still because she didn't understand reality. Dolores knew an important secret; that one pubic hair on a woman's body is stronger than the Atlantic Cable. Carrie, not possessing this knowledge, operating with false illusions, was doomed to failure.

Dolores gave herself a final once-over. She smiled again, satisfied that everything was in order and running according to plan.

* * *

When Eve showed Charlene David's photos of her, Charlene was full of praise. "I just can't get over how relaxed you've become in front of the camera," she said.

"I owe it all to David," Eve said. "He's the most wonderful photographer, Charlene, the most talented, the most fantastic—"

"Oh, ho!" Charlene exclaimed. "So love has hit our little Eve Paradise!"

Eve blushed.

"Don't be embarrassed, honey! It's the most natural thing in the world. When the chemistry's right, a girl blossoms. I'm glad it's happened to you; it'll do you a world of good. Have a good time with it."

Eve would have liked to confide her ambivalent and confused feelings to Charlene, to tell her about the time she and David had gotten so excited on the couch, and to ask for her advice. But she was too embarrassed. What if Charlene thought her cheap, or untrue to her religion, or thought that she was trying to use David in order to get ahead in modeling?

* * *

A few days later, Eve was sitting in the outer office waiting to see Charlene. She had just finished a job at the Coliseum with Leslie Savage, one of the models at the agency. It was Leslie's voice she heard coming through the open transom. "God, Charlene," Leslie said, "Bruno is the most marvelous lay I've ever had."

"For heaven's sake, Leslie," Charlene said, "don't let Ralph Winston find out, whatever you do. You've got to keep him on the string at least another month—that account means twenty thousand dollars in commissions to the agency."

"Don't worry, sweetie, I delivered the account last year, didn't I?"

"Right, and Rex and I are counting on keeping it this year."

"Well, Ralph Winston means a whole lot more than twenty thousand a year to me, Charlene. You don't think I'm going to let him stop keeping me just to ball another guy, do you? What has Bruno got to offer besides a cock?"

"Good, Leslie, I was sure you'd say that."

"I'll just sneak around with Bruno."

"That won't be easy," Charlene said. "You know how jealous Ralph is. He practically has a full-time detective force on you."

"Well, I'm counting on you to beard for me, Charlene."

"Any time, honey, any time. I know how it is."

"I'm not going to stop screwing Bruno. He's too sensational."

"Honey, you don't have to tell me. A really exceptional lay can be the greatest milestone in a girl's life."

Eve was shocked. From everything she'd been taught, she believed that only an immoral tramp would talk like Leslie. But Leslie was a lovely girl, refined and sweet. And Charlene! To think she had worried what Charlene might think of her own actions with David.

Something in Eve sank. She felt left out, left behind. All those teen years when other girls had been out having fun, she'd been fat and out of it. Now those girls had the jump on her; they had experience and know-how, while she was shy and unsure of herself.

Maybe her father was wrong. Maybe the Catholic religion was wrong. Maybe if a girl was really in love . . .

Oh, to be in David's arms again—and just let things take their course!

All Eve could think of was the magic of the time she had been with David, of the sweetness and the awareness of power and love. And now—emptiness, nothing.

Several times she walked past his studio, hoping to catch sight of him through the window, or better, to run into him on the street. Twice she even entered the building and knocked on his door, but he didn't answer.

Then, one evening at the beginning of the next week, she

111

approached his studio—and her insides nearly fell out, for there he was, right in front of her, about a half block away, and turning the corner with another girl.

* * *

The snow flurries began Saturday evening, and by Sunday morning Manhattan was enveloped by one of the worst early November snowstorms in history. Eve, having been unable to sleep, was up early and out on the windy streets. The city was a blinding river of whiteness: wires, flagpoles, and lampposts were covered with snow, ledges piled with it, streets banked.

She was thinking of David again. Why had she handled things so unadroitly? If only she could have been more adult; if only she had been able to show David she was a woman. She thought of the sickening image her parents had tried to perpetrate on her: "S., S., and G.," sweet, simple, and girlish. Ugh! If only she could climb out of the shadow of that curse. If only she hadn't been so fat, then she'd have experience behind her and she wouldn't be so afraid.

She ordered breakfast at a depressing place in the west forties. To cheer herself, she was tempted to order griddle cakes, but she resisted, telling herself all wasn't lost, she still had a chance.

When she left the restaurant she bought a Sunday paper and took it back to the Longacre House to read. But she couldn't concentrate on it, or on anything but David. About ten o'clock she could no longer control the urge to go and knock on his door, pay him a surprise call. Afterwards she would entice him, and they would neck again.

The snow had stopped falling, but the wind was still strong. Frozen from the walk, Eve mounted the dingy old stairs to David's studio and knocked on the door. She waited, and hearing no sound, was about to knock again.

Just then the sound of soft voices issued from the studio. Eve tensed, her ear pressed to the door. For close to an hour she stood that way.

She heard the voices continue, heard them turn to sighs, to moans, to whispers, to screams; she heard David's words, and

the girl's—words of love and desire and passion and culmi-
nation.

Only when silence at last came from within did she trem-
blingly turn to go. Tears filled her eyes as she met the cold
day once again. She knew the pain, not of having lost, but
of never having possessed, never having known or been
known. She recalled the way Leslie and Charlene had talked
together. I wish, I wish, she thought helplessly, I wish I were
a real woman.

She felt the wind biting at her face and legs, whipping at
her, smashing into her stomach, and attempting to blow her
off the street. Oh, how I wish I were a real woman, her
insides cried, as she felt fresh flurries of snow mingling with
her tears.

I'm hungry, she thought wildly. I'm so hungry I can't stand
it. She stopped at a corner drugstore, and despite the weather,
ordered the biggest, gooiest, most fattening banana split in the
entire city.

Chapter 8

CARRIE'S NOTEBOOK

December 4. *A miracle has happened, making me part of
eternity and the inner workings of the universe. I'm pregnant!*

*Mel said not having children of his own was the biggest
tragedy of his life—and now this beautiful miracle has happened. I can't wait to see his face when he hears.*

*It's all been strange. First month I even had my period. But
now I have all the symptoms, and there's no mistaking it.*

*At first I was worried, then the joy came upon me and
grew. A baby! It's not the natural order of things. But it happened this way, and I know everything will be all right.*

* * *

December 9. *I wish I could tell Mel in person, but the news mustn't be kept any longer. Besides, Mel is always saying he's coming to New York and then is delayed.*

I called his office in California, but he's in Europe. I had no idea he was going. Makes me feel strange, me here bursting with this beautiful thing, and Mel so far away when I want us to be sharing this together.

* * *

December 10. *I must reach Mel. There are problems to be solved. I called his office on the Coast again, and they told me he's at the Lancaster in Paris. Called the Lancaster but he's been out all day.*

* * *

December 11. *Have called several times, two days in a row now. Finally I made a definite appointment to call him day after tomorrow at 6 p.m., our time. I can hardly wait!*

* * *

December 13. *One minute everything can be so beautiful; the next it's turned ugly. Earlier, walking in the streets in the crisp evening, I wanted to savor the air, drink it deep. I was full of the knowledge of life growing inside me, and I was so happy. Now all that has changed.*

When I told him, his voice, an ocean away on the other end of the wire, fell silent. Then he said, "Have you been to a doctor?"

And still joyful, I bubbled to him, "I don't need to see a doctor, I can feel it. A woman can tell."

"Make sure, okay?"

"If you really want, but—"

"If it's true, you'll have to see about an operation."

This time it was my turn to lapse into silence. I wouldn't, couldn't face the implication of that remark. "Look," I said finally, "we love each other. You know you've always said we'd be together, no matter what. While you're getting the divorce, I'll stay in the background to protect our families. No one will know."

But he wouldn't let me finish. "No, it wouldn't work," he said. "Besides, I don't know what you can be thinking, Carrie. Didn't I tell you I was sterile? This can't possibly be my child."

"You used to be sterile," I said. "But you're not anymore. A miracle happened. We love each other, so everything changed."

"This was no miracle. This is another man's child."

"There hasn't been anyone but you," I said. "How can you say it can't be yours? It is!"

"I know it's not mine."

"How could you possibly say that?"

"Because just this past summer I took tests, and the doctors said there'd been no change in my problem."

"Maybe they can't tell."

"Don't be absurd, of course they can tell."

"Then maybe since last summer it's changed."

"This whole discussion is getting us nowhere. It's beside the point. The problem is, you're pregnant. Now, cookie, you have a friend in me you can trust, and I want to do what's best for you. You're a very emotional girl, and you need guidance."

"But Mel—you don't understand—" I stammered, thinking of how he had said he was my friend. It seemed wrong to use that word, all wrong. I stammered, "You said you wanted to be with me—always—"

"It's not possible now. Later, yes, when the divorce comes through. But now is not the time for it, don't you see that?"

I began to weep then. "But I want to have this baby, it means so much to me, you can't imagine . . ."

And then he said, "In that case I guess this is the end of the line."

An iciness gripped my heart. "What do you mean?" I asked, dreading the answer.

"I've never had anything to do with a pregnant woman before, so we can't go on together if you decide to go through with this whole thing."

The unrelated thought went through my mind that it was I who was paying for this long distance call, as Mel continued,

"I think, in any case, it will be very foolish of you if you do go through with it. You have no means of raising a child alone yourself."

"I work; I make good money—"

"Please, Carrie, talk like an adult," he said. "It wouldn't be fair to the child. It's selfish. And it's selfish not to consider me. You say you love me? Well, I don't want this child, it's not mine, I refuse to recognize it—"

"Mel, Mel," I cried, "I can't do what you're asking. I can't do it—"

"Honey," he pleaded, "if you'd only listen to reason. I don't want us to end either, but I want you to be realistic."

"I want the baby!"

"You've got to follow my advice, sweetheart, you're confused and emotional about this, you're incapable of thinking straight or knowing what's best, but later on you'll see I was right, how this is the only way—how it's the best thing for our future together."

"Mel—"

"Do it for me, angel, for us. I'll call you in a few days, and we'll get things settled."

"But I want this baby. . . ."

"You'll have a baby, dear." His voice was reassuring, cajoling. "We'll have other babies. Babies that are ours."

"How? If you keep thinking you're sterile? I mean, how can you have a baby with me later on, and you can't now . . . if you're sterile?"

"I'll have that operation. And it will be so much better then, because it will be ours. Now, honey, pull yourself together and stop crying. We'll always be together, and you know it. But you must see about an operation. Then in the spring, do you know what? I'm taking you to Europe with me, and we'll have a ball."

"I don't want to go to Europe. I want to have the baby—" My voice broke. Why did he tell me he was sterile? I could have been careful, but I didn't think I had to be. Now he doesn't understand.

"Cookie," he said, "we'll be together, but this is the best thing. Now I have other calls waiting, so I'm going to have to get off the line. I'll phone you in a few days, to see what you've done."

116

He hung up. Then, a few minutes later, Dolores arrived home. I was sitting near the phone, crying, and when she asked why, I told her.

"Pregnant," she said. "How?"

"I don't know."

"Weren't you careful, for Christ's sake?"

"Mel told me he was sterile. He said there was nothing to worry about."

"The son of a bitch. I told you you'd end up getting screwed, but I never thought this would happen. Honey, the only time a woman gets pregnant is when she wants a hold on a man. In this case, you made a lousy choice. Mel Shepherd won't let himself be gotten by the balls. The bastard schmuck. You're in a helluva mess."

Dolores lit a cigarette. "My first instinct," she said, inhaling deeply, "is to tell you to try and blackmail him, ask for fifty or a hundred grand. But I know you'd never do it. Anyway, when you come down to it, he'd just use the sterility bit; his wife would back him up; and they'd make you look like an idiot. So . . . the only thing you can do now is try to get the mess over with as smoothly as possible."

"I don't want it to be over with. I want the baby."

"It's out of the question."

"No."

"Oh, come on, Carrie."

"No."

"There must be a way. There has to be a way."

Chapter 9

Carrie, Dolores, and Charlene lunched together at the Forum the next day.

Charlene, on her third cocktail, insisted, "Carrie, it's not that tough an operation. It's very simple, and it's painless. How pregnant are you?"

"Nearly three months, I think."

"A little longer," Dolores said, "and it would have been too late to do anything about."

Carrie said, "Will you get it through your heads, you two, I don't want to have an abortion."

"Darling," Charlene said, "nobody *wants* to have an abortion. Will you get that through *your* head? The point is, you're a young girl in trouble; you have to think not only of your own future but also of the future of the child. Mel's married; he won't acknowledge the child. He's told you he'll have no part of it. You can't count on him."

"Yes," Carrie said, "but . . ."

"You're thinking only of how happy you'd be," Charlene went on. "You're not thinking of how unfair it would be to the child."

"Charlene's right, Carrie," Dolores said. "You're being selfish. You couldn't possibly bring up a child properly in your circumstances."

Charlene's iridescent-tipped fingers guided a cigarette to her orchid lips. She exhaled slowly and said, "The only possibility would be if you could go home to your mother."

"No," Carrie said firmly. "I wouldn't want to ever have her know."

"She'd have to know eventually," Dolores said. "What would you tell her?"

"And," Charlene asked, "what would you tell the child about its father? Do you think it's wise to be a mother who'd have to be lying and making up stories?"

"Let me tell you from experience, Carrie," Dolores said, "that a girl begins to despise her mother when the two of them are alone and the mother can't give the child the kind of home normal kids have."

"I know it's a tough thing to have to face, honey," Charlene said. "Don't you think I don't know. I went through a couple of abortions myself. It's no joke, but it's the only way. Listen, if you weren't so gorgeous, you'd have the guy who knocked you up wanting to marry you, but because you're beautiful, you attract the no-goodnicks. Plain Janes are the lucky ones in life. They get the nice steady guys who love them, the homes, the families, and the happiness. Beauties are the ones who suffer. You've got to watch it, Carrie. Everyone's out to devour you. You've got to be ahead of them, and not let it all get to you."

Carrie poked at the food remaining on her plate. "I don't know how I can help but let it get to me," she said.

"I know a doctor who can do it legally," Charlene said. "That's the best way, instead of some kind of shady office deal. This way you'll be in one of the city's leading hospitals. It's a whole procedure, involving seeing psychiatrists and gynecologists, getting a board to approve you for a legal curettage. It'll run you over fifteen hundred dollars, but it's worth it. It's the cleanest, easiest, safest way of doing things. I know you don't like to face things like this, Carrie—nobody does—but the major factors are (a) you don't want to involve your mother, and (b) if you're to have any future, with or without Mel Shepherd, you can't have the baby."

So plain, Carrie thought. So practical. So reasonable. Having the baby really was an impossible dream. Sometimes a person's deepest wishes don't count. Why? Why?

*   *   *

"Eve Paradise!" Rex screamed when she walked into his office that afternoon. Charlene was still at lunch.

"My God," Rex said, "I've been trying to get hold of you for hours! Don't you *ever* check with your service? I've been going simply out of my mind!"

"Oh, I'm sorry," Eve said. "I was just—"

"I've got somewhere to send you. It's a last-minute go-see. I want you to hurry over *right* this *minute!*"

He gave her the address, and she was off, sandwich, coke, book, satchel, and all.

Eve was a full-fledged model now. She had quit her part-time jobs and her days were spent on a continual round of interviews, call-backs, and wardrobe fittings. The job she was seeing about now was a soap commercial. The company was making a taped screen test of every candidate. From the experience she'd thus far had in modeling and commercials, Eve had acquired a relaxed and pleasant manner in front of the camera, and she was confident she would do well.

When the test was done, she caught Stan Walters, the

agency producer, winking at her, and knew she had cinched the job.

December 15. *Mel flew the polar route yesterday. Today he phoned from California and said, "I promise I'll have the operation. As soon as my divorce is final we can have as many children as you like. But don't you see that, for now, it's doing things in reverse?"*

"I know," I said. "But . . ." As if there were still some hope.

"There'd be hell to pay if Margaret's lawyers ever got wind of this," Mel said. "Don't you realize how much trouble I could be in? You've never gone through the agonies of working out a property settlement. Please have some consideration for me. I'm up to my neck in problems."

"Mel," I said, "no one would ever have to know. . . ."

"I can't accept it." His voice was firm. "I told you I wouldn't be able to continue seeing you if you went ahead with this."

There was a pause.

"Did you hear me, Carrie?" he said. "I can't argue anymore. Unless you do as I say, it's the end for us."

As he spoke, it seemed my whole life was at stake. The thought of losing the baby—I don't know if a word exists to describe it. Yet without Mel, what kind of life could I give it? And losing him would leave life meaningless. I couldn't blame him for his attitude; all the years he'd been sterile made it logical for him to feel as he did. There was nothing I could say, no way to make him believe it all happened exactly as I'd told him it did.

"Mel," I said, "are you absolutely certain everything will work out the way you say? That you'll have the operation and marry me and we'll have other babies? Because it would hurt too much to be left with nothing. As it is, I don't know if I can do it. You don't know, it's like tearing my heart out, even the thought of it."

"Yes, I know. I'm swearing to you, promising you everything will work out, cookie."

"It's the only condition I could possibly do it under."

"Trust me," he said, "and have faith." Then he hung up.

*"Let not your heart be troubled, neither let it be afraid."
These words from the fourteenth chapter of John always
meant so much. Jesus, help me! I'm trapped. I want to just
fall asleep and not feel anything. Let it be over quickly, God,
please; please be merciful and let it all end soon, this night-
mare. I feel I can scarcely go on another day. But I must.
I must.*

* * *

December 16.   *Christmas cheer is in the air all over town,
everywhere but in my heart. It's so cold out. Traffic crawls at
a dilatory snail's pace, crowds are six thick in each direction,
twelve abreast, noises screech at 90 to 120 decibels, and inside
I scream help, help! My heart is dangerously near collapse. I
keep thinking, oh, give me the happiness, let me treasure and
savor the happiness awhile longer yet, the thought of this
child.*

*My heart is split, half of it knowing the joy of life, of being
an instrument of God's creation, not wanting to let go of that
link of spirit with matter. And the rest of it is menaced by the
awful knowledge of what lies ahead, what I must do—exami-
nations, sessions with doctors, and then the hospital.*

*I stride past 5th Avenue bells and holly, wreaths and col-
ored lights and Salvation Army bands. There is a mist ahead.
Glistening car tops, halted, snarled, honking, congest the path.
All around me are tired, harried faces, their owners carrying
packages, trudging, nudging, inching, and fighting along the
avenue. Bare branches are sparse and cold, cold—*

*Is Christmas really on its way? The spirit of Christmas, the
spirit of love born in the heart—and all I see, all I feel, is the
spirit of death, of loss.*

* * *

December 17.   *Charlene's doctor sent me to two gynecologists, and two psychiatrists, who wrote out certificates to make
it legal. I had to tell the psychiatrists I'd commit suicide if I
couldn't have the abortion. I paid them all in cash—a total of
several hundred dollars. There'll be another seven hundred
to a thousand for the hospital. The board will review my case*

and approve it, Charlene's doctor says; then I'll be told when to go to the hospital. I'm doing my best not to think this is taking place.

Dolores said, "You're doing the right thing. It's the only thing you can do. You can't have the baby, Carrie. Don't worry, it's a D and C, very sanitary, very clean, no pain at all."

But I keep thinking, It's losing the baby, isn't it? But I mustn't think; I mustn't. . . .

"I'm sorry I won't be able to go to the hospital with you," Dolores said, "but I've had this date to go to Montego Bay for some time now, and I can't pass up the opportunity. This could really be a live one, Carrie."

"That's all right," I said. "I don't mind going alone."

Chapter 10

Eve had not misinterpreted Stan Walters' wink. The job was hers. A soap commercial! She was thrilled. Rex had told her pharmaceuticals, cigarettes, and soaps, in that order, were the best-paying commercials. And now she had nailed a soap. It was a great boost to her morale.

She loved being the center of attention during the shooting, standing there in a filmy negligee in front of so many males: the director, the producer, the clients, and the agency men, plus all the crew—the cameraman, the A.D., the lighting director, all the technicians and grips. She had to do a sensual routine at a washbasin, then one near a bathtub. It seemed ages ago that her parents' wish that she not appear in a negligee had nearly ruined her life. What a long way she had come since then! They'd wanted to keep her a little girl, but she was on her way toward becoming a woman.

Stan Walters was eying her closely, smiling and making cracks all the time, praising her after every take.

"Hurry up and let's get this stuff in the can!" the assistant director yelled to the crew. "We've got twenty minutes till we have to break for lunch or we go on meal penalty."

It was the second day of shooting.

"Did you have a good lunch?" Stan Walters sidled up to her.

"I stayed in," Eve said. "I'm covered with body makeup, and I didn't want to get myself all messed up." She smiled at Stan, at his ruddy, boyish blond attractiveness; she was flattered by his concern.

"Well, did you at least order something sent in?"

"I wasn't too hungry," Eve said.

"There are some bagels in a bag over there. Let me get you one."

"Bagels? What are bagels?"

Stan did a double-take. Then he said, "Eve, would you like to have dinner with me tonight? I've always wanted to take out a girl who didn't know what a bagel was."

"I'd love to," Eve said.

*   *   *

That night, following a dinner at the French Shack and a drink at Chucks' Composite, Stan suggested they go back to his place, where he'd show Eve his collection of sailing trophies. Sailing was his hobby, he said, and he kept a twenty-five-foot ketch in Larchmont.

*   *   *

Stan had the perfect solution to the problem of how to be cozy on a cold evening. Just light a fire and snuggle close.

"I dig you, Eve," he said softly, taking her hand.

Eve smiled, feeling warm and happy. There was a comfortableness in being here with Stan, and she felt the first touch of unknowing vanish as he kissed her and lights from the fire played across his face.

He held her gently for a few moments. Then one of his hands reached inside her blouse, and the other began unfastening the buttons, while at the same time, his tongue found her ear.

Before Eve knew what was happening, they were entwined in a prone position, and she was moaning with pleasure.

"Stop it," she cried hoarsely.

"I can't," came his smothered reply. His hand reached up her skirt, and a second later, he'd pushed the skirt to her waist and rolled himself on top of her. She shook with emotion as, despite herself, her knees involuntarily came up and encircled him.

She felt the taut hardness of his body against hers. How she wanted to go on, to experience the sweetness, the delirium—but this was wrong. She couldn't; she hardly knew this man. Oh, how could he do this to her, make her feel this way, give her feelings she ought to have only with a man she was in love with, who wanted to marry her? Oh, God!

"Please, Stan," she said, trying to pull away. "I—I can't—"

"Baby; oh, baby," he crooned, licking the inside of her ear with his tongue again.

She responded with a shuddering cry. More, more, she wanted to beg for more—but she couldn't, she mustn't. This wasn't love; it was *sex*. It wasn't right.

Then Stan became gentle again, and she didn't want to remove herself from the safety of his arms. But when his hand slid up her thigh and inserted itself into her panties, she froze.

"No! Oh, no! Stan, please! I can't; I have to stop. *Now!*"

"Why, baby? Why stop?" He was unzipping his fly.

God, no, she couldn't. She tried to free herself, but Stan held her firm with just one hand. With the other, he struggled to unhook his belt.

"Please, Stan!" Eve begged, feeling at his mercy now, and beginning to cry. "Oh, please don't *rape* me!"

Stan pulled away with an abrupt jerk, and sat up. Eve couldn't resist a look at his open fly. She saw something very big, vaguely rosy, both fascinating and horrifying. But she was able to get only the briefest peek, for Stan immediately hiked up his pants and put it back in again. She noted the way he touched it, the tender way his hands cupped himself.

"I—I'm sorry, Stan," she said. "But I really have principles. And I can't—I couldn't let you. I don't want to be just a girl who's used for sex—I want a man to have respect for me, and—"

"Look," he said, "I'd never have tried if I thought you were so hung up this way. *Rape*—I mean, for Christ's sake, I've never had to *rape* a girl in my life!"

"Well, you see, I'm—I'm different than most girls, because I'm very religious, and—"

"You sure *are* different."

"I'd really like to. I think you're very attractive, Stan." She didn't want to tell him she wasn't in love with him; she didn't want to wound his ego. "I really would *like* to—but the thing is, it's a mortal sin—"

"Mortal sin? What the hell is that?"

"Well, you see, I'm a Catholic, and . . ."

"Do you know what Magellan said about the Catholic Church?"

"No."

"He said, 'The Church says the earth is flat, but I know that it is round, for I have seen the shadow on the moon, and I have more faith in a shadow than in the Church.' That was way the hell back in the fifteenth century."

"Well, I—I really don't see . . ."

"The whole rigmarole against fornication is just a misinterpretation. The Jews wanted to keep their progeny straight, and in those days there was no contraception, so they had to invent a law, 'Thou shalt not commit adultery,' so the patriarchs would know who their own kids were. The Catholic Church has never kept pace with the times, and girls like you, who potentially could really enjoy sex, end up paying the penalty."

He stood up and put on his jacket. "Come on," he said, "I'm taking you home."

Eve followed him, thinking miserably, will I ever learn how to act with men?

Chapter 11

December 20. *Confusion. I'd come to the point where logically I understood what Dolores and Charlene were trying to tell me about Mel. Yes, Mel had been acting like a prick all along—he'd conned me, hadn't wanted the responsibility of the baby. I understood.*

But I thought I'd see him just once more—in a very businesslike way—to set him straight about everything.

We met in the grillroom at the Pierre. And for all my fine resolutions, I found the old feelings returning. Though I tried to fight it, I still had that fatal attraction to him. I tried to convince him again the baby is a miracle, that fantastic as it seems, it really has happened this way.

But as he spoke, I realized once again his history of sterility makes his point as logical as mine seems fantastic. Once again I became certain Mel really believes he's blameless. I don't know what it is about him—his looks, his words, his attitude—but in his presence all my convictions fall aside, and he is right and I am wrong.

It seemed I had no choice but to follow him into the elevator and up to his room. Yet all the while, I was full of dread, fearful of the heavy weight inside me, of what I must do alone, and of the burden of having to be adult. I wanted to hold on to the last shreds of what Mel and I had shared together, just hoping against hope—for what? Comfort, love, affection, closeness, recapturing the past . . . ?

Forever, it seemed forever I'd been longing for him, wanting to be touched by him, to feel that exorbitant mania that only he brings to my being.

But Mel didn't sense my need for tenderness and concern; he was bestial.

And later, The baby, Mel, it's our baby, we can't—don't you see; let's be happy together about the baby; it was meant to be this way; God intended us to be parents of this child.

No, Carrie, I told you this is the end of the line unless you agree—

Tears don't suffice; Mel's arms don't suffice; nothing helps at all. And I don't know what to do. Oh, God, I can't bear this. All right, I'll try to be adult.

Yes, Mel, yes; I know there are things that are ugly that we have to go through for the sake of something better later.

And then the night wore on. Lying awake, I heard the traffic rumbling outside. And watching Mel as he slept, his lip slightly curled, I felt he had receded somehow, slipped away from me.

A Salvation Army band was playing "Deck the Halls with Boughs of Holly" and "Joy to the World" outside the window this morning—the brassy notes echoing in the thinness of the wet air, a forlorn, tinny, sad, distant sound.

Just before I left Mel this morning I broke down, and there was a terrible scene.

"You can't back out now," Mel said. "You have to go through with it; it's the only solution. It has to be done this way. Pull yourself together, Carrie, for God's sake." *And I did. I was ashamed of myself for losing control, for acting like a baby in front of him.*

"You promised, Carrie," he said. "When I make a promise I keep my word—how about you, Carrie, are you a girl of your word? Doesn't your word mean anything?"

I got control of myself, and I gave in again. "Yes, yes, I'll do it, Mel."

Oh, God, against everything that was compelling me to do otherwise, I have gone ahead. Why is it everyone knows better than I what is good for me, when all of my insides cry out in protest against this outrage?

It's an easy operation, Dolores and Charlene both said. One out of every three women goes through it at one time or another. It's no big deal. You're making a mountain out of a molehill.

Mel had a breakfast date. Walking me to a cab, he said, "I'll be in touch." *He gave me a brief kiss, then said,* "Courage," and I almost broke down again. But, no, I have to be strong now. He said so, and I know he's right.

The hospital—yes, yes, I'm here.

A big Christmas tree decked with tinsel and lights and colored balls greeted me in the lobby. I got in line, trying to play the same game with myself I've been playing the whole time now—I am not having an abortion.

The floor nurse took my money and rings; they don't allow valuables in the rooms.

Now I'm lying in bed, staring at the white plastic identification bracelet they gave me. My name's printed on it in purple capitals: CAROLINE RICHARDS. The vintage radiators of the old hospital bang and croak and creak and whine. Across the street is a lovely sketchy ash tree etched against the mist of the already melting snow and watery air. All over, festive Christmas lights shine, injecting the atmosphere with impending gaiety, and here in this bed I want to cry out that my heart is bleeding.

Only of what use would that be?

*   *   *

Noon.   "Carrie, luv"—it was Charlene on the phone— "how are you feeling, baby?"

"Fine. I just got here."

"Wish I could keep you company for a while, but I've got to get Kurt to the vet. He's got a bad stomach. I'll buzz you later on."

I took up the Sunday Times crossword puzzle, to try to take my mind off everything. I got a word that had been stumping me since Sunday, kangaroo court. I got it and then I started to cry again.

2 P.M.   The doctor came in a minute ago. One of the gynecologists who signed the statement, the one who's going to do the operation for me.

"After the operation you'll need a few days to recuperate," he said. He was puffing on a pipe. "It's not the operation itself, but the anesthesia you'll have to recover from. And of course there are the psychological implications."

I tried to look composed, as if I were really adult and able to face things well, not the coward I really am inside.

He said, "No matter how much you want to have it done, there's still the psychological effect. Sometimes you don't feel it till afterwards."

I feel it now! I thought violently. But I smiled at the doctor and thanked him for his counsel.

Mel, I cried to myself as he left, oh, Mel, why does it have to be like this?

*   *   *

4:30 P.M. Soon someone will come to do the shaving. It's getting late. Outside, it's almost dark now.

Nurses have been filing in and out of the room all day. "Is your husband here?" one of them asked me, and I looked blankly away. "Is anyone from your family here?"

"No, no, I'm alone. When will they give me a sleeping pill? I want a sleeping pill."

"Soon."

Tomorrow they'll wheel me out at eight in the morning.

No, my baby, I don't want to think of you as alive, or as mine, as being any part of me. But, God in heaven, what must I do to silence the terrors inside me? Will they never end?

*   *   *

6:30 P.M. A nurse came with a pan of soap and water— and a long razor. Shorn, helpless and vulnerable now, like a little girl. But I'm not a little girl.

The pain my pleasure has caused! I keep hearing Mel's final word to me: "Courage." And again and again, it's made me want to yell out and break completely. But I mustn't. These things have to be faced alone; there's no one who can help you bear them.

Oh, God, I can still perceive Mel's odor, even though I've had two baths and the lathering for the shave since we made love yesterday. It's as though he's such a part of me that his trace is indelibly imprinted on me, forever.

*   *   *

7:25 P.M.   *I lie still, waiting, hurting.*

*   *   *

8 P.M.   *Outside the air is crisp and drizzly; it's beginning to rain. I can hear the splatter of drops against my window. Oh, these New York winters!*

The shave wasn't really close enough, and the thin nightie they gave me is rubbing irritatingly against the stubble. I'm beginning to feel an easing of tensions though. Must be the sleeping pill.

How strangely comforting the noisy radiators are. Their oldness seems to affirm that there is some continuity to life—except when I'm reminded that tomorrow I'll be wheeled on a table into the operating room. Then I want to scream, no! and split apart with the realization of how joyful it would be to be going there to give birth to the child that's growing within me, instead of denying it life, cutting it out of me.

Oh, don't think; don't think.

*   *   *

Midnight.   *All night long the man down the hall has been screaming from prostate trouble. "Help me, help me!" And somewhere nearby comes another patient's angry rebuff, "Shut up, do you want to wake everybody up?"*

"No, no," the man sobs, "I don't want to wake nobody. Oh, help me!"

*   *   *

December 21.   *It's all over.*

I feel as though I were nothing more than a shell. What happened? I'm trying to remember.

Morning arrived. Perhaps I had dozed an hour or two. Through the screens they hadn't taken down for the winter, wispy vapors rose from a thin smoke-stack across the street. They came and gave me a shot to calm me and prepare me. Oh, I don't want this, I don't want this at all, I cried with everything I am.

I tried to ignore my heart—to deny the presence in me.

White sheets, orderlies, interns, and the glucose needle in my arm, all tied to a whole big apparatus with a large transparent bowl on top—

I was on a table, being wheeled along a hall. How impersonal it seemed; it's as though you lose yourself and become just a thing. I joined the line of patients on tables outside the door labeled "Surgery." It all seemed inhuman and unnatural, the mechanical way they just take your body and do things to it. I kept feeling we were like a line of helpless lambs being led closer and closer to the sacrificial altar.

I am going to the slaughter, I thought; I am an animal on its way to be sacrificed. But I was detached. Let them kill me, I didn't care. Isn't it merciful what drugs can do?

Yet I still couldn't stop thinking of the baby. A doctor—I think she was a doctor—was near me. I reached for her hand and squeezed it hard. I could feel her smile down at me. Soon they would wheel me inside. There was no turning back now.

All through my mind, pictures and words were floating, in slow and steady rhythm. Something kept going through my head, from old Bible readings at home, and I remembered how Father used to say each man had to build his own Tabernacle in the Wilderness, where one had to become both the priest and the animal sacrificed, to enter behind the veil and find the symbol of the Tabernacle transferred to the home of his heart.

My heart is a wilderness. Even despite the sedation, there was still the will in me coming out strong now, crying no, I don't want to do this, I can't—it's a mistake—I wanted to tell them it was all a mistake, that this was not me acting, that everything I had agreed to do was because I had been thinking of others, not me, and now I wanted to be me and do what was right for me, and I didn't want them to cut the baby away from me, and I tried to rise off the table, but I couldn't, the needle and the wires were holding me down; the anesthetist smiled at me and though I tried to speak I couldn't do that either—and then—euphoria, twilight, sinking into oblivion, blissful—splendor and heaven and singing.

And then, as if no time at all had elapsed, I awoke to semi-consciousness, thinking I heard many people calling my name, "Carrie, Carrie, Carrie," oh, it sounded tender and miraculous, so infinitely full of love. Beauty, joy, glory, love, all so near and so real I could reach out, I really thought I could grasp them and hold on to them forever, and then, horrendously, agonizingly, excruciatingly, I was fully conscious again, leaning over and vomiting till I thought I would die of it, with the tears hot and choking me. I felt a hand supporting my neck and I groaned. I had thought I was dead, and now I knew, it was not I that was dead, but that life that had been inside me and now was no more. I retched harder and gagged, full of it, hearing some distant frantic voice in me begging for help, and I heard a voice say, "It's all right, honey, it's the anesthetic, that's all."

I must have slept awhile. When I woke, facing me in a chair with her knitting, was Nurse Grossman. She smiled. She's short and plump, with sad eyes and a habit of prefacing most of her remarks with "In my candid opinion" or "This is my personal opinion." She told me that the law required that I have a nurse with me at all times, since to get the legal curettage, I had had to be declared a potential suicide.

"My sister is a Chinese dancer," she said. "She's also a writer. Her present husband's a businessman. They fight all the time. She goes to adult education courses in the town they live in—Yonkers. In my candid opinion, she should never have married this man. Her first husband was a brilliant theatrical writer, Harvey Ross. He was in that thirties bunch, that WPA theatrical group. Ten years they were together, so she had her basic training in theatrical writing. She got it from Harvey. In my candid opinion, she'd never be writing today, or doing these dances either, if it wasn't for Harvey. That's one link I have with show business. In my personal opinion, it's a very interesting business."

I listened to her politely, even smiling sometimes, but divided inside, my stomach and heart taking all the pain, and willing my mind to be strong.

"I could never compromise with a man," Miss Grossman said. "I was a virgin till I was twenty. I had an abortion too. I was in my early twenties—about twenty-one. Do you know where it was? It was in Miami, Florida. He was so hurt when I didn't tell him I was pregnant, but I said, 'Why should it make any difference? Why base a marriage on that?' So, you see, I could never compromise. Maybe I should have married him. I went all the way to Miami to be with him, so I must *have loved him. My life might be different today. But I could never compromise with a man."*

Yes, yes, I nodded. I see, yes. Mother—I thought of Mother. Soon it would be Christmas and I'd be seeing her again. She must never know. I did what was right. Mother—and the baby too—would have had a rotten deal if I'd backed out, if I'd been selfish and not gone through with the operation. I did the right thing . . . the right thing. Then why do I feel this way, like my life is over, like it's the end?

"But after that," Miss Grossman went on, *"I've been so careful. And suspicious. I've never felt the same since then. I'm always wondering if it's really me the man wants, and not just . . . that."* She held up her knitting and peered at it. *"But still you have the basic biological urge, and the emotional needs. I don't know if I'll ever meet the right man. I often wonder if I will. I'm over forty now. I've waited a long time . . ."*

Mel! Has he called? I wondered.

"My main pleasure in life is my painting. I live in a big three-room apartment in Brooklyn. I'm working on a very big canvas now. Sixty by eighty."

"Did I get any messages, Miss Grossman?"

"No, honey."

"Oh."

"In my personal opinion," Miss Grossman continued, *"Einstein's theory of relativity is fascinating. Time for me has had an interesting connotation. Living with my paintings, I sometimes feel the reality of ten years ago even more keenly than the reality of yesterday or last week."*

Call soon, Mel, I prayed. Oh, please, God, let him call soon and ask how I am.

"Once I had a boyfriend for seven years. He was a jazz musician, so that was another link of mine to the show world, you might say. Do you like being a model? What commercials could I see you on?"

Mel, Mel, please call. . . .

And then I knew. Just like that, I knew. Mel wouldn't call.

"Do you feel like sleeping again, honey?"

Yes, I thought, I want to sleep. Please tell me that all this, this thing called my life, is not real. They took the baby, and *it's too late for anything now. Too late. Nothing can ever bring it back.*

The doctor entered. "I see you're feeling all right now," he said.

I gave him a smile, and a thank you, yes, yes, doctor, everything is fine.

Chapter 12

Rex bent over some titillating shots in the latest issue of *Physique Pictorial*, feasting his eyes on a particularly striking photo of a good-looking male in a G string. He read the description: "6' tall; 175 pounds; waist 33⅝ (pulls in to 30⅛); biceps 13⅜; forearm 11⅛; wrist 7½; neck 15⅝; chest 41 (expands to 43); hips 37; thigh 21⅛; calf 15⅛; ankle 8⅞; shoulders 43½; leg 34⅛. Got his build from farming."

Then the phone rang. "Dalton, darling." Rex's voice was low, intimate. "I'm doing my best to get you in on a Gillette Right Guard. . . . I'll meet you for a steam in half an hour."

He looked up to the image of himself in the mirror. How dashing he looked this morning, wearing his new periwinkle coachman's coat and a yummy lime tie. As he was adjusting his collar, Charlene appeared at the door.

"Honey, do you have the number for Phil Santuzza's studio? I thought I had it in my card file. Only it seems to have disappeared."

"I'll look."

"Poor Lu Ann Jackman's there. That lech photographer chased her all over the whole studio. Imagine, a naïve kid like Lu Ann. The poor thing finally had to lock herself in the dressing room and call me from the pay phone there."

"Here it is."

"I'm going to call that son of a bitch. Corrupting the morals of young virgins!"

"They don't stay that way very long in this business." Rex yawned, and returning to the mirror, began to comb his hair in preparation for his appointment.

*   *   *

Carrie went straight home when they discharged her the next day. The apartment had never seemed so empty or quiet. She was wishing Dolores hadn't gone to Montego Bay, when the phone rang. It was Charlene with an important go-see.

"You've got to pull yourself together and go on an interview this morning, Carrie," she said. "Just this one won't hurt you. After that you can go on home to bed again. . . . Can I count on you? . . . Good."

But Carrie nearly fainted in the street. When she returned to the apartment, her knees buckled under her and she collapsed. For a length of time she lay motionless on the floor, her head pounding, blood swimming against her temples and the back of her brain, hitting her as if with a hammer. Feeling had left her hands and feet. It was as if all the blood in her body had centered in two spots: the head, or the other end of her where it now came gushing out in streams.

She stirred. An eerie sound was coming to her ears as if out of another universe. The telephone!

With difficulty, she pulled herself up and answered it.

"Carrie, dear, sorry not to have phoned at the hospital, but you know how bad it would be for anyone to connect us." Mel's voice sounded far off, a part of a past life. "Listen, cookie, Margaret and the kids are coming for Christmas. It's just for the children's sake, to keep up appearances. I know you won't be a *kvetch* about it, that you'll understand and trust me and know everything will be fine."

"Yes, of course," Carrie said, a catch in her voice. When she hung up, she knew she had never felt more empty in her life.

*   *   *

"Where'd you go for lunch?" Rex called out as Charlene and the dogs entered the outer office.

"La Fonda del Sol."

"Yummy!" Rex licked his chops. "Hot bitchin'. They've got groovy *paella*. What'd you have?"

"I wasn't hungry."

"Honey, you're going to have to start eating. By the way, Valerie du Charme was up here looking for you."

"Why does that broad keep expecting I'm going to get her a commercial? She never quits. Pushing fifty and still acting the starlet. She's a terrible actress besides. She's always complaining she ought to be submitted instead of Leslie Savage, when Leslie's only twenty years younger."

"You know Valerie's the blindest broad in town, and the one with the most nerve. God, even *you* knew when to quit."

Charlene twisted her mouth into a large magenta smile. The words stabbed, but she'd be damned if she'd let Rex get to her. In carefully measured tones she said, "Valerie doesn't seem to understand she's not the right type for commercials. Even if she tried for the housewife image instead of the glamor girl—"

"The thing that gets me," Rex interrupted in his swishiest bitch, "is her trying to pass herself off as French. Of course, everyone in town knows she's a Lebanese Jewess. Not that I'm prejudiced, but it is rather amusing. She's been wining and dining casting directors all over town, taking them to Twenty One and the Côte Basque, thinking it's going to help." He cocked his head to one side. "She doesn't seem to know some of the shops only hire WPAs. I thought everyone knew you had to be a white Protestant American to get hired over at GFEP&D. I guess everybody but Valerie does."

Charlene removed the dogs' leashes and patted their heads. Warren rolled over on his back, paws in the air, exposing his belly. Kurt, paws perched on the window sill, stared at the winter spectacle below. He was fine now, the stomach ailment completely cured. That had given her a scare.

Valerie du Charme indeed, Charlene thought. My nemesis, my poltergeist. Shades of what happens to us all. She gazed up at her pictures. Once I was that, and today I am what I am. Oh, this business, it goes on and on, like a disease—first because of your needs and your dreams and the naïve conviction you'll find the answer to your life here, then because you're stuck and can't ever get away from it. As Rex always said, "Starlets twinkle till they wrinkle." Only the terrible thing was . . . they went on and on, even after they were over the hill.

It just happens that you're in the business, it's in your blood, like a cancer. The business is a worse sickness than alcohol, even.

A drink. How about a little post-luncheon one?

Charlene reached inside the filing cabinet. And the pain came again, the sharp, shooting pain below her right breast. Damn that liver, it mustn't give out on her now. She cupped it in her hand, feeling its swollen hugeness. You're really sousing it up pretty good these days, Charlene, a voice inside her said. Hell, no, another part of her retorted, all I take is a nip here and there to keep my wits in the face of all these things: my life that's crumbling into the last lap before God knows what; all the problems of today, business and money and aloneness—the intensity of life going on smothered this way, leading nowhere, and nobody cares any more.

Did anyone ever care? When I looked the way I did in those pictures, did anyone care then? Shit, no! Those guys just wanted me for their goddamned egos: have Charlene Davy on your arm, and that's your emblem of success. The hell with her as a person. Just give her presents to keep her in line, give her presents because you can't give her love. What beautiful woman is ever loved?

To have to live out your life with a beautiful face is a curse; it's a handicap you go on and on paying for.

The phone rang.

It was Carrie, saying she was feeling better.

Charlene said, "You just take it easy for today, honey." It was nice, she reflected, she'd been able to help Carrie get the abortion.

Abortion—it was so long ago that her own body had been violated that way. It seemed like another life, a whole other eon out of a whole other time span, that pain of 1927 or '28 or thereabouts. I shouldn't have done it. I wouldn't have if I'd known it would destroy my insides for good. Today they don't ruin you for future babies like they ruined me.

Now she was hating herself for having been forceful and domineering with Carrie, for having influenced and dictated to her. All because she, Charlene, was jealous and didn't want

137

Carrie to bring life into the world. Oh, I hate myself for all this.

There was the pain, growing over the years, over and beyond all the child-bearing years. Charlene wondered if there was a point where all the old pain ever vanished. Did it recede into wispy little clouds and disperse, or did it just stay inside you in hard cruel lumps, and remain with you until death took care of it?

She finished her drink and sighed as the shadows crept over her desk and the phone buttons flashed red.

Chapter 13

Broadway—West 44th Street to be exact. Dolores checked the name of the theater on the marquee, stepped around a puddle of melting snow in the alley and opened the stage door.

A homosexual with a pad and pencil and an officious manner stopped her.

"Your name, please?"

As if he were trying to keep her out of the theater, as if she didn't belong.

The nerve of the bastard. "I'm *Dolores Haynes,*" she said, and with an air of importance, forced her way past him.

"Just a minute, you can't go in there!" The fag with the pad ran ahead of her and blocked the path.

"I beg your pardon. I have a reading with Mr. Messina scheduled for eleven."

Another homosexual with a pad and pencil appeared. The first fag said to the second fag in a complaining tone, "This girl just barged in, Ballard. I tried to stop her, but she wouldn't listen."

Dolores said, "Oh, are you Ballard Baird? My agent gave me your name. I have a reading scheduled for eleven."

"Your name, please?"

"Dolores Haynes."

"It's all right, Stewart. Miss Haynes is on the list. Come this way, Miss Haynes."

Dolores turned and glared at Stewart, then followed Ballard Baird, who led her to a stair well and handed her a script from a pile on a table. Out of the corner of her eye she could see the stage in semidarkness. A girl stood waiting in the wings. The house was dark and utterly quiet.

"We're running a little behind schedule, Miss Haynes," Ballard Baird said. "Just try to bear with us. The part is Amanda. We'd like you to read over the second act and be prepared to do the first part of the scene with Emory; prepare the next scene too, the end of it, where Amanda's father comes in with the ax. Just make yourself as comfortable as you can down in the basement. We'll call you as soon as we can. Mr. Messina will begin shortly."

Dolores went downstairs and found a chair. She inspected the girls who were ahead of her. They all looked alike—typical New York actresses, definitely not pretty, decidedly unkempt, and with an air of poverty about them. They probably all lived in thirty-dollar-a-month cold-water flats in the Village, saw their analysts twice a week, slung hash to make ends meet, slept with lovers who were as hard up financially as they, and studied in Lee Strasberg's classes. They all had that Strasberg look of intensity and desperation. One or two of them were downright dirty, the others clean, but totally without style.

"Susan Styron?" Ballard Baird called from the top of the stairs. "We're ready to hear you read."

Dolores listened as one by one the girls were taken on the stage to read their lines. Every one of them sounded the same; they all seemed to be aiming for naturalism, but ended up arch and mannered and breathlessly phony. Just let me get on that stage, Dolores thought, I'll show them!

"Miss Dolores Haynes." It was Ballard Baird calling from the top of the stairs.

Dolores swept out on stage with a dramatic entrance she had practiced in front of the mirror at home. She smiled at the unseen audience, and said in her most mellow voice, "How do you do?"

"Miss Haynes, this is Mr. Alan Messina."

"Hello, Miss Haynes," a voice came from somewhere in the darkened house. "Nice to meet you. What's your first name?"

"Dolores. It's nice to meet you too, Mr. Messina."

Damn, if she could only see the frigging guy.

"This is Mr. Boruff, our playwright, and Mr. Finkelstein, the producer."

Dolores nodded. "How do you do, gentlemen."

Her eyes were gradually becoming adjusted to the dark house and the single work light on stage.

"Would you care to turn to page forty-three, Miss Haynes?" Ballard Baird said.

"Certainly."

"I'll read the other parts with you."

"Emory, please!!!" Dolores screamed loudly on Ballard Baird's cue. With her free hand, the one not holding the script, she began tearing at her hair. She also executed a dancing movement, to indicate backing away in fear.

Just then, in the middle of the page, Alan Messina said, "Thank you, Miss Haynes."

Dolores floundered. "But I haven't finished—there's the scene with the ax. I thought I was supposed to read that one too—I prepared it—"

"That will be fine for now, Miss Haynes."

Humiliated, Dolores turned to walk off stage.

"Would you leave your script on the table, please, Miss Haynes?" It was Ballard Baird's insipid, irritating fag voice behind her.

Haughtily, angrily, Dolores dropped the script on the table and stalked off.

Outside the theater again, she suddenly felt disoriented. She had no appointments for the rest of the day, and oddly enough, she didn't feel like shopping. Nor did she feel particularly hungry. All she could think about was the insulting way she'd been treated by Alan Messina, and by that stupid pansy stage manager. They wouldn't even let her read the best scene in the whole crummy play, where she'd really have had a chance to show histrionics. With the wild bit she was planning in that ax scene, no one else would have stood a chance for the part. What did that bastard have against her?

The other girls had been permitted to finish; they had all read both scenes. Why not her?

She would get Charlene to work on it, to make them give her another chance.

*　*　*

Warren and Kurt wagged their tails in appreciation of the tidbits their mistress fed them from her palm. Charlene, feeling the warmth of their saliva on her hand, said, "You two are about the only decent guys in the world." The dogs looked at her and seemed to understand.

A button flashed, and Charlene picked up the phone. It was her astrologer.

"Marcus, luv!" she said. "I've been trying to get you for hours! Where have you been? . . . Well, thank God you called me back, because I've been dying to talk to you. . . . Now that it's after the New Year, I want to have my chart progressed. But for now, can you fill me in on how things will be going for the next couple of weeks, till I can get in?"

She made pencil notes on the pad in front of her, then, after hanging up, put a notation on her calendar of an appointment two weeks hence. When she looked up from her desk Dolores Haynes was standing in the doorway.

"Where did you come from?" Charlene said. "I thought you had an audition."

"I did. Charlene, what a rotten deal. I've got to tell you about it. Come out and have lunch with me."

"I don't know if I should leave right now. . . ."

"Oh, come on, you don't have to stick in the office all day, week in, week out. Let Rex handle the fort and come to Sardi's with me."

"Sardi's . . . well, maybe that's just what I need—so I can drown my sorrows over the retrogressed Saturn squared Mercury that's going to be lousing up the next two weeks of my life."

At every vertical on the half-block way to Sardi's East, Warren and Kurt left calling cards. Walking slowly, Dolores told Charlene the story of how she had been treated unfairly at the reading. Charlene pulled the dogs away from a parking meter, then promised to call the production office and try to rectify the situation by getting Dolores in for the call-backs.

Now the two of them sat in Sardi's, Charlene on her second cocktail. "Don't worry about it, Dolores," she said. "Whatever happens, it's going to be good for you. I can tell. I've watched girls over the years, and I know who's going to make it and who's not. You've got what it takes, honey."

"I know I have it, Charlene. I *know* I can make it."

"Sure. You've got the will and the drive. Talent is pretty secondary in this business, you know that by now. Guts and perseverance mean the most. You score on all counts, honey. You'll go a long way. I had the drive too. . . . I wonder where women like us get it from?"

Dolores looked at Charlene and thought, My God, was she ever as young as I am? How does age happen? How does it creep up? How does it just get hold and ruin everything beautiful? It's not fair.

"I know about me," Dolores answered. "I never had anything as a kid. My mother had to work to support the two of us. My father left us when I was six—left my mother and me, just left us in the lurch. She was a sap, my mother, a real fart in the wind. Well, he took off, and I thought she hadn't known how to hold him. But how about me? I thought. I've never been a fart—I'm strong—and still that son of a bitch, my father, didn't give a damn. It took me awhile to figure it out, but I got the message."

"Yes?" Charlene leaned forward, twisting her glass.

"Men can't be counted on for anything. They'll never give you a damn thing unless you really get them by the balls. They'll never stick around." Venom flashed in Dolores' eyes. "Oh," she said, "maybe an old guy who's really tired would. . . ."

"Are you kidding? These jokers never get tired."

"You're right. Well, let me say, I determined at an early age to sell body and soul to get what I wanted out of life. If you don't take in life, you get taken."

"Sure," Charlene agreed. "Men are all out for what they can get. They use you if you don't use them first."

"Right. So I just made up my mind I was going to have things on my own terms. To really be somebody important and have everything."

142

"Independence is the best policy in life, you're right there," Charlene said. "I wish I'd had your wisdom when I was your age."

"Oh?" Dolores prompted.

"The thing that fouled me up," Charlene confided, "was love."

"Oh, Christ!"

"I wish I'd known forty years ago what a fraud it all is. I had to go and romanticize everything, and look for sublime feelings and all that shit." Charlene absently stirred her drink with her finger. "It's because I'm a Pisces; Pisces people always get loused up that way."

Dolores shook her head. "Love is crap," she said. "When I was six years old I knew that. You know, the only man who ever made me cry was that fucking father of mine. I made up my mind no other man ever would."

"If I had it all to do over, I'd follow your tactics. I'd fuck my way through life, and let it go at that. The hell with emotional security. There ain't no such thing." Charlene took another swig.

"At least you must have had chances for wealth, Charlene —I mean, along with all the love shit you believed in."

"Oh, sure, I've had settlements and alimony, jewels, furs, beautiful clothes; I've lost money in real estate and stocks; there've been lots of ups and downs . . . and here I am. . . ." She finished her drink in a gulp and motioned the waiter to bring her another. "But the thing I wanted more than anything else—the thing all women like us want—is glory. To be an eternal goddess. And that's dangerous."

"You've had four husbands," Dolores said.

Charlene nodded.

"You're three up on me," Dolores went on. "But no doubt I'll match you one of these days."

"Sure, I'll bet you will. Tell me about the one husband you've had. I presume it's over and done with."

Dolores chuckled. "For ages. I only did it because I needed security at that stage of my life. He was a stepping-stone. See, after high school I wanted to model—this was in Chicago. I tried, but didn't have enough cash to finance the initial stages —getting the pictures, living without earnings for the beginning. So I had to quit and get a regular job. To try and save to start again, I sold hosiery at Marshall Field's for six months." She laughed again. "Would you believe it? That's a part of my life I'd like to forget. Then I met Lou. He was a photographer. I'd just begun trying to model again. We started living together, and then Lou wanted to get married. Fine, I said. Not that he was any great catch, but what the hell did I have to lose? I was only eighteen or nineteen, and at that stage of my life, marriage was a big boost."

"Sure," Charlene said. "There are times in a woman's life when marriage is the only solution."

"I did well at modeling, but I always had my goals set higher. I knew where I was headed. It took me a couple of years, but gradually I got better and better pictures. Then I began sending them to agents and studios in Hollywood. One of the agents called and said he was interested. By then I had a few thousand saved, and I was off."

"When did you get the divorce?" Charlene asked.

"Right after that."

"What happened in Hollywood?"

"What happens to everyone?" Dolores said. "You're a new face; you get the red carpet; your agent sends you all over, and every studio wants to give you a term contract. So you listen to your agent, who makes you a deal—and there you sit. They give the real parts to the established stars, and throw junk, if anything, to the contract players." Dolores did not wish to tell Charlene that her option hadn't been picked up. "I had to get out," she said. "It would have been the death of me. New York is the answer. Here's where the action is. You've got to make it on an international scale today. From right here in this town, the roads lead everywhere that's worth getting to."

"You're right," Charlene said. "New York is the hub of the world. Things happen here. In Hollywood you sit, just sit on your tail, unless they've grabbed you from Broadway or London or somewhere. Hollywood doesn't create stars anymore."

"I'm glad I came here," Dolores said. "I'm convinced that from here my whole life's going to take shape."

"And that's a very exciting feeling to have."

"You bet it is."

"You've got it, Dolores," Charlene said. "You've got the

144

formula. Besides, you're a Leo, and Leos always make it big, plus which you've got Scorpio on the ascendant. My hat's off to you. Well, what do you say we toddle along? This has been divine, angel."

Chapter 14

Rex Ryan picked up the phone. "Hi, luv," he said in an intimate voice. It was Siegardner St. Lorraine, his latest flame. This thing between him and Sie had been going on less than a week, but Rex was convinced it was the real thing. So was Sie.

"Baby," Sie cooed over the phone, "I'm in love. And you know something, I think what we've got together is pretty unusual. I've been reading C. S. Lewis' *The Four Loves,* and the fact is, you and I have all *four* of them together—*storge, philia, agape,* and *eros.* Now that is really rare, for two people to have all *four.*"

Rex agreed vehemently, his eyes dancing, desire gripping his body. But the buttons for his other phone lines were flashing, and he had to sign off and take some of the calls. Business was really swinging. The Ryan-Davy Agency had never been more successful. Every ad agency in town gave it priority, knowing it could always be counted on to come up with the best people. Ryan-Davy models this season were kept busy with sometimes six go-sees a day, every day of the week, and were being booked for commercials back to back.

*   *   *

Carrie sat rigid and still inside the apartment, feeling as frozen as the winter scene outside the window. Numbness overtook her, as if a defense protecting her from pain too acute to bear, pain compounded from the waiting and the trust and the loss—loss of Mel, loss of the baby. The baby! If only he'd left her that.

Dolores was away again. I must pull myself together, Carrie thought. Do something. Oh, someone, something.

Distractedly she picked up a postcard and read it again! "Trinidad: Sun, sand, sex, and a Spanish nobleman. What more could a girl ask for? Olé! Dolores."

New York in winter, snow tires and chains plodding on a thinned-out crosstown street; and now it was much later, it was four in the morning, and outside was the lush hush of winter whispers, the vibration of icy pavements, the high tension hum and zing of frozen phone wires.

Gathering the sum total of herself, the dispersed fragments of her sad spirit, the reflections of her soul, she sighed and decided to take a bath.

And then there was a moment, lolling in the hot tub, where her toe squeaked on the porcelain, a moment then where her whole being, conscious and subterranean, going way deep and back and far, far ahead, was focused precisely in one suspended moment of time: that moment where her toe squeaked on the porcelain, where she faced the knowledge that all over the city at this hour lovers clasped each other, and that awaiting her on the outside of the door after her tub was next morning's unread *Times*, her future feast, her something. Just as she could hear the snow flurries falling mutely, and taste the cold, she could see the tears dripping from her heart as clearly as if they had been blood from an open and visible wound.

In spite of herself, she relived the romance, the days and nights of love, of comfort, belonging and sharing, of giving and tenderness, of beautiful lovemaking. Mel, Mel, she cried.

If only he had left her the baby, if only he hadn't insisted on that deprivation. But no, he had made sure not a trace would remain of him for her . . . so that she would ultimately come to this desolation, this vacuity.

*   *   *

"Cut! You did just great, honey."

Eve looked up from the toilet she had been leaning over all day. Her knees were killing her; her back ached from hours of bending and stretching and straightening, playing a new bride who discovers the merits of Blue-Bowl Toilet Freshener.

"It's a wrap," Ron Thompson, producer-director of the commercial, announced.

As Eve turned to gather her belongings, he caught her arm. "How about a drink in my private powwow place before you go home? I don't know about you, but I sure could use one."

*　　*　　*

The walls of Ron's pine-paneled office were lined with certificates. Eve read: "Special Citation, Desserts"; "Second Place, Confections and Snacks"; and "Golden Palm Award, Detergents and Cleansing Agents."

"Like my Cleos?" Ron asked.

"Cleos?"

"The statuettes." Ron indicated his shelves. "They're the equivalent of Hollywood Oscars."

"Oh!" Eve was proud that Ron Thompson, darkly attractive winner of so many honors, thought enough of her to invite her to his private office.

"You're the sexiest little toilet-bowl-cleaning broad in New York," Ron said, downing the last of his Scotch and rising for a refill. "Allow me," he said, and reached for Eve's glass.

"Oh, no," Eve protested. "I couldn't. I swear, I'm so hungry one more drop of alcohol would put me out of commission."

"Well," Ron said, "we'll have to remedy that situation. How about a steak at Chucks' Composite, or a hamburger at P.J.'s?"

"The only thing is . . . all this heavy pancake makeup. I hate it."

"I have a bright idea. We'll stop at my pad, and you can freshen up there. I have all the facilities." Ron winked. "Then we can either go out or order in from the Dover Delicatessen."

Eve was tired and would have liked to go home and relax in a hot tub, but she didn't want to lose the opportunity of a date with Ron Thompson, one of the most important people in the business. If she refused this, he might not ask her again.

*   *   *

Eve followed Ron into his apartment, and went straight to the bathroom, the walls of which were covered, above gray tiles, with yellow burlap. Hanging on a hook on the back of the door were a paisley robe and a douche bag. She washed her face, applied fresh makeup, and in minutes, joined Ron in the living room.

"How about a brandy or a B and B?" he asked.

"All right," Eve said, not wishing to seem unsophisticated. She'd never tasted brandy. She accepted the snifter of it timidly, and was so shocked by its burning she nearly choked. "Oh, excuse me," she gasped. "I—I've had this cough—"

"Why don't we order," Ron suggested. "It's getting late, and I want to watch TV at nine-thirty. What are you in the mood for? Shall we call the Gold Coin or the Dover?"

"Anything. Anything you say." Suddenly Eve's head had begun spinning.

"A commercial we made is being aired for the first time tonight. It'll be up for a Cleo next year, watch and see."

Ron went to the telephone. When he'd finished his call, he held out his hand to her and said, "Come on, let's watch television."

She followed him to the bedroom, her dizziness increasing with each step.

"Man, this's got to be the grooviest commercial ever made," Ron said. "There's a shot with the model hanging out of a skyscraper, being held by the elastic in her bra— it's the coup of Madison Avenue."

"How did you ever do it?"

"Wires," Ron said. He turned on the television set, and slipped off his shoes. They sat on the bed together, waiting.

"How did you dig it?" he asked when the commercial was over. "Groovy, huh?"

"Oh, yes," Eve said, "groovy. . . ."

"I think it really says something."

"Yes, yes, it certainly does." Her spinning head was ach-

148

ing now. She wished Ron would shut off the television, but he didn't.

"Well," he said, turning to her with a glint in his eye. "That's taken care of. Now . . . down to the more pleasant business at hand." He pushed up the sleeves of his sweater and moved closer to Eve, pressing his body against hers. "You sure turned me on bending over that toilet," he whispered. "Your dress kept hiking up—man, did that turn me on." Eyes half closed, lips parted, he buried his head in her neck.

How lovely and soft his lips felt, how smooth his tongue, how strong his hands. Eve wanted to melt. . . . But she scarcely knew him. Why was it always this way with men, why did they always try to take you by surprise? And then her doubts and reservations vanished as Ron guided her to him, and she allowed herself to be led.

"Come on, let's get comfortable," Ron said, pulling off his turtleneck.

My God, is he going to take off all his clothes? Eve's thoughts raced, seeing the naked chest with its sprinkling of hair.

He bent and kissed her chastely on the forehead. "Let me," he said, and began to undo the buttons on her blouse, while planting kisses all over her face and neck. His breathing was loud and excited as he opened the waistband of her skirt. Eve felt her mind floating out in space, away from the rest of her.

He pulled his trousers off, his shorts. Something was pounding against her temples. Her eyes could scarcely focus. She felt nauseous.

Then, naked, Ron lay on the bed beside her. She tried to protest, but he had found her mouth again, and was trying to pull off her skirt. She squirmed. Then she felt his hand inside her pants, stroking her where she was all silky wet. Eve moaned. "Ron," she begged, "please . . ."

"Oh, honey, honey."

"Something might happen. Something awful."

"What that's awful could happen, hon?" he asked, kissing her gently. "I'll be careful; I'll be exactly the way you want me to be."

His finger found its way inside her, and she struggled

against the sensations that raged in her body as he caressed her. It was all happening too fast. She didn't want it to happen so fast. She wanted to wait and see. Then, maybe . . .

She had to say something. "Ron, I—I like to neck with you." Her voice sounded unnatural and strained. "I just wanted to tell you—please be careful with me. . . . I mean, don't get carried away—because—because I—I'm a virgin, and . . ."

"A virgin! For Christ's sake, we'll have to put an end to that."

"I can't—not just yet."

"Why the hell not?"

"I don't know. I just can't . . . yet. Also," she said, feeling even sicker now, "I'm a Catholic, and—well, I used to think I'd only do it on my wedding night, but now I've changed. I mean, if I were in love and he really loved me too. . . . But—I don't know; it's too soon to tell with us, and . . ."

"What do you want me to do?" Ron snapped. "I got a pain in my gut, for Christ's sake."

"Well, I—"

"Why the fuck did you come up here? Why didn't you say something? I thought you knew the score."

"I didn't know this would happen."

"Why the fuck did you lead me on? What in hell are you, a goddamn prick tease?"

"A what?"

"I thought we were gonna get laid. Shit!"

"I'm sorry, I—"

"Well, the very least you can do, if you have any class at all, is to give me a little head."

"What? I—"

"Suck it, baby, I gotta get sucked off if I'm not gonna get laid."

With catlike agility and speed he reversed his position on the bed. Suddenly, before she knew what was happening, Eve felt him thrusting into her mouth with jerky up and down movements. His moans came sharp and loud. She started to choke and gag, and the realization came that Ron had absolutely no feeling for her, that she was being used like a machine. Sputtering and coughing, her eyes full of tears, she abruptly pulled away.

"Why'd you stop? Honey, come on—I gotta get my rocks off. Give me a good hot suck."

Eve sobbed.

"Goddamn!" Ron's voice bellowed above her.

Eve closed her eyes. When she opened them again she saw Ron's hand moving deftly along the shaft of his penis in fast, even strokes. She heard him cry out. Then he cupped the sheet around the tip, wiped himself, and said, "Button your blouse and go get your makeup on."

Still sniffling, Eve did as she was told.

Ron was waiting at the door. Before he let her out he stared at her a moment and said, "It might interest you to know, Catholic broads are the hottest lays in town."

Part

Three

Chapter 1

Another July, and the tempo of the town was loose and easy. Dolores, well entrenched in the commercial field by now, was presently tied up on shampoo, tooth paste, soap, detergent, coffee, and appliances, and was waiting to hear the results of three recent commercial efforts: Action Chlorine Bleach, Dale Hideaway Bathroom Deodorizer, and Zud Rust Remover, as to whether they would run. Though print work sometimes netted her a couple of hundred a month, she disliked doing it; it meant too much rushing around, and she preferred to save her energy for social engagements—parties, cocktail dates, luncheons, and the like.

She hadn't forgotten what Charlene had said last November, when she, Charlene, and Carrie were having Sunday brunch: "Get yourself a live one." The words had been directed to Carrie, who'd answered with prattle about love. Dolores knew better. And now she knew it was time she found the right man to keep her. Up to now, she'd been holding herself back—accepting money for dates with out-of-towners and playing things cool with the New York men —for she hadn't wished to be identified with anyone until she was certain he offered the right situation for her.

Standing on Eighth Avenue, she looked about for a cab. She'd just come from a rehearsal for an acting class and felt exhilarated because the last scene she'd done had involved making love to a strong, youthful partner. But the neighborhood she was in made her nervous. Looking at the dingy tenements and the unkempt little ragamuffins in front of them, she cursed the fact that there wasn't a free cab in sight.

In a drugstore phone booth, she checked with her answering service, which had a message from Charlene. A go-see had just come in, Dolores learned when she called Ryan-Davy.

A few moments later she found a taxi. Gazing out the window at the noon swamp of crowds filling the streets, rushing and pushing and shoving, she wondered how many of them would be around next year, how many would have changed jobs, or moved away, or died. And in twenty years' time, where would they all be then? Where would *she* be?

Dolores didn't like to think that in twenty years' time she would be forty-six. It revolted her that people got old, that flesh changed its appearance and betrayed its possessor. The whole process was nothing short of a dirty trick.

The taxi pulled up in front of a steel-and-glass skyscraper. The man she was to see, Nathan Winston, head of a liquor firm, was personally choosing a girl to be the "image" for one of his products. The executive offices were on the twentieth floor: when Dolores reached them she was shown immediately to Nathan Winston's large and expensive-looking private office. Light and color played over one wall in a giant kaleidoscopic effect. The furniture was Japanese.

A tall, unsmiling, middle-aged man stood up, shook her hand and invited her to sit down. Nathan Winston introduced himself. He had longish white hair and burly hands, full lips with uneven outer rims, large, long-lashed hazel eyes, and a striking profile dominated by a Roman nose that was presently inflamed, presumably from catarrh. He stared thoughtfully at Dolores in a way that made her stare back in insolent self-defense. Dolores read him as a secretive person who had gotten ahead by forcing others to assert themselves and being noncommittal himself, never offering a straight answer, making use of others' weaknesses and assets by clever manipulation. Though taciturn, there was an unmistakable toughness about him, she observed.

"Tell me about yourself," he said at last, not taking his eyes off her.

Dolores obliged.

Nathan Winston rubbed his palms together and said, "You're exactly what I'm looking for." He turned his head, his eyes leaving her for the first time and focusing on the kaleidoscopic wall. "Exactly." His eyes returned to her; they seemed to bore through her. *"Exactly,"* he repeated.

Silence fell, and it seemed to Dolores that the man was trying to cast a spell on her.

Finally Winston broke the silence by inviting Dolores to join him for lunch, which his personal cook would soon be preparing in the office.

Before Dolores could reply, Winston had risen and opened a door. He beckoned her to join him. Through the open door was a small dining room with a low Japanese table raised only a couple of inches from the floor.

"We eat here," Nathan Winston announced.

"Do you ever eat at regular tables?" Dolores asked.

"At restaurants, at friends' homes . . . when I have to." He shrugged. "But I prefer sitting on the floor. It's much healthier."

Dolores noted his tightly clenched fists. She was certain there was a great deal more to Nathan Winston than met the eye. Regretfully she couldn't stay to discover what. She had another appointment, she explained, but she'd be happy to take a rain check for the lunch.

If Nathan Winston was distressed, he didn't show it. He closed the door to the dining room and led Dolores back through his office to the outer door. Then, placing a hand on the knob, he suddenly did a swift turn, and Dolores, momentarily startled, thought he was preparing to lunge at her.

But he resumed his air of imperturbability and said, looking straight into her eyes, "You may not know it, but meeting me has been a major event in your life."

She could hardly help smiling at the pomposity of his remark.

"I want nothing from you," he said. "But you'll see, if you will listen to me, your whole life will change . . . as if by magic."

She frowned, thinking Winston overconfident.

"I don't want you to tell anyone what I've said today." Winston's eyes were suddenly fiery. "If you do, you will regret it, do you hear? Did you ever hear of Pandora?" He moved closer to her, and she felt his breath, hot and strong.

"Pandora opened the box," he hissed, "and mankind was afflicted with misfortune afterwards. If you open Pandora's box, you too will be afflicted with misfortune. If, instead, you choose to heed my advice, you will be a very lucky girl; you will find yourself endowed with untold benefits." His eyes were fixed on her, the pupils hypnotic. Without another word, he opened the door.

When she returned home at the end of the day, she found a huge basket of flowers awaiting her. She reached for the card.

"Do not open Pandora's box," it said. There was no signature.

* * *

Another boring cocktail party. By now, I should know better than to come to any of Edmund Astor's doings, Carrie reflected.

The host approached her, and as usual, having forgotten they ever met, repeated his standard invitation for her to visit his estate in Bucks County to shoot pictures over the weekend. Carrie shook her head; then Edmund put his arm around her and said to Quasar Litwin, who was standing nearby, "I'm in love with this girl."

"You can't have her, Edmund," Litwin said. "Worth spotted her first, and *he's* in love with her!" Worth was Litwin's employer, Worthington Middlesex, a Manhattan eccentric with the reverse of the Midas touch; everything he touched turned to dross.

"Well," Edmund said, "since this is my house, I should at least be entitled to *droit du seigneur*."

Carrie felt her skin crawl as Edmund kept squeezing her shoulder, practically winding himself around her in the process. Don't these men have any respect for a girl's right to keep her body to herself? she wondered.

"Very well, Edmund," Litwin said, "you can have her for this evening, and after Worth manages to abduct her from your territory, then she's his."

The same dialogue, the same grabbing, the same come-ons and put-ons—Carrie bore them graciously. Then Simon Rogers appeared. Short, fat, bald. Cigar. Edmund introduced him.

Simon Rogers operated the East Coast office of a major Hollywood studio. "You could be a big star," he said. "You

158

know that? You've got what it takes. God, you're gorgeous. Why haven't you been grabbed up?"

"I'm not an actress."

"You don't have to be. You think any of those dumb broads on the Coast are?"

"Well, I . . ."

"Acting, schmacting."

"I've never been submitted for a film."

"Don't let those agents bullshit you. They haven't got anything to do with who makes it and who doesn't. You know how a girl makes it in pictures?"

"How?"

"This business is all favors. You go to a picture and see some girl in a part, and she's not Liz Taylor, not an established star, then you know some guy's behind her. Loan-outs are all based on favors."

"I see."

"What you need is a guy behind you." He leaned closer to Carrie. "I'm in a position to help you. I can make it happen for you." He flicked the ashes off his cigar and proceeded to puff hard, but the light had gone out and he had to strike a match and ignite it again. "Why don't we get together and discuss it? How about a drink after the party?" he suggested, giving her a sly look.

"I'm sorry, I have to get up early tomorrow."

*   *   *

At eleven-thirty that night, the phone rang. Carrie answered.

"Please," she said, "I don't like to be disturbed at this hour." Then she hung up.

"Who was it?" Dolores asked.

"Simon Rogers."

"Are you out of your mind? Do you realize who he is?"

"I don't care if he's important. He's obnoxious. I'm sick of having to defend myself against these creeps. They're all empty, conceited, shallow, superficial, impossible, impotent—"

"Sure," Dolores interrupted, "that's what makes them such great targets." She posed in front of Carrie. "How do I look for my late date?"

159

"Enchanting," Carrie said. "I don't know how you manage to keep it up."

"I love every blessed minute of it." Dolores blew a kiss. "Well, *ciao*. I'm off to meet my latest Daddy Warbucks."

*   *   *

"Whoopee!" Rex exclaimed as Eve walked in the door. "You got 'Take a Crack'! Whee!"

"Wonderful!" Eve cried.

"I'm so pleased, Eve," Charlene said. "I know you'll appreciate having the steady income."

"Will I!"

"It's always good to have something you can rely on coming in each week," Charlene went on, "and 'Take a Crack' is one of the better game shows."

"I know. This is like the answer to a prayer."

"You're not putting on weight, are you, Eve Paradise?" Rex asked.

Charlene frowned. "You do look like you've gained some, Eve."

"Maybe a couple of pounds, but . . ."

"Honey, don't you know you can't afford to let yourself get out of shape? You're lucky, these game show people like the *zaftig* type, but for other work, you'd better slim down, honey."

"Well, I stopped taking the diet pills, and . . ."

"Better start in again," Charlene said. She paused to nod at Rex, who was on his way out of the office; then she continued, "And your skin could stand a good cleaning. Let me make an appointment for you with Dr. Behrman. It's the soot in this bloody city. The place is a poison belt. You should be going to Dr. Behrman twice a week now that you're earning a good income. Remember, in this business you *have* to take care of yourself. There's always someone newer coming along. Youth is your greatest asset. What I wouldn't give to be in your shoes today, knowing what I know. You kids just have no idea of the advantage you have."

Eve sighed. "I sure wish my youth would help me to get a few things. My problem is"—she stared at the floor—"I get very lonely. I guess that's why I've put on the weight . . .

because I've been eating too much. I just wish I could meet somebody. . . ."

"Well, I never!" Charlene said. "Who'd ever believe that a beautiful young dish like you would have trouble meeting people in New York City?"

"I guess I'm shy," Eve said. "I guess I think all these other girls have more to offer than I. I try to have confidence, but I always end up thinking, Eve Petroangeli, you're a big phony."

Charlene peered at Eve sympathetically. "You should have said something sooner, darling. It doesn't do a bit of good to have you walking around with an inferiority complex. It's utterly ridiculous for you to feel inadequate. You're every bit as good as any of the other girls. You've made a lot of progress, and you've had a great deal to overcome."

"But some of the girls—Charlene, you just don't know! Like Dolores Haynes, for instance: every time I see her walk into a room, it's like she owns the place. She just has this attitude that everyone else should step aside; I never saw anything like it. She makes me feel about two feet high."

"You should have one-tenth of Dolores Haynes' nerve. That girl has gone farther on less equipment than anybody I've seen in a long time."

"How do you mean?"

"I mean, a great beauty she's not, or a great talent. What she's got is belief in herself. She expects things. And she gets them. Jobs, men, money—anything she wants!"

"I think Dolores is very attractive."

"She's well-turned-out, honey, but it's all contrived. Nothing's genuine. Now take yourself, Eve. You're something entirely different. You *are* genuine. But there's something in you that persists in negating it, in not believing in your own power. So this is how you end up. Alone at the Longacre House. *Oy vey!* My God, luv, I don't understand you one bit."

Warren, who had been sitting at Charlene's feet, suddenly stood up, looked at Eve, and began to whimper. Charlene roared. "You see, even my dog can't understand you, Eve Paradise!"

"But I feel like I'm trying to fool people . . . and that when they find out, I'll be . . . embarrassed."

"Listen to me, honey"—Charlene bent forward, and her

161

eyes bored into Eve—"you *are* Eve Paradise. You created her, and you *are* she. Understand?"

"Yes, but . . ."

"You created her because you didn't like the limitations an accident of birth imposed on you. There's no law saying we have to accept our limitations, and you know that's the truth, Eve; you know it."

"I guess . . ."

"Sit, Warren," Charlene ordered. "Down with Kurt like a good fella. . . . There's my boy. Good!" She patted Warren's head, then Kurt's, then turned to look at Eve again. "Okay, honey," she said, "back to you now. You really are a case. What are we going to do about you?"

Eve shook her head.

"Well," Charlene said after a moment, "I have one idea."

"What?"

"Move you in with Carrie and Dolores. Something might rub off."

Eve's jaw dropped. She was speechless.

"They have plenty of room for another girl. I'll give them a call and let you know if it works out."

*   *   *

Still half numb from her conversation with Charlene and the possibility of the new turn in her life, Eve practically glided all the way to Uncle Nappi's shop.

"Uncle Nappi," she cried the moment she got inside, "guess what!"

The old man looked up from the haircut he was giving. "You got a big new commercial. You're gonna make a million!" Shears poised in midair, he said to the customer, "This here's my little niece, Evie. Her picture's all over my walls. You see what a beautiful little doll my niece is?"

Eve sat down with a magazine, waiting for her uncle to finish. Eight eleven-by-fourteens of her now graced the walls; Uncle Nappi had had them all framed.

In a few minutes, when the customer left, Uncle Nappi turned to her.

"Uncle Nappi," Eve said, "I may be moving in with the most glamorous, sophisticated, popular girls in New York!

They know everybody in the jet set; they go to all the most exciting parties; they know all sorts of rich people! Isn't that fantastic, Uncle Nappi?"

"In a while you won't even talk to your old uncle any more." He shook his head. "You gonna be too good for the Petroangelis, getting so fancy and coming up in the world."

"Never, Uncle Nappi!"

Uncle Nappi smiled gently. "Just so long as you never forget your old uncle."

Eve gave him a kiss and said, "Never, Uncle Nappi. Never."

Chapter 2

Two weeks had passed since Dolores met Nathan Winston. During that time he had sent flowers every day; evenings, he took her to parties and to dinner in Manhattan's most expensive restaurants. His being rich and unencumbered made him a most desirable target, and it delighted Dolores to be seen on his arm and to have important people notice her.

Nathan's plans for the future included entering politics, and he was well connected for the power game. The fact that he was both a gourmet and oenophilist was to his credit. His main attribute, however, was undeniably his wealth.

Nathan Winston, Dolores found, was a peculiar man, almost removed from the world at times. "What did you mean by Pandora's box?" she asked him several times; but he shook his head and refused to reply, as he always did when she wanted an answer to something specific.

Once, when he had been speaking about his son, Dolores had asked him, "How many children do you have?"

"Three," he'd said, his thoughts far off.

Later she had asked, "What are they, two sons and a daughter or a son and two daughters?"

Nathan's eyes had enlarged, and for an instant Dolores had

thought she read fear in them. Then, in perfect control of himself, he'd said, "I have a son and a daughter."

"What about the other child?"

"Which other child? I told you I had *two,"* he said.

Dolores allowed the subject to drop and continued being puzzled by Nathan. The hidden areas in him she could not approach irked her, for they made plotting her campaign more difficult.

* * *

At the end of the third week of Dolores' acquaintance with Nathan Winston, the second week of their affair, Nathan invited her on a spur-of-the-moment trip to Europe. The advertising campaign his company had planned, for which he'd promised she would be given special consideration, had been canceled. The trip seemed designed as some sort of consolation.

* * *

"Oh, honey, I left my shoe buckles on the dresser. Could you hand them to me?"

"Sure."

Eve leapt to Dolores' service. She was floating in the clouds since moving in.

"Thanks, kid." Dolores secured the buckles to her patent pumps.

"I think it's so exciting, your going to Europe," Eve said, her eyes round and envious.

Carrie entered, threw herself down on one of the beds, and kicked off her shoes. Indicating the small overnight bag Dolores had open on the bed, she asked, "Is that all you're taking to Europe with you?"

"Sure. Everything else I need Nathan can buy me there. What do I need with a lot of old crap?"

"How can you be sure he'll pay for everything?" Eve asked.

Dolores laughed. "Kid, did you ever hear the joke about the *yenta* who went away to the Catskills without her husband? When she came back she said, 'Morrie, you know that part of me you always said was such a nice place? Well, you're wrong, that's no nice place—that place's a gold mine.' "

"That's a joke?" Eve was perplexed.

"Well, never mind, kid, if you don't understand. I can see from just two days under the same roof with you, a swinger you're not. Maybe it's just as well. Less competition."

Carrie sat up and said, "Be sure to let us know where you are, Dolores."

"Sure. No sweat."

"I think this is so exciting," Eve said. "I wish I knew a rich man who'd take me places. Imagine, Paris, London, the French Riviera. . . ."

"I'm really going to buy out France and Italy. Wait till you see the bills I'm going to run up on old Nathan."

"Gee."

"Hey, that's the phone, kid. It's probably Nathan. Answer it in the living room and say you're my secretary. I told him I have a secretary. One more expense I can sock him with."

Eve went to the living room to answer the phone. Carrie, wearing a pale rose negligee, had risen and was bending over the dresser, fishing in a drawer for fresh underwear. The outline of her firm breasts was clear. Dolores watched, unable to look away. When Carrie held up a pair of flowered see-through panties, Dolores' breath came quicker. She imagined Carrie stepping into them, imagined Mel Shepherd or some other guy—there must have been lots of men—Carrie was hot, she could tell that—taking them off. Picturing what Carrie would be like lying naked in bed with a man on top of her, Dolores gripped her palms tight. They were sweating.

Suddenly the feeling she'd had when she first met Carrie returned strongly. Resentment flared in her, and she was seized with a jealousy and envy that made her feel hot all over.

Angry, she went to her overnight case and tucked a month's supply of Enovid in the lining. "What a real dumbbell kid that Eve is. Would you believe her?"

Eve stood in the doorway. "Nathan Winston is on the phone," she said.

Dolores hovered at the door. "Oh, Eve, dear, do me a

165

great big favor and get me my douche bag from the john so I can pack it."

"Gee," Eve said after Dolores was gone, "isn't she something?" For a while she sat in thoughtful silence. Then a question came to her mind. "What's a *yenta?*" she asked.

Chapter 3

"Caroline, *mon ange!*"

Carrie and Eve entered the ornate hallway of Geoffrey Gripsholm's town house. Geoffrey bent and kissed Carrie's hand in pseudo-Continental style. Then he stood her at arm's length and exclaimed, *"Comme tu es belle ce soir, ma chérie."*

"Eve Paradise," Carrie said, "I'd like you to meet Geoffrey Gripsholm."

"Oh, *c'est elle! Comme elle est belle! Une vraie ange!*" Geoffrey picked up Eve's hand and bestowed a liquid kiss on it. "Do you speak French?" he asked.

"No, I'm afraid not," Eve said, feeling self-conscious.

"Is he half French?" she asked Carrie as they went to leave their wraps in the bedroom. "I mean, he speaks English well."

Carrie laughed. "I can assure you his English is far more fluent than his French."

They entered Geoffrey's large bedroom, in which the *pièce de résistance* was a huge lubricious Louis XVI bed covered with a shocking-pink satin spread; four pink-gold Della Robbia *putti* decorated the canopy.

"Geoffrey has one of the most outstanding collections of Boucher, Fragonard, Watteau, and Vigée-Lebrun this side of the Louvre," Carrie told Eve as, leaving the bedroom, they proceeded back through the hall, then down the winding marble staircase, around a corner, and into the living room, which was, Eve saw, filled with clusters of people in evening attire. Suddenly Eve was seized with dread. Her legs felt like

166

jelly, and her stomach churned. She didn't know a soul in the whole room! What would she talk about?

Geoffrey Gripsholm was coming toward them. "Ah, *mes belles, mes chères belles amies!*" he exclaimed, extending his arms dramatically.

Since Carrie had known Geoffrey his French had not progressed much. She knew that during the past several years Geoffrey had skied in Saint-Moritz, Mégève, Klosters, and Gstaat and passed part of each summer on the Côte, and she'd often heard him claim that, having been so used to speaking French with his *copains*, he was forgetting all his English. If anyone dared ask, "How long were you in France?" Geoffrey would automatically look the other way and exclaim, *"Qu'est-ce qu'il y a là-bas?"* in order to get out of having to reply he'd spent a mere two weeks in *la belle France*. This, as all would have agreed, was hardly time enough to forget one's native tongue.

Carrie had seldom heard Geoffrey speak a sentence in French containing both a subject and a predicate. Yet he capitalized on the various phrases he knew, had the nasals down pat, and threw in a few "eu" sounds, as though he were searching thoughtfully for just the right way in which to express a complicated thought. Thus had Geoffrey gained a reputation among the nonlinguistic. Columns cited him as "suave Continental-mannered Geoffrey Gripsholm, renowned for his parties and for his art collection," and columnists noted that they had observed him chatting in "rapid, fluent French" at this restaurant or that.

Geoffrey's living room abounded with paintings, predominantly of shepherdesses and milkmaids. The ceiling, ornately carved, had been brought over from France. Much of the furniture was ebony. There were tables with inlays of metal and tortoise shell, or of semi-precious stones with gilded bronze mounts, and marquetry in floral designs in amaranth, satinwood, tulipwood, and kingwood, with attenuated sprays, tendrils, scalloped shells, garlands, and flickering flames. The guests turned intermittently toward the art in reverence.

Taking Carrie and Eve in tow, Geoffrey introduced them to several of the other guests, most of whom Carrie already knew. She noted the presence of a parvenu toilet-fixtures tycoon and his wife, of a dress manufacturer named Lenny

Lee who had moved up the social ladder by becoming a Broadway producer, and of a society columnist; also, of some Europeans, a pair of Hollywood-type males, several expressionless female models, and a fourth-generation Italo-American who'd once been known as Frank but now called himself Francesco and tried—with some success—to pass himself off as a count.

"One thing strangely out of keeping with much of the décor of my *petit pied-à-terre*," Geoffrey said to Eve, "is on display in the library. Perhaps you would care to view it?"

Eve followed him to the library, where he pointed out his greatest treasure, a Seurat, and said, "Although I have a natural bent toward the ornate and voluptuous, best exemplified by the eighteenth-century rococo style, I nevertheless could not resist this rare treasure so exquisite in its *pointillisme*." Eve later heard the painting was insured for $200,000.

"Carrie!" Lenny Lee, the ex-cloak-and-suiter, came up behind her, and as she turned to face him they nearly collided.

"You never call me." Lenny pouted. "I've been waiting for you to call." His beady eyes and high-pitched voice made Carrie shudder.

"Thought you might be interested in seeing the new spring line," Lenny said, rotating his drink between two fleshy palms. He still kept semi-active in the dress business in order to use it as bait for girls. "If you'd like to buy a few things, I'll give you a good price. Why don't we have lunch tomorrow and go over to my office afterwards?"

"I'm sorry, Lenny, but I can't. Things are terribly hectic these days."

"Been working a lot, huh?" His voice was his worst attribute, nasal and nerve-racking.

"Yes," Carrie said, turning away.

Fred Ackerman, the toilet tycoon, was talking to a French baroness, and gesturing widely to cover up his lack of fluency in French. His wife, Laurine, who despite nine summers at their villa in Cap Ferrat, still could not speak a word of French, let alone issue a coherent statement in English, stood close by, giving him the fish eye.

As Carrie breezed past, Fred caught her arm. "Long time, no see," he said, holding her at his side. "Sometime"—he turned again to the baroness—"I'll have to let you see *our* art collection. It may not be as extensive as Geoffrey's, but it's a lot more exclusive and *recherché*. Wouldn't you say so too, Laurine?"

"Yes," his wife answered, staring blankly ahead of her.

"We have a Picasso," Fred boasted. "And we also have a new acquisition—really a collector's item, isn't it, Laurine?"

"Yes."

"It's a Rauschenberg." Fred swelled with pride. "Only cost ten thousand dollars. A steal. And it's tax deductible. I just declare it's owned by my Foundation."

"How marvelous," the baroness said.

"You have to see it. Laurine and I will be having some people over soon, when we get back from Europe."

The baroness nodded; then, lapsing back into French, she excused herself and left. Fred and Laurine moved to where Lenny Lee stood with a girl in a white brocade pants suit.

Geoffrey Gripsholm, seeing Carrie alone, flitted toward her. "Eve is *absolument ravissante!*" he said. *"Une vraie ange, non?"*

Carrie spotted Eve on the other side of the room, surrounded by men.

On one glass of champagne, Eve was giddy, garrulous, astounded at her own wit and poise and dizzy from compliments:

"You're one of the best-looking girls in New York, do you know that?"

"How come I haven't met you till now?"

"You're a fresh face. There's nothing like a fresh face."

"I can't believe you've been around a year. I thought I knew every beautiful girl in town."

And just a moment ago a Hollywood publicity man, the well-known Hy Rubens, had said, "You ought to be a star."

A star! Hy Rubens' words were pure nectar to Eve. She listened avidly as he told her he was intrigued with her "quality," that she was star material, and that he could spot potential when he saw it.

"What have you done?" he asked now.

"Well," Eve said, "I've done commercials. Right now, I've got several running: Rinse Away Dandruff Shampoo, Gaines Dog Food, Tropicana, K2-R Spot Lifter—"

Hy was nodding brusquely. "The thing we'll have to do with you is line up some publicity. Break things in columns, get some action going. Let me give you a call. What's your number?"

Trying to control her excitement, Eve told him.

"You're a natural for pictures," he said, jotting it down. "I know you could make it big."

The movies! Eve had never dared hope! She had imagined Hollywood as a whole other world, a foreign country, practically, where the actresses were all discovered in drugstores or imported from England. And now this man, Hy Rubens, who really knew what he was talking about, said *she* had what it took to make the grade, that she was a "fresh face" and a great type. A big Hollywood press agent had discovered her! He believed in her! He wanted to help her! A whole new world was opening up for her.

To think that when she had first entered Geoffrey's living room she'd been frightened and worried! And now—just two hours later—she had countless invitations to lunch and dinner, had been asked to three parties, had been offered clothes at a discount, and best of all, was going to be promoted to stardom by a famous Hollywood publicist. She couldn't believe her good fortune. At last things were happening as she had dreamed they would.

A moment later, Fernando, the Philippine houseboy, signaled to Geoffrey, who clapped his hands together to summon the guests to dinner. One by one they descended the narrow stairway to what Geoffrey called his *"cave."*

The teak floor was partially covered by an Aubusson, the walls adorned with eighteenth-century drawings. A large French window offered a view of the garden beyond, where a tent had been put up for after-dinner dancing.

Geoffrey's menu consisted of *pâté de foie gras*, vichyssoise accompanied by a 1957 Montrachet, *mouton à l'Alsacienne* served with various vegetables and Château Haut-Brion, tossed salad, and dessert—*mousse au chocolat* and petit fours with 1962 Dom Perignon.

Eve listened to the society columnist discuss skiing in Saint-Moritz. He said that last March he'd been grossly disappointed in the crop of personalities on the slopes and in the cocktail bars. "Saint-Moritz just isn't the way it used to be," he lamented. "The wrong element is ruining it."

Geoffrey agreed. "*C'est de la merde, ça me fait chier.*"

After dinner Fernando was serving demitasse in the living room. Carrie walked over to the couch where Eve sat talking to Geoffrey and one of the Hollywood men, a fellow with a brutal head and the mouth of a dolphin.

"Carrie, I'd like you to meet Hy Rubens," Eve said.

Carrie was surprised that Hy stood up upon greeting her; however, it turned out that he'd risen not out of social courtesy, but because he was leaving the party. Geoffrey followed him to the door. Eve watched for a moment, then said, "Carrie, everything is just perfect. I've met so many interesting and intelligent people. Everyone has been so nice to me. They all want to help me! Oh, thank you, Carrie, thank you for introducing me to all these wonderful, exciting people!"

Geoffrey returned. "I'm simply mad for that publicist," he told Carrie. "Isn't he the gauchest person you've ever met in your life!"

Chapter 4

The social whirl was beginning! Eve met Lenny Lee for lunch the next day at Twenty One. She was intrigued when he told her he owned a Ferrari, and impressed with the way the waiters treated him, calling him by his name and acting glad to see him. But she did not like the loud voice in which he called across the room to other customers or the flip way he gave orders to the waiters. Still, being at Twenty One, which she'd heard so much about, almost made up for Lenny's presence.

After lunch she went to his office and chose two suits and two dresses, which he gave her at cost. He seemed rather put out that she had to dash off as soon as she'd paid for the

171

clothes. She had another appointment, she said, and she was also busy for dinner.

"I'll call you tomorrow," he said. It sounded far more like a threat than a promise. "Maybe we'll grab a bite together."

* * *

From a pay phone in the lobby of Lenny Lee's building, Eve checked with her answering service. A call had come in from Hy Rubens at the Waldorf Towers, she was told. Immediately, she rang his room.

"Honey," he said, "I was trying to get you all morning. It's after four o'clock now, and I gotta catch a plane to the Coast. Hey listen, I'll tell you what. Come on over for a drink right this minute, and we'll ride out to the airport together."

"Oh, I'm sorry, Hy," Eve said with regret. "But I have an appointment at five."

"Well, cancel it."

"Oh, I couldn't. It's an on-camera call-back for Johnson's Lemon Pledge. They've narrowed it down to six girls, and I'm one. It's very important."

"Oh." Suddenly Hy sounded distant, as though he had more important things on his mind. "Well, I'll call you when I get back to town then."

When Eve placed the receiver back on the hook, she was worried. Maybe she'd said something wrong: Hy was so enthusiastic last night, but he didn't seem that way now. She was sorry she couldn't drop everything and meet him.

Well, at least she'd made a dent in the New York social scene. All eyes had been on her last night. Charlene was right: she really did have something unique and extraordinary. And at long last people were beginning to see it. She picked up her book and satchel, left the phone booth, and started over to Dancer-Fitzgerald-Sample and her final appointment of the day.

* * *

Cherry Grove was where the action was. Goldie's was packed, smoke filled, and full of titters, twitters, and quips. Everyone who was anyone in the gay world was there, rushing around greeting each other, strutting, cruising, and making new contacts. There were designers, choreographers, hairdressers, chorus boys, singers, dancers, all discussing the incoming fall Broadway productions in breathless, excited tones. Outside, young flesh, gobs of it, oozed along the boardwalks and the beach. Rex was in seventh heaven. The Beach Hotel teemed with beautiful male bodies. Dancing under the stars at the Pines, bronzed young gods clung to their boy friends during the ballads and bounced enticingly during the go-go numbers.

It was during one of the latter that Rex spotted his weekend catch, a black-haired, dark-skinned, blue-eyed, built-like-a-brick-shithouse specimen of pure masculine sexuality in clinging low-rise sailor pants and a pale pink turtleneck. One glance at the physique, one sniff of the animal vitality, and there was no doubt in Rex's mind: he wanted that boy.

Rex saw the boy approved of his taste in clothes, and was glad he had worn his new hipster slacks, his Countess Mara fly-fronted shirt and paisley silk ascot from the Cardin Boutique.

He sidled up to him. "Hello there," he said. "My name is Rex Ryan. I'm an agent."

"Sinjin O'Shaunnessy. I'm an actor."

Rex read the hungry look in the boy's eyes. Of course. He should have known he was an actor.

"Sinjin? That's an unusual name."

"Actually, it's short for St. John."

"Do I detect a British accent?"

"I'm from Dublin, actually."

"How fascinating. Why don't we get together and talk. May I have this dance?"

"Why, certainly."

Their bodies rubbed enticingly as the music began a suggestive crescendo.

"Tell me about your career," Rex said. "Are you working?" That was always the bitchiest thing to ask if it turned out the actor wasn't.

"I'm understudying."

"What's that?" Rex said. He could barely hear Sinjin above the din of the noisy band.

"Understudying! Off-Broadway!"

"Oh! What's the play?"

" 'TIS PITY SHE'S A WHORE! I understudy the incestuous brother!"

"I can scarcely hear! Let's go to my room and talk!"

*   *   *

Later that night Rex and Sinjin, satiated, lay stretched out on the bed. A dim bulb burned behind Sinjin, lighting a slim volume of Yeats, from which he read:

> He longs to kill
> My body, until
> That sudden shudder
> And limbs lie still.
>
> Oh, what may come
> Into my womb
> What caterpillar
> My beauty consume!

"That's wild!" Rex exclaimed. "That Yeats sure could write poetry. You read well." His hand squeezed Sinjin's knee. "I can see you have talent."

"I have," Sinjin agreed. "I ought to be doing a lead on Broadway."

Rex turned over on his side and traced a design on Sinjin's back. He said, "I never browned a Black Irishman before."

Sinjin said, "I hope you'll come see me when I get to go on in the part."

"Sure, sure I will," Rex promised. "And I'm going to submit you for lots of things. I have you in mind for a part in a TV show."

"Which one? When do I go on it?"

"Call me Tuesday in the office, and I'll let you know. Now, come here again, you beautiful, sexy, wild, erotic hunk of male pulchritude!"

*   *   *

The weather in London had been superb. Evenings were a constant round of visits to Mirabelle's and the Ad Lib, the

'21 Club, Dolly's, Les Ambassadeurs, and the Colony, where Dolores won two hundred pounds gambling.

At Casa Pepe Nathan sent back a bottle of 1963 Château Lafite declaring it to be under par. Dolores basked in the stir they created, then went back to thinking about all the new clothes Nathan had already bought her—and about how the fun was only just beginning.

In Paris they stayed at the quietly luxurious Lancaster; they ate at the Tour d'Argent and under the stars at Lassère; they visited Chez Castel, and Nouveau Jimmy's on the Boulevard Montparnasse, and Régine, *naturellement;* and went to the Palladium and to Bilboquet, very *yé-yé,* with its wild orchestra and dazzling Paris young—who made Nathan look like Methuselah; and they visited Au Pied de Cochon near Les Halles, and of course Maxim's, and the Deux Magots and de Flors Verts, and had tea and cakes at La Marquise de Sevigné on the Place Victor Hugo.

What a drag Nathan was! Sure, he'd been generous enough, buying her clothes, perfumes, and accessories, then a diamond bracelet with matching earrings at Van Cleef and Arpels and a mink at Réal. True, he never flinched when she spent his money. But there wasn't much else you could say for him.

In Rome the night scene was the Piper Club, Shaker, Il Pipistrello, the Club 84, the Caffè Doney, the Caffè de Paris, the Caffè Rosati, and Tre Scalini, as well as La Cabala, the outdoor Helio Cabala, and the Casina delle Rose. During the day, Dolores would haul Nathan onto the Via Condotti, where he signed away numerous traveler's checks for, among other things, a diamond necklace at Bulgari, which Dolores insisted she needed to match her other diamonds.

No, it wasn't generosity Nathan lacked, it was *chutzpah.*

It wasn't long before Nathan's taciturn, enigmatic manner, his penetrating eyes, his indifferent noninvolvement, and his apathy began to wear on her. By the time they reached the south of France, she'd had her fill of him. Clearly, the man was in his decline. On the beach flabby Nathan compared most unfavorably with the shiny bronzed men who paraded by, young men with healthy virile bodies, sex teeming from their pores, their breaths reeking with it.

At night Nathan, tired from sun and wine, his body exuding odors of chemical unbalance and unpleasant emanations of a

175

disordered nature, suffering from chronic ailments of the eliminative, digestive, and secretory systems, would fall asleep while Dolores silently cursed him and his cold, clammy, moist hands and feet. Only two or three times since the onset of the trip had he made sexual overtures. He had gotten into the habit of apologizing with a sleepy yawn, saying, "Maybe I'll feel like fucking you tomorrow night. Right now I'm too beat." The next morning he invariably rose without a thought of sex, early, so as not to miss the sun (he harbored the illusion it was youth-restoring). Later in the day, Dolores, seething, would get him to sign away more traveler's checks than she might otherwise have asked him to.

One morning—it was late August now—while Nathan was busy making transatlantic phone calls, Dolores left their suite at the Old Beach Hotel in Monte Carlo and went outside to lie in the sun. She felt like scratching Nathan's eyes out.

* * *

"*Pardon, madame, mais est-ce que vous savez l'heure, par hasard?*"

Dolores looked up to see a tanned, muscularly handsome young man in his early twenties standing over her.

"Do you speak English?" she asked, not wanting the young man to go elsewhere with his question.

"Oh, you are not French then?" The voice was sexy, early Charles Boyer.

"No. I'm American."

He grinned, exhibiting brilliantly white teeth. "If you will pardon me, I have been observing you for several days now, here on the beach where you usually come with your father. One cannot help noticing so beautiful a woman."

"Why, thank you." Dolores lifted herself up on her elbows. The sun was hot on her thighs.

"I was certain a woman of so much charm and *savoir-faire* must assuredly be European—most likely French."

Dolores smiled, flattered.

"I should never have taken you for American," the young man continued.

Dolores stretched her legs out enticingly, feeling herself powerfully drawn to this magnificently sexual creature. She

176

looked at his lean, sculptured body, his vital square hands, his face (the well-developed nostrils were those of a true voluptuary). And of course she was not unaware of the superbly bulging genitals stuffed inside his skimpy bikini.

"Your father is not with you this morning, I see," he said, referring to Nathan. "May I sit down?"

"Please do," Dolores invited.

"My name is François," he said, sitting very close to her. Lifting her sunglasses gently, he peered into her eyes. "And yours?"

"Dolores."

"Dolores! How beautiful! Dolores! You have magnificent eyes, Dolores. A woman with eyes as beautiful as yours should never hide them behind dark glasses. You must never deny the world the privilege of seeing your lovely eyes."

Dolores smiled in a sultry manner. "But it's precisely for this reason I wear the glasses," she explained, "in order to *save* my eyes for the right man—for the man who knows how to appreciate them."

"You are the most charming woman on the beach, the most charming woman in all of Monaco this season, and the loveliest American I have ever met."

An hour later they lay naked together in the narrow bed at François' pension. How wild François was—lean, magnetic, vigorous, like a young stallion drunk on aphrodisiacs; and he said such deliriously exciting things in French as he made love to her. It didn't matter that she didn't understand what the words meant, she relished the intoxication of their sound.

Dolores and François continued exploring one another's bodies until lunchtime, when Dolores reached in her bag, extracted 200 francs, handed them to François, and made a date to meet him again later.

When she joined Nathan on the outdoor terrace at the Old Beach he was silent, as usual, and hid behind the *Wall Street Journal* until they were served a light lunch of *langouste*, salad, and Chablis. Finally he asked, "Did you have a good morning?"

"Yes, darling," Dolores purred.

*   *   *

She could not get enough of François. It was insanity: a combination of sun, wine, sea air, the Mediterranean climate —and having been left so ungratified by Nathan Winston.

Dolores lived for the moments when François would touch her, penetrate her, make her feel alive and womanly.

It was a headiness never before known, this voluptuousness, with the softness of romantic French ballads drifting through the window. The air was permeated with pine, palm, mimosa, and bougainvillea; and there was the taste of salt on their skin.

She relished François' paying her homage, the sensual delight of his oblation; it was like the renewal of an ancient rite, herself cast in the role of siren, the enchanting, beguiling Lorelei.

Mediterranean sex—it was languid at first, a subtlety that grew, and ended with primitiveness and savagery and a welcomed pain. Everything inside her surged, her nerves clamored and rose in spasms and wails demanding, rapacious in the fever of driven desire.

How strange it was that when she was in a position of power with a man, when it was she who was doing the buying, she became like a tigress out to kill her prey. With old men, like Nathan, she had to act the courtesan, to pretend a passion she did not feel. With François the roles were reversed and Dolores felt the overwhelming thrill of conquest. So this is the way old men feel, she thought. No wonder they pay so dearly.

As her satisfaction with François grew, her contempt for Nathan Winston doubled and redoubled.

*   *   *

For the day before Dolores and Nathan were to fly back to New York Dolores had arranged a final clandestine meeting with François. From the moment she woke that morning she had had one thought on her mind: to rip off her clothes and hungrily devour François with all her body and being. Showering, making up, she could scarcely wait another instant.

When she left the bathroom, she found Nathan standing by the door, poker-faced. The *Wall Street Journal* was folded under his arm. "What do you say we take a drive?" he said. "I'd like to go up to Cagnes-sur-Mer."

"We just drove there the other day."

"Well, at any rate, let's drive up in the hills."

What could she do? It was impossible to plead a headache; she'd already told him she was feeling marvelous, and if she should pretend sudden illness, he was liable to stay and watch over her like a hawk. She had no choice but to yield to his wishes. Perhaps when they returned she could squeeze in a quickie with François.

*   *   *

She thought Nathan looked strange as they drove along the Upper Corniche. "Is anything wrong, darling?" she asked.

But he was silent.

At length they arrived at a small hill town. Sloping down a steep ravine, lush green plants converged with clusters of flowers. Nathan parked the car, and they got out and walked over to a roadside balustrade. Below them, an old dog was beginning a slow climb upward.

Nathan hadn't spoken in some time, and Dolores was uneasy. "Is anything wrong, darling?" she asked again.

Without warning, he turned on her. "I know about you and that French gigolo!" he hissed.

"Nathan!"

"Whore! *Whore!*" His face was contorted, his fingers dug into his palms. Then he lunged at her and struck her with the side of his hand.

Dolores reeled.

"Filthy whore! Using my money to buy yourself a lay!"

Dolores screamed, "You son of a bitch! Who in hell do you think you are?"

"Who the hell do you think *you* are? Two-timing tramp!"

She regained her composure enough to smile at the spectacle of Nathan's egocentric anger, and spat out, "If you were a decent lay in the first place, this never would have happened, and you know it!"

"Shut up, you cunt!"

"I will *not* shut up!" Her voice rose in anger. "I'll give

179

you the truth, Nathan! You're washed up as a man! You're old, Nathan. *Old!*"

He stepped toward her again, his face livid and twisted. "You slut! Stop it, I tell you!" He tried to shake her, but she kept her body rigid.

She pulled away and smoothed her hair. With nonchalance she said, "You're finished, Nathan. Do you think you can satisfy a woman? An old man like you? Don't make me laugh."

Nathan's whole body shook.

"A dried-up schmuck like you is good for one thing only, to pay the freight."

The color Nathan had worked so hard to acquire had drained out of his face. Dolores reached into her bag, one Nathan had bought her at Hermès, and extracted a gold compact, another of his gifts. She began to fuss with her makeup, ignoring the quavering man by her side. With complete disdain, she said, "An old bastard like you is lucky to have the company of a beautiful young girl like me. The only way you could get it would be to pay for it. Don't you know—women lay and men pay?" She closed the compact with a firm snap, and deigned to look at Winston. "And that means you have to pay for *all* my kicks, baby, material and physical. It's for sure you can't begin to accommodate me in the fucking department. Do you think I ever enjoyed your touching me, the few times we did it?"

He lunged at her again, but she dodged evenly, sending him crashing against the balustrade and down to the ground.

Looking at him stretched out in the powdery dirt, she smiled smugly. "Anyway, Nathan, will you tell me, what's the difference between us? I did what *you* did. You bought me, and I bought myself a Frenchman. Big deal. We're two of a kind."

Nathan's pasty face was now tinged with green. She thought he looked sick as he drew himself up and brushed his clothes off.

"I'm a healthy girl, Nathan; I need kicks—real sex, and lots of it. The hotter the better. How *dare* you get angry because I fucked a Frenchman! So what? You know damned well if you were any good in the sack, it wouldn't have happened. So why make a big issue of it?"

"You conniving cunt!" He was gasping for breath. "You tramp—you'll pay for this!"

Blindly, he stumbled toward the car. For a moment, Dolores didn't move. Let the bastard bide his time for her; she'd be there in her own good time. He was lucky she'd ever paid any attention to him in the first place, the old fart. Let him cool his bloody heels.

Leisurely, she began to stroll toward the car, which was about fifty feet away. Nathan was now at the wheel. She heard him start the motor, and had a moment's apprehension.

"Nathan!" she called.

The car backed up, swerved into a U-turn, and sped down the road, leaving a cloud of dust swirling behind.

* * *

It was night before Dolores managed to find her way out of the hills and back to Monte Carlo. She walked for several hours, until some German students finally picked her up. Riding in the back seat of their Volkswagen, she thought with grim anger of the crazed actions of Nathan Winston. Wait till she saw him again. She'd make him pay.

Tired, disheveled, and hungry, she arrived back at the hotel—to find that Nathan had checked out and let the rooms go. There were no accommodations to be had for the night; her overnight bag—the one she had taken with her from New York—sat in the lobby. Suspiciously, she noticed that the luggage Nathan had bought her at Hermès was missing.

"Where are the other bags?" she asked the concierge.

"Monsieur took many bags with him. This one little one is all that remains. He said it was the only one belonging to madame."

François! He would help her. And to be in his arms again would be just the tonic she needed.

She went to a telephone, and after some delay, reached him.

"I am sorry," came his apology. "I have an engagement this evening."

"But François, you don't understand! The pig took everything—all my new clothes and my diamonds and—"

"I regret," François said, his voice oily and insincere.

181

There was a click at the other end of the line. That proved what Dolores had always known: no man could be counted on . . . unless the woman were in the driver's seat.

Not wishing any further embarrassment at the hotel, she had the concierge summon a cab to take her to the airport. She'd wait there until her plane left the next morning. Thank God she still had the airline ticket in her purse.

When she got to the airport, she took her overnight case to a bench in one corner of the terminal. Then she opened the bag and examined its contents. Just as she'd suspected, of the clothes, the jewels, the perfume, and the other things Nathan had bought her, nothing—not one item—was there. He had taken every single thing, the prick!

In spite of herself, Dolores smiled. She really didn't know why. Probably to keep from crying. Closing the overnight case, she leaned back and shut her eyes for a moment. She felt the caressing warmth of the Riviera air that drifted inside the terminal, smelled the scent of pine and bougainvillea, and that of the salty sea, listened to the sounds of the arriving and departing passengers around her.

She opened her eyes and looked about. Except for her, everyone in the terminal was with someone else. Except for her, everyone was about to begin a holiday, or had just finished enjoying one. She gritted her teeth.

* * *

Not until her plane was halfway across the Atlantic did Dolores remember that she'd never found out what Nathan had meant when, in the beginning, he'd spoken about Pandora's box.

Must've been something dirty, she decided. Dirty like Nathan. I'll get him. I'll get the pig if I never do anything else in this life. I'll get that son of a bitch Nathan Winston and fix him for good.

Chapter 5

"Damn those License Bureau people. If they think they can fool me, they've got a lesson to learn."

"What's the matter?" Rex looked up from his desk to face a seething Charlene.

"This is the fourth time in four months it's happened."

"Not again. Another spotter?"

"*Another* one."

"What happened?"

"A mature man this time. Good-looking. Told me people had always thought he ought to go into modeling. Of course I knew he was a spotter the minute he walked in, but I played along with him. He asked me where he could get pictures, portfolios, clothes, lessons; just *waiting* for me to trip up and recommend a place I'd get a kickback from. I finally told him I was tired of being insulted by people from the License Bureau. 'This agency has a double A rating,' I said. 'We deserve it, and you people don't have to keep coming around to try and trip us up.' "

"The thing is, they *have* caught some of the other agencies recently, and fined them too."

"I know, Rex. But I'm sick of having to go through the same scene over and over again. Sorry about sounding off so. . . . I guess it's been a hectic week. What are you up to?"

"I'm looking for a Wonder Woman."

"For personal reasons?"

"No, dear, for a commercial."

"Sorry."

"She has to be an expert tennis player, ski, do high diving, and jump horses."

"I think Carrie Richards does something—swimming or tennis, or is it skiing?"

"Does she ride?"

"I don't know. But Dolores Haynes must ride. Didn't she do a Western in Hollywood?"

"Honey, they want English riding."

"Oh, well, in that case . . ."

"I'll have to go through my files. The girl I need has to be an expert in *all* fields."

"Speaking of the devil, look who's here, Rex."

"Carrie! We were just talking about you."

"Come on in my office, luv. I have a check for you on the roach killer you did."

"Thanks, Charlene. I can use it."

* * *

"Here you are, honey," Charlene said, holding out the check.

Carrie dropped the check into her satchel. "Did any money come in yet on my Corman's Crackles?" she asked.

"Oh, didn't I tell you about that? They decided to Schwerin it."

"Schwerin? What do you mean?"

"You've been in the business a year and you don't know about Schwerining?"

"Never heard of it."

"I guess you've never had a commercial they decided to test. What they do is, they screen it for audiences in, say, the South or the Middlewest. They see what effect the commercial has, whether it gets the message across or not. They often do this with a new product or a new advertising campaign. No residuals."

"Too bad," Carrie said. "I sometimes count my money before it's hatched."

Charlene regarded Carrie closely. It seemed she had changed considerably since her experience with Mel Shepherd. "How are you, honey? I often worry about you."

"Okay, I guess, Charlene. The business keeps me active. I'm grateful for that."

"That's the spirit, luv. Now I have somewhere to send you tomorrow, so get your appointment book out. I want to send you up for a Kraft Herb and Garlic French Dressing. Then, right after that, Green Giant . . ."

Carrie fished her notebook and a pen from her satchel and started writing.

* * *

"Charlene," Rex called after Carrie had left, "do you know anyone with bursitis of the arm?"

"Sorry, not offhand."

"The FCC is sure complicating things. Oh, and luv, you never paid me the dime you borrowed the other day for the coke."

"Take it out of petty cash," Charlene snapped, and picked up the phone.

* * *

"It was a brilliant idea to come here. I've been hearing about this place for years."

Carrie gazed into the clear, honest eyes smiling at her, belonging to Dr. Peter Talbott, who was sitting opposite her at P. J. Clarke's.

"It took you to bring me here," he said.

It could have sounded square, but coming from him, it was charming. Carrie laughed. "I thought everyone in the world had been to P. J. Clarke's."

"Not *every*one."

"I'm sorry, I didn't mean to sound blasé."

"You're forgiven," Peter said.

His smile was open and candid. Nice, nice boy, Carrie thought; the kind of son any mother would be proud of—sweet and good and real. A trifle young and unformed in appearance yet—as though he hadn't been shaving long—but mature inside. There was something substantial about him. The pipe he smoked was an amusing affectation, a whimsical touch. How different he is from the men I've met in the business, she thought; he's like a breath of fresh air.

"I'm glad you asked me to join you, Peter," she said.

"I wasn't sure you'd come. It took nerve."

"Why?"

"You're so beautiful. I never would have thought I had a chance. I'd have thought you had a dozen dates lined up for tonight, all more exciting than one with a poor resident on his way to Vietnam with the American Friends' Service Committee."

"You wouldn't believe how far from the truth that is. You don't know what the men I know are like," Carrie said ruefully. "It's an unusual experience for me to be out with you. I don't ordinarily meet doctors, particularly dedicated young ones on their way to volunteer in Quan Ngai."

"Some people would call it draft evasion," Peter said.

"I know with you it isn't."

"You're right. Even if I weren't a Quaker, there's something in me that would still make me want no part of this or any other war."

What a fine person he is, Carrie thought, feeling sad at the thought of his leaving. We just found each other, and now . . .

"It's not fair," she said, "you just about get finished with residency, and now you have to go over there."

"You go where the need is greatest. That's part of being a doctor, part of being a Friend . . . and part of being a human being." He re-lit his pipe and puffed on it. "Tell me about your writing," he said.

"I wish I had more time for it. As it is I keep notebooks—"

"Notebooks?"

"Yes. For instance, I record thoughts and events, character sketches, descriptions, impressions. But you need a stretch of time to develop a full idea. The agency keeps me so busy with appointments I can't do things the way I'd like to."

"Couldn't you arrange your time to do more writing? I went through med school and wrote a lot of poetry at the same time."

"You did?"

"Of course it's not quite the same type of undertaking as doing a whole book."

Carrie was thoughtful. "The trouble is, I'm not sure what I want to write *about* yet."

"Well, in the meantime, your career sounds fascinating. It's great you're so successful. Think how many girls would love to be in your shoes."

"Because they think it's glamorous. In reality it's trivial.

You use so little of yourself. Sometimes I worry about contaminating myself by staying in the business."

Peter gave a hearty roar. "Never," he said. "What you are shines through. If you lived in a whorehouse for a year, you'd still be you, and nothing could change that. By the same token, the business hasn't spoiled you at all. You come from a good background; you're a levelheaded girl; and nothing's going to contaminate you—don't worry."

*　*　*

A heaviness had found itself into her chest. She wished she could have had the opportunity to know him better. They had met only one day ago, and tomorrow he would be gone.

Violet shadows touched the solid wall of skyscrapers that towered above the gritty brownstones with their roof-gardens. It was a full moon, and all the stars were out tonight. There was a muffled feeling to the air outside, and then a breeze seemed to enfold them in a gesture of grace. They walked in quiet to the river and watched the phosphorescence of shadows melting into the dull waters.

"There's a bond between us," Peter said. "Not just because we both have Quaker backgrounds. It's more than that."

The ache in Carrie's heart tightened. How sad, she thought, how sad is might-have-been.

Chapter 6

"Carrie, darling," Charlene said, "I'm glad I got you at home. Tell me, can you play tennis?"

"Well," Carrie said, shifting the telephone in her hand, "I'm not exactly in shape for Wimbledon, but . . ."

"But you *can* hit the ball, can't you? And serve, and things like that?"

"Yes."

"Good. I want to send you somewhere. It's for Yuban Coffee, over at Benton and Bowles. You're to see Rosalie Walton. Tomorrow at nine-forty-five. Look athletic, outdoorsy, and wholesome. Got it?"

"Right."

"Then I have a couple of other things. At noon, I want to send you on a Halo Shampoo. Be sure your hair is clean and shiny. Wear it up. Look sophisticated. Early twenties. See Bill Cassidy at D'Arcy."

"Okay."

"Two more to go. I have a three o'clock for you over at Compton. You did get a release on that Lux, didn't you?"

"Yes."

"Well, this one's for Ivory. Go out and get it. Look about eighteen."

"Right."

"Then at four-thirty they want to see you at BBD&O. It's for Pepsi, so you know how to look."

"The Pepsi look."

"Sure, I don't have to tell you. By the way, they haven't made a decision as yet on the Pepsodent. You looked too young on the Westinghouse. I'll have word on the Pepsodent tomorrow. Then I have something coming up for Friday. I haven't got a time on it yet, but it's for a Noxzema over at DCS&S. I'll let you know."

"Okay."

"I think your test for Gerber's has been postponed. Alex de Paola had to fly to the Coast. They'll do it as soon as he returns. Well, luv, that's it for today. Drop by and see us soon."

"I will," Carrie said, and hung up.

Dolores looked up from doing her nails. "Damn, I've only had three interviews since I've been back from Europe."

"You haven't been back that long. Only about a week."

"I know I should have been up for Campbell Soups. And Drano too. I was perfect for what they wanted. Did you get the Star-Kist Tuna commercial?"

"Haven't heard yet."

"What about the Saran Wrap one?"

"Still waiting on that too."

"Where's the kid?"

"Out with somebody she met at Geoffrey's."

"Would you believe she's still a virgin?"

"How do you know?"

"She told me. Nineteen years old, one year in New York, and still a virgin. She's a big Catholic though. I guess that has something to do with it. How do my nails look?"

"Fine."

"I used a new shade. Do you think it's pearlized enough?"

"Plenty."

"I couldn't get an appointment with Roxie today. Had to do them myself. You're sure they look okay?"

"They're fine."

"I don't want to have a hair out of place tonight. Edmund's big blast. I just know I'm going to meet a live one. You're sure you won't reconsider and come with me?"

"No, thanks."

"You'll be sorry." Dolores shook her hands in the air to make the nails dry faster. "Did I tell you I ran into Simon Rogers last night? Know what he says about you?"

"No. What?"

"Says you're a lesbian. Because you wouldn't see him, of course. Typical male ego ploy. You reject them, it's got to be your problem." She picked a speck of polish off her cuticle. "I don't understand Rex and Charlene. They ought to be doing better for me. They call you all the time."

"We're different types."

"That's for sure. Different types when it comes to men too. Who was that baby you were out with last night?"

"Peter Talbott."

"Who's he?"

"He's a doctor, a resident. I met him at the Friends' meeting."

"Residents never have any money. I'll bet he hasn't even served time in the Army."

"No. He's a C.O."

"He'll end up a jailbird. You really can pick them. Have you screwed this kid yet?"

"No."

"Well, I'm surprised. A girl who loves to fuck as much as you—"

"Cool it, Dolores," Carrie snapped.

189

"What the hell's the matter?"

"Just cool it, that's all."

"Okay, okay, so why take my head off?"

Dolores sidled up to the mirror and examined her face. François and the Riviera sun had done her a world of good. "Yep," she said to her image, "I'm about due for something really big. Tonight's going to be the night."

* * *

The elevator doors opened directly into the foyer of Edmund Astor's spacious Fifth Avenue duplex. "How do you do." The shriveled corpselike man standing beside them grinned distortedly, exhibiting a mouth full of gold dentures. "I am your host, Edmund Astor. And you—you are beautiful, my dear. What is your name?"

He must be blind, Dolores thought. How could he not remember me?

"I'm Dolores Haynes." She extended her hand. "But you don't mean to tell me you don't remember me?"

"Of course, of course, how very gauche of me to forget. You must forgive me."

Edmund's smile was a frozen grimace. He walked as if every step were his last. His small, dull eyes made a brave attempt to flash. "In a while we shall talk, you and I," he said with a note of salacious conspiracy in his voice.

Dolores knew the inside scoop on Edmund, a naturalized citizen who had made his first fortune selling ammunition to Hitler. Now in his dotage, the man was receiving due measure for his heinousness in the form of diabetes, dropsy, and various other physical ailments, not to mention senility. Edmund, Charlene had told her, was a notable cheapskate, good for one thing only, his parties, where one might happen to stumble across a more generous man than he.

All around the flat were photographs of pretty girls sitting next to Edmund (at various stages of his life), mostly at night clubs, usually El Morocco. The photos made Dolores shudder in much the same manner that Charlene's rogue's gallery at the agency did. She wondered what had become of all the girls.

Dolores surveyed the scene in the living room. None of the

girls were any competition for her. The men were all safe bets, old and unattractive, most of them over fifty, many spilling into the sixties and seventies, except for Geoffrey Gripsholm and one or two other oddities.

It was Geoffrey Dolores gravitated to.

"I read in the *Guardian* the other day," he was saying to a swarthy, corpulent man, "that the Frenchwoman spends twenty-four minutes a week with her lover, whereas the Frenchman spends twenty-four minutes a *day* on—er—'other obligations' was the way the *Guardian* phrased it."

"Yes, yes, how charming."

Dolores eased her way into the group around Geoffrey, who turned to her and said, "This is Miss Haynes, Mr. Constacuntacropolis."

Constacuntacropolis! Of course! Spiro Constacuntacropolis, the well-known peripatetic Greek shipowner, with homes in Athens, New York, Paris, Lausanne, Biarritz, Sardegna, Cap Ferrat, Palm Beach, London, and so on, ad infinitum. What a stroke of luck.

"How do you *do?*"

As they shook hands, Dolores gave an extra bit of pressure to Spiro's sweaty palm and looked him straight in the eye, projecting the thought, I'd sure like to climb in the sack with you, honey.

Spiro grinned in response.

"You're looking very Madame Récamier," Geoffrey observed.

Dolores smiled her most charming come-on smile, directing most of it to the obese Spiro, eager to become better acquainted.

A moment later Geoffrey left the fold, and Edmund Astor joined them. "What an exquisite girl," Edmund said. "Isn't Miss Martin exquisite, Spiro?"

"Haynes," Dolores corrected. "I'm *Dolores* Haynes."

"I must invite Miss Hays to my home in the country. We could do some outstanding things there. My hobby is photography, you know."

"Isn't everyone's?" Dolores said, and smiled.

"What type of camera do you use?" Spiro asked.

"A Graflex," Edmund said, his eyes devouring Dolores' cleavage. "I have a large estate, a *very* large estate, in Bucks

191

County. I would be most pleased, Dorothy, if you would be my guest there for the purpose of photographic research."

"That would be very nice," Dolores said, wishing the old fogey would go away and leave her with the Greek.

"Edmund, Edmund," someone called from across the room, "we need your opinion! You must tell us . . ."

"Excuse me; I must tend to my other guests," Edmund said, and left.

Spiro Constacuntacropolis stared long and insolently at Dolores, as though he were undressing her. She returned the look.

He said, "What a wonderful surprise, to come here tonight and find you. You are a rare gem indeed."

"Why, aren't you just too sweet for words."

"I should love to see you again, to have you be my guest at dinner," Spiro said.

"Wonderful." Dolores looked deep into his eyes.

"I regret we have met only this evening, the day before my departure for Europe. But may I call you on the next occasion I come to town? At that time I should be honored to have you as my guest for dinner, if you would please me by accepting."

"I would be utterly delighted, Mr. Constacuntacropolis."

"Call me Spiro."

"Spiro."

Spiro took out a pen and a slim gold-embossed Moroccan leather address book.

Whoopee! she rejoiced as he was writing down her phone number. I knew I'd meet a live one tonight! Conviction is all it takes, and you can have anything you want in this world. I'm keeping my claws out for this one.

*   *   *

Rex reached into the bottom drawer of his desk and extracted his favorite cologne, Woodhue, by Fabergé. He poured several drops of it into his palms, doused his face and hair, combed his copper-toned locks, and sniffed the perfumed air. Ready. Ready for his Wednesday night oratory at the Mattachine Society, where he was an ardent campaigner for the repeal of the Anti-Sodomy Act.

192

Sinjin O'Shaunnessy was to be Rex's special guest tonight. The affair with Sinjin had lasted longer than most—three and a half weeks now. Rex was sure Sinjin would be impressed with his speech, and he was right. Later, sharing a candlelit dinner in the Village, Sinjin was full of praise and complimented Rex lavishly on his impassioned delivery.

From the restaurant the two proceeded to Sinjin's digs around the corner, where Sinjin read some poetry, then spoke of his interest in etymology.

"The English language is in the process of change," he said. "Words have lost their power, we've sucked them dry of their original meaning. We need to have new words, or else to bring obsolete ones back into common usage."

"I see," Rex said.

"Take the word *fuck,* for instance."

Rex perked up.

"It's been used for *fornicate* so often that it no longer has the drive and force it once had. Now . . ." Sinjin continued, "I suggest that in the future one ought to use the word *fuck* in its original sense, to *plant.* In other words, one would fuck an oak tree in one's garden; one would fuck petunias, one would fuck tulip bulbs—but no longer would one fuck *people.*"

"Well, you'd have to have a word for it, still and all . . . I mean—"

"I have the word," Sinjin interrupted.

"What is it?" Rex asked.

"*Swive!*" Sinjin proclaimed.

"*Swive?* I never heard of it before."

"It's a fine old Anglo-Saxon word. Chaucerian. The word is listed in Webster's second, and in the Oxford Dictionary."

"That's pretty good—*swive* . . ."

"The *Secreta Secret* says, 'Don't bathe on a full stomach; nor swive.' "

"Ha! Ha! We know better!" Rex sniggered.

"We certainly do," Sinjin agreed.

The two boys looked at each other with mutual adoration, having just swived on a full stomach.

Sinjin leaned forward eagerly. "When are you going to check to see if the film people have made a decision?" he asked.

"I'll call tomorrow," Rex replied. Then, feeling a new surge of desire, he reached for Sinjin and exclaimed, "Swive me, baby; swive me!"

Chapter 7

Eve's life had never been more beautiful. She knew in short order she could have her pick of the town's most eligible bachelors. Work was going well too: she'd just stopped up at the agency and collected $1,200 worth of residuals from three new commercials: Jif Crunchy Peanut Butter, Dentyne Cinnamon Gum, and Kellogg's Bran Buds. In addition to that, she had the steady security of her job on "Take a Crack," plus some print work. Traipsing all over town for odd forty-dollar-an-hour photography jobs was exhausting, but steady work at a catalog house, paying a couple of hundred dollars a day, often came her way in season.

Most of the day's activity had for some time been centered around interviews for projected commercials rather than for print work. Even more pavement pounding was involved, but the pay was better—much better. After an interview at Y&R, below Grand Central, she might race over to Elliot, Unger and Elliot, far in the west fifties, then on over to Compton on Madison and Sixtieth, then to MPO across the Park near Amsterdam, then on down to SSC&B on Lex and Fiftieth. It took time to fight the traffic, and more time was wasted sitting in reception rooms. Thus Eve was usually exhausted by the end of a day.

Whenever possible she would take a half-hour's nap before a date. But there were days—like today—where her busy schedule did not permit a moment's relaxation. Up at seven, she had given her hair a quick wash and set, then sat under the dryer sipping coffee and reading *Vogue*, *Mademoiselle*, *Bazaar*, and *Glamour*, catching up on the latest fashion trends and what was happening in the pace-setting world. She read avidly, with the half-envious feeling of one who had been shut out of the mainstream of life for a long time.

After she'd combed out her hair, Eve packed up her satchel, grabbed her book, hailed a cab, and headed down to J. Walter Thompson in the Graybar Building, for a Ford interview.

The procedure at J. Walter involved signing a paper saying you were free on the product; you also had to list any commercials or print jobs you'd done for any other brand in the same product group. After that the casting assistants saw you quite promptly (unlike those at some places, who were known for staging cattle calls—and kept you waiting over an hour, without even a place to sit). J. Walter was one of the nicest agencies in town, and Eve always felt at home there, especially in the morning, when the coffee wagon came around.

Her interview at J. Walter was at nine-thirty. By ten she was out and walking over to DCS&S, a few blocks away, at Fifth and Forty-fifth. Here the interview was for a Cutex commercial. After seeing the casting director, Eve was taken in to meet the account man, who raved over her pictures and said he'd call her back. As she was about to leave, he told her on second thought to wait, then picked up the phone and spoke to someone named Jim.

"Have you got a few minutes?" the account man asked Eve. "Would you like some coffee?"

Eve said, "Yes, thank you," and the account man rang a secretary and told her to bring in three cups of coffee.

"One's for Jim," he explained. "Jim's the copywriter on the commercial."

The coffee and Jim appeared simultaneously. Ignoring his coffee, Jim looked through Eve's book, and nodded in approval. "Very good book," he said.

Eve glanced at her watch. It was now 10:45, and at 11:15 she was supposed to be at Norman Craig and Kummel for a Hertz interview. If she were late, it would make her fall behind schedule, and her afternoon was crowded.

"Can you wear your hair any other way?" Jim asked.

"Yes, I can do different things with it," she said. "I have different styles in the pictures."

"Let's see how it would look up," Jim said, putting his fingers to his mouth in thoughtful contemplation.

Though Eve was worried about getting to her next interview on time, she didn't want to ruin her chances for the Cutex, so she did as she was asked. Taking a brush from her satchel, she brushed her hair up; then she took out a hairpiece and secured it on top of her head. Both men relaxed into smiles.

Eve put the brush and hairpiece back, shook her head, and combed through her hair with her fingers. There was no time now to worry about how it looked, so she tied a scarf on it and dashed out to catch the Madison Avenue bus up to Fifty-second Street, where Norman Craig and Kummel was located.

Five girls were waiting ahead of her in the attractive gold and white reception room. Four more arrived shortly. Eve gave her name to the receptionist, took the script which was handed to her, sat down, extracted a large mirror from her satchel, wiped the soot off her face, applied fresh powder, and rearranged her hair. Then she settled down to the business of silently rehearsing the lines.

She read—well, she thought—for Maxine Marx, the casting director. But by the time she'd finally completed her business at Norman Craig and Kummel it was past twelve o'clock.

She ordered a sandwich and Coke at a drugstore on Madison, ate hurriedly, then hopped the Fiftieth Street crosstown bus as far as Tenth Avenue and walked the few blocks up to the old Fox Studios, where she had a 1:15 on-camera test for a Colgate commercial. The competition had been narrowed down, in the course of three interviews at Ted Bates, to eight girls, two of whom were waiting when Eve arrived at the studio.

When the makeup man got to Eve he instructed her to remove all her street makeup. He then proceeded to apply Max Factor's Pan-Stik number 6N. The whole process— makeup, rehearsal, test, saying thank-yous, goodbyes, and hope-to-see-you-again-soons—took an hour and a half.

Then she was off in a rush again, for she had a go-see at Benton and Bowles, 666 Fifth, for Pepto-Bismol. *"Get* this one," Charlene had told her. "The pharmaceuticals are the best payers."

The rush never ended! She had to look like a teenager for

a Pepsi interview over at BBD&O at 4:30. This took a little doing. Her hair had been swept up for the Pepto-Bismol interview, since for this spot the agency wanted a glamorous image, and she was still wearing the Max Factor and false lashes from the Colgate test. Hurrying into the ladies' room at Benton and Bowles, she redid her face and hair and changed clothes, replacing the dress she was wearing with a crepe blouse and checked mini skirt from her satchel. Her face was bare now, save for a bit of eye makeup.

Her hair (styled by George Michael of Madison Avenue, who gave the best blunt haircuts in town) fell free and nearly straight, topped by a headband.

She'd scarcely had time to check with her service all day. Finally, after the BBD&O interview, she wearily gathered her forty-pound satchel and her twenty-pound book, one in each arm, went downstairs, found a drugstore, and phoned. Six people had left messages. She couldn't possibly get back to all of them now, so she decided to just call the agency.

Rex had some good news for her. She was booked for the following Wednesday at the Elliots' on a Yuban Coffee commercial, an interview she had been on the day before, again at Benton and Bowles. Also they were very interested in her at Foote Cone and Belding for Clairol and loved her hair color. They had told Rex to be sure to tell her *not* to touch it! However, the people at Compton liked her for Duncan Hines, only thought her hair too blonde and wondered if she would darken it a shade.

"The thing we have to reach a decision on," Rex said, "is which would be the better payer, in the event there's some conflict. Assuming we *get* both jobs. But for the time being, honey, I'd say don't touch the color."

* * *

Eve, nearly worn out, took the Madison Avenue bus up the few short blocks to her street, descended, and trudged home. She threw her book and satchel down, kicked off her shoes, loosened her clothes, and collapsed into a chair. She was acutely conscious of the ache of too much walking, too much strain. For about a minute she sat in exhausted relief. Then, seeing it was nearly six o'clock, she picked up the phone and called Geoffrey Gripsholm to say that she was running behind schedule but would meet him in half an hour.

*   *   *

"Hello, Rhinehart, darling," Eve heard Dolores coo into the phone. "Many thanks for the St. Laurent, dear; it's perfect."

Eve stepped into the shower. When she came out, Dolores was posing in her new gown. "How lovely!" Eve said.

"It's nothing," Dolores shrugged. "Just a little remembrance. It's the least Rhinehart could do, with all his dough."

"I thought you were interested in Spiro what's-his-name."

"A bird in the hand, as the saying goes . . ."

The phone rang again. "It's for you, kid," Dolores said, holding the receiver toward Eve. "A guy with a funny accent."

"Hello, Uncle Nappi." Just when she was rushing. She listened impatiently to his invitation to go to a *festa* in Little Italy. "Uncle Nappi, I'm in a terrible hurry," she said, feeling irritated and ashamed. "Can I call you back tomorrow?"

Why did he have to call and have Dolores hear the way he spoke English? Eve was mortified. Dolores already thought she was a complete square for being a virgin. She was sorry she'd let Dolores worm that information out of her. She should have kept her big mouth shut.

Exposure to the New York social scene had made her aware of so many things. But it wasn't only her family background she was ashamed of, it was her own inadequacies as well. For instance, so many people in the jet set used words she didn't understand. To try to compensate she'd bought a book on vocabulary building and determined to master a new word every day. Today's was *billingsgate*, a word she adored. The previous four days' words were *rodomontade, intrepid, ineluctable,* and *vociferous.*

She finished dressing, grabbed her Emanuelle Khann purse, hailed a cab, and after five minutes' ride up Park, pulled up in front of Geoffrey Gripsholm's town house. Approaching the iron gate, she reminded herself to be sure to use sentences

198

in which her new words appeared. That way Geoffrey would find her intelligent and interesting.

* * *

"I must say, you're looking extremely dishy," Geoffrey greeted her. "Really shipshape and Bristol fashion."

"Thank you," Eve said. "You look very nice too." She looked at his maroon velvet smoking jacket and turquoise silk ascot, and at his rose velvet slippers, shaped like gondolas.

He led her to the library, where he rang for Fernando and ordered some Iranian caviar. Then he asked, "What libation may I offer you?"

"Oh—er—"

"Scotch?"

"Oh—I—n—no. Make it a Harvey's Bristol Cream on the rocks." She tried to imitate the way she'd heard Dolores ask for her favorite drink.

Geoffrey went to the bar. "It seems but yesterday I returned from France and *Angleterre,*" he said as he poured two glasses of sherry, one for Eve, the other for himself. "And now I await with bated breath another such jaunt. I shall spend a fortnight in the City of Light, enjoying the most delicate and refined cuisine in the world."

He handed Eve her glass and joined her on the sofa. "Ah, *les français!*" he exclaimed. "They truly know how to satisfy the palate, with their *savoir-faire* in culinary matters . . . their expertness in choice of vintage."

"I think the French people are *ineluctable,*" Eve said.

If Geoffrey was impressed with her vocabulary, he didn't show it. "I shall also spend just a *soupçon* short of a week's time in London," he continued, "to partake of West End theater fare and attend fashionable Mayfair functions. This youth craze is ruining Britannia. Of course, I consider myself above it, don't you know."

"Oh—yes!"

"What I find so terribly amusing about London," Geoffrey reclined on the uncomfortable antique sofa, placing his sherry glass on the coffee table, "are the marvelously *soigné* Sunday afternoon champagne parties, where one is served a truly magnificent champagne, *premier cru, naturellement.*" After another delicate sip of sherry, Geoffrey regarded her for a moment, and said, "On my next trip I would be pleased to have you along for company, *ma chérie.*" Sherry glass poised in hand, his free arm resting casually on the sofa, he subjected her to another few moments of silent scrutiny. Then, smiling, he muttered, "We shall discuss the possibility of this later, as we come to know one another better."

Once more he was silent—this time for so long that Eve began to worry about getting the conversation going again. In her mind she conceived a sentence with the words *intrepid* and *billingsgate* together, but before she could get it out, Geoffrey spoke.

"It becomes necessary," he said, "for me to speak of the fourfold rhythm of life, to instruct you, as you are still a child, and as yet, do not know."

Eve leaned toward him, puzzled.

"Prurient people—such as myself—have long been aware that only in a carefully induced state of *suspension* can the natural rhythm of life be invoked," he said. "Yes, it is important to recognize both the beauty and *value* of the sordid. While still at Harvard I discovered this great secret of life, unknown to the masses, a purely esoteric phenomenon . . . open only to the most licentiously receptive. Do you follow me thus far?"

Eve nodded, but without much conviction.

Geoffrey moved closer to her and said, "The moment I met you was for me a *coup de foudre,* for in you I instantly recognized an appetite for perversity—as yet unawakened, but nevertheless *there.* In you I saw a partner in depravity, I understood this part of you, and knew you to be a true *vicieuse,* do you understand?"

"I think so."

"What I find so adorable and rare in you," Geoffrey continued, "is your *fin de siècle* quality. There is something totally *déclassée*—and thus enticingly corruptible—about you. I responded furthermore to that quality you possess of the demimondaine: you have the demimondaine's hunger for life and love (as if you refuse to believe in the abyss between souls and insist on reaching out in all possible directions to satisfy your deepest cravings). I can help you; I can help you do that."

"Yes?" Eve said.

"Let me explain. I spoke of the fourfold rhythm of life. Now, each living cell must germinate and bud, build up tension, grow to its fullness, and then die. Within the framework of moments—aye, seconds—in the life of each man, this principle is likewise in force. However, it remains for us to find a way to rediscover the natural rhythm of life, which is only found, as I said, in a state of suspension. Only in the sweet ecstasy of *perversion* can the mind wander, distracted, and allow the full force to culminate. The tension must build in order to attain its full release. This is a great secret.

"How is this accomplished? I will tell you: it behooves us to create a flow. And this is done via a channel—for this two people must be ideally suited as to purpose, preparedness, and intent. This is the role in which I envision you, *ma chérie:* you are my vestal, the vehicle who can make the revelation possible for me—and I in my turn can make it possible for you. What a charming liaison awaits us! You recall I spoke of the beauty of the sordid. Yes, how beautiful and *insidious:* slowly mounting, yet motionless, soundless—a primordial stillness, a hallowed benignity . . ."

Geoffrey's voice had grown softer and softer.

"Yes," he said now, so quietly that Eve had difficulty hearing him. "It's like this—a whisper. Shhh! Nothingness. Oh, yes, slow . . . slow . . . slow. And still: Nothingness—until—yes—VIOLENCE BREAKS LOOSE!" His voice reached a frenzied pitch. "Unleashed, voracious, terrible, marvelous—it's *everything!* It's the whole of creation, yes! The great spirit is free at last!"

He relaxed and blinked. "But," he said, "it must be *evoked* by a channel, by the vessel. It must be aroused from where it lies dormant. It must climb slowly and stealthily, rising in spirals, evoked by the Vestal of Scatological Perversion. And this great force I speak of responds only to the *base,* for only through the base can its true nature be evoked and thus emerge."

Eve glanced at her watch. It was nearly eight o'clock. In another instant the precise time was established by Geoffrey's collection of cuckoo clocks. Within seconds of each other, tweeting, twirping, coo-cooing figures poked their heads out of bird houses and chalets and began circling and singing out in unison like a chorus of dodos.

When the last cuckoo was silent and returned to its enclosure, Geoffrey said, "This is a most unique service, yea, privilege, one can accord another, and requires enormous *savoir-faire* in undertaking. The climate of Europe, particularly that of the Mediterranean, is ideally suited to initiation. Are you free to accompany me in October?"

"Well," said Eve, not wishing to get in bad with Geoffrey or to seem unsophisticated, "you see, I have to work . . ."

Geoffrey brushed her statement aside with an elaborate gesture. "Shall I tempt you with trinkets, baubles, bijoux?" he asked. "Name your boon, and it shall be granted, fair lady."

"Well, the thing is, fall is always a good season for commercials . . ."

"Ah, I understand. The sinews of war are the lagniappe you seek. Very well, so be it. Ofttimes these pecuniary matters can be so indelicate, eh, what? Out with it, *ma chérie*, what is your figure?"

"I beg your pardon?" asked Eve, not comprehending.

"Combien? You shall make on the swings what you lose on the roundabouts, never fear. I shall see to that."

"I—I—"

"Shall we phrase it in a more agreeable fashion: what do you anticipate the sum your losses would amount to, should you immolate yourself and abandon these shores? I say *immolate* facetiously of course, for in short order you shall be grateful to me for the rest of your life, of this I am certain. Ah, sweet delights! Golden moments of bliss, of knowledge of the arcane, the scatological, the utterly low—man's true nature! I shall teach you—teach you all that is perverse! I should like to train you to suck my special way." Geoffrey regarded her with haughty condescension.

"You see, my dear, the vessel becomes worn out. Inside of two years it becomes necessary to find a *new* vessel—a new vestal, as it were—and this is my current situation. A man must replace a woman every two years, like a motor car. Assembly-line scatology. Yes, a man has a great need of youth, of newness, of change—and this is how a woman resembles a motor car."

"Well," Eve said, "if you say a man has to replace a

woman every two years, that a man needs youth, what happens to a woman, after that . . . eventually?"

"*Sic transit gloria mundi,*" Geoffrey replied, raising silken arms to the rococo ceiling.

"Is that French?"

"No, ducky, it's Latin. You did say you were Catholic, didn't you?"

Not waiting for a reply, he continued, "Other men will not give you what I can. Other men will seek to *penetrate* you. They will make you a slave to this vice, to the unnatural vice of sexual intercourse, and you will come to develop a need to be penetrated by the male phallus. This will never happen with me, for I am a latter-day D'Annunzio, finding solace only in scatology. My penis is too sacred to soil with women by the penetration. Nay, my penis is more than sacred; aye, it is inordinately sacrosanct. Therefore I could not soil it in the penetration, for women are all dirty—they have dirty caverns. It is I who seek to soil, to render them even dirtier than they are—thus to liberate them as well as to liberate myself. Yes, as I say, my penis is far too sacrosanct for that. This I can give only in the holy rite with a fellow Brother of the Left Hand; then, and only then, with him, can my penis penetrate—but this doesn't concern you. *À nos moutons.* Come, 'Sweet Helen, make me immortal with a kiss!' Marlowe understood. D'Annunzio understood. Eleonora Duse understood. She was the liberating force for D'Annunzio. This is what Dr. Faustus sought from Helen of Troy. 'Was this the face that launch'd a thousand ships?' It was this way when I saw you, that same *bouleversement.* The perception of the corruptibility, the willingness to be corrupted, the quality of the true *vicieuse,* the hunger of the demimondaine, her fever for life and love—the purity of her reaching out. Aye, purity—the purest virgin is often too filthy for me. I need purity, do you understand? I need to ruin it, to corrupt it—and thus free it and free myself."

Eve did not hear all of what Geoffrey was saying. She was too busy wondering what a "brother of the left hand" was.

"What I understand and face in myself," Geoffrey went on, "is a thing I have been aware of, as I said, since my Harvard days. I know I am Medusa, just as you are Medusa, and every man is Medusa. This is the other side, the side we hide and refuse to look at. But I, unlike my fellowmen, call Medusa forth. I invoke her; I welcome her. I look her in the face without fear. And the only way to call her to appear is, as I explained, through completion of the execution of the fourfold rhythm of life, brought into being when one is in this state of suspension, where one is free to participate passively at first, with the building up of tension, which happens in scatology. This is the great lesson I can teach you. This, then, can become the apotheosis of your life, of your little existence here on this planet in this lifetime—this flicker, this fragment, this moment between two eternities. For in the innermost kernel of man resides the sexual guilt—call it original sin if you must, for you are of the Roman faith—from which most men shrink in horror. Thus they do not find truth. But I do not shrink. I face the truth in myself; I recognize my sexual self." Geoffrey finished his sherry and went to the bar to pour himself another glass. "May I give you a refill?" he asked.

"No, thank you," Eve said.

Geoffrey returned to his place on the couch. "My theory of bursting catharsis is this," he said. "Civilization has lived in a bottle too long, and now insanity and brutality are being ushered in, liberating the human spirit so long imprisoned. This is a healthy sign, and the more violence, the more scatology, the better. It comes to us as a purification, offering us the balance and solace of our other nature, our dark side, Medusa. I am one of the rare people who truly understands. I hold the onerous secret which can set us free. Onerous, yes, because knowledge implies responsibility—it must be used." Geoffrey sighed. "Therefore, I am burdened, burdened by a soul that knows too much—too much truth."

He was silent a moment. Eve, feeling uncomfortable, wondered how she could break the lull.

Then he spoke once more. "And what are you thinking, pray tell?"

Should she feel flattered or insulted? Whatever in the world did he have in mind doing with her? Regardless of the fact that he said he'd give her anything she wanted, she certainly couldn't go along with his schemes. He was cracked.

"I don't know," Eve said. "If I had more time—but you see, it's after eight now, and since I'm meeting Carrie and some people for dinner at eight-thirty, I really have to be going now."

Geoffrey looked annoyed. Walking her to the door, he said, "Of course, I have every promise from you that what has transpired between us will be kept strictly *entre nous.*" Then he bent and kissed her hand. "You are a bijou, my love," he said. "I look forward to carrying our discussion one step farther upon our next meeting—very shortly, I trust."

Eve nodded, wanting to get away as fast as possible.

"I believe it's our destiny," he said. "I also believe, as La Rochefoucauld said, that the passions are the only orators that always persuade. Ergo, your natural predilection as *vicieuse* must be dealt with accordingly. *À bientôt; enfin, à tantôt.*"

He waved from the entryway as Eve descended the stone steps and reached the pavement.

Chapter 8

"Would you throw me my hairbrush, kid? Thanks." From the spot at the mirror she had occupied for the past half hour, Dolores smoothed her hair, cocked her head, stood back, and, posing, surveyed her image.

Eve, looking on with a mixture of envy and admiration, said, "I think it's so exciting, Dolores. You have the most glamorous boy friends."

"Just you watch how I'm going to zero in on old Spiro. I've really been sweating it out, waiting for this guy to come back."

Carrie was soaking in the tub, scrubbing her back with a long brush.

"Do you have a date tonight, Carrie?" Eve asked.

"No. I'm staying in."

"There she sits in her goddamn tub—when she ought to be out doing what I'm doing: screwing her ass off to land a millionaire." Dolores shook her head in disdain.

"I want to do some work tonight."

"What are you writing about now, Carrie?"

"She's been writing the same damned thing since I've known her, and it's never getting finished. Something about her family and her farm in the South."

"Wrong. I put that aside. For a while."

"You just keep jerking off. Why don't you just write a sexy book instead—one that will sell and make lots of money." She patted her hairpiece. "How do I look?"

"Fantastic."

"Boy, have I been looking forward to this. Do you realize how many girls in New York would give their right ovary for a crack at Spiro Constacuntacropolis?"

Pirouetting, Dolores gave herself a final admiring glance of approval. Then Spiro's chauffeur rang the bell and escorted her to the waiting limousine.

* * *

Spiro and Dolores had danced, dined, and lunched together at le Mistral, the Italian Pavillon, Maud Chez Elle, the Leopard, Arthur's, the Royal Box at the Americana, the Persian Room of the Plaza, and the Blue Room at the Roosevelt. Now they were lunching at the Colony.

Over *coquilles de cervelle au gratin,* Dolores asked provocatively, "Tell me, Spiro, what is the significance of your name, Consta-*cunt*-acropolis?"

The lusty Greek sniggered. "Come with me to my suite at the St. Regis and I shall explain it to you," he answered, chewing his *selle de mouton* with gusto.

"That would be lovely, darling," Dolores purred. "But first let's stop at Cartier. It's practically on the way, and I saw something absolutely superb in the window I know you would just love to buy me."

That afternoon Dolores became both the owner of a ruby necklace as well as Spiro Constacuntacropolis' newest bed partner. The necklace was comparatively modest in price (only $4,000), but it represented a beginning. Better things would come soon.

*　　*　　*

Three days later, she made Walter Winchell's column:

Ubiquitous Spiro Constacuntacropolis of the Greek shipping fortune, who can have his pick of New York's lovelies, squiring beauteous model Dolores Haynes around town. Looks promising for Dolores. Spiro's quite a catch.

I'm making it, Dolores rejoiced. It won't be long now, and everything will open up—Broadway, films, fame—everything I've ever wanted. Standing in front of the mirror, she watched the lights of the rubies play upon her face, bathing it in pinkish light. Beholding her new radiance, she knew she must acquire more and more gems—as many as she could—in order to realize her full potential as a woman.

Her thoughts went to the last chance she had had and muffed. Damn that frigging Nathan Winston, she muttered under her breath, damn him for taking away my diamonds. Never would she forget the insult and humiliation Nathan had caused her. Someday, she vowed, someday she would pay Nathan back.

CARRIE'S NOTEBOOK

November 7. *This afternoon Charlene sent me up for a three-week TV job, to replace a weather girl during the holidays. Got it. Nearly $400 a week. Since Mother will be going to California to see Peggy's new baby, I wouldn't have been going to Virginia anyway.*

Last night, a party chez an ex-Follies girl (seventies, playing about fifty years younger), married to one of the young male models at the agency. Rex and Charlene were there; as well as some Mafia men and some voodoo people, and Roger Flournoy, the famous writer.

"The short pudgy fellow over there's Porco San Tomasso,"

Roger told me. "He's visiting from Naples. Practically runs Italy. The tall ugly one's Scar Scaravaglioni. I'm surprised you didn't recognize the Scar. He had rather a lot of publicity last year—when someone tried to rub him out."

Without warning, the lights were lowered, and right in the middle of Manhattan, a voodoo ceremony began, with colored dancers wearing loincloths, red handkerchiefs and bells, beating hide drums. There was a box with a live snake slithering in it. It was when the voodoo people drank blood that the Mafia men left. Roger says they're terrified of the malocchio.

Looking at Roger—at his skinny, slight frame that caved in in the middle and his freckled, thinned-out skull, the eyes with their layers of wrinkles—it's hard to believe this is the same man who wrote all those banned books forty years ago, who used to be such a Casanova. In his dotage he's forsaken writing for painting and says he'd like to do my portrait.

It should be fun posing for him. He says he'll be ready for me in a few months, when his present commitments are out of the way. Meantime, I have the weather girl thing to look forward to. I've wished I had more time to write; and perhaps this three weeks of steady work will help.

I've been looking for a theme or focal point, and I believe I may have found the germ of an idea to develop, a topic I feel close to. The theme would center around beauty, and in particular how hard it is to be a woman if you are beautiful.

I want to do more thinking about it. I think I could have something here.

WEALTHY GREEK DROPS DEAD

Nov. 10. Spiro Constacuntacropolis, 69, Greek shipowner, suffered a fatal heart attack this morning in front of the St. Regis Hotel, where he was staying. At the time of his death, Mr. Constacuntacropolis, who had been preparing to embark upon a holiday in Guadalupe. . . .

Eve read the ensuing paragraphs open-mouthed. "Gosh, that's terrible," she said.

"Any time, any time can happen such things," Uncle Nappi said.

"Poor Dolores. She wanted to marry Spiro, too."

"An ugly bastard like him? What the hell for?"

"Oh, Uncle Nappi," Eve said, "you just don't know! A man like Spiro who went everywhere and knew everybody in the world—I mean, a man like that is—is . . ." She searched for a word.

"Is an ugly old bastard," Uncle Nappi said. "Sure, your girl friend want one thing." He gestured with his fingers. "*Soldi. Vuole soldi.*"

"Money is a very important commodity," Eve said. As Uncle Nappi picked up some newspapers and threw them in the trash can, her eyes went to the framed pictures of her that he had hung on the walls. Each few months, as her test shots had improved, he'd replaced the old pictures with newer and better ones. She studied them absently for a long moment. "Uncle Nappi," she said, "why don't you fix the shop up? You could get a better class of customers if you did."

"I'm happy with what I got. The same people been coming to me for years and years. Is okay for me."

"But you could be doing better business. You could raise your prices."

Uncle Nappi shook his head. "I'm an old man, Evie. Things as they is is fine by your old uncle."

"You ought to have a really fancy shop, Uncle Nappi, like the Carusos. They hang out a sign that says *parrucchiere* and everybody goes, and half the clientele can't even pronounce the names right. Do you know most of those dumb models call Enrico *On*rico! But everybody goes there, and do you know why? Because the Carusos are fancy, they have style, they have—"

Uncle Nappi laughed. "I'm surprised at you, Eve. You know your old Uncle Nappi's only a *paisan*. Born *paisan*, *paisan* he gonna be till he die."

"Uncle Nappi, if the Carusos can do it, so can you. They're Italian too."

Uncle Nappi shook his head. "Always since you get fancy yourself you want your uncle to get fancy with you, to go society. Impossible. I'm just a plain old guy, Evie. I can't do like you want."

Eve thought she saw a tired sadness in her uncle as he gathered his combs and scissors together and placed them in the sterilizer.

She stared at the walls in silence. What was it that was

bothering her? It wasn't just her wish that Uncle Nappi have a better shop; no, it was more than that. It was—it was . . . well, what would some of the important men she knew say if they ever came past and saw her pictures on the walls? They would certainly wonder about the connection between her and Uncle Nappi. He'd say, "That's my niece, Evie Petroangeli," and then what? She would be mortified if Geoffrey Gripsholm or someone like that, someone rich and important, with class, knew her uncle was a barber.

She watched Uncle Nappi's tired, bent form as he began to sweep the floor. He worked so hard. All the Petroangelis had worked hard for their living. It made her feel sad for them all—sad for her parents, sad for her grandmother, sad for Uncle Nappi, and she suddenly realized, sad for herself too. She had to tell him, she had to protect herself.

"Uncle Nappi," she said, "in case anyone asks you about me . . . I mean anyone who looks like he might be important . . . or rich." She hesitated a moment. "Well, the thing is, I know lots of people in the jet set, and I'm accepted at all the best places. And I have my career to think of—I have my life ahead of me, and . . ."

Uncle Nappi looked up from the dustpan. Slowly he raised his wearied limbs. Eve thought she saw a hurt look in his eyes.

She continued. "I mean, in this business there's a lot of stress on certain things—and lots of people are prejudiced, and . . . well, the agency *did* make me change my name, and . . ." She was stumbling, trying to explain.

Uncle Nappi said quietly, "I always tell you someday you gonna be ashamed of your family."

"It's not that, Uncle Nappi, it's . . ."

The old man studied her for a moment. Then he said, "Okay, you like, I take down all the pictures, so no one never sees or says nothing."

He strode over to the wall and reached up.

"Oh, no!" Eve grabbed his arm. "You can keep the pictures up, Uncle Nappi. It's good *exposure* for me. It's good advertising, I don't mind if you keep the pictures up, it's just—"

Uncle Nappi looked genuinely perplexed. "What you want me to do? You tell me what you want, Evie."

"You can leave them, Uncle Nappi. It will make everyone see me and notice me. I just don't want them to connect us, that's all."

"What you want I should say?" Uncle Nappi asked in a toneless voice.

"Well, just say I'm a girl, that's all—I'm the daughter of one of your customers."

Her uncle nodded his gray head. "Okay, okay," he said softly, "if that's what you want, Evie. Uncle Nappi does what you say."

Chapter 9

Rex had taken a few minutes out from his daily routine to help Corrie Harris, a new girl he was grooming, learn to walk properly. Wearing an Edwardian coat and ruffled Palachio shirt, he swung his hip out, his hand casually poised on his waist, head cocked to one side, eyes slightly downcast. The phone rang. He glanced toward his desk and saw that one of the buttons on the phone was lighted. "Tomorrow, luv," he said to his pupil, who smiled and left, walking somewhat better than she had when she'd come in.

Polly van den Heuvel was on the other end of the wire. "Rex," she said, "I want to see three girls, no more than three. You know I hate having my office cluttered with excess rubbish—so send only the best. The girl for this commercial must have *natural* color hair; she must be a *natural* beauty. Do *not* send me any dyed heads. A touch of a rinse and they're out. You will send them to me beginning at exactly ten minutes to eleven tomorrow morning."

Charlene hovered in the doorway. "Porter, Tailer, Gilbert and Tribble are furious with us, Rex," she said.

"What about?"

"Gillian Hughes. She was booked for a laxative commer-

211

cial. Said she could swim; got there and couldn't. I told them, how am I supposed to know? I haven't got a pool in my office."

* * *

A half hour later Rex appeared at Charlene's door and asked, "Charlene, what shall I do? Barbara Longworth just called. Says her husband is sick and can I send a hundred dollars over to help?"

"Have they decided about the Moderna Soap commercial yet?"

"No. Barbara says she likes Sandy Holder and wants to push her for it, but—"

"You didn't send the money, did you, Rex?"

"No, but suppose we don't, Charlene? What then? I don't want to ruin Sandy's chances for the commercial. If I refuse Barbara, she may get sore and knock Sandy off the list."

"Rex, how can you even consider sending Barbara the money? Don't you see, honey, this is bribery? We've got a double A rating with the License Bureau these past years, and we're not about to jeopardize it now."

"I guess you're right, Charlene," Rex said, and went back to his desk, dejected.

* * *

"Eve, what you did to Uncle Nappi was cruel." It was the voice of her mother on the phone. "I just found out. How could you?"

"I didn't mean anything, honest—"

"What a snob you've become. You're ashamed of your own family."

"No, Mom, I—"

"You don't know how Uncle Nappi loves you. You hurt him, Eve, you hurt him terribly."

"I didn't mean it. I just didn't want people to get the wrong idea. Mom, you don't understand how hard it is to get somewhere. I have to be careful and protect myself."

"You *are* a snob. You're too good for the Petroangelis."

Eve sighed, feeling guilty and full of remorse. "I'm sorry,

Mom. I was thinking of myself, and I didn't realize the effect it would have on Uncle Nappi." She started to cry. "I wouldn't want to hurt him for anything. What can I do?"

"The damage has been done."

"What can I do, Mom? Tell me, what can I do?"

Her mother sighed. "I don't know, Eve. Maybe you better just let things ride a bit. Then in a few days or a couple of weeks you can go in and see him."

"Okay, Mom."

"But try to pay more attention to your uncle. When you've been stopping in so seldom on top of what you did to him, what can he think? He has to think you're ashamed of him."

"Okay, Mom," Eve said in a small, humble voice. She felt like crawling through the woodwork.

* * *

Another winter was approaching, another busy season would start in the modeling business. In just a few weeks all the catalog houses would begin photographing for their summer issues, and the advertising agencies would be flying people south to the sun spots to film the next cycle's commercials.

Frustration was growing in Dolores. She knew that the instant she appeared in a good role in a movie there would be an impact heard round the world. But why had the opportunity been so long in coming? True, there were few parts to be had in New York, for most films were made on the Coast. But Dolores knew only too well what a trap Hollywood was. A new face there had carte blanche, but if you didn't make it in six months you were an old face and everyone lost interest.

New York was the place to operate from, the city where you could find the optimum of action, contacts, and money. Its more democratic approach in contrast to Hollywood's caste system offered social interchange with all kinds of intrigue and opportunity. But preparing a banquet full of hors d'oeuvres, what Manhattan failed to deliver was the entree and the dessert.

She told Charlene, "You know I keep getting the commercials. I just finished a Dairy Council of America. I just did an Isodettes—and a Delsey 2-Ply Bathroom Tissue. Next week

213

I'm doing a Mazola Oil. I'm one of the best girls in the business, and so what? In Hollywood you get to plateaus. You're known for the level you're on, and you have a corresponding reputation, a corresponding price. In New York every call that comes out, you have to keep going back to see the *same* people at the *same* places, competing against the *same* girls each time. You can earn fifty thousand a year five years in a row here and not be established. Every blessed time you have to go out and fight for the job all over again. Every time."

"That's this business," Charlene said. "I never recommend it to anyone who doesn't have a strong stomach. Remember, we discussed it before."

"I remember, but that doesn't mean it isn't driving me crazy. It's been nearly two years now, Charlene."

Yes, she well knew the commercial business could not be relied upon as a steady means of support over a period of time. It was, as Charlene had so often said, the means to an end. It was a living for now, and that was all. The idea was to find the right man and use him as a stepping-stone.

Easier said than done. Unfortunately she had struck out twice, first with Nathan, then Spiro. Now? Men appeared on the scene constantly, men in from Europe, from the Coast. New York was perpetually turning itself inside out; a girl could exhaust herself running all over, grabbing dinners, cocktail dates, evenings out, attending parties, premieres, theaters, charities, accepting weekend invitations to the country.

A beautiful girl was in constant demand, everybody wanted to take her to bed—but sleeping with men just for sex was a losing proposition. The men left town, passed on to new amusement. More men appeared—it was a constant sea of faces—and then what? Where did it lead or culminate?

It was easy enough to intrigue the Hollywood producers who came to town, to have them be attentive and interested. All males, in an instinctive reflex action, were susceptible at first. They even feigned interest in your career. "Are you a good actress?" they'd ask. Then they tried to lay you. Sure it was great to have them easily accessible for vamping without their wives breathing down their backs. But to get them to give you the needed opportunity was another thing entirely. There were just too many girls around: the men had seen so many over the years they were jaded. One girl was the same as the next to them. For a few days, or maybe a few weeks, they could be held attentive, but then they'd leave town and forget as easily as they'd been enticed.

Dolores knew she had the necessary talent to make it on Broadway and had expected to land a part there long before this. The fact was, however, fewer and fewer opportunities existed for new talent. Always the same plaguing problems. The Broadway casting people were leery of the fact that her acceptable acting credits were practically nonexistent. Each time she read for an off-Broadway play or one of the few dramatic TV shows out of New York, the nances doing the casting all acted snotty about her experience.

Charlene had asked her to consider doing summer stock, saying if she wanted to act, this would be invaluable experience. But it would have taken her away from her social contacts and the possibility of meeting someone who could help her.

Clearly, what she needed was a man behind her, a person of wealth, position, and influence. Then she'd be able to write her own ticket. If she could only find the right man and get him by the balls.

* * *

Henry Haupt arrived in her life like a godsend. Appearing in a red satin kimono and matching mask at a Chinese costume party, he sat next to her and complimented her on her likeness to an Oriental empress. To her delight, she found that he was not only an affluent financier but also a heavy investor in Broadway shows. He danced with her twice that night and said he would like to call her.

"Call me soon," she said. Beholding Henry without his mask, she saw his skin was pasty, his head sprinkled with thinning white hair. He had unfortunately thick lips, droopy eyelids, and gaunt cheeks. His manner, however, like so many men in their mid-fifties, was gentle and fatherly.

"Call me *very* soon," Dolores said.

* * *

Henry called the next day, and Dolores saw him three times that week. The next week, as their fourth date (dinner at La Grenouille, dancing at Le Club) was nearing an end, Dolores whispered in his ear, "Henry, darling, why don't you take me home with you. I'd love a nightcap . . . just the two of us."

He hesitated a moment; then, guardedly, he said, "All right."

*　　*　　*

They entered a large two-story foyer full of paintings, Louis XIV furniture, and plants.

Leading Dolores into the library, Henry showed her his collection of eighteenth-century Chinese snuffboxes, Thomas Webb cameo vases, Early American cigar-store Indians, and art nouveau spoons; in another he showed her his glass-encased displays of primitive spear tips, arrowheads, bones, blades, hides, horns, harpoons, tools, drums, ceremonial masks, and other artifacts.

Leading her into the library, he asked, "Would you like a drink?"

Dolores accepted a glass of white port and reclined on the strawberry-colored silk pillows that covered the couch. Henry was standing up, looking at her. She took off her shoes, curled her feet under her, and smiled at him. "Come over here, darling," she said.

Shyly, almost fearfully, Henry obeyed. And a few moments later their lips were locked.

At length Henry drew away, and staring morosely at his fingers, said, "There's something I have to tell you. You have a right to know."

"Yes . . . ?" Dolores said.

Henry twisted his fingers, attempting to collect himself. Finally he said, "I was married to a woman I hated for a number of years. She came from a wealthy family . . . and I was poor. . . .

"Yes, I married her for her money. Helen was everything I loathed: she was fat; she smelled bad; she had the face of a hawk; her voice grated on my nerves. I cheated on her all the time. Finally, I couldn't take the marriage any more, and we got a divorce. By this time I was well on my way, thanks to Helen's capital, toward becoming very rich in my own right.

"I married again, and almost as soon as the ink was dry on the license my second wife began to remind me of Helen." He tried to take a deep breath and nearly choked. "She smelled bad, although I had previously been attracted to her odor. Her voice was almost unbearable. The worst thing, though, was her drinking. I lost interest in her sexually, and started playing around." He looked up with a hangdog expression.

"Well, that's understandable, Henry," Dolores said. "After all, no one could feel romantic toward an alcoholic."

Henry shook his head. "No," he said, "you don't understand. I cheated on Donna incessantly. She just kept on drinking more and more, and I'd come home at night and find her in a stupor. Twice I shipped her off to the farm; twice she came back and started boozing all over again. Well, one night I was out fucking—excuse me." He hit his head, as though chastising himself for having used an improper word in Dolores' presence. "I was out *sleeping* with another girl, and I came home at four in the morning. I walked in, and there was Donna, lying on the floor by the staircase. She'd been drunk and had fallen down the stairs.

"Later the doctor said she'd been lying there a couple of hours." His voice caught. "She was dead. You see," he whispered, his contorted face imploring Dolores to say something to ease his guilt, "I killed Donna!"

"Oh, Henry, that's ridiculous. It wasn't your fault she drank. You did what you could. You sent her to the institutions. You tried to help her."

"No, don't you see, if I'd only *been* there! The servants never heard! It was too late, and they were way in back! But if I had been there, it never would have happened! If I hadn't been out fucking—I mean *cheating* on Donna—it never would have happened. It's my fault she died." He looked away again; then, his voice barely audible, he said, "Since then . . . I . . . I've had a—a *sex* problem."

"I understand how you feel, Henry. But I don't want you to worry, darling." Dolores took his tightly clenched hand.

"I—I just feel so rotten," he said.

"Don't, darling!"

"Goddamn it, you're a wonderful girl, desirable and lovely, and what can I offer you?" He pulled his fist from Dolores and sent it crashing down on the French eighteenth-century satinwood coffee table.

Pulling him toward her, Dolores tried to calm him. "Don't worry, dearest," Dolores said. "Everything will be all right. It will work. Just relax and it will work."

"I can't!"

*　*　*

Patiently she endeavored to arouse Henry, but he did not respond to her subtlest caresses or her highly developed technique of fellatio. Always his penis remained shriveled and limp.

Each time they indulged in sex play, Henry would wail, "It's my fault. It's my fault. Oh, God! What's a beautiful young girl like you doing with an incompetent, impotent, worn-out, wasted old man like me?"

"Hush, darling. . . ."

Henry would rise, pace the floor, and in a boiling rage, throw objects, many of them quite expensive, into the marble fireplace.

*　*　*

"You wouldn't like to come back to my place and try again, would you?"

Always the same line, without variation, as if he expected her to renege and were offering the out. And then, in Henry's king-sized bed, the scene was invariable, until one night he burst out, "Why do you *bother* with me? *Why? Why?*"

"Because I love you."

"You couldn't—"

"I do."

"How could you, it's not possible—"

"Well, I do love you, darling, and if you'd trust me . . ."

"I *do* trust you. But I can't see what you see in me—I can't satisfy you. I can't fuck you! You're a young woman—you have needs—how can you stand this?"

"Don't you see, darling? My love is more important than mere physical gratification."

"I disagree. Sex is very important. A woman needs it, both physically and emotionally."

Dolores smiled to herself, wondering what Henry would think if he knew of her daytime trysts with other men.

Henry sighed. "I just don't see how I can *allow* you to keep on this way, Dolores. It's just no good for you."

She said almost sharply, "If you'd trust me, darling—"

"I do trust you—"

"No, if you did you wouldn't be so tense."

"I'm tense because I have no release—"

"You've got a mental block. But it's *not* your fault she died. *You* couldn't help it if she was a drunk."

"I shouldn't have been out *fucking* all over town, don't you see? They say everything comes back to you. Now I can't fuck. It's my payment for what I did."

How tiresome he was. And now the talk of nobility and not wanting to subject her to the further torture of his impotence. Clearly, something would have to be done, and soon.

She could not afford to let this slip through her fingers. She knew if she could solve Henry's sex problem, he would be indebted to her—and anything she wanted would be hers. Yes, something *had* to be done.

But what?

*   *   *

"You're sure you don't want me to bring you anything?" Rex hovered in the doorway, dressed in earmuffs and hip boots, his head cocked to one side.

"No, thanks, honey. I'm just not hungry."

"But, Charlene, you never eat a thing any more."

"I'm too busy to eat!"

"Well, okay, if you insist. But I worry about you."

"Don't, honey. Look we've got company. Dolores Haynes!"

"Hi, there, luv."

"Got any residuals for me, Charlene? Hello, Rex, how goes it?"

"Not bad, honey. I'm just on my way out to lunch. Bye

bye!" His shoulders shimmied as he walked away with bird-like steps.

Charlene leaned over the desk. "You're looking fantastic, Dolores!" she exclaimed. "The coat's gorgeous."

"Oh, Spiro Constacuntacropolis bought me this before he croaked. Say, Charlene, I've got a problem. Can you help me?"

"I'll try."

Dolores told Charlene about Henry Haupt. "I've gone to the library and read everything I can find on the subject of male impotence. I even made an appointment with a psychiatrist. No luck in finding any help so far. But I have an idea you can help me."

"Me? How?"

"Where can I find an aphrodisiac? A strong powerful one—like the kind the French courtiers used to put in chocolates or the roots the Latin American men use."

"What makes you think I'd know?"

"Charlene, if anyone in this town would know, it would be you."

Charlene roared. "Well, luv, I just might be able to help you at that. Sit tight a couple of days. I'll have to do some checking."

"Thanks a million, darling. You don't know how much I appreciate this."

* * *

Dolores watched as Eve was packing two large valises. "All set to go on your big job up in Vermont, kid?"

"I can hardly wait! Imagine, two whole weeks. I'm going to earn over a thousand dollars."

"Won't they mind your not being able to do 'Take a Crack'?"

"No, they're being so nice about it. They've given me a leave of absence."

"And when do you start your weather show, Carrie?"

"In a couple of days."

"You're going to have to hold down the fort alone."

Carrie looked up from the evening papers. "You mean you're going away too, Dolores? Since when?"

"That sweet divine Henry is taking me on a trip. Only he doesn't know it yet."

"Where are you getting him to take you?"

"Oh, we'll see. . . . I'm going to let him know tonight. Somewhere exotic."

"Like Palm Beach?" Eve asked.

"Or Nassau, or Jamaica, or Grand Bahama, or somewhere —the important thing is sunshine and relaxation. Oh, there's the phone, and it better be for me. I'm waiting for a call."

Eve had started for the phone. She stopped and let Dolores get it.

"Hello," Dolores said. "Oh, Charlene! Boy, it's good to hear from you. . . . You did? Give me the details. I'm all ears."

*   *   *

The following morning Dolores made a trip to the bank and then trudged to Harlem, to the address Charlene had given her.

She paid $600 in cash to a fat, scarlet-frocked, chocolate-skinned woman with clinking gold jewelry, and in exchange, was given a small bottle.

That night she managed to slip a few drops of the liquid in the bottle into Henry's predinner drink. The potion began working at the table, when a strange expression came over Henry's face. "You wouldn't like to come back to my place and try again, would you?" he said.

*   *   *

Dolores had chosen a restaurant close to Henry's apartment. Within minutes they were in bed, and Henry Haupt had his first erection in three years.

Later he was ready to give Dolores anything in the world she wanted. For starters, she suggested a trip to Jamaica and a sable coat.

The reservations were made and the coat was purchased the next morning, and that night, feeling the sable caress her shoulders as she and Henry huddled together at Orsini's, Dolores said, "You see, darling, you were living in the past."

221

"I know that now. Oh, how is it that *you* knew it all along? How is it you were so wise and so patient—that you refused to give up? And how did you finally bring about this miracle?" Henry's eyes were moist.

Dolores smiled diabolically.

Chapter 10

CARRIE'S NOTEBOOK

December 10. Dare I believe it's possible, that I have found an eligible male I'm really attracted to?

It happened last night. An opening night party at Sardi's. Buffet dinner, people milling around with drinks. He was standing at the other end of the room, and our eyes met. At first I was sure we knew each other, but the second glance told me it was only wishful thinking. And then suddenly I was embarrassed, embarrassed for wanting and needing to belong to someone like this without even knowing him. But here was a real man, and Lord knows there are few of them around.

He couldn't be available, I was telling myself that, and had almost reconciled myself to it when he came over and introduced himself. "Hello, I'm Gordon Leigh."

I was struck by his command of himself, by his unmistakable confidence and masculinity. He's not much over thirty, but a sprinkling of prematurely gray hair gives him added years, and there's depth and maturity in his deep brown eyes.

"Caroline Richards," I said. "I thought I knew you, but I guess I don't."

"Didn't," he corrected. His smile was warm and friendly, and we looked at each other as though we'd known each other always.

Less than an hour later, we sat together at Mama Laura's. Oh, let this be real, I kept thinking. It's been so long. I wanted to place my feelings, my whole being, in Gordon's hands.

"I'm much happier here," he said, leaning on the table. "It was a terrible party. Being at a flop-play party is always depressing."

"You've been to many?"

"Too many. I used to practically live at Sardi's."

"And where do you practically live these days?"

"I moved to California two years ago. Just after I was divorced. Gave up the theater scene. New York is wonderful; I love it; it's a—"

"Great place to visit?"

"No, no, I'd live here if I could. But in my line of work, directing and writing, there's more opportunity on the Coast."

"All those television series—the ones I do commercials for and never watch—do you write and direct those?"

"That's right. But I do watch them."

"Are you doing a show here? There are hardly any dramatic shows out of New York anymore."

"No, I'm just here over the holidays to see my daughter."

"How old is she?"

"She's five." His face lit up. "The sexiest five-year-old you ever saw."

We were full of things to say to one another.

Then, at the end of the evening, something peculiar happened. He asked me, "What do you want out of life?"

A pleasant surprise of a question. Mel would never have asked that. "Marriage and a family," I replied.

Then came an odd thing, his reaction. He raised his eyebrows, seemingly taken aback, and said . . . nothing.

I was disturbed by his quick dismissal. Then he gave me a light peck, promised to call soon, turned quickly, and was gone.

Let him call soon—please.

* * *

December 14. Two days of getting to know each other better. I met Gordon's daughter, Susan, and she's a doll. Would I ever love to have a little girl like that. We took her

223

—or rather, she took us—to Central Park, the children's part where adults aren't admitted unless accompanied by a child.

Later we had sundaes at Rumpelmayers and saw Santa Claus at F. A. O. Schwarz.

There's so much joy in life I'm not a part of. This modeling stuff is just so meaningless. I think I'm ready to end that whole phase of my life—and to become a part of something real.

And now Gordon. He is it, what I've waited for. How simple.

There was a little fight in me—you know the way it is when you know you're going to be hooked and you think, oh, Lord, I'm scared he won't feel as I feel, he won't care as much as I care—but then, you say it just doesn't matter. All that's important is that I care, that I express how I feel. When it's been so long since there's been anyone, the need to love is what takes over despite any worry and doubt.

I want Gordon to care, I want this to be perfect for him too. I am so hoping he'll love me. But even if he doesn't, there's something in me that says I must, absolutely must go ahead anyway—and settle for whatever he will give.

*　❀　*

December 15. *Gordon picked me up at the studio at seven. We were invited to dinner at some friends'.*

A charming, tasteful apartment on the West Side, near Lincoln Center. I loved it the minute we entered; cozy, scads of books piled to the ceiling in the living room, children's art framed in the halls and bathroom and kitchen; it was a roomy and old-fashioned place with high-beamed ceilings. A fire was going. There were children's voices.

Gordon even knew the maid and everybody was so glad to see everyone else. All the while I kept thinking that this is how it's supposed to be, just like it used to be in our family.

After so many months of nothing but New York phonies and playboys, I'd forgotten how easy it is to be happy and satisfied. All it takes is the company of down-to-earth people who enjoy each other and share with each other. I told Gordon this after we left.

"They're really not that way at all," he said, looking at me with an odd kind of forced smile. "That's just their party manners."

"You can't fake genuine happiness."

"They've both been around the theater long enough to be thorough experts in front of company. But don't kid yourself, they have their problems."

There was tension between us. I tried to make my voice light. "Oh, everyone has problems."

"Married people more than others."

"What have you got against marriage?"

"It's an unnatural state."

"Unnatural? Why?"

He looked irritated. "Any number of reasons," he said.

"Such as?"

"It's impossible to be faithful to one person for any length of time. It's highly unnatural."

"Not if you're in love."

"What is love? People outgrow one another."

"Not if they're really matched."

"That remains to be seen. Of course it's easy for you to talk—you've never had the experience."

"Well, I've seen some wonderful marriages. My—"

"I haven't."

"That doesn't mean they don't exist."

"I was married once. I don't intend to get trapped again."

He said it with such cold finality! My heart sank, but I tried not to show it—or to let it affect me.

The apartment seemed empty and silent without Dolores and Eve. But when Gordon's smile reached me, it was as if the whole room were filled. I ached for him.

"You're very unusual," Gordon said. "I've never met anyone quite like you."

The remark, flimsy compliment though it was, pleased me.

"Do me a favor?" he asked, placing his drink on the coffee table.

"Yes."

"Look into my eyes."

I was all trust, all desire, melted and soft, and seized with a loneliness and yearning. I wondered if his eyes read that in me.

"What do you see?" he asked.

His eyes were incredibly liquid and gentle. But I was aware of the strength in him—and the desire. Words couldn't express how I felt.

And then we were lying side by side on the couch, kissing deeply. He drew me out, and I gave; it all poured out of me, all that need to give what was inside.

His mouth was a vast cavern to be explored, a secret chamber of velvet and silk. In its depths a current was sucking me in, stinging and biting and evoking me, and soon he had found my breasts under the thin wool of my dress. My body was under his, and I was submerged in him, feeling his weight, his substance, his essence.

And then, as if coming up for air, we both opened our eyes, and looked at each other and smiled, knowing we were very good together, and I asked in a breathless whisper, "Do you want to come to my bedroom?"

His voice was tender and soft. "Yes."

Together, slow at first; there was the winding and coiling of our bodies, the finding each other as he began to invoke my rhythm and we were caught in mutual intensity. Our pungent kisses tasted as though they were drenched in the small of life, and he was reaching deeper and deeper within my body, our limbs were entwined, and he was crushing me and I was crying out for more, more.

I wanted to suck his very life into myself and never let go of it. As we rose higher and higher in those ecstatic involuntary rhythmic movements, catching the wave and the poetry, the music and the dance of each other, two primitive pagans reaching, straining, giving, receiving, how good it was, and how starved I've been for all that. I couldn't get him close enough, it seemed, or have enough of him or give him enough of me. It was all reaching upward, and sighs and moans and the subtle wending and weaving, all beauty and joy and gladness and transport, too much for earthly words, so much it made me cry and shake all over.

And there was that first hushed joy in apartness, after the ecstasy, lying close to each other, having belonged, oh thank thee, Lord, for that, for that harmony and peace and fulfillment, and giving from the bottom of me, the way I felt was absolute; he had felt it too. And then, just as I was about to drift off into sleep, he moved away and lit a cigarette.

It was then there came that tug at the heartstrings, seeing him there smoking, wishing he were still holding me; that was when the memory of his words against marriage came. And I was telling myself, don't let me hurt again. Why did he say those things? Forget now. I suppose the experience itself should be enough. Ideally. But what then? What about tomorrow—and next year? What about the way I want to make a man happy, and share with him, and make him a home, and have a center for the two of us and our children? What about all this? Where does it fit in?

I wished Gordon had stayed close, that he could have locked me in his arms all night.

The red ash glowed in the dark.

"It's strange," Gordon said.

"What is?"

"I don't know. I didn't count on you. I've never felt quite like this before."

I touched him lightly. "I haven't either."

It sounded trite, but are there words, I wonder, to express this degree of gratitude?

* * *

December 18. *Days and nights with Gordon—happy days and nights—continue. Knowing the miracle of love, I wonder if I would have been able to go on if Gordon hadn't come along when he did.*

* * *

December 20. *Last night—in the bitterness of the cold and the wind, I was like a frail reed, but my hand was in Gordon's, and I was safe, huddled close to his large warm body. His blue fuzzy-gloved hand held my leather one, and his other arm encircled and guided me through the winter blast.*

We finally found a cab, and then back here, as I had thought about all evening long—his arms were tenderly holding me, his red cold cheek pressed against mine. There we were, two icy cheeks numb against each other, and he was unbuttoning my coat and unknotting my scarf and kissing my

227

neck, and then soon we were pressed naked together between the flowered sheets; my teeth were still chattering, and then the teeth hushed, and we were warm and hot together.

* * *

December 21. *We were with Susan all day today. Went to the Museum of Natural History—she loved the mummies and the dinosaurs! Then to the space show at the Hayden Planetarium. Susan and I get along beautifully—hope Gordon is taking it in!*

* * *

December 22. *Christmas nears. Mother will be going to California to help Peggy with the new baby. It gives me a lonely feeling, knowing I won't see any of the family. But then I have Gordon, so everything's all right. Well, almost. I keep expecting him to say something about Christmas—where, and plans about being together—but he hasn't.*

* * *

December 24. *We exchanged gifts. I gave him gold cufflinks; he gave me an ounce of Réplique.*

He said, "I'll see you in a day or two."

"You mean we won't be seeing each other for Christmas?"

"Oh, didn't I tell you? My parents are having the family to dinner. I'm taking Susan out tomorrow morning. I'll miss you, honey." He planted a kiss on me lightly.

My blood boiled. "Damn it, Gordon," I flared, "you hand me a bottle of Réplique, peck my cheek, and patronize me—when you know damned well I'm alone, that I have no family here, and it's Christmas. What do you expect me to do, go to Horn and Hardart's? Sorry, Gordon, but this is no way to treat anybody."

He looked startled, scarcely offered any argument, and left, his tail between his legs. I've been crying with rage ever since. The skunk.

* * *

December 25. *A thoroughly miserable Christmas. The phone rang all day, but I was damned if I'd answer. If it's Gordon, let him stew. My Quaker training may have taught me to turn the other cheek, but there comes a point where you have to put your foot down, when it's a question of being stepped on. I may not have known with Mel I had the right to get angry, but I sure know Gordon is out of line.*

Almost midnite. I was mad all day long. Then after the weather show, the book I had in mind on beautiful women seemed to become clearer to me, and I sketched a rough outline. It almost seemed as though from Gordon's working me into a temper, things had been brought to a sharper focal point in my mind. Don't tell me I have him to be grateful to.

* * *

December 26. *"Carrie?"*
Silence on my part.
"Carrie, it's Gordon. Don't hang up. Look, I'm sorry. I don't know how to ask you to forgive me, but please believe me when I say I thought you had to stay in town for the weather show at six forty-five, and that it would have been impossible for you to have made it out to Long Island. I would have loved to have spent the day with you, but my daughter—a father does have responsibilities to his child— I . . ."
"Yes?"
"I did think of you all alone, and I was worried. I called. There was no answer. I missed you."
I was filled with a great tired sort of ache. Gordon had so represented an oasis to me.
"Don't be mad," he said. "It was a misunderstanding. Let's not have any misunderstandings so close to New Year's."
So we are seeing each other again. But there's that ache in me, and something is missing.

* * *

December 27. *The ache is still there. I know now what is missing—it's his heart, and you can't force that in anyone.*
I've done a lot of thinking about us, about him. Gordon is

229

a virile, sensual, sexual man. Mentally we're ideal, and there's much we have in common. But he's self-centered. Despite his affection, his companionship, his lovemaking, his attention remains focused on himself. Susan is the only woman who really figures in his life.

How hard it is to accept this. There are so many unfulfilled hopes in me, but I'm helpless to change the situation. This is how it is.

There's no one I can depend on but myself. That's what my inner voice tells me. If Gordon won't make me more important than he has, if I can't count on a man's love and honest caring, I must find another avenue. Maybe after the holidays I'll be able to do something toward developing the idea I had for the book. I must do something that expresses myself, what I am.

* * *

December 28. *Gordon and I discussed my book. I told him how I get discouraged in the business—not doing anything worthwhile, just looking pretty, period—and how I want to do something challenging and fulfilling with my life.*

"Do you have a subject?" he asked.

I nodded. "Women."

"That's a bit broad, *darling, if you'll pardon the pun. It would help if you could be more specific."*

"Beautiful women."

"You mean the problems confronting the beautiful woman that don't confront the ordinary woman?"

"Yes. I guess that's sort of what I mean. I mean, being in the business has exposed me to this problem. You wonder sometimes, what's the percentage in being beautiful? There's a premium on freshness and youth, but how long can one keep going on that alone? So few men will allow a woman to be anything else but what she is physically. You know there are men who won't go out with a woman unless she's beautiful? That's their criterion."

He nodded thoughtfully.

"The beautiful girl is a victim in a society that feeds on beauty and youth."

"I think it's a pretty sound idea. Go on."

I continued, feeling my way along. "There are various types, of course. There's the tough kind who's out for all she can get and hates men. There's the good-natured kind who keeps having bad luck, being used, and having bad experiences with men. And there's the kind who settles with someone she doesn't love—just to get out of the rat race and lead a quiet life—because she can't take the pressure and the hurt of being used."

"I see."

"Even the supposedly smart ones suffer, because they lose themselves. They sell out their birthright. For what? For a dream of glory."

"Go on."

"There are many fascinating variations within these types, many stories to be told."

"What's the point? The connecting theme?"

"For one thing, that beautiful women have more trouble finding happiness than others do. That they're at the mercy of people who feed on them; that they're used, made victims. And the thing is, of course, that they go right along with it. They allow it to happen."

"Why do they allow it?"

"Various reasons. They think they can escape the penalty, that they'll succeed where others have failed. There's an element of ego, I'm different, I'm appreciated for myself, not just my looks. They tread tightropes telling themselves things are going to work out the way they want, eventually. Maybe for a while they'll use their looks, eventually they'll be in the position they want to be in."

"I think you should write it."

"I will."

"Don't just say you will. Really do it. I think it could be very interesting."

"You really do?"

"You've got a good idea, and the background to write it. I think it would sell."

"You really think so?"

"I certainly do." He grinned. "Then what would you do with all that money?"

I smiled back. "I don't know." My smile turned sad, for as I looked at Gordon, I couldn't help thinking—all that money—for myself alone? Mightn't there be just a chance for us? Deep down I knew that that hope was vain; I wanted so much to be in his arms, to feel love and reassurance, yet I knew it wasn't going to go beyond the now, the right now.

Why is all this so important to a woman, and how is it a man can be immune, can be a part of it all, yet not a part?

* * *

January 5. New Year's. Had I been looking forward to that with dread or anticipation . . . or what exactly?

I didn't have one at any rate. Gordon got a call from the Coast to begin an assignment on a new show. He had to go back right away for conferences with the producer.

"Darling, it's been marvelous," he said to me at the airport two days before New Year's.

As I watched his tall figure disappear down the ramp, I kept thinking, I had no choice. I needed to give. I knew it would end this way, but I had to go on. I couldn't have not had the affair.

Why can't I take life for today? Why can't I just want to live for the moment? I can't. I can't because I know there is so much more to be had, so much that is deeper and richer.

Gordon's talk against marriage should have been my cue to run. Right from the start, I knew it would come to this. But I needed those days of closeness, my only ones in so very long; I needed them to sustain me through another long winter, to feed me and keep me from total starvation.

When I first cried after he was gone, it was because he could take it so lightly, while for me it meant so much more, and after that I was angry. How dare he, how dare he treat me like that? He had no right to do that when I cared so much, when I'd given my heart.

But, oh God, it was good, the way he made me feel. God, it was good. Maybe I ought not to have given like that. But it couldn't have been otherwise. It had to be from my heart. I had to give him my heart.

Chapter 11

Henry Haupt had been lonely in his large triplex, but now Dolores had come to fill the apartment—and his life—with love and warmth. He told her what a difference she made.

"You know, Henry," she said pointedly, "I think some men were meant to be *married*, and I think you are one of those men."

"You know, I think you're right." Returning her smile, he looked like a seventeen-year-old boy enraptured with his first love.

Two weeks later, Dolores became Mrs. Henry Haupt. They were married twice: first by a rabbi, in the presence of Henry's family; then by a judge friend of Henry's, attended by twelve hundred of their friends. Dolores wore a Mainbocher gown and the emeralds and diamonds that were Henry's wedding gift to her. Her picture appeared in all the New York papers the next day.

Carrie was her maid of honor, and looked, as *Women's Wear Daily* noted, "dreamy and ravishing in citron chiffon." Eve was a bridesmaid, "appealing and pretty" in pale yellow. But no one could take the limelight from where it belonged, on Dolores Haynes, the new Mrs. Henry Haupt, whom the same writer called "the bride of the season . . . a fashion personality and arbiter par excellence, witty, bright, cheerful, fun FUN FUN."

Charlene showed up with the two dogs, of course, wearing a gold nail polish and royal-blue eyeshadow, magenta lipstick that practically lit up ten feet away, together with a kelly-green floor-length satin dress and ostrich plumes. She poured bourbon down her throat in praise of the match and Dolores' great success in nailing Henry.

Rex was agog. His constant searching looks and cruising of the reception room, everyone knew, were in hopes of finding a rich gay boy friend. As he consumed more champagne than usual, becoming increasingly swishy, Dolores remarked to Charlene that Rex was in reality a frustrated bride himself.

Living proof of mind over matter without knowing it was Henry Haupt, for once they were married, Dolores stopped using the love potion she had purchased in Harlem, and her groom was capable of performing sexually nonetheless. All he had needed was the initial restoration of his confidence, and after that, as the old saying went, success breeds success.

If you could call it success. For as to what type lover Henry was, that was another matter altogether. Even at his most feverish, he was too plodding, too dull and pedestrian for Dolores' taste.

I married a fool, Dolores thought contemptuously, and soon she was again taking virile young lovers, mostly stud types from her acting class.

How she loved the moments when she throatily commanded, "Worship me, you prick," after which she would lie back, and the young man would do her bidding like a lackey, like a male concubine. She needed the homage, the worship of her as divinity incarnate.

Meanwhile, apart from her clandestine life, her days were full with shopping and fittings, sessions at Kounovsky's gym and daily comb-outs at the hairdresser, singing, acting, dancing, and speech lessons, as well as meetings with her new press agent. There were lunches at La Caravelle, La Grenouille, the Colony, and Le Pavillon, and continual go-sees and appointments for commercials. Life had never been fuller for Dolores.

* * *

"Jobs are pouring in for Leslie Savage. Carrie Richards is tied up on so many products there isn't much she's available for. Vince August is getting his release on Chesterfields soon; we'll have to get him another cigarette . . ."

"We've got Eve Paradise on the game show, Anita Suzanne in a Broadway hit, Lois Daniels on a panel show. Diane Rose will have a Broadway show soon, with Fleming Todd backing her . . ."

Rex and Charlene were having their monthly conference

reviewing the status of the agency, deciding what things needed to be done for whom.

Charlene said, "Commercials booked this week: Shinola, Gulf, Enden, Spic and Span, Esquire Shoe Polish, Mustang, Black Flagg, Mr. Bubble, Twenty Mule Team Borax, Benson and Hedges, Pan American—"

Rex said, "We're doing all right, considering money's tight, and that we're into the slow season."

Charlene said, "Irene Lord is coming along well. Nothing fazes that dyke. She's got nerves of steel. By the way, I've been meaning to ask you what happened to that cute fellow—what was his name?—who used to come around last summer. Sinjin?"

Rex shuddered. "Don't ask! I don't ever want to hear that name! It's a dirty word!" He covered his mouth to protest the indelicacy of Charlene's question. Then, stepping over to the window, he pulled the cord of the Venetian blind, and before Charlene knew what was happening, a ray of sunlight struck her face.

Instantly her hands went to her eyes in a gesture of self-protection.

"What the hell are you doing?" she reprimanded sharply.

"It's so dark in here," Rex complained.

"Well, that's the way I like it. Pull them down again."

"Okay, okay, so don't get so nervous."

Bastard fag, Charlene thought; he did it on purpose. But she wasn't going to give him the satisfaction of knowing she knew. With studied aplomb, she continued the conference. "Then there's Dolores Haynes—"

"Laurie Glory has been bugging me lately," Rex interrupted.

"Poor Laurie. Another one who doesn't know when to give up."

"She had her chances. But how do you tell a girl she's over the hill?"

Charlene was thoughtful. "It gets undignified," she said. "Undignified to have to keep up the struggle and keep trying to sell yourself over and over. The saddest thing of all is when a girl doesn't know she's had it."

*   *   *

Charlene was pondering her own words when, about an hour later, Laurie Glory appeared at the door in a dress a little too cutsey-poo, dyed red hair overdone, too teased and fussy. Her pancake makeup had cracked around her crows' feet and eyes, and there was a slight yellow, porous quality to her skin.

"Hi, Charlene," she said. "Anything going?"

"No, honey, it's quiet. Rex just stepped out for a steam. You're looking great." Liar, she told herself. Laurie had been one of the busiest models when the Ryan-Davy Agency began, but she'd had it now. Fresh faces like Carrie Richards and Eve Paradise were the ones getting the jobs these days.

"I heard about an interview for Rolaids," Laurie said. "How come I wasn't sent?"

"Honey, that was for eighteen-year-olds."

"I can go eighteen. Here, look, Charlene. I just had some new test shots done. Take a look at these contacts."

"Who did them?"

"Aaron Kenter."

Charlene recognized the name. Aaron Kenter charged $150 a sitting. A few years ago, numerous photographers would have jumped at the chance of doing tests of Laurie for nothing.

Charlene examined the contacts with a magnifying glass, and located the bags, circles, and lines in the face.

"Which do you like?" Laurie asked anxiously.

In all the pictures Laurie was reaching, straining to look younger. Charlene knew there was a span of a good ten to fifteen years after being a young beauty where it was difficult to make the transition to character woman or mature housewife. During these years, it was nearly impossible to find work in the business unless the model had established herself as a spokeswoman or actress. Only then would the makeup and camera people fuss for you. *Fresh* unknowns were the only unknowns who had a foothold in the business. Over the hill has-beens like Laurie, no matter how hard they tried, were a lost cause.

"And see—my old pictures are still good," Laurie said. "Take a look at my book, Charlene, and see how you like it."

Charlene remembered Laurie's portfolio. Most of the pictures looked out of style. Didn't it occur to Laurie that the

Madison Avenue casting people looked for up-dateness in a model's book? She turned the pages idly.

"I guess you heard I got a divorce and moved back to town," Laurie said. "I hated being in the suburbs. I'm so glad now I can be more available to be active in the business."

"That's nice."

"Well, I have to go to the hairdresser now. I'm having my hair lightened."

"Yes," Charlene said, "blondes get more work."

* * *

It was late enough now to open the window blind. Charlene got up and pulled the cord. Yes, her face could take the light at this time of day. Standing near the window, she opened her compact and surveyed herself haughtily. For a woman of sixty-never-mind-what, she was in damned good shape. Middle-aged spread she had checked. Despite the drinking she had managed to keep her weight down. Only naked did her body show signs of wear. The lumpiness which had developed in her legs had been surgically removed last year. Pierre was a wizard; the hair color he had invented especially for her never varied even a fraction of a tone and facials twice a week kept her skin in condition. Still, her mirror hinted it was getting about time for another sanding. The pouches under her eyes, despite an operation three years ago, were noticeable, and in another year or two, she'd have to start thinking about further cosmetic surgery.

She snapped the compact shut and poured herself a slug of bourbon. Sounds of the Manhattan traffic and crowds drifted up from the street. The city goes on, Charlene thought, and all of a sudden you're old.

How she despised that word, *old*. She wouldn't use it in connection with herself. Charlene Davy would never be old. Well, all of a sudden you're not as young as you used to be, then.

That's right, no one's feeling you up, no one's sticking hands up your skirt in restaurants anymore. Now you watch men doing to the younger girls what they once did to you. You hear the same lines, you realize it's the same story year in, year out, and you feel revolted at the thought that when

237

you were unsurpassably beautiful you never had a clear picture of how things really were, that you believed all the garbage, that you never knew you were being used—yes, used—by all of them, by all the dirty old men and the dirty young men, the playboys, the perverts, husbands, lovers, not one of them giving a damn about you as a person, only basking in the reflected glory of what being with a beautiful woman could do for their egos. It was all just a part of a total picture a man had of himself, all you had amounted to was an adjunct, an extension of himself.

She poured another slug of bourbon and slammed the bottle down. Warren, asleep under the desk, growled. Kurt regarded him quizzically, ears pricked up.

"Oh, you two!" Charlene howled. "I can always count on my two favorite males to give me a lift!"

She sighed. Once again she allowed her hands to pass over the surface of her body. Her liver was even bigger than it had been last month.

"Hi, Charlene."

Carrie Richards stood in the doorway, carrying her book and satchel, wearing owl sunglasses, her hair pulled back with a man's handkerchief.

"Carrie! Just the girl I want to see. I have some residuals for you." Charlene reached into a drawer and thumbed through a stack of checks. "Here we are. General Foods, Class A, use number 2, gross seventy dollars; Colgate-Palmolive, Halo Shampoo, Class A, gross a hundred and fourteen dollars. Both received from D'Arcy. Now here's one from J. Walter Thompson: Lever Brothers, Lux Soap, Class A, program buyout, thirteen-week cycle, gross seven hundred fifty dollars. And that's not all. Also from J. Walter, they're using the Lux on spot too: three hundred eighty dollars and four hundred ten dollars for Triple A and wild spots. Then I think something just came in for you from SSC&B or DCS&S —but we haven't had time to get to those yet."

"This is just what I needed," Carrie said, stuffing the checks into her satchel.

Suddenly Charlene remembered something. "I've been meaning to speak to you, Carrie," she said.

Carrie looked up. "Oh? What about?"

"You have a slight Southern accent—almost imperceptible.

But I hear it on words like *pin* and *pen*. I think you should work on it."

"All right."

"Everyone who stays in the business takes classes," Charlene said. "When a girl first comes to town she can make it on freshness and youth. There's nothing like a new face in this business. But after you've been around awhile, you've got to compete. You have to deliver the maximum amount of professionalism. I want you to start voice training with Bert Knapp twice a week. He's the best in town. Also, I want you to take ballet and acting classes, have facials with Dr. Behrman, and go to Kounovsky's gym."

"How much are all these things going to cost me?" Carrie asked.

"The whole thing shouldn't run much more than a hundred a week. It's deductible. You have to spend money to keep on making it. Relax, and others will pass you by."

"I know you're right, Charlene. But . . ."

"But what? What's the matter, honey?"

"Well . . . look at what my life is like, being in this business. I never have a moment to myself. I rush, rush, rush—you go on twenty or more interviews just to get one job. Then you have to worry, will the commercial run or will they hold it and tie me up? And if it runs, will it be a money-maker? What kind of a life is it, dashing all over the place, waiting in reception rooms, hopping cabs clear across town, just hoping the whole time you have that indefinable something they want for the product's image. It gets so tiresome, sometimes, because the real me is frustrated. I keep waiting for the big money-maker, the job that's going to make the big difference, the one that's going to put me ahead financially, so I can lead my own life. Because I know I don't belong in this business. I'm using nothing of myself, nothing really worthwhile. The only thing that counts here is looks—"

"Type," Charlene corrected.

"All right, type. I mean, all along I've been looking forward to Independence Day—marriage, hopefully, or at least having the time and money to travel and write."

"We all have our dreams."

"But I really want these things, Charlene. I don't want the business."

"Honey, what else could you be doing? How else can a girl earn twenty, thirty, forty thousand a year?"

"I know, I know . . ."

"I thought you'd been writing all along."

"No. Keeping notebooks. Now I've got this idea I want to really work on."

"What's that, honey?"

"It's a book, Charlene. A book about women. I've been doing notes for it, and it really excites me. It's primarily about beautiful women, and the penalty of beauty, about the beautiful girl in a society that lays stress on the physical. For instance, I'm trying to show how little chance we get to be *human*—how we're exploited for the surface of us—"

"*Bravo!*" Charlene said. "It's time somebody told the truth."

"If only I had the money and the time. Expenses are so high. And now more expense. I wish I could apply myself to it wholeheartedly right now, instead of having my energies go out in a hundred trivial little directions."

"You have years and years ahead of you, Carrie."

"I know, but . . ."

"You'll write that book someday. Writing, you can always do. But now's the time that's important in terms of yourself. Youth. You've got the biggest commodity going."

"Where am I supposed to go with it? Look at the men, Charlene, the men you meet in this business. All right, getting back to my theme, these men a girl meets because she's beautiful—they're jokes. The girl is only there for show. But how about her? It's the glib line the beautiful woman gets, not the heartfelt thought. In this business, in life, men expect us to be poised, sophisticated, hip, with it. We're supposed to be turned on to everybody else's scene, because they're the power people and we're the servers. Madison Avenue tells us to lose our accents, dress eighteen today, look outdoorsy tomorrow, have the Gem Razor Blade look at three o'clock and the Pepsi look at four-thirty. Then, later on, the dates, the parties—it's the same thing: more catering, more smiles, more yeses.

"You start wondering what the hell's going on. Who am I? Am I anything more than a yo-yo? I'm chattel, waiting in those offices to turn on my Pepsi or my Palmolive look, or whatever. I'm tired of being *on* every minute. I think maybe girls are attacted to this business because they want a certain kind of acceptance and admiration. They even think they're getting it at first, when they get praised for their pictures and their profiles. But soon something starts gnawing away, and you know this isn't where it's at. I'm not sour grapes, Charlene. I'm only trying to find some kind of norm . . . because there's just no reality here. How long do you think I'll be able to maintain my equilibrium if I have to go through these ordeals, grappling with creeps and never receiving an ounce of genuine appreciation or affection or anything even vaguely resembling love?"

"I agree, honey, it's not easy. The only thing you can do is to get wrapped up in yourself, in your profession, and stop worrying about the private life. Don't make it so important."

"But I want to lead a *meaningful* life."

"What's that?"

"It's everything. Emotional fulfillment, intellectual satisfaction, the physical, the spiritual—everything together. It's being a part of the times, a part of life in a constructive way— being able to make a contribution, belonging, being what I'm capable of being."

"Youth, youth!" Charlene shook her head. "You'll learn."

"I want a fruitful existence, not this kind of sterile, artificial life." Carrie's eyes sparkled. "I want love; I want a good husband. I want a home, Charlene; I want a family. I look around at the people I meet and I can't believe what I see. I don't want all *this*—being there just for decoration, having all I really am ignored or overlooked."

Charlene lit a cigarette and smiled condescendingly.

"And you're right about fresh faces," Carrie went on. "I know what happens to girls in this business after a few years. How long can I go on being at the top? I keep hearing how beautiful I am, how wonderfully I photograph . . . but how long can that last?"

"Honey, the way you look, you've got a good ten or fifteen more years, provided you take care of yourself. That's what I've been trying to tell you—"

"But who wants all those years in the business? The business is okay for girls driven by ambition, or for the teenagers, who think it's exciting. But . . ."

"Do you want to get out and go into another field? Work steady hours and make a snappy hundred a week—if you're lucky? Someday you'll look back on all this and be sorry time has passed, sorry you're not right here anymore."

"Never. When I'm a little old lady with a shawl, sitting by the fireside with my ten grandchildren, then I'll know life has been everything I've ever wanted it to be. And I'll never once think about all the phony emptiness of this business."

"Girls like you don't become little old ladies with shawls and ten grandchildren," Charlene scoffed. "You want to know what happens to girls like you, Carrie? They never let go. Can't. You'll cling and cling to your looks, because you know they're what *make* you what you are—what people see in you and expect of you and want in you. You'll be doctoring up your looks and trying to forget there are younger and prettier girls coming up every season."

"That's ridiculous."

"That's what happens when a girl looks like you do, honey. The only salvation's in being clever. Dolores had the right idea. Make sure you get the big security, and the rest of your life will take care of itself."

"How?"

"You'll have affairs, like everyone else. That's the answer. When a dame has a good affair going, she's flying. It's the only way you can survive in the world. Learn to take care of yourself like every other woman does. Don't be foolish, Carrie. You've got a chance now; don't throw that chance away."

Carrie said, "I just wish I could afford not to work in this business."

"Nonsense," Charlene protested. "You've invested too much money and time in the business. You've put in the groundwork, posed for hours to get your book in the shape it's in. You've done a good job of public relations all this time. You can't let it all go out the window. It's all going to pay off in a big way; you'll see, honey. And Rex and I have invested a lot of time in you, Carrie; don't forget that. We can't afford to lose a top girl like you."

"I know," Carrie said. "But . . ."

"Carrie, where could you do better than you're doing here? You love clothes; you like being your own boss, making your own hours, being able to come and go as you please."

"True. In that sense the business has me hooked."

"It's got us all hooked. None of us can ever leave it. When the residuals pour in, this business looks like the best in the world."

"The trouble is, how long can I last this way? What will become of me if I go on being treated this way? It's love I need, Charlene, don't you understand that?"

"You'll find a husband," Charlene said. "Just stick, and it will happen. Keep yourself in shape, go on your interviews, and sooner or later things will happen."

* * *

Charlene sat alone now, alone in the shadows of the dying day and in the shadows of years, creeping memories and deadness and mistakes and regrets. Smart girl, Carrie, she thought. She sees the handwriting on the wall, which is more than I did at her age. What happened? What went wrong for me? Where could I have changed things and made them come out all right? Or were the cards just stacked against me from the start, because of the mere accident of being born a woman with a beautiful face?

I never made the really big security scene. Too stupid when it was possible. Too busy having fun, thinking the golden days of wine and roses lasted forever. And now? The loneliness, the fear. Life is closing in and what is on the other side of life? Tawdry glitter like here, is it a tinsel veil, a champagne bubble—or is it nothingness?

I hate being alone, I hate it, I hate it. I hate everything. Hate the noises and the shadows, and the newspapers telling you life is something more than you've ever known it to be, and here I am alone, getting older and older, and there's this awful sense of impending doom—and my face! My face has wrinkles. God, God, my face. No, no, oh, God, how I hate looking in the mirror sometimes. Look at those pictures, just look at them, look at the way I *used* to be. What am I going to do? And my goddamned liver. Oh, what? Whatever? Call somebody. Who can I call?

A man, that was what she needed. It had been so long. If only Rex were here now. A few times he had gotten the

243

masseur from the steam bath to come up and give her a treatment, and for an extra sum, a "special."

That's what I need now, Charlene thought, a special. But Rex wasn't in and she didn't have the number of the steam bath, and who knew if the same guy were there now or if—oh, the whole thing was too damned complicated.

She poured more bourbon into her tumbler, and after a swallow, suddenly remembered that she'd been so busy she'd forgotten to make her yearly appointment to have Marcus progress her chart. She picked up the phone and dialed.

"Marcus," she cried into the phone, "I *have* to see you—as soon as possible. It can't wait!"

Part

Four

Chapter 1

In May, at the start of Dolores' third year in New York, it could be said she had status and security. She was Mrs. Henry Haupt, and due to star in a Broadway play, which Henry was backing for her. The part was that of a femme fatale who was on stage almost the entire time. Dolores was certain the play would be a tremendous hit, and her performance a tour de force that would propel her to Hollywood.

Early in September, after considerable out-of-town trouble —including the firing of two directors and the male lead's quitting, then returning with an increase in salary—the play reached New York, was panned by all the critics, and folded after four performances. Dolores had to face the fact that, except for a few words about her wardrobe, her own notices had been none too complimentary.

Vexed, she blamed production problems, and announced to Henry her intention to do another play as soon as possible.

No sooner had she made her intent clear than she found herself pregnant, an unforeseen event.

"I've decided to go through with it," she told Carrie over lunch at Twenty One. "Motherhood is a link. This'll give me a much tighter grip on Henry." With her left hand she smoothed her hair, purposely making an ostentatious display of the twenty-two-carat diamond engagement ring Henry had given her.

"How did it happen?" Carrie asked. "I thought you were on the pill."

"I skipped one day, and this is the result." She lit a cigarette with the new gold lighter Henry had given her from Tiffany's that had cost several hundred dollars, and noted with pleasure that Carrie was envious of her condition.

"You're still thinking about that abortion, aren't you, Carrie? Well, don't. Practically every woman has an abortion at one time or another. Lots of women have several. Forget about it. You could get married and have a baby tomorrow if that's what you wanted."

"Who would I marry? I wouldn't be in love . . ."

"Will you ever get over the illusion, Carrie?"

"Illusion?"

"Love is crap."

"Dolores—"

"Take my advice, Carrie, you've got to move in on guys who're ready to be moved in on. Now, take Henry Haupt, for instance—"

"Dolores . . ."

"Just remember—rich guys do it too."

*   *   *

"This is a shitty business, Charlene, you can't depend on it." It was the end of the day and Rex was pacing up and down in a state of high irritation after having lost a top model he and Charlene had invested a lot of time in.

"Calm down, Rex, things like this happen."

"You spend months grooming a girl, you knock your brains out for her, and she ends up leaving you and signing with another agency."

"There are a few rotten apples in every barrel," Charlene said philosophically.

"Well, I'm sick of it, sick of knocking myself out. For what? Goddamn models, they hate our guts. We do all the work and collect ten per cent of shit. We should get ninety per cent. What the hell do they contribute? You teach a girl how to walk, get pictures for her, teach her how to make up, send her to see everybody in town—and all that goes down the drain. What a bunch of ungrateful bitches. They'd screw their own mother. I'm about to join you in a bar tonight. I wanna get drunk as a skunk."

"Rex, I get worried when I see you like this. You know you shouldn't get so excited, and you shouldn't drink."

"Look who's talking about drinking."

"That's different."

"Well, I'm sick of things. We ought to have our heads examined for going on this way. I can't keep putting up with this shit. I'm going to look for another way."

"What kind of a way?"

"Some kind of investment project . . . or another business. I don't know. Some way of getting an income so I don't have to spend my whole life in this rat race." Rex wrung his hands and banged his temple with his fist.

"Please, Rex," Charlene begged, "calm down. You know you shouldn't get so excited."

"Knock it off, Charlene."

"You know I promised your mother I'd watch out for you."

"Keep my mother out of this!"

"Your spells, Rex—"

"*Shut up!*"

"I'm only fulfilling an obligation. I worry about you as if you were my own son."

"Well, don't! I don't need it."

"All right, have it your own way," Charlene said, and stormed out of the office.

* * *

Eve reached into her satchel, took out her appointment book, and read over what she had done during the day: a sitting for test shots, four go-sees, a fitting, a stop at the agency. She'd also made several phone calls, and left undone about six things that were on the list she'd made the previous night. Now she went into the living room, found a pencil, and made the next day's list: "9:00—booking at Binder and Duffy; 11:00—Norman Craig and Kummel; 12:30—Claudia Walden at Grey; 1:30—Ruth Levine at Benton and Bowles; 2:45—fitting for catalog house; 4:00—final audition at MPO (that was cutting it close since the catalog fitting was bound to take at least an hour and MPO was way over on the west side); pick up check at the agency, call five photographers to set up more test shots, buy acetate sheets, buy dress at Bonwit's."

The phone rang, and she picked it up.

Charlene had another appointment for her for Thursday, a call-back on a coffee.

"Boy, does that surprise me!" Eve said. "It was a bad scene the last time I was there."

"What happened?"

"First of all, they kept me waiting almost an hour. When I finally got in, the director and the producer were sitting around with beer cans and cigarette butts all over. And the director, he was in his shirt sleeves and playing darts. I screamed, 'Look out!'—and this dart comes flying past me. I could have been killed."

"Some of these people are infantile idiots."

"And then they joked and tried to act cute and asked me questions like, do you have a boy friend? how do you look in a bikini? and things like that. I got so mad."

"I don't blame you, honey. You should have told me sooner. If anything like this ever happens again, be sure you let us know right away."

"I will. Anyway, I'm sure surprised they want to see me again. I was very cold to them."

"And how *do* you look in a bikini?"

"Oh, Charlene, I really am going to take off those seven pounds. I promise."

"Well, I may have a new system for you. I'm finding out about it later on today."

"A new diet?"

"No, a system that balances the body, that equalizes anything that needs to be equalized. It would be a natural, painless way of reducing."

"Sounds fantastic."

"It's a Chinese method. It's called T'ai Chi Ch'uan. Marcus put me onto it. I'll let you know about it as soon as I find out. Have you seen about the acting class yet?"

"I called the man, and—"

"You mean John Sacchetti?"

"Yes. I'm visiting the class next week to see if I like it."

"Good, honey. It will be a great help to you. You weren't ready for John Sacchetti before, but you are now. He's just what you need. The classes will give you polish, help you to acquire more presence, and you'll have a technique to work with."

"I'm looking forward to it, Charlene. I didn't think there were enough hours in the day to do all this, but I'll find the time somehow."

"It's the only way, sweetheart. If you don't work at keeping yourself on top, you'll slip, and other girls will take your place. You've got too much going for you to let that happen."

CARRIE'S NOTEBOOK

September 19. Dichotomy. On one hand I ought to be pleased the business has been quiet; what I've been yearning for is more time to devote to the book. On the other, however, I'm sorry there aren't more interviews, for the money situation is getting worrisome. I'm tied up on four commercials they're holding and not using. I wish I could get ahead, create a backlog of funds, have more residuals coming in.

It seems there ought to be more interviews—unless I'm an old face. Could I be slipping? To myself I still look the same, but can I trust my own opinion? Can others see things I can't?

I called Charlene, and she said I'm utterly crazy to worry, that of course I'm still everything I ever was—and more; it's just that the business is slow, and I'm tied up on so many products.

"Our people can come out all right," Charlene said, "between industrials, trade shows, market week, training films for the armed forces, stock, and so forth, but the returns aren't what they used to be. The tight-money situation is getting worse and this is the poorest year we've had in a long time. People who make the commercials are getting smart—they've been going to Florida and the Coast a lot more—finding talent there—writing the trip off as a business expense—gives them a chance to play away from home base—or they can even go to Europe where they can get away without paying residuals. It's out of SAG jurisdiction."

So I guess it isn't me. Though it really makes a dent in the bank account when your income drops. But it has given me a chance to do some work on the book. I really believe I have something here, and I'm going to see it through.

* * *

It was her first acting class, and Eve was nervous. She hardly knew what to expect as she climbed the three flights of stairs in the decrepit old building off Sixth Avenue.

At first the method workshop studio seemed completely dark, but gradually her eyes became accustomed to the dim light and she perceived a long and narrow area filled with some thirty chairs. A small stage contained a platform raised a couple of inches from the floor, and in back was a smaller room separated from the main theater section. A faded mauve curtain partially blocked the view, but she could see the glowing ends of cigarettes and hear muffled voices coming from inside.

Several actors sat in reverent silence as though in meditation or church. Most were informally dressed. When the evening's work began they formed a quiet, respectful audience.

First on the agenda was an exercise called "moment of privacy," where the actor was expected to behave as though he were alone with no one watching him, and do something he would normally never do in front of people. A slovenly woman with mousy brown frizzled hair rose, went to the stage, and for some time merely paced. Then she took off her sweater and skirt. Eve drew in her breath.

The woman, standing in her bra and half-slip, seemed to be gazing in an imaginary mirror. She patted her buttocks, looking upset over her proportions, then passed her palms over her bare midriff. She paused, shaking her head, trembling visibly, from time to time touching various parts of her body until finally she raised her hands to her face, let out a deafening shriek, and doubled over in sobs.

Recovering quickly, she announced, "That's it," and put her clothes back on.

"What do you want to tell us, Mary?" John Sacchetti asked from his seat in the front row.

"I used a specific setting, and from there I worked on sight and touch," Mary said. "I looked at myself until I couldn't stand it any longer . . . because I'm so ugly."

"Good, good," John said. "Class"—he stood up and turned to face the other students—"Mary has just done what every actor must do. Her preparation worked for her, and she reached into the depths of her emotional resources. She

252

found realistic honesty and release from fear. More important, she knew when to stop."

Eve was conscious of the fact that she was shaking inside. I'd never be able to do that, she thought; I'd make a fool of myself.

"I can't stress how important the moment-of-privacy exercise can be to an actor," John went on. "You'll find your work in scenes becomes simpler once you've broken through your emotional barriers." He turned toward the stage again and said, "I'm very proud of you, Mary. Your work is coming along just beautifully."

Two actors who had gone into the back room to do some last-minute rehearsing emerged. Their names were Bruno Abadessa and Cynthia Laslo. They announced an episode from Flannery O'Connor's *A Good Man Is Hard to Find*.

The scene dealt with a bum masquerading as a Bible salesman who seduces a girl with a wooden leg in a hayloft.

Eve had a feeling of revulsion as she watched the enactment of the scene. It was terribly perverted, she thought. She was particularly amazed that the seduction was carried to a horrifying length of believability, with Bruno actually mounting Cynthia and the two of them moving together in the rhythms of lovemaking, moaning and clutching at each other like primitive animals.

Some of the tittering students in the audience stood up in order to get a better view of the spectacle on the floor of the stage. An unseen boy directly behind Eve said, "It's a real dry fuck."

How could anyone be so crude as to make a remark like that? Eve was embarrassed, and at the same time, fascinated, in awe of Bruno and Cynthia's abandoned movements and cries. She had never seen sexual energy at such a peak and it made her feel left out. She wished she was in on things, a part of life. If only she could find a man—someone.

"I used my first sexual experience as an emotional memory," Cynthia said after the scene was over.

Eve was astonished by Cynthia's uninhibited honesty, and by John's praise of the actors for their realistic performance. Good Lord, if her father ever knew!

The next scene, the last before the coffee break, was done by a curly-haired actor who wore a shirt open to his waist.

He stepped to the stage and announced he was going to do an emotion memory.

Eve learned later that John had the actor, Andy Silverman, on a program of emotion memories to increase his sensitivity and release his inner resources. The emotion memory, Eve discovered, had to be of a disturbing experience that had happened at least seven years ago. The actor had to sit with his eyes closed at first, and make his body relaxed all over. When he began to speak he was supposed to recall the specific place in which the experience happened.

Andy described the curtains, the furniture, the smells, sounds, and textures of a room. "It's afternoon," he said. "About five o'clock. The light's fading." He went on to evoke more of the setting. Then he began to relive a fight with his sister in which he threw a dart at her, hit her close to an eye, and went so out of his mind with fright and anger that he seized the cat and began to throttle it. He'd started the exercise fully relaxed; he ended it screaming at the top of his lungs, jumping about, and waving his arms in uncontrolled frenzy.

The second half of the evening began with a scene from *The Catcher in the Rye*, in which Holden Caulfield watched the boy down the hall popping his pimples, squeezing pus out of them, and applying a white liquid medication.

Next, two other students, Scott Lawrence and Nina Martin, having finished their scene, were completing their discussions on preparations. Nina Martin, Eve thought, looked like a prostitute, with her cheap dyed red hair, overdone eyes, flashy tight clothes, and the way she threw her body around. Nina was saying that she felt the reason she had not fully executed her intention in the scene was that she had a sex problem.

"Don't you enjoy it?" John asked.

"Oh, my God, yes!" Nina said. "I go crazy, John, I just love to get laid!"

"Well, then, what's the problem?"

Nina brought her fingers to her mouth, and for a moment, despite her hardness, she looked like a little girl. "The thing is, John," she cried, "I enjoy it too much. I don't think it's right to like it the way I do, and I always feel funny about it, as though I shouldn't be enjoying it so much, you see?"

What next? Eve wondered, and then a troubled-looking

young man named Marty Sachs stepped onto the stage and stood silently scratching his head and staring into space—in order to get in the mood, Eve supposed.

"Now I am alone. O! what a rogue and peasant slave am I," he intoned at last, in a voice that reeked of New Yorkese.

He had gotten no farther when John interrupted him and told him to start over again. Upon reaching the end of the same line, John once again broke in. When the same thing occurred the third time, John asked Marty what he was "using."

"It's something personal," Marty said.

"What?" John prodded, and Eve saw the color drain from Marty's face.

John persisted. "What made you want to do Hamlet?"

"Because," Marty cried out, "because Hamlet is just as fed up with this lousy, shitty, fucking world as I am! I can't stand this goddamn crap-filled life any longer! I want to die, I want to die!"

He collapsed on a chair, buried his face in his arms, and began to sob. "I'm so ashamed. I'm so goddamned ashamed."

A current of embarrassment hung heavy in the air. The class was silent. It was as though everyone were both sorry and appalled by the breakdown.

Gently, John asked, "Why are you ashamed, Marty?"

Digging his fingers into his scalp, Marty said through clenched teeth, "Because I'm so goddamned fucking lonely! Nobody cares, I ache so, and they don't give a shit—none of them give a lousy fucking shit, and meanwhile I'm dying I'm so goddamned fucking alone!" His voice, which had started low, rose to a scream. "Christ, oh, Christ above, good Christ in heaven, do you know how goddamn fucking *lonely* I am?"

"*Now!*" John said. "*Right* now! Begin the scene again."

"I can't!"

"Begin—*now!*"

"I can't. I can't!"

"*Now!*" John commanded, and Marty, yielding at last, slunk like a whipped dog to the center of the stage.

Faltering often, swallowing at intervals, choking, shuddering, and wiping tears from his eyes, he delivered the speech. This time John did not interrupt, for despite his distracting and out-of-place New York accent, Marty was interesting to listen to. Eve thought the reason was probably that he was thinking about what he said this time.

Marty left the stage, and John, donning a rakish tweed hat, announced that class was over for the evening. He went to the door; then he saw Eve and waited. As she approached him, she realized he was a little man, but energetic as a tiny moth. His features were Sicilian, and she'd noticed earlier that he spoke like someone who'd been influenced by the gestures and inflections of an Italian family. She felt a bond of tradition and nationality uniting her with him.

"I'll give you something simple to do as a beginning," he said. "Maybe the *Rose Tattoo*. Playing virgins is always the easiest beginning."

Eve laughed, trying to appear loose and with it. But when she left the studio, all she could think was, Oh, God, what would John think, what would those actors think, if they knew she really was a virgin. If only she'd meet someone! Someone to sweep her off her feet. Someone to change her life.

* * *

Eve lay silently in bed that night listening to the hum of traffic on the street below. Gradually tears came, rolled off her face, and plopped on the pillow. Her body shook. She thought of Marty Sachs, the actor who'd broken down in class. She understood.

Chapter 2

"Carrie Richards!" Charlene greeted her. "Just the girl I wanted to see. How's the book coming?"

"Pretty well, Charlene. For the past three weeks there've been so few interviews that I've had a chance to do lots of work. I've got pages and pages of notes. I'll be ready to start putting it together soon."

"Honey, I've got somewhere to send you—and this could be exactly the thing you've been looking for!"

"What?"

"It's for a very important campaign. The agency is looking for a girl to be the image for the product. You'd be paid a base salary of twenty thousand dollars a year, plus residuals, plus travel expenses."

"Hallelujah!"

"The beauty of it is that it only requires about three days' work a week. You could get ahead financially and still have the time to write."

"Charlene, I *have* to get this job!"

"There's dialogue. They want to tape an on-camera audition. You're to go over to Porter, Tailer, Gilbert and Tribble and pick up a script. Then work on the material with Bert Knapp. They'll tape you next week."

"Oh, Charlene, keep your fingers crossed for me!"

"I certainly will, honey. This could be the answer to everything you've been hoping for."

*   *   *

Charlene collapsed into a wicker chair under a Chinese lantern at Elliot Woo's T'ai Chi Ch'uan Studio. Across from her, the wall was decorated with yin-and-yang charts, Quan Yin goddesses, and fat Buddhas; tea brewed on a hot plate on one corner of the desk, under which Warren and Kurt slept peacefully, indifferent to the lesson their mistress had just completed.

Elliot Woo, wearing a black turtleneck, black trousers, a black cap, horn-rimmed glasses, and a sly smile, leaned over the desk. "You've done very well for your first lesson," he said.

His unlined face, his firm trim body, were those of a man in his thirties, and there was something animalistic and sensual about him.

Charlene grinned. "I've got a good teacher. Ha, ha! Not bad for an old girl, was I, Elliot?"

Elliot drew himself up quickly. "Never say old! In T'ai Chi, there need never be any age."

"I must say, all this is really fascinating." Charlene accepted a cup of Ginseng tea. "And you're too much, Elliot. You don't have a line in your face."

"I owe it all to T'ai Chi. Cream or sugar?"

"Neither, thanks. Tell me more, honey. I'm all ears."

Elliot filled his own cup. "T'ai Chi is an ancient form of Chinese health dancing and exercise. It originated in Buddhist, Taoist, and Confucian monasteries and was practiced by the old emperors and by sages of Oriental lore as well as by monks. Its daily practice will keep you looking young forever. It has the power to rejuvenate."

"Doing the exercises felt terrific, Elliot. But tell me, just how does T'ai Chi accomplish all this?"

"It equalizes the *chi*, or energy, in the body. It unblocks the nerves and balances the centers, thus creating a flow in harmony with the natural rhythms of the body. It achieves the proper body dynamic. Look at me."

Charlene stared with appreciation at Elliot's tall-for-an-Oriental, olive-skinned, muscular body, at his solid square shoulders. Behind horn-rimmed spectacles, his eyes were inscrutable.

"Look at me," he repeated. "I'm an old man. Who would ever believe that ten years ago I was potbellied, white-haired, and sickly? Today I have the body of a healthy man in his thirties, thanks to T'ai Chi."

"How long do you think it would take me to do what you've done?" Charlene asked.

"Inside of six months, Miss Davy—"

"Call me Charlene."

"Charlene—a beautiful name. As I was saying, Charlene, inside of six months you'll be looking ten years younger. In two years you won't know yourself any more. You'll be a young woman again in five years."

"I'm especially concerned about my calf muscles," Charlene said. "They give out on me sometimes."

Elliot waved her worry aside with a quick graceful gesture. "I promise you," he said, "that your body will be restored to its natural state. People weren't meant to get old. Aging is

only the result of ignorance. In China, the sages who practiced T'ai Chi lived to be three hundred years old. Practice
T'ai Chi, and you'll stay young forever. Who would ever
believe I'm sixty-eight?" He executed a slow-motion T'ai Chi
movement with fluidity and precision. "T'ai Chi is the answer," he said.

"This is absolutely the most sensational thing I've ever
heard of. It's fantastic!"

"I can also help you in interrelated ways," Elliot said. His
mouth spread into an equinelike grin, showing a double row
of large yellow teeth. "The Chinese have several things the
West has been slow to catch on to." He took a gulp of his
tea. "There is also acupuncture."

"What is acupuncture?"

"It's a puncturing treatment with needles, based on the
meridian system. You have to know exactly where to press.
If you're even a tiny fraction of an inch off, it could result
in failure."

"Well, what's it supposed to do?"

"This is another Chinese system of rejuvenation, to be
practiced along with T'ai Chi. It frees the flow of current in
the body and restores equilibrium."

"Is it painful? It sounds painful."

"Not at all. The pressure is so gentle, the action so quick,
you hardly feel it."

"I don't understand. How does all this—this acupuncture—
make a person young again?"

"It balances the yin and yang," Elliot explained. "That's
the whole problem in aging; the positive and negative forces
in the body get out of balance, so disease and decay set in.
What happens when the yin and yang are off is the nerve
endings are blocked. Using a combination of T'ai Chi and
acupuncture, you get speedier results."

"In other words, I don't just need T'ai Chi, I need this
acupuncture too?"

"It would be very helpful."

"Where can I have it done? I'm interested in the fastest
results possible."

"I myself do acupuncture," Elliot said. "My fee is fifty
dollars a treatment."

"If it does all you say, it's worth double. When do we begin?"

* * *

"I'm glad you dyed your hair back to its natural color, Carrie," Eve said. "That was terrible, the color you had to go last week for Adorn."

"I guess it will photograph okay though."

"Any word yet on the audition you taped over at Porter, Tailer, Gilbert and Tribble?"

"No, but Rex says they've narrowed it down to six people. I'm holding my breath."

"Oh, I almost forgot, Carrie. You have a message from a Jerry Jackson. Who's he?"

"Vice president over at Hart, Schofield, Moran, Pinkham, and Cook. Remember when I did that Speedy-Whip? He's the producer. He offered to get me a print, so I went to pick it up the other day. He made his pitch."

"Do you like him?"

"I'm attracted to him physically. He's masculine and strong-looking. But he lives in Stamford."

"I guess that means he's married. Too bad. You working on the book tonight?"

"Yes."

"Some of the things you're saying are so great, Carrie. Like how we're not playthings, we're real people with real feelings. And how so few men come on to us in human terms; how so many won't go out with a woman except if she's beautiful; and how they're advertising the fact they need an ornament. I've felt that way—with people like Geoffrey Gripsholm, for instance. I mean, I don't think they have a clue who I am or what I am."

"Join the club," Carrie said.

"Well, I must say the fellas in my acting class are completely different. They're all so superhonest it's scary."

"I know what you mean. It's an inverted kind of thing."

"Wish me luck tonight, Carrie. I'm rehearsing with a new partner, and I'm scared."

"Don't be. What's the worst that could happen?"

"I don't know," Eve said, "but I sure hope I don't have to find out!"

*　　*　　*

At eight P.M. sharp a taxi driven by Marty Sachs pulled up to the curb where Eve stood waiting. She opened the front door and was about to step in.

"What are you," Marty said, "some kind of a nut? You wanna get me arrested?" He closed the front door and pointed to the back.

Eve's stomach was churning as she entered the cab, and nervously contemplated Marty. Darkly greasy, sinister, and oily, he had sweaty, pock-marked skin, black pomaded hair, and a mouth framed by thick lips. His presence frightened yet thrilled her. She wondered what it would be like rehearsing her first scene for the class. Marty was sullen.

"I didn't know you drove a cab," she said, trying to make conversation.

"I do it part time, for bread. When I make it in acting I won't do it any more."

"Can you more or less make your own hours?"

"Uh huh."

In the three sessions she had attended at the John Sacchetti Method Workshop, she had never seen Marty Sachs in attire other than the clothes he wore now; faded jeans, black leather jacket, and a frayed navy T-shirt. She thought of the embarrassing way he'd broken down the first time she saw him, and she wondered if he were still lonely.

Marty brought the cab to a halt on Amsterdam Avenue, near Ninety-eighth Street, and Eve opened her purse to pay him for the ride.

"Forget it," he said. "It's on the house."

*　　*　　*

Marty's small apartment, located near Amsterdam and Ninety-eighth, consisted of a studio living room, kitchen, and bath. A couple of rattan chairs were the only furnishings other than a low coffee table, a few Japanese lanterns, and a double bed covered by a bright Indian blanket.

"I dig Vivaldi," Marty said, pulling a record from its jacket. "Okay by you?"

Eve had no idea who Vivaldi was, figuring only he must be an Italian, but she nodded from her seat in one of the rattan chairs. Afterwards, when the place was flooded with music, Marty drew the copy of his script out of his jacket pocket, and began sliding his thumb along the outer margin of the book, pensively contemplating outer space until he finally looked at Eve and asked, "Wanna start work?"

"Okay."

He suggested they try "to put the scene on its feet."

Eve thought that was a strange way to phrase things when almost all the action took place in bed.

Following Marty's direction, she climbed on top of the Indian blanket, and they ran through the scene twice. Then Marty suggested they take a break.

He lit a cigarette and stared at the ceiling, watching the smoke rise. "I dig you," he said, still looking at the ceiling. "You're not just a pretty girl. You got it here." His hand beat the place where his heart was.

Then he put out his cigarette, folded his arms on his chest, and looked at Eve. "Man," he sighed.

Eve felt uneasy. "Why don't we do the scene again, Marty?" she said. "I can't stay too much longer."

He looked at her strangely. "Sure."

Eve's part required her to pretend to be asleep until Marty entered and initiated the dialogue. After a considerable while, when he still had not made his entrance, she opened her eyes and saw him standing in the middle of the floor, staring into space. "Marty?" she said. "Are you coming?"

"Just give me five minutes." He walked over to the bed and sat on the edge. "I gotta work on my preparation."

After more minutes of staring into space, he looked at Eve and asked, "Am I correct when I say I think your sex life stinks?"

Eve's mouth opened to retort. But Marty, apparently not interested in listening, stood up and said in a detached voice, "Let's take it from the top."

The scene went well until it came time for the kiss, an action they'd brushed over in the previous run-throughs. Now Marty reached for her, planted his heavy wet lips on hers, and kept them there so long that Eve wondered if he'd forgotten his cue. She broke away in order to remind him.

His head rested on the pillow, his lips touching her ear. "I think we know the scene okay." His voice was subdued. "I just want to stay here a minute and hold you like this."

His arms were strong and protective. He did not push or rush her. Instead, he seemed to be seeking her out, attempting to discover something about her, and offering her the opportunity to respond and find him. It was relaxing in his arms, but she had to close her eyes in order not to see his ugly face with its pockmarks and pustules.

"Do you dig it?" he whispered.

"Hmm?"

"I mean, do you dig the action?"

"Oh, I . . ." Her words were smothered as his lips again pressed hers. At first, she responded. Then she was struck with the thought that it was wrong to allow herself to be receptive to an ugly taxi driver who spoke with a horrible New York accent and lived in the middle of the slums.

She drew away. "I'm sorry," she said, "I didn't realize how late it was getting. I have to go now, Marty."

"I can wait." His eyes were insolent.

Eve stood up and smoothed her hair and her skirt. What could she have been thinking of, lying there on the bed with someone like Marty Sachs? If she wanted sex, she could have it with a rich and important man, one who'd help her, who'd elevate her in life instead of dragging her down.

Marty had begun to pace the room. "Maybe you think I'm just interested in you for sex," he said. "If that's what you think, you are *so* wrong. You know, the best part of it's just *being* with somebody, you dig? You're the kind of chick I'd spend an hour making love to *afterwards*, you dig? There aren't many chicks around you can feel that way about, but you're different."

He lit a cigarette and stared at the ceiling, blowing a series of thick smoke rings and watching the fumes disappear into wisps. "I dig you," he said, his face still to the ceiling. "It wouldn't end with my shootin' it into you; it would just go on and on, ya know? Man, it'd really be swingin' with us. I can tell. Can't you?"

Eve was silent, feeling uncomfortable and embarrassed. She

no longer considered Catholicism a valid out; by now she was well aware that Catholics *did*—but the question was, oughtn't she to be in love with a man to consider anything intimate? She could never be in love with Marty, of that she was certain. He was too common. But why, then, did he unnerve her so? Why did she feel this way now, all trembling?

"What's the matter?" he asked, peering at her as though he could see through her.

"Nothing," she said with a small forced smile. "I—have to go now, Marty."

"Sure."

They walked side by side to the cab, and when they got to it Marty held the door open. As Eve was starting to get in she saw his face in the bright light of a street lamp. Besides the deep acne scars, he had several odd-looking red marks. She climbed into the cab and didn't say anything.

"Like my cigarette burns?"

"Cigarette burns?"

"Yeah." Marty chuckled. "Crazy dame." He started the cab.

"A girl burned you? Deliberately?"

"Yeah."

"My heavens, why?"

"Gets her kicks that way."

"It sounds perverted to me."

"Cynthia Laslo did it. You know her. The chick from class. You just watch from now on. Every time that chick does a scene you just look at the guy and see if he doesn't have burn marks on his face. Crazy chick. Her bag is she can't act unless she mutilates you first. But Cinnie's got a lot of talent."

"I don't understand that at all."

"Everybody in the world's got needs. We all got a need for love. Some people gotta take weird trips. Cinnie's just doin' her thing, that's all."

Eve thought about Geoffrey Gripsholm and the perverted things he'd talked to her about. Was the whole world crazy? Or was she herself abnormal not to understand it all? She looked at Marty's face in the mirror. It seemed uglier than ever. How could she ever have kissed him?

She decided not to press him for any more information on Cynthia or any other subject. The fewer confidences they shared, the better. He was not the sort of person she ought to cultivate.

And yet . . . and yet she couldn't deny that when she was in his arms and kissing him she'd *liked* it. With her eyes closed, she was very attracted to Marty!

When the cab pulled up in front of her apartment, she thanked him for the ride.

"Don't mention it," he said, his fat lips twisting into a smile. "Just remember, any time you need it, you know where to come."

The cab zoomed down the street.

Chapter 3

As a beauty, one is so seldom treated as a person, a human being. Self-respect is hard to come by when one is considered a commodity. One of the major problems is one of identity; to discover who you are, feedback is needed, the honest reactions of others confronting you in human situations. However, with the beautiful woman, a man is reacting to presuppositions, and spontaneity is therefore not present.

The trap is, you never find out who you really are, because that honest interplay of reactions is not there.

The average nice guy doesn't want a beautiful woman. He's too sharp on self-knowledge, and it's his self-knowledge that tells him there would be too many ahead of him. Of course, he doesn't realize those other men, the so-called glamorous playboys, are all empty, shallow, and unable to relate in human terms. It doesn't occur to the nice guy that another human being with compassion and understanding is what the beautiful woman wants and can't find.

The phone rang, and Carrie put her pen down and answered.

"Carrie, luv," Rex said, "you know the taped audition you did over at Porter, Tailer, Gilbert and Tribble?"

"Do I ever. I've been sitting on pins and needles ever since."

"Well, it's ninety-nine per cent sure you got the job. We should know definitely tomorrow."

"Oh, Rex, I can hardly believe it. The waiting's going to blow my mind."

"Relax, honey. I'm sure we'll have a definite commitment by tomorrow."

Carrie could scarcely sleep that night.

* * *

Two days went by, and still no word.

Finally Charlene called and said, "I'm sorry, luv. The agency decided to drop the whole campaign. I know it's a big disappointment. But we'll get something else."

It would have been so perfect, Carrie thought when she'd put down the phone.

Then determination rose in her. She went back to the desk where her manuscript lay. This is what really counts, she told herself. I know I can shape it into something. I know I can.

* * *

With the tip of his tongue Rex wet his ring finger with a small quantity of saliva, and watching himself closely in the mirror, smoothed down first one eyebrow and then the other.

"Let me see you, honey!" Charlene called.

Rex, wearing tight crimson matador pants and an elaborately decorated turquoise, white, and gold bolero jacket, white silk stockings, and buckled shoes, picked up his three-cornered toreador hat and his polished sword and sashayed into Charlene's office. Warren and Kurt barked seeing him dressed so bizarrely.

"Marvelous, luv," Charlene applauded. "You'll be the hit of the party."

266

"Where's my mask? I forgot my mask." Rex sauntered back to his office to pick up his silver-sequined disguise.

"How divinely wonderful to be going to a masked ball," he said. "Dickie is simply ecstatic I've invited him to go as my guest."

Dick Getsoff, Rex's latest boy friend, was meeting him at his father's office, where Rex had a late appointment. Dr. Getsoff, a noted proctologist, was helping Rex with his hemorrhoids.

"Elliot's coming to the office," Charlene said. "Rex, you really ought to take up T'ai Chi. It would do you a world of good."

Rex let out a delicate roar. "I can just see me doing those exercises."

"It would be the best thing that ever happened to you."

Rex giggled. "Well, I'm off, honey!" he said, and waved sweetly from the door.

Alone now, Charlene straightened the desk and threw the dogs a couple of tidbits. Confronting her image in the mirror, she reassured herself that she would be looking much younger soon. Soon she'd look forty again, and then even younger. God, would that be the day for rejoicing. Reaching into the filing cabinet, she took a bottle and poured herself a shot of Jack Daniels.

Warren and Kurt pricked up their ears. There came the sound of the elevator doors parting, and a few seconds' footsteps brought Elliot Woo, wearing his all-black outfit, to the threshold of the door.

His mouth spread into a grin exposing the rows of yellow horse teeth. The eyes behind the glasses narrowed down to slits. "Hello there," he said. "Ready for your massage?"

"I thought you were going to give me acupuncture."

"Yes, but the massage comes first."

"Oh, fine."

Charlene disrobed, put on a silk kimono, and lay down on the couch.

Elliot hovered over her. "May I open the robe a bit?"

"Sure."

Perching on the edge of the couch, he began massaging the back of her neck, the shoulder blades, and the vertebrae, moving lower to the coccix and down by the rectum.

"I want you to be perfectly relaxed for the acupuncture treatment," he explained.

As his fingers deftly manipulated her flesh, working the muscles with his strong hands, Charlene moaned with pleasure. She could feel her body becoming limp and responsive under his sensual and invoking touch.

"May I remove this robe?" he asked.

"Sure."

She lay naked now, looking up at Elliot while he searched through his attaché case.

"What's that?" she asked, as he held up a long, thin device resembling a pen.

"We use this for the acupuncture."

"I thought you said it was done with needles."

"This is my own personal method. I use this special invention of my own, which is similar to the needles others use, but more effective."

Beginning with her fingertips, Elliot gently pricked her with the device. The quick nips gave a pleasurable tingling sensation. In some places tiny red marks were left on the skin, and it was in these areas, Elliot said, the treatment was most needed. Next he proceeded to the toes, followed by the back of the neck, the knees, the shoulder blades, and the back.

"There, you've had your first acupuncture session," he said. "You may dress again now."

"That was marvelous," Charlene purred, too relaxed to move from the couch.

"I'll come again next Friday," Elliot said, as Charlene slipped the robe on once again. "You'll be ready for another treatment then."

He returned the acupuncture device to his attaché case, then turned to Charlene and said, "How long since you have had sexual intercourse?"

The question took her off guard and seemed an insult. "I don't see—"

"No, no, I don't mean this in a prying way," he said. "But this may have some important bearing on our case."

"Well, I—I . . ."

"I see . . . it has been quite some time. When you were in the habit, how often did you practice, and what was the usual duration of the experience?"

"Now, just a minute, here—"

Removing his spectacles, Elliot blew on them and wiped them with his handkerchief. Without his glasses, his eyes looked small and beady. He said, "I can tell a great deal— *everything*, in fact—about a person from my knowledge of the human body. I can tell about you from what I know of your body."

"What the hell do you know about my body?"

"Everything."

"Ho ho!"

"Furthermore, I am aware of what needs to be done to repair the damage." He began to pace the office. "Your whole nervous system is out of kilter. This is what causes aging. T'ai Chi and acupuncture are both wonderful to repair the nervous system, but as an adjunct to them"—he put his index finger under the glasses and rubbed an eye—"in your case I would recommend Tantra yoga."

"What's that?"

"Tantra, the Yoga of Sex."

"Oh?" Charlene allowed her robe to slip off her shoulder and partially exposed her breasts. "Tell me."

"It's an esoteric form of sex," he said, taking a seat on the opposite end of the couch. "For centuries it has been practiced by Tibetan and Indian initiates."

"Well, what's so special about it?"

"Tantra is far different than the way sex is practiced in the West. Actually, if the truth be known, sex as practiced by most Americans does more harm than good to the nervous system. But Tantra realigns the body. It balances all the centers. It is the harmonious yin and yang, the magnetic female and the electric male forces coexisting in perfection. If more people knew and understood the principles of Tantra, the world would be peopled by youth."

"I still don't get it."

"You see," Elliot proceeded, "Western man is too aggressive and has his orgasm far too soon. The important male-female, yin-and-yang, bioelectric current has no time to be brought into play. And Western men have too many orgasms. The male only needs to have an orgasm once a month, otherwise he should conserve his fluid in order to preserve the life force within him." He smiled. "The female may have as many

269

orgasms as she pleases, as there is no fluid involved in her case."

Charlene nodded, considering his words. "It sounds interesting as hell," she said.

"I myself have no great need of orgasm," he said, and smiled again. "In the first place, I'm an old man. As I say, once a month is enough."

Charlene stared with envy at his uncanny youth.

"In Tantra the most important thing is to build up the bioelectric current. This can only be done through a slow, patient, complete togetherness, lying for the most part quietly together, the genitals united, for two hours at least."

"Two hours!"

"Certainly. A passive state is necessary for at least one hour prior to movement. This is the only way the bioelectric current can be aroused. Western sex leads to aging. The reason so many people cheat, and so many think—mistakenly— that they're oversexed, is that they never achieve true gratification in sex. Oh, yes, there is the temporary release of orgasm, but *orgasm is not enough!* People are forced to keep seeking and to perform repeated sex acts, involving a waste of energy and only partial satisfaction, because what's absent is the bioelectric current. They haven't sought the inner essence, yin-and-yang fulfillment, balance. The yin needs the yang, the yang needs the yin."

Without quite realizing it, Charlene was staring at Elliot's fly.

Seeming not to notice, he went on, "Not just anyone can perform Tantra. In the first place, it requires great staying power. Now, you take Westerners. Even when the female does reach orgasm, it is, more often than not, mechanically brought about, either through physical means or through mental concentration on erotic thought. Seldom does it derive from the experience of male-female, eternal components of the deity. In India and Tibet, vestals are brought in for the Tantra practitioner. Together, the couple offer themselves to the cosmos. Sex is practiced for the glorification of the divine principle of the universe."

"You make it sound like some kind of religion."

"Exactly! For the Tantric, sex is the highest mystical experience open to man. In this rite, untold energies from the higher realms are poured onto the practitioners. Only one who knows the secret rite can teach it to another. You must be trained, and thus the secrets are passed on from master to disciple. You see, it's not merely a matter of prolonging things; other things are involved—special positions, invocations, psychic currents, et cetera."

The robe had slipped farther off Charlene's shoulders. Her left breast was now fully visible.

Elliot said, "I'm not simply recommending you practice sex relations, understand, but this *special technique*. It would be a great help in your rejuvenation program."

Charlene said, "Where would I ever find a guy who knew all this?"

Elliot moved closer, his eyes on her bare breast. His grin was that of an engaging little boy. "I have studied this special technique with a Tibetan master," he said. "Therefore I myself give Tantra treatments. My fee is a hundred dollars a session."

He stood up and began to unbuckle his belt. He said, "Would you like to see T'ai Chi legs?"

"What the hell, it's worth a try," Charlene said, removing her robe altogether. "I thought I'd seen and done everything. Ho ho!"

Elliot stood in his shorts, his penis erect.

"But for a hundred bucks," Charlene said, "baby, you better be a damned good lay."

* * *

Marty Sachs had been on Eve's mind since they had rehearsed. Why, she did not understand. He was neurotic, ugly, Jewish, and poor, the antithesis of anyone she'd ever dreamed of wanting. Why was she thinking about him so much? Marty Sachs, darkly greasy, with pock-marked skin and pomaded black hair—why Marty?

"I think you're really very attracted to Marty, but you won't admit it," Carrie said.

"But how could that be? He's everything I don't want."

"You have an image of the kind of man you think you ought to find. Somebody wealthy and social."

Eve blushed.

"But Marty is your physical type. He turns you on."

"I don't understand why."

"Chemistry. You can't fight it. Marty is the type of guy you'd like to sleep with."

"Oh, Carrie," Eve said, looking sheepish, "I'm embarrassed to tell you this, but you see, I'm still a virgin, and—well, the trouble is, I'm not sure if it's really Marty or the fact that I'm just ignorant about *sex*."

"Well, don't you think it's time you found out?"

Eve sighed. "I always thought—used to think, that is—that if I lived up to all the stuff I'd had rammed down my throat, men would respect me for being a good girl and really want me. God, was I brainwashed!"

"You couldn't help it; it wasn't your fault."

Eve thought for a moment. "I wonder," she said. "The thing is, I really am eager to have an affair now, to make up for all the lost time. But I wonder, is Marty the one?"

"You're attracted to him."

"Am I? I mean, where does love come into it all? Am I in love with Marty?"

"Do you know what love is?"

"I guess not. I guess I'm going to have to expose myself to life more to find out. But the thing is"—she screwed up her face—"I keep thinking if only I didn't have to look at Marty in the light. Does that sound stupid? I feel embarrassed. I don't know, there's something about his appearance—and also about his being lower class. And of course, his voice. Well, he could always work on that, I suppose, like I worked on my voice. He could lose his accent. And he could have his pockmarks sanded, couldn't he?"

"Sure," Carrie said.

Eve sighed again. "You know," she said, "I think I will. I think I will lose my virginity with Marty Sachs."

Chapter 4

The phones had stopped ringing, and Rex was taking a breather. He called up the Brick Shed House to order some new nylon net bikini underdrawers, then applied colorless lacquer to his toenails while he dreamed of the cruising he was going to do as soon as the day ended. Ever since the raid on his favorite steam bath a few weeks ago, when his name had been put in the police files, he'd had to play it cool, but now, horny for new action, he felt he'd waited and been discreet long enough.

On his way to the john he encountered Charlene. She said, "Valerie du Charme just called. She just never gets wise. If she'd at least consider going housewife—"

"Sure," Rex said, "look at Lucille Granger. Made the switch and got an Anacin commercial."

"Lucille's going to make twenty thousand on that Anacin. I'm always delighted when anyone gets a pharmaceutical. By the way, honey, aren't those pants too tight?"

"No."

"They show *everything*."

"That's the way I like it," Rex retorted, and breezed past her into the john. Bitch! Who the hell did she think she was, telling him how to dress and what part of his anatomy to show—as if it were morally wrong, or something, as if he *ought* to hide his treasures and ruin his chances for sex.

But when Rex lowered his gaze to his fly, something caught his attention—it did look like there was a bigger bulge than usual. And yet he did not have an erection. Hurriedly he unzipped his fly.

"Gloryoski!" he exclaimed. "My bird is all swollen up! It's twice as big as normal!"

Worried, he rushed to Charlene's office. "My bird is twice as big as normal!"

"That should make you happy."

"But it's *soft*."

"How the hell did that happen?"

"Don't be funny, this is serious!" Agitated, Rex reached for the phone. "I'll have to see a doctor immediately!"

The next day Rex's penis was down to its customary size, but his testicles had swollen. The doctor told him he had a rare disease known as blue balls. A day later, in order to recuperate, he left town for a vacation at a gay hotel in Puerto Rico.

*   *   *

Traffic whizzed past, but Eve was aware only of the back of Marty Sachs's head. Nervously she stared at the incisions and red holes on his neck where large pustules had once been.

Her legs shook as she stepped onto the pavement. She couldn't bring herself to look at Marty now. A whole terrain of an unexplored frontier stretched before her, waiting to unfold itself to her trembling lips and arms and legs and breasts and hips and belly, her insides, all of her, and how she had waited for this, how ready she was, but how frightened.

"Your apartment is very nice," she said when they got inside. "I didn't tell you last time."

Marty said nothing. She wished they could hold an enlightened and meaningful conversation, but felt at a loss for words, and unsure what she wanted to converse *about*. Feeling foolish, she asked, "Do you know your lines?"

Marty took off his jacket, threw it on a chair, and nodded.

"How come you wear that leather jacket all the time?" Eve asked, and the minute it was out, realized how stupid it sounded. Quickly she tried to cover. "I think I know all my lines, and I've got a good thing I'm using, an emotion memory—you see—"

"Would you like anything to drink?" Marty said. "Coke or anything? I have some Scotch."

"Yes," Eve said. "That would be nice. I'd like a Scotch." She sat down. Her stomach was a mess. Why couldn't she relax? Well, it wasn't every day a girl set about to shed her virginity. She supposed it was all to be expected; but it seemed so appallingly abnormal, really, to go to a man's apartment deliberately intending to be seduced, but not telling *him* anything that was going through your head, and just sitting there and waiting.

The icy glass Marty handed her froze her fingers. Uncomfortable, still trying to become more at ease, she asked, "Do you like New York?"

"Yeah. It really *kvells*."

She took another gulp of her drink. Oughtn't she to know a little something about Marty . . . so they'd be less strangers when they ultimately got into bed together? "Tell me something about yourself, Marty," she said.

"Not much to tell. I'm twenty-five, born in the Bronx, divorced—"

"You're divorced? I didn't know you'd ever been married."

"Yeah, I was. I been divorced three years now."

"Do you miss it? Marriage, I mean? Or her?"

Marty took a slug of the Scotch he was drinking straight, and paused thoughtfully. "No, I don't miss *her* or being married," he said after a moment. "The only thing I miss is my kid."

"Well, don't you ever see your child?"

"My kid's dead," he said.

Eve heard herself gasp.

"That was the main reason for the breakdown I had in class that time. Remember? When I fell apart? Man!"

"I'm sorry."

He picked at his cuticle. "That's the way the matzo ball bounces," he said, draining the last of his drink. "Wanna start?"

Eve went over to the bed, preparing to get under the covers.

"You gonna play the scene like that, or what?"

"Like what?"

"Like with dress, jewelry, shoes, stockings, girdle, bra—all that crap on? When we do it in class, I mean."

"Oh, no; I guess I'll wear a bathrobe."

"Honey, this chick'd never be caught dead in a bathrobe."

"What do you think I should wear, then?"

"A slip."

"Okay, if you think so."

"Might as well get the feel of it. Let's rehearse it the way we're gonna do it."

He turned his back to begin his preparation. Eve felt embarrassed but reminded herself Marty was not looking at her. Hurriedly she removed her clothes, watching Marty's back out of the corner of her eye, and then quickly dove into the bed, wearing only the new underwear she had bought expressly for the occasion. She wondered if he would appreciate all the trouble she'd gone to.

Then the scene began, and all during the dialogue, she could think of one thing only: what was ahead of her. She hoped Marty didn't notice her nervousness.

The moment had arrived; Marty kissed her. She felt the weight of his body, the strength of his arms; their kisses became prolonged and deep; she tasted his thick lips, and was aware of a warm smell in the room. The lights were blazing. She closed her eyes. She did not want to spoil things by seeing Marty's face.

His hand explored her body. Part of her enjoyed what was happening, but the other part was fearful. She drew her breath in sharply as she felt him pressing against her. His urgency to enter frightened her. He seemed so enormous.

"You're dry as a squeezed lemon," he said.

Suppose she were too small to accommodate him? Suppose he ruptured her and caused an internal injury? Suppose he got stuck inside her and couldn't get out? She had heard a story about a couple on their wedding night where the man had gotten stuck inside the woman, they'd had to call an ambulance, and both had died in the hospital.

Though shaking with fear, she knew she must go through with this. She had waited so long to be a woman.

"Relax; you're stiff."

"I—I'm sorry . . ."

"Maybe I oughta get some Vaseline."

"Vaseline? What for?"

"You're pretty tense. Not much lubrication to speak of."

"Oh, oh, I'm really sorry, I—"

"If you'd just relax it'd be a helluva lot easier."

"I'll try—I—"

"Wait, I'll go down on you. That'll help you loosen up."

Minutes later Eve's stiffness melted as her legs and torso intertwined with Marty's head and shoulders and she lost herself in the most delirious and exquisite sensations she had ever believed her body could feel.

She was ready for Marty on any terms now.

*   *   *

"Hey," Marty said later, gazing at her tenderly.

She could look at him now and take no mind of his pockmarks. She was conscious only of the light in his eyes, and of the gentle curve of his mouth. Somehow she thought of her mother and father. She had always wondered why her mother had chosen such a crude type of man to marry. Now, lying in Marty's arms, she understood.

"It'll get better." He caressed her softly, kissed her neck, her ears, her eyes. "You were a little stiff. We don't know each other well enough yet—but it's going to be great—you'll see."

How warm and cozy it was to lie in his arms, their fingers entwined after the intimacy they had shared. How wondrous to feel his breath close. To be a part of that body that moved with such suppleness, to feel his heartbeat and sense the rhythm of his chest moving up and down. How beautiful to touch his skin and feel the hairiness of his chest, to find a resting place for her head between his shoulders and neck. How lovely to fit together with someone! Finally!

It was everything she had expected . . . and more. She was glad she had chosen Marty. There was something about him—was it his loneliness, the pain of his loss?—that made him sweet and loving. He stood apart from the other men she had met.

And yet, with the newness added to her life, something had left her—too. What was it, this bittersweet sad nostalgia she felt? She thought of her parents again. Once, when they were young, like she was now, they had conceived her. She had started out as a little tiny speck, became a full-blown baby, and had grown to this moment leaving all that had been, behind. But what of those past moments that had created what she was today? It was sad to think that all that had receded and lived only in her memory. And one day this too would be a memory.

She looked at Marty. He was sleeping peacefully, smiling. She smiled too, and an instant later fell asleep.

Chapter 5

Rex had left the letter lying in the middle of his desk.

Dear Rex,

I stopped up at the agency today again, admittedly to see you. You say nothing has changed, but I must disagree violently, because much has changed.

You know I love you because of what you are, who you are, and all the things which combine to make you Rex Ryan. It just so happens that the more I see you, the more I love you. My love has not changed; it has grown. And if you wonder why I feel as though I must emphasize this point so strongly, it is because of the change in you. Since your return from Puerto Rico you have become acutely aware of certain aspects of your sexual behavior even where you feel you must impress it on my poor ignorant mind. I knew you were gay before I knew your name was Rex. That was the reason I agreed to meet you in a gay bar. The facts remain I have been your friend, your lover, I have confided in you constantly, cried on your shoulder and loved you through it all more than words could ever express. Now I've met another side of you that I love even more, and you are scared. You say you know what you are. Well, bully bully for you, so do I and I don't give a damn. As far as I'm concerned, the differences between homosexual and heterosexual are just about as extensive as those between the men's and ladies' rest room. Some law says there must be two rest rooms, but the only difference is the signs on the doors. Inside they are the same. Heterosexuals do not enjoy normal sex relations. Homosexuals can and do derive sexual satisfaction, and thereby hangs the tale. Of course so many so-called heteros do something to themselves, but I guess that doesn't count, huh? Anyway, I fail to see your logic, and I don't think it even matters. Why are you afraid of love? What makes you so self-conscious? It would almost seem that you are ashamed to love me. I only ask one thing of you. Give me a little credit, will you? I'm not a child, I know about life. Don't push me away; that, I cannot bear. And I don't believe it anyway, even though it is just the balm you need to salve your guilty conscience. You are such a wonderful man with so much love to give, it's almost selfish of you to keep it all inside. I only want to avoid the tension I could feel in the air. I want to see your face shining and your eyes aglow when you look at me. Do you realize that until last Wednesday, a kiss was as normal as a song, and then you refused to kiss me? If it is not fear or guilt or self-consciousness or a combination of all three, then you tell me what has changed between us?

ORATOR

Charlene felt creepy as she read the letter. All these years of closeness to Rex, working with him, his deviation was something she had taken for granted. But now, this somehow gave the deviation a new reality, almost an intimacy. Charlene felt herself shudder.

Rex had a right to his tastes. But he had no right to parade them, to involve people who didn't share them. He should keep his gay friends and their letters to himself.

A phone button lighted. Charlene picked up the phone on Rex's desk and said, "Hello. . . . Oh, yes, Larry, how are you?" It was Larry Reed, one of the vice presidents over at Hinsdale, Kingsland, Tager and Smith.

"Charlene, for the love of God, don't send me any more of those *faggots!*"

"Faggots? What faggots? I never send fags."

"Well, who sent them, then?"

Rex again; damn him. Damn him and his fucking faggots.

279

"I'm sorry, Larry," Charlene said. "It must have been a mistake."

"No more faggots! Don't send me any more of those *faggots!*"

Charlene wondered about her partner, about how she had mothered him; what kind of a monster had she created?

Wearily Charlene picked up the phone again. No word from Polly van den Heuvel of Ackerman and Bruce for more than three weeks now. That was strange. She'd have to check on it.

"Charlene, my dear," Polly's frigid stilted voice came. "But, of course you must know why I haven't phoned. When I specified I wished to see no more than three girls for an assignment, you sent me twelve."

Rex again. Damn his boo-boos.

Charlene went to her filing cabinet and poured herself a shot. She had just drained her cup when Carrie appeared at the door.

"Hi, honey," Charlene said. "There's a fellow who's left a couple of messages for you. Jerry Jackson."

"Oh, yes," Carrie said. "He's been calling me at home too."

"I trust it's *not* business."

"I trust."

"What have you been up to? Anything interesting?"

"Posing for Roger Flournoy. Remember meeting him at that crazy voodoo party? He didn't forget he wanted to paint me. We've had one session."

"That old lech."

"Aren't they all."

"Flournoy especially. Has he given you any trouble?"

"Not so far. He's quite a treat, actually. Talked about the literary scene of his day. He's alert and charming, with a lively memory, and quite a gift for anecdote."

"How's the writing coming?"

"Fine. I'm getting more and more done. Sometimes it's hard to find the time; then a quiet period comes, and I get a large block accomplished."

"Just keep plugging away, luv," Charlene said.

*   *   *

Somehow Charlene could not get that letter out of her mind. It bothered her all day long. She shouldn't have told Rex to go on ahead and take that steam. He should be working, helping her. It had been a bitch of a day, and she was in a bitch of a mood—a mood for fireworks.

When Rex finally got back to the office, it was with Bradford Schwartz, his latest affair. "I've got to talk to you, Rex," Charlene said.

Sensing her upset, Rex asked Brad to mind the dogs. Then he said to Charlene, "You and I'll have a little pick-me-up at Walgreen's, honey."

"Don't you ever take *anybody* anywhere decent?" Charlene snapped. "Woolworth's, Walgreen's, Rexall—"

"All right, all right. We'll go somewhere else."

"It's not so far from dinner, after all . . ."

"You want dinner?" Rex glanced at his watch. "It's five-thirty. We'll go to Hector's Cafeteria. They have a special on."

*   *   *

"Look, Rex," Charlene said, "you've got to watch it. If you had your way, God only knows what would happen to the agency." They sat over beef Stroganoff at Hector's. "First of all, I haven't forgotten such boo-boos as your wanting to send Barbara Longworth the money when she said her husband was sick—if the License Bureau had heard about that one, we'd have lost our double A rating. I saved your neck that time. Now, recently you've been going overboard, sending a whole troupe of girls to Polly van den Heuvel when she asked for only three—"

"I'm sick of that bitch."

"We both know you have to cater to Polly, but the way you've been handling things with her, we've been losing her business. Then, Rex," Charlene glanced from her lemon chiffon pie to Rex, "there's the matter of the fags."

Rex frowned, annoyed.

"The minute one of those fag friends of yours walks in, he's dead. You ought to know that by now. I'm sick of having to compensate for your mistakes, making excuses for you and bailing you out of trouble, *and*," Charlene cut her pie with venom, "I'm sick of your goddam cheapness too. You

281

ought to be ashamed of yourself, Rex. What would your mother say if she could see you?"

"Don't bring my mother into this," Rex flared. "I'm old enough to do as I please. Who the hell do you think you are, telling me things and ordering me around? I'm Rex Ryan!"

"Bully for you, God the Father."

"Shut up, Charlene! Shut up, or you'll be sorry."

"I will not shut up. I've stood for this long enough. It's thanks to me the agency runs at all. I've had enough of your childishness, your irresponsibility, enough of your goddamn cheapness, and enough of worrying about you, little boy."

"Quit bum-tripping me, I don't need this."

"You send those boys because you want to *make out*. It's ridiculous. No one's going to hire them. You're risking our reputation. I've put too much effort into this agency to have you ruin things just because of your lousy sex life."

"You cunt! You're jealous! You're jealous because you're an old bitch, because your cunt is old and shriveled and you couldn't get a lay if you gave it away. Don't talk to me about *my* sex life, you old cunt, you're just jealous because you have to pay for it."

Charlene's eyes blazed. "You lousy—"

"You think you can take over my life. Well, I'm sick of it, I don't need any more mothers. Just leave me alone."

"Without me, you'd be nowhere, you faggot."

"Damn you—"

"Faggot! Faggot! Goddamn fag—"

"Shut up, you cunt! I'm warning you—"

"Fag! Fag! Fag!"

"Shut up!" Rex picked up his table knife and pointed it at Charlene. "And I mean it this time, you goddamn cunt!"

"Are you out of your mind? Have you gone totally crazy?" Half from genuine fear, half acting, Charlene covered her mouth and began to whimper in a loud voice. Patrons of Hector's were staring.

"You take back what you said," Rex said, still pointing the knife. "Take it back, or you'll be sorry."

"Help! Help! He's gone crazy! He's having a spell! Oh, Rex, your mother was always worried sick over your spells! Help! Someone, please help!"

"Now you're gonna get it, bitch!" Rex lunged across the table.

Before he could reach her, a man from behind caught him around the shoulders and restrained him. Charlene was still whimpering.

"Oh, thank you. Thank you for saving my life!" she exclaimed. She gathered her belongings hastily, anxious to escape.

Rex, red with fury, still pinned, screamed after her, "I don't *ever* want to set eyes on you again, you cunt. Stay out of my way, or I'll kill you!"

* * *

Chapter 6

The large studio was covered with mirrors from floor to ceiling. The sounds of "Meditation" from *Thais* came softly from the stereo speakers. Roger Flournoy emitted strange noises while he sketched, wheezing, coughing, clearing his throat periodically, and saying hmmm, hmmm every few seconds. He was wearing an old tweed jacket with an open shirt and V-neck sweater.

Intent on his work, he squinted alternately at Carrie and at the portrait of her he was painting.

Finally he exclaimed, "Aha!" and seemed to relax. "I've found the groove I was seeking," he said.

From then on, he was garrulous, recounting anecdotes dating back half a century.

* * *

"And then there was the time I met James Joyce," Roger said.

"How marvelous," Carrie said. "That must have been fascinating."

"I remember very little about the occasion because at the time I was in love with a beautiful Iranian girl. Hmm hmmm. Can you tilt your head up? . . . Yes, fine. . . . Hmm hmmm."

Suddenly Roger's eyes seemed to narrow as if he were seeing her born anew before his eyes. He was silent, staring at her from underneath the multi-wrinkled, hooded lids. He scratched his freckled, bald scalp and lit a Phillip Morris. His hand was unsteady. "That's all I'll do today," he said.

Walking Carrie to the door, an odd look came into his eyes as he put his quaking hand on her shoulder. "Hmmm, hmmm," he repeated over and over staring at her with patronizing amusement. "You do have a beautiful face. Beautiful eyes, beautiful. Yes, yes, yes. A beautiful girl. Hmm hmmm."

It wasn't the artist in him speaking, Carrie reflected, but the lecher of forty years ago, who wrote the dirty books.

Then he moved in closer and took her face into his hands. Poor man, Carrie thought, he's old now. I can't refuse him this. It would be too cruel not to kiss him. She would be charitable.

The whole time he wheezed and said "Hmmm, hmmm," and she thought, poor Roger. It was as if they were spanning decades reaching into the shadows and dust of the past; reaching through yellowed book pages and pressed flowers and coffee-stained doilies, and it was sad, she thought, that wizened figure caved in in the middle, the way skinny men got when they were really old and shriveled, his skin like a mummy, bony hands shaking from trying to clasp her tight while he wheezed away and muttered hmmm, hmmm.

It made her think of the end of life, and how silly great lovers became as it drew near. She was glad the portrait was almost finished.

*   *   *

Charlene tried to turn over on her side and felt the stabbing pain under her right breast. Goddamned liver! And here she lay in the bloody hospital, jaundiced and miserable. Cirrhosis. Shit!

284

The phone rang.

"Hey, Charlene!" It was Dolores.

"How's the expectant mother?"

"The hell with me; I'm fine. You're the sick one. What happened to you?"

"It's my blasted liver. My feet are all swollen; I'm waterlogged; my liver is huge. It was those damned eggs, honey; I never should have eaten those eggs."

"What eggs?"

"Leslie took me for brunch, and like an idiot, I ordered eggs Benedict. It was a damned fool thing to do. I knew bloody well it would cause a cholesterol disturbance. My damned liver can't take that kind of thing. Now I'm all jaundiced."

"What do the doctors tell you?"

"All sorts of crap. Like my sgpt and sgot enzyme tests are highly elevated and shit like that."

"Well, honey, shouldn't you be going easy on the booze?"

"Are you kidding? They tell me if I keep on, I'll die. But I figure I'm going to die anyway, so what the hell."

"When are you getting out of the hospital?"

"Don't I wish tomorrow. But I guess it may be a few weeks till they get me dried out. You should see what a mess I am. But at least it brought Rex and me back together again."

"Oh?"

"We had one of our annual blowups. But he called, and we patched things up."

"Nothing serious, I hope."

"No. Just the usual. It happens once a year, and we always make up."

"Good, I'd hate to see you two break up."

"How about you, luv? What's new?"

"Getting along fine. Wish I didn't have to carry this load around. What a drag. But after this kid is born, I'll really be ready to move. Wait till you see, Charlene."

"I'll be looking forward to seeing you, honey," Charlene said, and feeling the pain knife through her again, placed the receiver back on the hook.

*   *   *

Eve was busier than ever, what with interviews, the game show, continual parties, and, of course, her love affair with Marty Sachs. In addition, there were her acting classes, and there was the T'ai Chi Ch'uan, at which Marty scoffed. He said it wasn't T'ai Chi but a steady diet of sex that was making her feel so vital—so much better than she'd ever felt before. But she believed Elliot Woo, who told her the T'ai Chi exercises were responsible for how good she felt and assured her that if she practiced faithfully every day, her nervous system would soon be perfect and would stay that way for the rest of her life.

One Tuesday Elliot took her around the corner for a Chinese dinner after the lesson.

"There is absolutely no need for aging," he said, glancing up from the menu. "None whatsoever. I only wish I had discovered this sooner. I was fifty-eight when I came to T'ai Chi, but I just keep getting younger and younger as a result of constant practice."

"I simply can't believe you're practically seventy," Eve said.

Elliot's big yellow horse teeth protruded as he opened his thick lips into a wide grin. "Do you like Foo Chow Egg Roll?" he asked.

"I don't know."

"We'll try it. I think you'll like it."

"All right."

The waiter arrived, and Elliot ordered. Then he leaned his elbows on the table and said, "You've told me you were once quite overweight. I can see the residual effects of that. It's still in your nervous system, the tendency to obesity."

"Oh, I hope not," Eve said. "Why do you think so?"

His glasses had slipped down his nose. "The body has no secrets from my eyes. I can tell everything about a person from the way he moves." He pushed his glasses up and smiled broadly. "But no need to worry; we will rid you of the tendency."

"How long will it take?"

"The yin and yang have to be completely balanced. Once that has taken place in the body, there will be no further inclination. In studying your case, I've given considerable attention to—"

"Yes?" Eve asked eagerly.

The egg rolls arrived. Elliot waited until the waiter had gone before he spoke again. "May I ask you a few personal questions?"

"Sure," Eve said, worried by the confidential tone and thoughtful frown Elliot had assumed.

"Do you have a boy friend?"

Eve blushed and nodded.

"And do you have sexual relations with this man?"

Her blush deepened. "Yes."

Ignoring the egg roll steaming in front of him, Elliot raised his head to the ceiling and pursed his lips thoughtfully. Then he looked back at Eve. "I think what you need is Tantra yoga," he said.

"Tantra yoga—what's that?"

"A special kind of sex yoga, employing a technique known only to the privileged few who've been initiated into the inner circle."

"I don't understand," Eve said.

Elliot's glasses had slipped once more. He took them off, blew on them, and rubbed them with his napkin. "Tantra is a way of balancing the body. It achieves harmony in the nervous system by balancing the yin and yang of the organism."

"I thought T'ai Chi was supposed to do that."

"True, true," Elliot said. "But what we're interested in are the fastest possible results, and this special technique would be an *adjunct* to T'ai Chi." He placed his glasses back on his nose and leaned forward. "Tantra is much different than ordinary sexual intercourse as practiced by the average Westerner," he said. "If the truth were told, the sex practices of most Westerners are harmful."

"Harmful?" Eve said, alarmed.

"That's right. Ordinary sexual intercourse can be exceedingly bad for the nervous system."

He finished his egg roll and wiped his mouth. "But the Tantra method would be the ideal all-around thing both in terms of health and also to lick your weight problem for good. I can see your body needs this special treatment."

Eve blushed again.

"You needn't be embarrassed. It's a very natural and healthy thing we're discussing. Western man marks sex with either prudery or licentiousness, both equally wrong concepts. But for the Tantric, sex is purely a health and religious practice. It is holy. A Tantra initiate studies for years with a master before he is ready to perform the Rite of the Five True Things."

"What's that?"

"I can't reveal the inner secrets." Elliot waved her question aside. "But suffice it to say, one of these is the *esoteric* way of performing coitus."

Eve poked at her food and considered. She said, "Of course I'm interested in getting my body aligned and my nervous system in shape, in order to control my weight and stay young and healthy. But if this special technique is so unusual, I suppose not very many people would know about it, would they?"

"No, they wouldn't."

"Then I guess it would be pretty hard to find anyone who—who knew how to—do it?"

"Oh, not so hard as you think." Elliot glanced around a bit furtively, then leaned across the table, and looking Eve directly in the eye, declared, "In fact, I myself give Tantra treatments."

* * *

There is so much material comfort, yet such a shortage of real homes. This is a woman's role, as the center of the home, the supporter and life-giver, spreading love, nurturing; she is the center, and from her womb and breast emanate the strength, the tenderness, and the sympathy that enable men and children to be stable and productive.

Few women in this day and age have begun to tap their resources. It is not an easy thing to do with circumstances as they are.

It's interesting to think that before the supremacy of the Olympian gods, motherlike figures were the supreme deities. Woman was the authority, lawgiver, and ruler in family and society. Then men subdued them, giving women the minor role, and women, always peaceable, accepted.

But look at the difference in the characteristics of the two types of society, matriarchal and patriarchal. Under matriarchal rule, what counts are ties of blood, reverence for life, equality; the aim of life is known to be the happiness of all men. Peace, unity, love, these principles prevail. It is under the matriarchal system the idea of the universal brotherhood of man develops, and a characteristic of all matriarchal societies is harmony.

Under the patriarchal system man-made law rules; man tries to change the natural order of things; there is competition, hierarchy, restrictions.

Clearly, higher ideals are expressed under the matriarchal system. If we could embody these matriarchal principles in our present society, life would be more worthwhile. It has to happen if we are to progress to a more civilized way of living, find harmony in our male-female relationships, and achieve inner happiness and growth.

Carrie interrupted her work to answer the phone.

"Come on over for a drink."

It was the fourth time Roger Flournoy had called since finishing the portrait.

"I'm sorry," Carrie told him, "but I've been working on my book. I'm in a good work period now—I've done from two to five hours every day this week."

"You need a respite."

"I wouldn't want to break the continuity."

"All work and no play makes Jack."

"I should think you'd understand, Roger. After all, you wrote books too."

"That's different," he said. She could hear him sneering over the connection. "You're a beautiful girl. The world deserves you."

Meaning him, Carrie thought. "I'm sorry, Roger," she said, hung up abruptly, and returned to her writing.

Chapter 7

"Eve? Eve Paradise?" The voice on the phone was strident, insolent.

"Yes . . . This is me, but who—"

"Hi, honey, how've ya been?"

"Fine." Though she strained, Eve couldn't place the voice.

"That's good. What's been happening? What've you been up to?"

She hesitated. "Uh—who is this?"

"Come on, don't give me that."

"I'm sorry; I can't place your voice."

"Don't act so sore. It's Hy."

"Hy? Hy who? Oh—oh, you mean—"

"Yeah. Hy Rubens. How's that for memory. I oughta hang up right now."

Guiltily Eve said, "I'm sorry, Hy. It's just that I haven't heard from you in so long. I thought you were going to call me before this."

"I lost your number. I just found it again. It was in the pocket of a suit I haven't worn in a long time. What're ya doin'?"

"Well, I—you mean, right now?"

"Yeah."

"I—I was just washing out some underwear."

"Oh, yeah? Sounds like a ball. Listen, honey, I'm just in from the Coast I'm at the airport. Why don't you stop by my suite at the Plaza in about an hour?"

"It's a little late." Eve said.

"Naw. It's only nine."

"Yes. but by the time you get in it will be ten."

"The night'll just be beginning."

"That's awfully late for me."

"Okay, if that's the way you wanna be about it. I was gonna talk about your career with you."

"Well, I'd love to some other time—"

"Okay. Meet me for cocktails at my suite tomorrow after you get off from work. Give me a blast first."

*   *   *

The door was ajar.

"Come on in, baby!" Hy called from the desk where he sat talking on the phone and jotting things down on a pad. "You're looking great, honey," he said; then he turned to speak into the telephone again.

Eve hesitated in the doorway till he motioned her to a couch.

"I spoke to Bernie on that deal just two days ago, Marvin," Hy was saying. "You know of course he's in London. We had a bad connection, but . . ."

She could see Hy shift his eyes sideways to get a view of her legs.

". . . the trouble is they wanna set the budget at five million, and as I was telling Bernie last week, that's sheer idiocy. They're making a big mistake having Henry direct. Bernie could save himself a lot of trouble if he'd listen to me."

Something about Hy's appearance bothered Eve: she recoiled at the sight of his navy suede shoes on the top of the desk, of his ostentatious gold cufflinks and pinky diamond, the Jay Sebring haircut, and the striped high white-collared shirt that fit his body so tightly she could see the outline of the hair on his chest underneath. The way he leaned and turned in the swivel chair and his loud deliberate talk made her uncomfortable. She wished he wouldn't try so hard to seem important.

He finished his call and placed the phone on the hook. Eve expected him to rise and greet her. Instead, he picked up a pile of papers, shifted them to another pile, jotted something down on his pad, lit a cigarette—and picked up the phone again. "Hey, would you be a real doll and get me a glass of water, honey?" His hand was over the mouthpiece. "Oh, yeah, operator, get me Mr. Abramson in Beverly Hills. CR 2-4699."

Eve returned from the bathroom with a glass of water, and

Hy, accepting it, deigned to offer her a condescending smile. "You're looking really terrific, honey, I mean it." He took his hand off the mouthpiece.

"What? Oh, he's not? Okay, tell the Beverly Hills operator to have him call me here. I'm staying at the Plaza."

Hy rose, went to the bar, and poured some Scotch into a glass. "How about a drink?"

"No, thank you." Eve met his hard, calculating gaze, and averted her eyes.

He moved into the bedroom, and she heard him calling room service for some ice. She wondered how she could broach the subject of publicity, since that was the purpose of her visit, and he hadn't mentioned it yet.

"Hey, baby," he called from the bedroom.

"Yes?"

"I'm *lonesome* in here alone. Come keep me company."

Eve hovered in the doorway. "When you phoned yesterday you mentioned you wanted to discuss my career," she said. "Last time I remember you mentioned you had ideas for layouts in gossip columns and things."

Hy, propped up in bed sipping his iceless drink, his palms rubbing the glass, did not reply to her question nor did he take his gaze off her. His eyes narrowed when he finally spoke. "Do you know a photographer by the name of Bert Klinger?"

"No."

"He's only the greatest photographer in the city."

Again, silence fell, and Eve was uneasy with his beady eyes climbing all over her body. "I thought you had a call to make," she said pointedly.

"I'm waiting for the line. The desk will ring." His eyes continued to bore into her, until finally she said, "Hy, if you don't care to discuss the matter I came to see you about, I'd better be going."

"You're cute when you get mad."

"I'm not mad, but you said—"

"Don't get so huffy. I'm only trying to find out what you're like."

She studied him curiously. "What difference does that make? You talked to me before, and—"

"I want to *really* know you—"

"But . . . I mean—well, why?"

"I like to feel I know a person before I work for him. Your reactions to me are very important. I have to feel there's a *rapport* between us if I'm going to help you." He flashed her an oily smile; then he reached for the phone, and without removing his insolent eyes from her body, he asked the operator to get Bert Klinger's number for him.

"Bert? Hy. Got a great little girl here for you. Remember, I promised I'd return the favor? . . . Yeah. Groovy kid, wild body. You could pitch for *Playboy* or *Cavalier*. Shall I send her over tomorrow? . . . What time?" He turned to Eve. "Four okay for you, honey? She says fine, Bert. She'll be there. . . . Don't mention it, you know I always think of you."

With a satisfied look on his face Hy replaced the receiver on the hook. "How's that for fast action, honey?" he asked smugly. "Never let it be said that Hy Rubens isn't a man of his word. Don't tell me this isn't the quickest action you've ever had, honey, 'cause I know better. Am I right, or am I right?"

Eve nodded halfheartedly, feeling partly grateful to Hy, and partly annoyed at him because he might be overestimating the importance of his contribution.

"So you see," he said, "already I'm working for you, and you aren't paying me a cent. Do you know how much my clients have to pay for a service like that? I don't think you could exactly afford to put me on a weekly retainer, could you?" He peered closely at her. "You've got a great body. Great tits. Your legs are fine, and you have a small waistline. Are you wearing a girdle?"

"Yes."

"Jesus Christ—go in and take it off."

"I—I really, I think—"

"Oh, stop being so goddamn puritan. I'm not going to attack you. I want to see what kind of a line you can get without the girdle."

She reappeared a few minutes later.

"Now stand ass-backwards with your hands on your hips, turn around, and face me. Hike up your skirt a bit. . . . That's it. Yeah, great, baby, wild. Think we can work out a *Playboy* bit with Bert, but I'll have to come up with some copy. Come over here." He motioned with an arm.

She didn't like the way he was staring at her. It gave her the jitters.

"What for?"

"I said come *here.*"

"But why?"

"I want to look at you close up to get a better idea of what to do with 'you."

Against her better judgment, she approached.

His fingers moved to her leg and lifted her skirt. Eve jumped.

"What the hell ya so nervous about? I was just trying to get a better idea—to see what kind of a picture layout we'll do."

Temporarily satisfied with the peek, he stood up. She moved away. Then, before she knew what was happening, he was in front of her, his arms were around her, and his breath was hot against her ear.

"Please, Hy," she begged, trying to pull loose. "I didn't come here for this."

His hoarse words bellowed against her skull. "I don't want to ball you, I just want to hold you. I want to feel close to you. I have a great need for affection."

"I—I really have to go now, Hy. I have another appointment." Eve wriggled helplessly.

"No, no, you can't go." His grip tightened. "Look, I just wanna hold you for a few minutes. What the hell's the harm in that? The least you can do for me's to show me a little affection after I've promised to help you with your career and start the ball rolling and all." He was inching her toward the bed.

"Hey!" All of a sudden she was on the bed and he was on top of her. "No, no!" she cried, smothered under his hot massive frame. "I told you I couldn't—"

"You don't have to do anything, baby. Just let me feel you and play with you and be near you. I don't care if you don't want to fuck me."

"My God!" Vainly she tried to raise herself to a sitting position. Feeling his hand rising up the smoothness of her thigh, she drew in her breath sharply. She reached for his face and pushed it away, her hands clutching at him and pounding his neck and shoulders.

"Wildcat!" he hissed. "Bitch! You wanna be raped. That's the way you like it, isn't it?"

"Let me go! Let me go!" She struggled with her legs and teeth and fists, but his hand had found the top of her underpants, and now, with a rough jerk, he ripped them off. Her skirt was around her shoulders.

She could see him fumbling with the zipper of his fly as she managed to twist free. Gasping for breath, she rolled away from him, and fell on the floor. She pulled herself to her feet, to find him standing in front of her, reaching toward her with an imploring look on his face. "Baby," he whispered, "don't fight it. It's bigger than both of us—"

Just then the telephone rang.

Hy reached for it and Eve heard him ask how the weather was in Los Angeles. Her head was dizzy and swollen. As quickly as she could she gathered her possessions together, missing her underpants, but scarcely giving the matter a second thought in her rush to escape.

Stumbling into the hallway, she heard Hy's voice calling after her, "Hey, wait a minute—come on back—" but she ran as fast as her legs would take her, rounded a corner, and made a beeline to the elevator without looking back.

Chapter 8

Charlene looked up from her desk. The door to the office formerly belonging to Liz Webster and now occupied by a woman named Martita Strong was closed.

It was all Rex's doing hiring that woman; if only she'd gotten out of the hospital two days sooner she could have been there to put her foot down; now it was too late, the forty-fivish equine-faced lesbian was installed. One look at the woman told Charlene she was poison; she resented her overbearing manner and mannish clothes, and couldn't imagine why Rex was on such friendly terms with her. "What's with this les you've gone and put in the photography department?" Charlene had demanded her first day back from the hospital.

"What do you mean, what's *with* her?" Rex had said.

"Where'd you find her; an ad in the Los Angeles *Free Press?*"

Rex looked annoyed. "Martita's a good worker," he said. "You know we needed someone to run the department. Good people are hard to find."

"Well, keep her in her own territory," Charlene warned. "If she gets underfoot, she's in for trouble. I don't like her."

Nothing had seemed quite the same since her discharge from the hospital.

And now Rex, just returned from the dentist, looked strange. Charlene wasn't sure it was merely the dentist that made his face appear unfamiliar. Ever since that Martita had come, he had seemed changed—different-looking, different in behavior and actions.

"Mrs. Daniels stopped by again," Charlene said, trying to establish the old bond of complicity in gossiping with Rex. "Wants to know why isn't Lois getting more commercials. If it isn't the mother, it's the boy friend."

Rex looked absent a moment; then he said, "You mean the hood?"

"Yes, he's really a terribly nice fellow, so mild-mannered and courteous. You'd never think he was a top gangster. Now the mother, there's something else again! You know Mrs. Daniels, luv."

"I can't exactly place her," Rex said.

"Pale mink, pale hair, flashy jewelry. He really takes care of that dame. The three of them live together, you know."

Charlene bit into the hot dog she had just had sent up from the drugstore, and made a face. "There's something wrong with this frankfurter," she said. "I'd better give it to Warren. He loves 'em, no matter what, mustard and all."

Rex looked toward Martita's office.

Charlene said, "Business has been swinging while you were gone: calls from J. Walter Thompson, Compton, Benton and Bowles, Warwick and Legler, SSC&B, Y&R; bookings on commercials for Leslie Savage, Bill Vincent, Stan Harris, Warner McConnell, Sue Lavery, and a hold on Eve Paradise, weather permitting, for Tuesday. Then"—Charlene's tone became more confidential—"you had a visit from Valerie du Charme. That pushy broad never quits." She laughed, expecting Rex to respond, to exhibit the common reaction they had always shared for Valerie du Charme.

But Rex only half smiled, almost politely. The laughter and complicity once so strong between them had become strained and hollow.

"She brought you a box of cigars," Charlene finished lamely.

"Oh," Rex said, glancing furtively in Martita's direction again. "Well, since I don't smoke . . ." His voice trailed off. "Excuse me, honey, I'd better check on Martita."

Charlene was sure she detected something akin to guilt on Rex's face.

*　　*　　*

Martita imbibed her Martini with a single gulp, turned to Rex in the dimly lit cocktail lounge, and said, "Look, luv, as I've told you from the start, we can be great friends, you and I. I dig you as a human being. You might say I feel like a sister to you—like you're the brother I never had and always wanted. Now, as you know, honey, I dig girls, so I'm hip to your scene. But the thing is, what's it all about?"

"What do you mean?" Rex asked.

"I mean, are you going to slave forever? And for what? No, honey, you want to enjoy life, right?"

"Well, sure . . ."

"Quit. Go off; do all the buggering you got a yen for— you know, get your rocks off plenty, have beautiful boys, never want for action. Flesh, that's what you want, isn't it, sweets?"

Rex nodded. "Yes," he replied.

"Okay, *that's* what it's all about, don't you see, sweets? Getting enough money! Then you can *buy* your way anywhere. You pay, people welcome you; they sit up and take notice. Get money, and your life is set. Am I right, or am I right?"

"Right," Rex said.

And then Martita outlined her fantastic plan, which would absolutely guarantee Rex's future.

* * *

"Hey, bitch!" Charlene confronted Martita in the ladies' room. "Bug off!"

"What do you mean?" Martita demanded, meeting Charlene's eyes levelly.

"Word has come to me you've been infringing on my territory, girl! You called an advertising agency and tried to send over talent for commercials." Charlene's eyes were blazing. "On top of that, you sent three of our best girls on a job for a photographer's party—forty dollars an hour to run around in brief costumes. Look, bitch, our girls are not cheap whores!"

"If they didn't want to do it, they could have refused," Martita said.

"How dare you push in where you don't belong!" Charlene retorted. "You may have Rex conned, but I see through you, you old bull dyke. You got any plans of taking over, put them out of your mind. If we weren't shorthanded, you'd be out on your ass tomorrow. You stick to photography, we do the commercials. Don't infringe on my territory. Stay out of my hair, bitch!"

* * *

"Why, Rex? Why?"

"She knows what she's doing, Charlene. She's a smart businesswoman. She can make us a million."

"Bullshit!"

"Listen, I know. And if you want her to invest for you too, I can persuade—"

"No, thanks," Charlene snapped. "And you'll regret it yourself someday—when you lose your shirt."

"Honey, you don't understand. She has inside information on the market."

"I'm telling you, Rex. Watch your step."

"I know what I'm doing. Now quit treating me like a child,

Charlene. I'm not going to go on slaving away. I need a steady income coming in, a set amount. Martita's acting as my business manager. She's got it all figured out. She's going to make it happen for me, Charlene."

"All right. All right, Rex. But I'm putting up with this only as long as she stays out of my hair. Just keep that cunt in her own corner. I want nothing to do with her."

Chapter 9

Eve was doing her makeup when Carrie returned from a late go-see for Jubilee Kitchen Wax. "Are you seeing Marty again tonight?" Carrie asked.

Eve looked up from the sink where she was concentrating on her eyeliner. "I like him, Carrie," she said. "But you know the thing that upsets me about him?"

"What?"

"It's his only being a taxi driver. I mean, he has no background, no position. He's more human than the jet set people, but that's not enough. Damn! If I could only combine the two elements."

"You can," Carrie said. "The jet set people still call you."

"I just love dressing up and going places," Eve said. "I can't compare the evenings I spend with Marty to the dates I have with the rich crowd. I mean it's quite a comedown getting in Marty's cab and heading for Phil Gluckenstern's on Delancey Street or making the scene at Ratner's or Rappoport's. If Marty has a late night, sometimes we go for sandwiches at the Stage; but about as glamorous as we ever get is the Russian Tea Room."

Eve stood back and surveyed the Twiggies she had finished painting on. "Last night we were at the Russian Tea Room, Carrie. The waiter had just delivered this dish, blini, that Marty had raved about. And then Marty pointed out Leonard Bernstein to me. Well, I wanted to crawl under the table. I was mortified, because I'd been introduced to Leonard Bernstein once at one of the jet set parties. God. I was scared he might see me and wonder what I was doing with someone as low class as Marty. Oh, well," Eve sighed, "forget about me. How's your writing coming?"

"Fine. I'm satisfied with what I've got on the first draft but I'm still going like crazy."

"I take it you're staying in again tonight?"

"Yes."

Eve sighed. "If only Marty were successful."

"Well, maybe he'll make it someday."

"I doubt it." Eve added a final touch of powder to her makeup and stood back to check her reflection. "It's bad enough Leonard Bernstein saw us sitting in the Russian Tea Room, but it would be even worse if I was out with somebody from the jet set and Marty should happen along and pick us up in his cab—and act like he knew me. I live in mortal fear of that."

That wasn't all Eve lived in fear of. Suppose Marty should ever find out about her two indiscretions with Elliot Woo? What a mistake those had been.

She recalled Elliot saying, "Tantra for the male involves self-control; for the most part there is no orgasm. Physiologically speaking, the male only needs to have an orgasm once a month."

It had been just her luck he had gone and had a climax anyway, after all that buildup. How was she supposed to know she'd be the once-a-month recipient of his sperm? His excuse had been she'd excited him too much—he hadn't been able to control himself. She had been expecting some special kind of experience, and all it was was ordinary sex, not even as good as it was with Marty.

And then, like an even bigger jerk, she had gone and agreed to try "Tantra" with Elliot a second time, when he'd explained he was out of practice and the next time would bring an improvement. It hadn't been much better than the first time; he'd controlled the climax, but that was the only difference. She'd been a fool to listen to Elliot, a fool to let him have that accident inside her. But then, she'd taken a few chances with Marty too, and it worried her. Everything in life was a mess.

At least Elliot wouldn't be bothering her anymore; he'd left for a lecture tour of the West Coast, with his wife (the dirty guy was even married). But in addition to worrying about not having been careful, she was also concerned about Uncle Nappi. She had really been a snob with him, and it wasn't right. Poor Uncle Nappi couldn't help it if he had no education, if he spoke poor English. It wasn't his fault. She had no right to expect him to do any better than he already had. Her uncle was an immigrant; nothing was his fault, and she'd acted horrid to him.

*　　*　　*

Eve's thoughts were filled with remorse as she turned the corner to her uncle's shop. It had been so long, too long, since she'd seen him; and that was wrong of her. But she had an hour to kill before her next appointment, and she was in the neighborhood anyway, so she would see him now and make up for it all, and everything would work out perfectly.

Absently she noticed an official vehicle parked outside the shop. A small crowd had gathered, and as she came close and her thoughts came into sharp focus, she was alarmed.

"You can't go in there." A police officer at the door barred her way.

"What's the matter? Where's my uncle?"

"I have orders. You can't go in till the coroner comes out." He turned away, refusing to look at her face.

Where's my uncle?

A man carrying a black bag exited. Wide-eyed, frightened, Eve persisted, "What's going on? I came to see my uncle! I don't understand all this! Please *tell* me—"

"There's the coroner now."

Terrified, Eve fought her way up to the man with the bag. "Please tell me what's the matter. *Where is my uncle?*"

At that moment two men came out, carrying a stretcher covered with a sheet. They walked through the aisle the police had cleared and placed the stretcher in back of the wagon. She ran up to them, crying, "What's happened to my uncle?"

They ignored her. Beside her, a police officer asked, "Are you a relative?"

"Yes! Yes!"

301

"There's somebody inside, an employee. Anthony Cavallieri. You know him?"

"Yes—Tony! He works for my uncle."

"You can go in and talk to him if you're a relative."

She approached the door, and the first officer barred her way again. The officer near the wagon called out, "It's okay, Kelly, she's a relative. Let her in to see the fellow inside."

* * *

Tony sat quietly in one of the waiting chairs, his head bowed, his hands clasped together.

"Tony!" Eve cried. "What's happened?"

He looked up, his eyes filmed over. "He's gone, Evie. . . . I'm sorry."

"No!" Eve cried. "I don't believe it. What happened, please tell me what happened, Tony. I just don't understand anything."

"He was shaving a guy. He fell. I don't know, honey; he hit his head on the steel of the next chair—"

"But, Tony, couldn't they do anything for him?"

Tony's shoulders shook. "They say he was dead before he hit the floor."

"Dead? How could he be dead? I don't understand. I don't understand how Uncle Nappi could be dead." Tears were streaming down Eve's cheeks.

"I cleaned up the blood," Tony said. "He split his head open."

"But . . . I mean, I mean if you said he was dead before he hit the floor . . ."

"I told him he oughta have gone to the doctor, but he wouldn't go; he kept putting it off . . ."

"Was he sick?"

"He had an internal injury. He never would go and see about it." Tony's eyes closed, as though he were trying to shut out a bad memory. "I don't know. I think he just had a heart attack. He's gone. He just keeled over, and he's gone."

"Uncle Nappi!" Eve ran outside to the curb.

The doors of the van were shut. The motor was going.

"I'm sorry, miss," an officer said.

Her body shook with sobs. She wanted Uncle Nappi there

beside her, his laughing good-natured presence greeting her, she wanted to hear his voice singing one of his Italian folk songs while he gave a haircut, to have him smile at her and call her Evie and tell her it was all right, that he forgave her. If only she could tell him she hadn't meant to ignore him all these months, hadn't meant to make him feel she was ashamed of him. How she wanted to tell him she loved him still and always would love him and be proud of him. If only she could take his old hand in her young one and infuse it with strength and life. But it was too late.

The wagon pulled away from the curb.

Chapter 10

Between calls to J. Walter and Compton, Rex rang Rel Taller-day, his latest love, to arrange a late clandestine meeting. It would have to be very *sub rosa* so that Harleigh Willingham Babcock didn't find out. Rex was due to meet Harleigh for dinner, having just made his acquaintance the previous evening through Martita.

That Martita was a swell gal. She was really coming through. Though it had always been difficult for Rex to part with money, he had given her $5,000 so far from his savings account. With such a certain thing as her investment plan, there was no reason at all to worry. Rex knew he'd get a substantial return on his investment when the stock went public, and opened at many times what he had paid for it. Getting in on the underwriting stage with Martita was a surefire thing.

But Martita wanted Rex to invest more than a mere $5,000. "You're going to need lots of money to retire on, sweets," she'd said. "Now, I don't want to drain you, but we've got to get the money from *somewhere* . . . and I have an idea where."

It was here Harleigh Willingham Babcock entered into things. The octogenarian millionaire textile manufacturer, a lifelong homosexual, was practically at death's door. He had taken to Rex immediately, just as Martita had predicted. ("You're exactly right for him, absolutely *perfect*, sweets; I know his type.")

That Martita was a genius, and now things were really going to pop, for last night, when Harleigh and Rex were arranging their dinner date, Harleigh had expressed interest in helping Rex with his investments.

"Don't forget to play it cool," Martita had said this morning. "It can mean a million dollars."

"Don't worry; I will. Are you sure he's that wild about me?"

"He's in love, Rex! You can do no wrong. Just get him to write you a check for five thou. Tonight, I *know* he will. He wants you, sweetheart!"

* * *

Christina Suzanne Haupt came into the world after causing her mother hours of miserable pain. The labor had been induced at seven months in order to spare Dolores the final two months of stomach expansion, which might have been a risk for her figure or might have left ugly stretch marks, or both.

During the last two months of her pregnancy she'd been worried by the appearance of veins in her breasts, for which her obstetrician had given her hormone shots twice weekly. Now she was glad the whole thing was over with. Never again, she vowed. Hardly worth the trouble. She made up her mind she would have her tubes tied as soon as possible.

As for the baby, Dolores could not imagine how *she* could have given birth to such an ugly creature. For several weeks she harbored a grudge against Henry. It ought not have been his sperm that impregnated her; she should have chosen someone attractive to be the father of her child.

But as Tina grew, her appearance changed, she became prettier, and Dolores accepted her as her own. However, the novelty of having a baby soon wore thin. It would have been too great a drag to change diapers, give bottles and

304

baths and coo "gootchey-gootchey-goo" all day long, of
course, so thank God for Tina's nanny. This left Dolores with
plenty of free time; she could get her figure back in shape at
Kounovsky's, have some work done on her face at Benne's
(somehow, pregnancy had changed her facial planes), and
see about getting her career going again.

* * *

"Hi, Claudia."

Charlene was on the phone as Dolores entered the office.
She waved excitedly, then went on with her call: "Seven-
thirty at MPO; bring three or four cocktail dresses, three or
four choices in medium-toned wool suits. . . . Good. I'll have
her there. . . . Bye, luv."

Charlene stood up, stepped over one of the dogs, and
clasped Dolores in a hearty abbraccio.

"Darling, it's so good to see you!" she shrieked, scarring
Dolores with her magenta lips, kohled black eyeliner, and
thick mascara.

"You're looking marvelous, Charlene."

"How's the baby?"

"Beautiful."

"You shoud have a baby a year. I can't get over how wonderful you look. I guess you're ready to go back to work?"

"As a matter of fact, I'm dying to get back to the business.
I can't wait."

"Well, you came at a good time, honey. It's busy right now.
Besides which, we've got a bonus for you. Checks!"

"Oh, goody!"

"Jonny-Mop, Texaco, Bold, and TWA."

"Just what I like to hear."

"I'll tell Rex you're back with us. He'll be delighted. He's
out right now, seeing clients."

"I don't want to do any print," Dolores said, "just
commercials. So don't bother to speak to the photography
department. What was her name who used to run it? Liz
something?"

"Oh, honey, Liz left ages ago. You've *really* been out of
touch. We've got Martita in there now. That Liz was terrible.
She promised all the male models jobs, just to get them to

ball her. Then they all got furious when she didn't get them any work. . . . Well, most of them were fags anyway, and, as you can well imagine, it killed them to have to get it up for Liz. But the one who *really* got mad about it all"—Charlene's voice fell to a confidential whisper—"was you-know-who."

"Rex?"

Charlene nodded. "She was infringing on his territory."

Dolores howled.

"So now Rex has found this Martita. No problem there. She's a dyke. Furthermore, Rex thinks she's some kind of financial wizard or something. She's been investing money for him in the stock market. Rex is convinced he's going to make a million."

"More power to him."

"Oh, say, I see that old boy friend of yours, Nathan Winston, is a candidate in the primaries. Wants to be a Congressman."

Changing the subject, Dolores asked, "Are there any commercials you can send me on in the next couple of days?"

"As a matter of fact, yes." Charlene looked at her book, then had to take four incoming phone calls before she could tell Dolores that she was to go to Grey, SSC&B, and Benton and Bowles on go-sees. She gave Dolores the times of the go-sees and instructions on how to look at each place; then she said, "I'm glad your life is taking shape, Dolores. So many girls haven't got your good sense. They hold out for fame, and turn their noses up at a good marriage when it comes along. They believe that when fame comes, it will be more important than anything in their lives. They haven't got your sense of proportion. . . . But you always were wise."

*   *   *

It was a crisp fall day, and Dolores, feeling frustrated, went to Saks and spent $200 on makeup. Then she headed over to Allen and Cole, where she charged $3,000 worth of clothes to Henry. She thought of calling someone to roll in the hay with her, but since she had her period, she decided against it.

Charlene's remarks about marriage and fame had nettled

her. As if she weren't meant for fame, and had been sensible enough to settle and marry Henry. It was disgusting. Of course, there was a good deal to be said for the fact that she had achieved security, which was more than Carrie or Eve had done. But she, Dolores, would do more—far, far more. With Henry's money anything was possible.

It was too late to get a play for this season—Tina had seen to that. But she could start looking for a vehicle. And she could prepare things properly, with the right publicity campaign.

Soon, soon, everything would come her way.

*　　*　　*

Just as Martita had predicted, Harleigh Willingham Babcock was glad to help Rex with his investment program and had written out a check for $5,000.

The next morning Rex cashed the check and gave the proceeds, in crisp hundreds, to Martita, who exclaimed gleefully, "Congratulations! This is only the beginning!"

But with the acceptance of the check, Rex found he had signed his life away to Babcock. The hoary old fossil would scarcely let him out of his sight. In fact, so possessive of Rex did he become that he had full-time detectives assigned to keep tabs on him.

Rex would never have known this if Martita hadn't warned him.

Now, over cocktails at the Spindletop, she whispered, "I'd advise you to lay off the boys till things get settled—"

"But I can't!" Rex said, horrified. "I need it! I need it to function, to stay sane!"

Martita shook her head. "Honey, I'm an old bull dyke, and I understand how it is—believe me, I do—but just look at things this way: for just a little while it's going to have to be mind over matter, just until we get enough money to secure your future."

"God! How long?"

"Not long, baby."

"Well, *how* long?"

"Only a few months, maybe—"

"A few *months!* I can't! It's only a few days, and already I'm going clean off my chump!"

"Is Harleigh that bad in the sack? He doesn't satisfy you at all?"

"Are you kidding?" Rex groaned.

"Well, Rex, let's be practical. Let's think this thing through reasonably—"

"Practical! I don't wanna think, I don't wanna be reasonable, I wanna have sex! *Now!*"

"For a lay"—Martita's voice was stern—"you'd wreck your whole future? No, Rex. You *know* you can't cheat on Harleigh; you're under constant surveillance. One false move, and all's lost. When there's so much at stake, it strikes me as positively infantile that you can't control these desires of yours long enough to—"

"I can't help it! I'm a very sexy, passionate fella, and I need three times the sex an average guy needs. I *gotta* have it. That's just the way I'm constructed."

"Well, think about all the extra blow jobs you'll have coming to you as a reward, later. . . ."

"You don't understand. I can't *wait* till later."

"This is ridiculous, Rex. You're acting like a child. A child expects to have all his wishes gratified; an adult learns there are times he has to do without the things he imagines he requires."

"This isn't imagination! I've got this terrible *irritation*, see, right in my—"

"All right, all right, but think about ten years from now—twenty, thirty years from now! You'll be old then, Rex. You're good-looking now, so you can find lovers, but when you're old you'll still have these desires, and then you'll have to be *rich* to get boys to do it with you. Be honest now. Would you have sex with Harleigh if it weren't for his money? You know damned well you wouldn't. Don't be a fool, Rex. Think about all the ass you'll be able to buy in your old age, and for now you can jerk off."

Rex stared at his drink, miserable. "I've never been in a fix like this before," he muttered.

"It's good for you," Martita said with a down-curved smile. "It'll help develop your character. How are you coming on the will?"

"I've hinted."

"It's not enough to hint. You have to make *certain* he includes you. It's a token of love. If he loves you, he *has* to put you in his will. You told me he likes the way you suck."

Rex nodded, wishing Martita would not remind him.

"When are you seeing him again?"

"Tonight; after here."

"Good. Make sure you get him to agree to add you to the will *tonight*. The old bird could kick the bucket at any moment. You have no time to lose."

Rex took another swig of his drink and said, "Okay."

"And maybe he can take away your hard-on," Martita said facetiously, staring pointedly at Rex's lap.

The most Rex could manage was a glum smile.

*   *   *

Eve was used to lugging forty pounds of equipment with her on her daily rounds. Still, by the end of the day she usually felt like her feet were ready to give out. This afternoon she felt even more tired than usual, and was very relieved to get to the hotel in which her new gym—the one she'd started going to just after Elliot Woo left town—was located. In just a few seconds she could dump her heavy satchel and book, remove her clothes, and relax and breathe again.

But as she descended the steps to the basement, where the gym was located, and the smells of disinfectant and sweat came to her in knifelike whiffs, she suddenly felt dizzy. All at once she was afraid she wouldn't make it to the bottom of the stairs. Groping for a railing, she felt blackness overtaking her.

Somehow, she stayed on her feet until she got to the bottom of the stairs. After that she was aware of nothing until she opened her eyes and saw two male attendants in identical white shirts and black trousers leaning over her with smelling salts and hot tea.

She would have to forego her workout for today. She hailed a cab and went on home. Carrie was out, and stillness prevailed in the apartment. She didn't like to think what the matter with her might be.

Perhaps she ought to call Marty and mention her fears. No, she told herself, this is silly. Just take some aspirin and go to bed. She must have the flu.

*   *   *

A week later Eve knew it was not flu. She was pregnant.

Her feelings about it were mixed. The physical reality of creation and the idea of her body being used as an instrument to produce a new life filled her with pride and happiness. But at the same time, she felt stigmatized.

She tried to pretend she was married, and imagined how wonderful it would be living in a big apartment, being very rich, and welcoming a baby. Yes, that would be a different thing altogether. Everything's different when you're rich.

Suppose the child was Elliot Woo's? Suppose it came out a Eurasian? That first time Elliot had *come*. Even the second time might have done it: she'd heard stories about girls who'd been impregnated by rubbing or even just taking a bath with a man, without the man even being inside. Even though Elliot boasted of having such great control (the second time) mightn't he have dribbled? One little drop was all you needed.

I've really fouled up, Eve thought bitterly. I was terrible to Uncle Nappi, and I'll never forgive myself for that. I got conned by a phony Chinaman, and now I'm pregnant and I don't even know who the father is.

But Elliot was not only out of town, he was married as well, so she wouldn't waste much time thinking about him. Marty was the one she'd have to go after and reckon with.

*   *   *

Tonight, tonight, Eve said to herself, tell him tonight. When she stopped in the drugstore to buy some toothpaste, smack in front of her was a whole shelf devoted to babies' products. What a huge immense project it was to have a baby. All the supplies—the powders, lotions, oils, diet supplements—all kinds of things she'd never known existed. It struck her as frightening, the whole undertaking that lay in front of her.

She bought her toothpaste and went out into the street

once more. The weather was getting colder. All around, in the shortening daylight and the dead leaves falling, in the fading autumn, were the signs of death. Death, death, all around, in the dry caking earth, in the increasing solemnity of New Yorkers. Why in the presence of new life surging within her, why was she so conscious of death?

Why all this morbidity? She couldn't figure it out.

*　　*　　*

"Marty, I'm pregnant." The only way Eve could get it out was to call it to him from the bathroom, from behind a locked door.

"Honey?"

Eve heard his steps, heard him stop at the door. She heard his breath, and she could almost feel his body against the door.

"Evie?"

She was nauseated, whether from pregnancy or nerves, she didn't know. She leaned against the basin, feeling her stomach in turbulent disorder, her whole body alternately hot and cold.

"Evie?" Marty called again.

She was glad she didn't have to look at him. Suddenly she wondered if she'd ever loved him, and if she loved him now. If a girl was really in love with a man, she'd be happy about having his baby, wouldn't she? If it *was* his baby.

Of course the baby was Marty's. The chance of its being Elliot's was remote. She must put Elliot out of her mind for good and concentrate on Marty.

But she didn't want to look at his pock-marked face. Nor did she want to think of having a swarthy baby with oily skin. Perhaps if she prayed to St. Jude, he'd give her a beautiful pink-and-white baby, a baby that had nothing of Marty in it.

"Honey, open the door."

"I will in a minute."

Well, she had to face him sometime. It couldn't be put off indefinitely.

Unlocking the door, she saw him standing there with a grin that stretched from ear to ear. He held his arms out, gathered her to him, and held her close. "Honey," he said, his body shaking with emotion. "Oh God, baby."

311

She lay her head on Marty's chest and clung to him. It was as if part of her were dead now.

"We'll get married as soon as they give us the license," Marty said. "Jesus, a kid!" He clutched her tighter. "Oh, honey, you don't know what this means to me."

She raised her head—and felt his sweat hot on her cheek. Then it occurred to her that Marty could very well have gotten her pregnant on purpose.

But she was tired of thinking. She sighed and put her head back on Marty's chest. Oh, it will be okay, she thought, trying to reassure herself.

As soon as she felt the baby stirring, she would be overjoyed, and when it was born she'd be beside herself with happiness. Then she'd be grateful for Marty, her husband. The world was really too much to contend with alone. She needed someone.

But then, looking up at Marty again, she had the decided feeling that somehow, no matter what, she would never be able to get away from the thought that she'd been cheated, that she'd had this marriage forced upon her, and she doubted that she would ever be able to forgive him for not being successful and rich, and a member of the world that counted.

Chapter 11

The will business with Harleigh Willingham Babcock had been settled.

Martita was annoyed that Harleigh had only included Rex for $150,000, thinking this a paltry sum under the circumstances, but Rex himself was far from displeased. Now, if only Harleigh would die, Rex could invest the money and make even more!

Of course that wasn't Rex's only reason for wishing Harleigh would drop dead. Everyone noticed how tense Rex was, how on edge and irritable he'd gotten lately. But only Martita knew the reason: the fact that he'd been forced to keep away from the fleshpots.

Martita was the one person Rex could confide in. Almost every afternoon she and Rex left the office together and had cocktails at the Spindletop, where Rex would complain endlessly about his sex life. Then Martita would spot someone at the bar and say, "Don't look now, sweets, but that's him—the plainclothesman. Careful, honey."

Rex would grit his teeth and pray for the day things would return to normal when he would be able to lead a balanced sex life again, and then Martita would give him courage, courage to face the awful deprivation that threatened to destroy his equilibrium. She would praise him and tell him how his character was being developed and that soon, soon, it would all pay off.

"When?" Rex demanded. "Do I have to wait for the old fossil to kick off? I can't wait that long, Martita. I *can't*."

"No, honey," Martita said. "Just as soon as Harleigh knows he can trust you, he'll take the detectives off you."

Rex looked at the bar, at the man Martita had spotted. Absently he wondered how she always infallibly knew which one it was. But he was too sick with his problems and frustrations to give the matter any serious consideration.

He gulped the remainder of his drink and said, "Well, I'm off," gnashed his teeth silently and rose, on his way to meet Harleigh.

* * *

Everyone came to the party at the agency, all the girl models, all the male models, commercial types and actors and actresses who worked through Ryan-Davy, all the character people, all the casting and advertising people, the producers of commercials.

Charlene was horrified when Rex, trying to save money, poured the dregs of peoples' drinks into the punch bowl. She tried to steer the important people away from the concoction, telling them it was poisoned, and offering them drinks from the private stock in her filing cabinet.

Warren and Kurt gorged themselves on cookies and cakes fed them by the guests. Then, toward the middle of the party,

Kurt threw up in sight of everyone. Making polite apologies, the crowd began to thin out.

It was about an hour later that Rex got really out of hand. Luckily all the big clients had left. Even Martita Strong had gone.

The trouble started harmlessly enough, with poor Rex desperately trying to prove he could swing with girls. He went after Lorna Carroll, who told him politely to cut it out. Rex, unable to take the rejection, would not leave her alone, but kept forcing his attentions on her.

Finally Lorna turned on him savagely and said, "Rex, now that's enough! Behave yourself!"

"Don't you talk to me like that!" Rex shouted. "I'm Rex Ryan, and you can't talk to *me* that way, young lady."

"Stop it, Rex! You're making a fool of yourself. You're being obnoxious!"

"You little bitch! Who do you think you are, talking to *me* that way?"

"Well, pardon *me*, they forgot to tell me you were God!"

"You get out of this agency, and don't ever come back! And don't ever ask me to help you find another abortionist, either!"

Lorna went white and stumbled off.

"Get out! Get out! Get out of my agency!" Rex screamed after her. He picked up a glass and threw it at a table in the corner, sending a shower of smashed bits and pieces crashing to the floor.

Charlene thanked her stars nobody important was around to see what followed.

For Rex, before anyone could stop him, picked up another glass, and screaming "Bitch! Bitch!" smashed it against the wall. "I'm sick of this business, sick of this life! I hate everyone in this stinking, fucking, lousy business, and I want them all to die!"

"Rex!" Charlene came up behind him, but he pushed her aside with fury.

"I'm sick of it all!" he cried, smashing another glass.

Glass after glass smashed on the table, the floor, the wall as Rex screamed and wailed, "I haven't had a decent lay in two months! That bastard keeps me a prisoner! I never get laid anymore! He's a lousy lay! the bastard! the prick! He has no right to curtail my sex life like this! I hate him! It's not worth it! I hope he dies so I can have a decent fuck! Goddamn it! Shit! Shit! Shit!"

Suddenly Rex was silent.

For Harleigh Willingham Babcock had appeared on the scene, a decrepit, shriveled, wizened figure, frailly clutching to the last threads and stitches of life, leaning for support on the door, his legs buckling underneath him, his face pure candescent chalk.

There was an instant when his and Rex's eyes met. And then the old man collapsed. He was dead on arrival at the hospital.

Rex, by the time he got the news, was at Charlene's sipping hot tea, having calmed down sufficiently to be sorry and to tell Charlene he didn't know what had gotten into him, to make him go berserk that way.

When Charlene told him Harleigh was dead, the first thing that came to Rex's mind was that now he was free. No longer would he have that old relic on his tail, never leaving him alone for a moment, keeping detectives on him, ruining his sex life. Now, for the first time in ages, he would be able to resume having normal sex relations. At last! He could really groove! It was then he remembered Harleigh's will.

The hundred and fifty thousand! It was his! He was rich! He had liquid assets! Harleigh's money would snowball! He would never have to worry!

Rex turned to Charlene with a broad grin on his face and said, "Let's pour us a drink for a Christmas toast! Merry Christmas, honey! This is going to be the greatest year ever!"

Chapter 12

"You missed two appointments, honey."

"I'm sorry, Charlene. Sometimes I get so wound up with my writing, I forget."

"Well, don't get so wound up you forget to come in and

collect your residuals. We've got checks for Easy-Off Oven Cleaner and Borden's Instant Non-Fat Dry Milk waiting for you."

"Great!"

"And don't forget you've got to plan for the future. In other words, *keep* the appointments we make for you, luv. I've got two places to send you tomorrow morning. Look eighteen. Write this down."

Carrie scribbled as Charlene dictated. "Got it."

"After that you have a call-back on Gleem. You're supposed to look early twenties for that one. It's at eleven at Compton. Then I have a twelve-fifteen for you down at Y&R. Want you to look sort of casual on that one. Then, in the afternoon, look sophisticated, early twenties over at . . ."

It went on like that, day after day. The interviews, the go-sees.

Sometimes I wonder where I belong in the world, Carrie thought. I can't bear that people want pieces of me, but no one wants the deepest, realest part. If only she would meet someone; being a part of someone else was the answer. You grew, you blossomed. The life she led was meaningless. Without the larger purpose, everything seemed shallow and silly. That's what modeling was all about. Triviality. And still she went on smiling for commercials, for clients, for agency people, like the trinket she was supposed to be. It was the same faces, going through the same motions and gestures year after year, and she was one of them. Nothing changed.

Carrie wrote:

There's an ominousness hanging over this business. Yes, the business tears us down. It claims our innocence and our beauty, physical, moral, emotional, spiritual. It robs us of our only weapon. It strips us. What do we have left, when our freshness is gone? And all the while it's happening, we try to live, knowing that outside is that tawdry world in which we are objects, yet inside is that world of beauty and the richness of the interior self; the self we know has such a capacity for love and is suffering so from want of expression.

316

There have been too many mistakes, she thought when she put down her pen. But I can make up for them. I will. I *must*.

*　　*　　*

Clear air, thin traffic. The snowfall stirred something distant, now with the city suspended in quiet hush. Riding in numb silence through winter's desolation, Carrie thought the icy concrete and wind and shivering trees were trying to convey some message to her, but couldn't discover what. She thought, if only I didn't feel so empty inside. And she was full of rhythms and feelings for which there seemed no adequate words, all flowing through her like a persistent prayer. I will have someone soon, she thought. And if he can't be all I could love and cherish, then he'll be someone who can at least take me away from all this bloody solitude.

As the cab plodded along across town, she stared out of the window at the colors reflected in the glass and the polished metal of the buildings, feeling cold but looking upward to the promise of beauty, yes, there is always that hope, she thought, the hope of what could and might be.

It kept snowing all afternoon while she went on appointments for Duncan Hines Cake Mix, Laura Scudder Potato Chips, and Ivory Liquid. The end of another day.

Darkness's enveloping mantle was closing in, slicing and cutting through the air. Claxons and echoes and reverberations of heavy trucks and shaking subways penetrated deep, resounded clear.

Home. The apartment was still. Not a sound of a voice or footstep save her own. The heating system had begun to clank, the radiator was taking up steam and hissing. She wanted someone now. Right now. Not in a week or a month or tomorrow but this instant.

Then the phone rang and it was Jerry Jackson. Carrie made a date with him for the next evening.

*　　*　　*

Rex was taking time out to watch a scene from *Cactus Flower* enacted in his office by one of the agency's girls and Rocky Esposito, whom he was now wooing.

"Man," Rex said, watching Rocky's timid approach to the actress, "you gotta have balls. What else's a guy got to sell but his balls?"

Rocky hovered close to Rex's desk after the actress had left. "What about work?" he asked.

Rex glanced furtively at the door. "I'm trying to get you in on a Command Tahitian Lime Deodorant for Men," he said.

"Well, what happened on the Williams' Lectric Shave?"

"They haven't made a decision yet."

"You said you were going to send me on a Hai Karate After Shave Foam, but you never did."

"Well, they changed the whole campaign."

"I need work, Rex. You said I'd be working all the time if—"

"I know, I know," Rex said hastily. Then the intercom buzzed.

It was Charlene. "They certainly are looking for people with false teeth these days," she said. "Would you believe this list I've got in front of me, Rex? Fasteeth, Kleenite, Dentu-Creme, Poli-Grip, Polident, Ezo Dental Cushion, Orafix Denture Adhesive, Efferdent Denture Cleanser Tablets—those have come in just in the past week. Can you imagine us finding that many people to own up to having three or more removable teeth?"

"Impossible," Rex said. "They all want you to think they're perfect."

"Yeah," Charlene said, "it might ruin their self-image. Ego, ego, ego. How are you coming on the Rokeach Gefilte Fish and the Streit's Matzos? Gone are the days of the WPAs."

"Yeah," Rex said, "the minority groups are taking over. By the way, we have the books to do. What do you say we make the scene at Bickford's?"

"Sounds like a ball," Charlene said.

*   *   *

"Hi, honey," Charlene said over the phone. "How's the baby?"

"Just fine," Dolores answered. "Would you believe she has two teeth already?"

318

"The little monkey! When are you coming up to show her to us? And when are you coming up to pick up your checks?"

"What's there?"

"Zud, Value-Pak Moth Crystals, Head and Shoulders—"

"I'll be up this afternoon."

"I called for another reason, too. Listen, luv, we have a director coming in from the Coast. Alan Messina—very nice fellow."

"Oh, him!"

"You know him?"

"Sure. Remember I read for him for that Broadway flop a few seasons back?"

"You've both come a long way since then, honey."

"Do you think he'll remember me? I wasn't at my peak in those days. My acting's improved fantastically since then."

"Don't worry, luv. I'm sure Alan Messina'd as soon forget that whole period himself. He's one of the hottest TV directors on the Coast now."

Dolores perked up. "What's he doing in town?"

"He likes New York actors. Wants to see our best people, our real talent. Can you come to the agency at five?"

*   *   *

Wearing khakis and an old velour shirt with the sleeves rolled to reveal hairy arms, Alan Messina sat at Rex's desk. Those seasons back in the darkened theater Dolores hadn't been able to make him out clearly, but now she saw him to be forty-five or thereabouts. Boyish, he had the look of a tennis player or karate expert, and, she noted, quite an evil twinkle in his eye. His gestures, like his mind, were rapid and fluid.

"Physically, you're just what I'm looking for," he said, "for a specific role."

"Oh? What is it?"

"It's the part of a tall patrician girl from San Francisco. Do you think you could do that kind of thing?"

"Yes, it would be just perfect for me."

"Have you got any film on you?"

"I'm afraid not," Dolores said. She didn't want him looking at her old Hollywood stuff, the dumb secretaries and nurses, those nothing bits she'd done four or five years ago. "But I do have Broadway experience. And I've studied a good deal."

Alan was impressed. He said, "Good. I'm glad you've got the experience. I'm getting tired of the same old Hollywood faces. If you can read well, you're halfway home. Here's the script."

She had finished less than a page when he stopped her and said, "Enough! That's just fine."

She waited, anxious to hear him tell her the part was hers.

"I don't have to hear any more," he said. "I know you can act. I'll be in touch with my people on the Coast and tell them I want to use you. We'll see what they say."

"When do you think you'll have word?"

"Maybe even in a few hours. Can I call you at home?"

She recognized that look, that unmistakable look in his eyes, and she returned it, offering no room for speculation that she would be one hundred per cent amenable to any and all casting couch plans he might have.

"Maybe we could have a drink later on?" he suggested.

Holding the undercurrent between them, she prolonged her gaze. "Fine, I'd love to."

"Give me your number, and I'll call you. Are you going to be home later on?"

"Why don't we set a time and place right now?" she said.

"It's a bit rough, with my schedule." He pursed his lips and scratched his head. "Isn't there someplace I can call you? Or do you have a boy friend who might get jealous?"

She flashed him one of her most tantalizing smiles and said, "I have a husband who might."

Under his breath, his eyes riveted to her, he said, "Can you meet me at my hotel later on then? Say around nine. That ought to be playing it safe. We can have a little drink together."

She smiled. "I'd love to."

* * *

Offering Henry the excuse that she was meeting Charlene, Dolores left their apartment and ten minutes later arrived at the seventeenth floor of the St. Regis, where an impishly smiling Alan admitted her to his large suite.

320

"Name your poison," he said.

She accepted a light Scotch, settled back on the couch, and waited for him to broach the subject of the part.

From the bar where he was mixing himself a vodka martini, he said, "I think everything's going to work out."

"Darling, you only *think?*" Dolores pouted, offering him her hand as he joined her. "What a shame."

"To your career." He looked steadily into her eyes as he raised his glass.

"To a prompt decision," she said, eyeballing him above her own raised glass.

Alan took a large gulp and said, "Tell me about your husband."

"How boring. I'd much rather talk about us."

"So would I, honey. But I'm curious about the rest of your life. What kind of a marriage do you have?"

"All right as marriages go." Her eyes devoured him, already feeling his penetration of her, his maleness possessing her, consuming her.

"You're opposed to marriage, then?"

"Not at all, darling, I think marriage is a marvelous idea. In fact, I firmly believe it's the only way to live. A woman needs a husband. But"—she lowered her voice—"a woman has other needs too."

A hush, a silence full of sparks fell, and Alan moved closer. "I know just what you mean," he said, putting his drink on the table. "I'm married too."

"Then you *do* know," Dolores said, likewise placing her drink on the coffee table.

"Sure, I know." He kissed her experimentally.

"My husband doesn't kiss like you," Dolores murmured between half-open lips.

"Neither does my wife."

"I just love the hair on your arms," Dolores said. "It's sexy as hell."

"How do you know I've got hair on my arms?"

"I know."

"Does that turn you on, baby?" Bending her backwards, he allowed his tongue to find her ear.

"You turn me on, honey; you turn me on!"

"You're a pretty sexy broad, you know that?"

321

"You don't know the half of it, baby."

"I'm gonna find out right now."

"And my contract, honey? My contract?"

"Don't worry, baby, the part's yours." He rolled on top of her.

"And the people on the Coast, what about—"

"Let me handle it, doll. Anything for a sexy broad like you, baby."

"Alan!" she moaned in his ear, "you're the most erotic, thrilling man I've ever met."

* * *

"Well, you see, luv, it all paid off. Now you'll be able to screw all the ass that comes your way," Martita said.

"That's just what I've been up to since Harleigh kicked off." Rex grinned lasciviously. He and Martita were having cocktails at the Spindletop after work.

"Well, never let it be said old Martita isn't a shrewdie," Martita said, mouthing the ripe cherry from her Manhattan and tossing the stem carelessly on the floor. "Now then, Rex, we've more business to discuss. I'd like us to invest another fifty thousand."

Rex went pale. Fifty thousand was one-third of his inheritance. He said, "I—I don't think I can give you that much."

"Well"—Martita shrugged—"it's your life. Order me another Manhattan, Rex. And then I have to go."

Rex said, "Well, look, Martita, I do have many expenses. I mean, I do have some unforeseen bills, and . . ."

She gave him a frigid stare. "Fine, Rex." There was a flatness to her voice. "You do as you please. In my opinion it's a mistake to be that tight, to hoard. In my opinion we ought to get the maximum out of this. We should go for broke. Of course, I know how cheap you are, so I'd never suggest investing all the money—"

"Well, I *would*," Rex interrupted defensively, "only I'd like to see some returns first. I mean, you did promise I'd have something by now, a dividend or something, I mean. You said the stock was supposed to go public last month, and—"

"I believe I explained all this before, if I remember correctly, Rex," Martita said. "Now just remember one thing: I do not need your money; I'm doing all this for *your* benefit, not mine. It's hardly my fault if the company delayed things. On second thought, I don't think I'll have that Manhattan. I'll be leaving now." She began to gather her belongings together.

Rex anxiously caught her arm and said, "Wait!"

She paused. "Well?"

"All right," Rex agreed weakly. "Suppose I give you forty thousand, okay? As a start? Then after that, as soon as the stock opens and I make some money, after that I'll give you more. Okay?"

Martita said, "Rex, I insist on one thing. I insist you stop saying you will give *me*, as though I'm taking your money for my own purposes."

"I'm sorry, I didn't mean—"

"You know why all this is being done. It's to help *you!* To guarantee your old age. To make sure you can quit while you're still young enough to enjoy life, so you can afford all the tail you want when you get over the hill."

"Yes, I know," Rex said, displeased with her phraseology.

"So in the future, remember that. For God's sake, I knock myself out for you and this is the thanks I get."

"I didn't mean—"

"I know, sweets," Martita said, dismissing the subject. "All right, order me that Manhattan. We'll toast to the forty thousand and to the firmer and more secure future you're going to have." She patted his cheek. "To the young boys of Mexico, the Riviera, Paris, Capri, and all over the world! To all the beautiful boys who're gonna get to bugger Rex Ryan, the American millionaire!"

Chapter 13

"I guess you wonder why I've kept calling you," Jerry Jackson said in French.

He had scarcely spoken a word of English all night long. It seemed to Carrie that he found relating embarrassing and that every time he wanted to convey something personal, he reverted to French in order to place himself at a distance so as not to expose himself.

He pushed his plate away and lit a long chubby cigar. "Originally," he said, puffing on it, "I never would have endorsed anything on the outside, but now . . . well, things change." He couldn't bring himself to look her in the eye. "There's no reason why a contract has to be permanent. Permanence is no test of a contract's ultimate value. A contract can last five hours, two days, whatever, and still be meaningful. Of course, I plan to stay married to my wife, and we both want more children. But I think we both realize that after eight years together, both of us need outside experiences."

"And that's why you called me. To take me to bed."

Jerry looked sheepish. She could see beads of perspiration forming on his face and around his collar. He puffed hard again and said, "Well, I don't know. I have my worries, my fears . . ."

"In what way?"

"I want something I can rely on." He looked at Carrie out of the corner of his eye with a certain reservation. "How do I know I could count on you? It worries me."

"Count on me for what? What worries you? I should be the one to worry, not you."

"Why would you worry? You're a beautiful girl. You can always find someone."

"Suppose I fell in love? You're a married man."

"Well, I wouldn't want you to fall in love. I'd want us to have a relationship—an understanding."

"What do you figure would be the advantage to that for me?"

"You know as well as I do, the moment we met, something special happened between us."

"But you're married."

"I can't help that. It's not my fault. It's the way things are. In almost every life there's someone in the background. But this doesn't solve a person's real needs. I do have needs, you know, and it's not very often I meet someone who could meet those needs."

"And what about *my* needs? Everyone is trying to pull at me and devour me. Do you think I can give myself to everyone?"

"I don't care about *everyone*. I care about *me*. It's an open field, and I want you the same as any man would. But don't try to tell me something special doesn't exist between us, because I know you know better. You ask what advantage there could be for us? You know how it is with us, how it could be. And you must also know how rare in life a Supreme Experience is. If two people find the possibility of a Supreme Experience, they owe it to themselves to live the experience to the hilt. Whatever beauty life offers us, we cheat ourselves if we don't take advantage of it."

"And what about my future?"

"You'll always make out fine. You know you're a beautiful and exciting woman. Just walking down the street with you, all heads turn. A girl like you'd never have any trouble. You'll have a million opportunities. If you're worried about your future, don't be."

"All that really matters to me is marriage and a family. And it's not at all easy to find."

"You're too beautiful for one man. You should be for all men. Don't you know that's what beautiful girls are for?"

"No, I don't know that. Nor do I believe it. Nor do I believe I could get by in the world in the life you describe."

"Oh, well, if you're worrying about money, I can always help you get work. That's no problem."

They always say that, Carrie thought. I'm sick of that line, of their unkindness in playing upon this need in us.

But there was another need too. And how conscious of it she had been for so long, trying to push it to the back of her mind. But she couldn't. She couldn't. It was as if this terrible lack propelled her to seek something, no matter how small, just a scrap to sustain. Yes, she would go through with it. She needed it. As Jerry was grasping her in the hallway, breathing loudly, holding her tighter and tighter, grabbing and nearly crushing the wind out of her, she knew she couldn't wait for the wonderful one who maybe didn't even exist. This was all there was now. Outside the wind was howling against the concrete, against the frozen stone, and she thought, yes, yes, I will. I will have something in place of nothing. No matter if my heart cries for more. I will be content with this, this all-there-is.

Later, lying silently beside him, a desire for tenderness overtook her. As she turned to face him she realized that all he had offered was bestiality. Why, she wondered, was love a woman's lifeblood and to man only a diversion? Bestiality hadn't been enough. And she knew she wouldn't see Jerry again.

*   *   *

The Boeing 707's engines roared, sending a shower of drizzle and a foam of snow flurries an area of twenty feet around its still-whirring engines. Dolores alighted from the first-class section and proceeded into the massive airdrome, where the early sun seeped in through slotted windows and noises were absorbed by thick red carpets. A taxi sped her to Manhattan.

Something was bothering her, something she could not define, a depression, a discontent, eating away at her insides. A cacophony of ice-cream-flavored doors lining a demolition pit caught her eye, with bricks, stone, wood, steel bars, cracked plaster, junk, and debris lining the hole. It seemed the sight of old things being torn down to make way for the new were a sign to her; her marriage, she knew, had outworn its purpose; Henry was hindering her goals. She, too, must do away with the old and pave the way for the new. Now that she had the footage from Alan Messina's show under her belt, she would have only to wait until the show was aired and she would be sitting in a fine position. But first Henry would have to go. He was a drag.

The triplex greeted her. Henry wouldn't be rising for a few hours yet, as it was Sunday, his day for late sleeping, breakfast in bed, and reading the papers till early afternoon. When she looked in on Tina, the baby was fast asleep in her crib, thumb in mouth. She buzzed for the elevator.

New York was still silent and deserted. The small trickle of traffic progressed with a silken flood of unhampered movements. Dolores strode down Fifth Avenue past the cluster of hotels on Fifty-ninth Street.

She stopped at the St. Regis to use the phone, emerged, and hailed a cab. Several blocks uptown an exciting erotic exploit lay waiting for her. What better way to be welcomed back to town early Sunday morning than this? She had been thinking about it on the plane, hoping nothing would interfere with the fulfillment of her sensual appetites, and luckily she had been able to get the appointment with Rick, one of her favorite lovers, at the stud service. Good old Charlene had been advised to beard, as usual.

Now, as Dolores climbed the stone steps leading to the sumptuous East Side town house in which the stud service was located, her desires rose in anticipation, and her breath quickened as she felt the heady, lush surging of inner fire.

Ginny, the chic young matron who booked appointments and ran the establishment, greeted her and indicated which room she was to use.

Two hours later, gratified and appeased after an especially active session with the darkly exotic young Negro, she paid $150 to Ginny ($50 for the house, $100 for Rick).

"Everything okay, honey?" Ginny asked.

"Just great," Dolores said, languid and relaxed. "That Rick is superdivine."

"You're telling me." Ginny winked knowingly. "He's getting so popular, every bitch in town has hot pants for him. They're phoning left and right."

"Well, book me again for . . . let's see . . ." Dolores got her appointment book out. "Wednesday morning. Say eleven. I don't think I'll be able to get in again before that. Just got back in town, and there are a million things to do. But put the Wednesday session down—I know I can't possibly hold out any longer than that. And then, how about Thursday at four? Okay?"

Ginny nodded and waved goodbye, as Dolores slipped out the door. Henry would be waking up now, most likely.

*　　*　　*

The winter season was on. That night Dolores and Henry attended a dinner party held in a large East River duplex. There was an orchestra, dancing between courses, floral decorations and beautiful china, crystal, silver, and linen. Wines and champagnes of the rarest vintages were served.

The next night they went to a premiere, where the usual crowd of young moderns, aging dowagers, and penguin-suited perennials turned out and sat rustling programs and nodding to each other.

Yes, the routine had begun again. Dolores Haynes Haupt, the young society wife, married to a wealthy and influential man, attending all the important social functions, lunching at the best-known restaurants, rushing between the hairdresser, boutiques, department stores, and the exercise salon; Dolores Haynes Haupt, the young wife with her clothes, her parties, her openings, her *Vogue, Town and Country,* and *Bazaar* spreads, her charge accounts, her at-home soirees, her dilettantism, her unfulfilled ambitions, her furtive sex life, back to normal again. Only now she knew it was time for the decision.

*　　*　　*

"I'm ready for a change, Charlene."

They sat eating cherrystones at the Four Seasons. Charlene looked up.

"What kind?"

"A life change. I'm getting ready to shed Henry."

"Oh, goody! We'll have to order a magnum of Mumm's on that."

"It's really been a terrible drag. You just don't know—"

"No need to explain. I'm surprised you stuck it out as long as you did. Waiter!"

"Now that I have a good piece of footage on myself,"

328

Dolores continued, "I have something to work from. I know I belong on the Coast, Charlene."

"Honey, let them come to you," Charlene insisted. "You go out there of your own volition, and you're just another broad trying to get a break. Stay here and be exclusive. Get some publicity going for yourself."

"Publicity. Charlene, ever since my marriage to Henry, I've been having it in *Vogue, Harper's Bazaar, Town and Country, Women's Wear*. You know that. I'm known as a socialite actress, Charlene, but somehow the title hasn't turned the trick."

"What you need is another play," Charlene said. "Let's get you one, then you'll be in a strong bargaining position."

Yes, Charlene was right in the fact that she couldn't go out to Hollywood and be thrown in with all the ding-a-ling starlets. She must maintain her own identity and dignity, remain distinctive and exclusive. Here in New York she could retain her image of being apart from the herd.

But that didn't change her decision regarding her marriage. Definitely, Henry would have to go.

It wasn't merely their sex life that was inadequate; it was the whole relationship. Henry was too old for her; she needed a man to keep pace with her own youth and style. Henry was too sedentary, too pedestrian, and besides, the marriage had never been intended as more than a steppingstone in the first place.

The following week, Dolores moved out of the apartment, checked into the Pierre, and served Henry with separate maintenance papers. Henry made no trouble at all and agreed to give her a million-dollar settlement, tax free. She was surer than ever the marriage had been time well spent, and now, all this behind her, she knew her true destiny lay just ahead.

Chapter 14

According to the birth announcement, Andrew Sachs weighed eight pounds, two ounces. His doting mother said he ate like a hungry tiger and judging from the baby's healthy pink chubbiness every time Carrie saw him, Eve was not exaggerating.

The early fall weather was warm; Central Park abounded with bright leaves, prams full of babies, and laughing children floating toy boats in the pond. Eve, her eyes moving constantly down to her baby son asleep in his stroller, looked the picture of serenity and happiness, Carrie thought.

Eve said, "I've just got to go back to work. Expenses keep mounting."

Carrie said, "It seems like the cost of living has gone up a hundred per cent since we've been in the business."

"And residuals haven't."

"Do you still have anything running?"

"Yes, thank God. I've got Aunt Jane's Ol' Timer Kosher Dills, Kingsford Charcoal Briquettes, and Hartz Mountain Dog Flea and Tick Killer. My Chef Boy-ar-dee Ravioli just ran out. How about you?"

"Weiman Furniture Cream, Fulvita Diet Breakfast, Wizard Bathroom Deodorizer, Tab—"

"Hey, not bad."

"But the commercials aren't running like they used to. They don't pay nearly as well. The tight-money thing's affecting the business. In the old days the number of commercials we've got going would have meant a fortune, but everything's off—and the trend nowadays is for plain, even ugly girls. Charlene always said the gravy train didn't last forever."

"That thought makes me sick," Eve said. "It used to be so easy. And now when you really need it—at least I do, with

330

this little one to think of—" She glanced down and cooed at the baby.

Carrie said, "What about Marty? Doesn't he help?"

"Are you kidding?" Eve said with disdain. "He just watches TV all the time."

"I thought things were fine between you."

"I think I've grown in that I don't require the richest guy in the world like I used to, but my Lord, this guy watching TV all the time, bringing in maybe twenty-five dollars a week? Well, it really bugs me."

"That's too bad."

"At least I've got Andrew. It sure was a good thing the Petroangeli northern Italian genes won out over the Sachs New York Jewish ones. But sometimes I worry about his name. I mean, Andrew Sachs! It sounds all wrong. Maybe I can change it legally. After all there's no reason for a poor child to be stigmatized with a Jewish name like Sachs. Andrew's no more Jewish than I am. He'll grow up to be a devout Catholic, just like me. How do you like Andrew Saxon? That's much more like it, isn't it? Or maybe even Andrew Paradise. Well, I'll have to decide. How about you, how's the writing coming?"

"Pretty well, I'm doing rewrites now."

"Great! Good luck with it."

"Of course, there's that anxiety. You need security. You spend residuals so quickly."

Eve said, "I know. Good Lord, there's photographs, taxis, lunches, doctors, gyms, facials—you name it."

"But did I tell you about my latest idea, Eve? I'm going to apply for a fellowship."

"A fellowship? That's marvelous, Carrie. Do you think you'll win?"

"I don't know, but it's worth a try. I'm going to give Roger Flournoy for a reference."

"Have you asked him yet?"

"No, but I'm sure he'll agree. He always liked me. I'm going to send him a sample of my work with a letter asking him if he'll do it. I'm sure he'll say yes."

"Perfect!" Eve said.

"Then I could really quit the business for good."

It was with a tug at her heart, seeing Eve once more look

331

down at her baby, that Carrie saw Eve's pride coupled with love, and her reluctance to remove her gaze from the baby for more than an instant.

"It's time for Andrew's feeding," Eve said. "Shall we go somewhere where we can have privacy?"

In a secluded spot behind some bushes, Eve opened her blouse, put the child to her breast, and held him there. His eyes were shut tight, his tiny fists clenched, and he made little sucking noises.

"Just wait till you have a baby, Carrie," Eve said. "There's nothing, absolutely nothing in the world to compare to it. It's the greatest happiness there is in the world."

Carrie looked off to where a German shepherd was chasing a poodle.

"It's such a beautiful feeling to nurse a baby," Eve continued, patting her child. "It just sort of grabs you right here in the stomach and rises and swells, until the whole of you is consumed with love."

Carrie felt her palms, her face, her body, struck with a paralyzing hot flash, but she nodded and smiled a forced, hurtful smile. All she could think of was, this could have been me if I hadn't listened to Mel Shepherd and Charlene and Dolores. Why, why did I do it?

"No woman is complete without this," Eve said. "Is she, Mommy's little love?"

The baby responded; he smiled, he laughed, he moved. When Eve burped him he sat up, looking wise and adult; when she changed his diaper, all he did was grin and laugh.

Eve smiled. "I guess I sound like a typical mother, but I'm just so excited about him I can't tell you. I'm a whole new person, and it's all because of this precious bundle."

Andrew let out some gas.

"Would you like to hold him?"

"I'd better not. I might drop him."

"Go ahead. We're sitting on the grass." Eve handed Carrie her son, that tiny, sparkling, silken-skinned child whose warmth penetrated her body, whose softness permeated her being and made her ache.

Later the memory was still there. Carrie tried but she could not erase Eve and her baby from her mind. If only I'd kept *my* baby, she thought. But she hadn't. And it made all the difference in the world. Eve had been so much wiser than she.

She remembered how, in the hospital, just after she'd awakened, after all that vomiting, the emptiness that had come, the feeling of being a vacuum, and the horror of knowing a part of her was gone that could never be brought back, no matter what. How she had wanted to call a halt to it—over and over—and then, when the glucose needle sent her into euphoria, it was all too late, too late, too late. What she had done had been irrevocable, and nothing could ever bring that lost baby back.

* * *

When you have a baby in Manhattan and you walk with your child, the past comes back to you; you face the stone walls of Sixth Avenue by the Time-Life and Equitable buildings where you used to sit and cool your feet in the fountain, you see how tacky the all-night beauty salon you used to go to looks in the daylight, and you pass the billboards of Times Square, reassuring yourself the man is still blowing smoke rings out of the Camel sign. You remember. There is the ache at seeing the flowers at Rockefeller Center, and the pavements blanched with sunlight, the clouds melting into the downtown buildings, the shrubs lining Park Avenue, and all the shops on all the crosstown streets. There is the sweet gnawing of nostalgia as you walk past the Ryan-Davy Agency. Then there comes the surging sadness, recalling those young hopes and the young pain, the dreams of a child in a woman's body so full of expectations. How poignant it seems now, the hopes from those days and how young you once were. And now how different everything seems with your perspective grown. Now you have a link, you have maturity, a purpose, you are a woman now.

Marty Sachs sat, at five o'clock in the afternoon, in front of the television set.

"What are you doing, watching TV again?"

"I'm learning by watching the working actors."

Eve looked away in disgust.

"It's really a groove. I'm learning so much watching these old movies. That Bogart sure had it."

Heaving a sigh of disgust, Eve went into the bathroom to do the baby's diapers. How often she thought with longing upon the old days, the days when she had created such a stir at all the important jet set cocktail parties. It seemed as though she had been cut down and shut out before she'd even had a chance to begin to live. And now, here she was, involved in a dreary marriage, when by all rights she ought to be out in the world, having rich men all clamoring at her door, taking her to all the "in" places and making her be noticed wherever she went.

Seeing Carrie in the park had aroused a feeling of jealousy in her. How lucky Carrie was not to be tied down, to still have her freedom. Of course there were compensations her own life afforded; she had something Carrie did not have: she had Andrew. It certainly was lucky Andrew had not turned out Eurasian, or even too Semitic-looking. He was perfect. Eve wondered how she had existed before, not knowing this tender love.

But as to the rest of her life, as to her marriage, whatever feeling she had originally had for Marty had paled. The more she turned the matter over in her mind, the more she analyzed it, the more it seemed the emotion she had mistaken for love had been no more than curiosity, together with a very conventional first sexual awakening, that it had been normal and to be expected that due to the restricting circumstances of her upbringing she would have assumed it to be love.

Whatever the feeling *had* been, it no longer was.

There seemed little further she could do to make the marriage work. She had tried.

Eve threw the disposable diaper in the wicker wastebasket. As she picked up Andrew to move him to his bassinet and opened the bathroom door the sound of the TV bellowed in her ears.

*   *   *

"I said I want a divorce!"

Marty dropped his fork and stared at her in disbelief. "But, baby, I . . . I . . . I don't understand. You and I, we . . . we . . . we have a real swingin' thing goin' together; we love each other and . . ."

334

"That's the way it's going to be, Marty. I mean it."

"But why?"

"Why? I'll give you a few good reasons. You want to stay in the same spot forever, just driving a cab and waiting. You believe someday Broadway's going to come begging for you to star in a big hit play. Well, it just doesn't work that way, Marty. I try to tell you, I try to help you. But you won't take any of the suggestions I give. Like your appearance, for instance. I told you you ought to have your skin sanded, but you tell me all my ideas are phony. Marty, I don't need a million dollars, but I need more than you bring in."

"Honey, you don't understand. The whole trouble with you is you're materially oriented. That's the whole trouble."

"I don't care what you think the trouble with me is."

"You're materially oriented. That's what puts a strain on our marriage."

Angrily, Eve indicated the sparse furnishings. "I want more than this. I want more, and I need more, and I've had it with this whole situation."

He said, "It seems to me, there's a whole level that passes you by completely. You're unaware. Everything with you is cut and dry, black or white, there's no in-between."

"I'm a person of decision. No fooling around," Eve said. "You, Marty, you're always taking your time, just waiting for things to happen. Well, nothing ever does *happen*, Marty. You have to *make* it *happen*."

"No, I *live* things. That's the difference between *being* and existing. I am me, and I *be*."

Eve was sick and tired of Marty's everlasting talk about honesty, sensitivity, being, and all the rest of the code he claimed his creed.

"You don't understand anything at all, Marty Sachs. I'm tired of all this nonsense. This is no place for me and it's no place to raise a child." Words tumbled out. She spat out all the pent-up frustration with a depth of feeling that surprised even herself. "I can't stand it anymore. You don't understand me. You don't care. I want more than this and I want my son to have more. And don't try to kid me, Marty. You think *I'm* phony, you think I've got false values, you think I'm conning myself in the modeling business! Well, don't con *yourself*, Marty. Don't tell me you're studying acting by watching television. Marty Sachs, I want a divorce. I'm leaving, and I'm taking my son. I want him to have more than this."

"Andrew's *my* kid too!"

Eve shook her head in exasperation. "It's only some sperm, for God's sake, Marty! Only some sperm!"

"He's my kid!" Marty hollered, his eyes blazing.

"Oh, for God's sake," Eve screamed back, "stop getting so excited. What a big fuss to make over some little sperm! *I* carried Andrew for nine months, it was *my* body he lived in and grew in, *I* gave birth to him, *I* nursed him. Your contribution was one fuck, one little sperm cell, besides which I didn't have to marry you, you know, I could have just had Andrew alone without you, and anyway, how the hell do you know he's *yours*? I might have screwed a few other guys, how would you know?"

Lunging, he caught her by the shoulder and shook her. "Shut up, you cunt!" he cried. "You take that back, apologize, you bitch, or I'll knock your teeth in. Andrew's my kid and don't you ever pull a cheap cunt thing like this again on me, ya hear?"

Eve had never seen him so excited. "All right." She drew away from him and caught her breath. "All right, Andrew is your child too. But that doesn't change anything. I still want a divorce, no matter what. And now, if you'll excuse me," she said grandly, "I have to go give mother's milk to *your* son."

She hoped Marty hadn't soured her milk. Damn him, he had no idea how much he had cut her off from. Imagine, to have to live this way for the rest of her life! To think she had once idealized marriage. Well, it was really grossly overrated, this whole marriage business, anyway. She was beginning to understand that the most successful marriage, the most desirable kind, would be one of convenience.

Dolores Haynes had known this all along. Why was it she, Eve Paradise, had been retarded? Well, she was still young, she would have another go at it, and the second time around she would be far wiser. Now that at last she was hip about sex she would be one of the most desirable girls in town.

336

Chapter 15

Dolores had checked into the Beverly Hills Hotel, and was due to start shooting another TV show shortly. Generally she relished her seclusion by a rosebush out at the pool, soothed by the steady sounds of balls bouncing on the nearby tennis court. Here she could read the trades and study her script.

Today, however, it looked as if her privacy were being invaded. A young man was approaching. She had observed him for the past week, wondering what it was about him that was so familiar. The youth, short of stature, slender and graceful in figure, had fine-textured delicate hands and feet, and perhaps the narrowest hips she had ever seen on a male. (She hated men with slender hips; nothing to wrap herself around, nothing to dig her heels into.) Shyly, summoning his courage, he drew closer. "I see you're reading a script," he said. "I hope you don't mind my being curious, but is it anything I could see you in soon?"

"Not for a while yet, luv," Dolores said condescendingly. "We only begin shooting next week."

What was it about that face? The expression? The large attentive hazel eyes with the long eyelashes? The slender neck? His flat retreating narrow chin? The full round cheeks? The Roman nose? The full, rough-lined lips with their uneven outer rims? What?

"You're the first actress I've met," the boy said hesitatingly. "Have you been here long?"

"About a week." Dolores went back to her lines.

The boy continued, "I've been here about that long myself. I just got out of the service. I was stationed in Germany two years **with** the Air Force. Now I'm trying to get readjusted to civilian life. I suppose you must be from out of town, since you're staying here too. I guess you must be a Broadway actress."

"Yes, dear," Dolores mumbled, her eyes not leaving the page.

The waiter came, bringing a tray containing her lunch: Neil McCarthy Salad, toasted bagels, fruit, and coffee.

"Let me get that," he rose to sign the check, as Dolores thought, oh shit, this semi-fag creep closet queen I need like a hole in the head and now the jerk probably figures on ruining my lunch with his presence just because he picked up the tab.

The boy held out his hand. "My name is Larry Porter." He pulled a chair closer. She hoped none of the motion picture potentates who convened around the hotel at lunchtime would catch sight of her with this skinny ex-soldier. "My tray should be arriving any minute now."

What a drag his conversation was, so banal, so ineffectual.

"I'm twenty-four years old," he said. "Today is my birthday. How old are you?"

Dolores gave him a frigid stare. "Don't you know any better than to ask a woman her age?"

The boy swallowed, then falteringly trying to get control of himself, asked, "Do you know many people in New York?"

"Of course," Dolores snapped. "I live there."

"Oh, that's right." He blushed and tried once again to gain composure. "I—I don't know too many people in New York myself, although I happen to have been born there. But you see, I left when I was quite small. When I was only three weeks old as a matter of fact. They sent me to live with my grandmother in Florida. You see, Mother wasn't well—and she—she died shortly after that."

"That's too bad." Dolores bit into a bagel, wishing the youth would go away and leave her in peace.

"I only get to New York occasionally—as I say, I hardly know anyone there. About the only man I know in New York is somebody who often invests in the Broadway shows. I wonder if you might know him too?"

"Who's that?"

"A man named Nathan Winston. I know him and that's about all."

Nathan Winston! And suddenly it dawned on her. Of course! Those large hazel eyes with their long lashes, the expression of the face, the rough-lined lips with their uneven outer rims—that profile, that Roman nose! Pure Nathan Winston! Identical! It was the structure of the body that had thrown her—the delicacy, the effeminate quality, his gracefulness, undoubtedly inherited from the mother; but the rest of him could have come from one source only, sperm belonging to Nathan Winston. She remembered the time Nathan had made the slip about having three children and then corrected himself to say only two. She was sure of it. The resemblance was too striking.

She had not forgotten Nathan Winston's bitter humiliation in the south of France over three years ago, and her resolution to one day make him pay for it. And now, as if the answer to a prayer, this opportunity to reach a vulnerable spot had fallen into her lap.

The waiter brought Larry's tray. "I wondered if you were free this evening," he said, "I thought we might have dinner."

She purred, "Do you think you can afford a woman like me, darling?"

"Oh, yes, I have plenty of money," Larry replied ingenuously.

*　　*　　*

"You know," Dolores said, as they sat that evening at Frascati, "I noticed something about you, Larry, something which leads me to believe Nathan Winston must be your *father*."

Larry went pale. "How did you know?" he gasped. "Nobody knows about it—even when they see us together, Nathan—he—he's always introduced me as his *nephew*—I—" the boy stammered. "How—?"

"Just looking at you, darling, I knew immediately."

"You must know him then."

"Not well. I've met him a couple of times at dinner parties. But I couldn't help noticing what an attractive man he is. Such a strong resemblance between the two of you. You inherited his good looks."

Larry blushed uneasily. "Thank you," he said. How guileless and callow he was.

Another thing about Larry was he couldn't hold his liquor. Wavering before the evening was over, he blurted out his

339

story: Nathan Winston, divorced from his first wife, had gotten Larry's mother, a young Broadway dancer, pregnant. Having promised to marry her, he reneged and she had to see it through alone.

Three weeks after Larry's birth, his mother had called her parents in Florida, asking them to take the baby, saying she would care for him herself at a later date, as soon as she was able. Instead, one week later she had committed suicide. It was then Winston had tried to get the baby to adopt and bring up himself. Larry's grandmother had agreed on one condition, that Nathan acknowledge Larry as his legitimate son and heir, but Winston had refused, saying were the true facts known they would hurt him in business. Over the years he had been generous with money, and Larry was invited to stay any time, as his nephew.

Dolores took Larry's hand and looked deeply into his eyes. She said, "You're such an attractive man, Larry, so witty and so bright, so wise and knowing. And I admire your taste in clothes. Who is your tailor?"

Larry blushed to the roots of his hair. "Well, I got this suit at Sy Devore," he said.

Her words were breathy against his smooth pink cheek. "Darling, I like you tremendously. Do you feel the same way about me?"

As he inhaled sharply, she could feel his stirring. "Yes," he said.

An idea was circulating in her head, but she needed more time, more information. She said, "Why don't we drive to Palm Springs over the weekend? I start my show next week, but we can have the next few days together."

*   *   *

Dolores snuggled close to Larry in the Mercedes. He had been ready to rent a Chevrolet until she had put her foot down and said with disdain, "No one would dream of expecting *Dolores Haynes* to drive to Palm Springs in a *Chevrolet*."

Now the vehicle made its way through a light sandstorm. The dying reflections of the sun foraged the sage-clustered mountains.

"Tell me about your paternity," Dolores said. "If you needed to prove it, could you?"

340

"Sure."

"What have you got as evidence?"

"Letters. And then I have a copy of my birth certificate. It has his name on it. Of course he's had the original removed from the files and destroyed."

"But you do have letters?"

"Sure, lots of those. Even letters from Nathan to my grandmother. And, of course, Gram saved my mother's suicide note. It talks a lot about Nathan." Larry's face showed a trace of bitterness.

"She made a last attempt to get him back and failed. Nathan dropped her, you know. He was willing to pay her off, and to pay for my care and upbringing, but he didn't want anything more to do with *her*. He paid off a lot of people to hush up the whole mess."

"Where are the letters you have?"

"In Florida. Gram had them put in a bank vault before she died."

"Haven't you ever thought of getting them out and using them against your father?"

"What for? Money? He's always provided for me. I have all the money I need."

Dolores contemplated the stretch of sand, the vast acres that reached out like an Arctic steppe extending to the ends of the earth. Terra cotta, burnt sienna, gray and yellow plants swayed in the strong wind and the tumbleweed flapped against fences. She said thoughtfully, "It seems to me I read somewhere Nathan Winston had gone into politics. Is that so?"

"Yes. He's running for Congress on the Democratic ticket. He's got lots of Tammany friends."

"I suppose he's got a pretty good chance."

Larry turned to her shyly and said, "I've never met a girl like you before. This whole trip has been so wonderful."

Dolores was due to report to work Monday afternoon. Monday morning she asked Larry to take her shopping in Beverly Hills. She needed some new lingerie, and allowed him to foot the bill for a few items at Juel Parke, the total of which was $3,000. Next they visited Marvin Hime on South Beverly Drive, where she chose a diamond and sapphire pin. Larry was mesmerized, transported into a world he had never dreamed existed. Her slithering, serpentine movements during their lovemaking left him breathless and drained.

It was at the end of the week, Dolores having carried the heavy load of both the television show and her romance with Larry, when they were sitting in the dim light and wooden paneling of Scandia, over *krefte,* that Larry timidly announced he would like to marry her.

She took his hand and pressed it to her cleavage. "That's the loveliest thing anyone's ever said to me, darling. Let's do it immediately."

Chapter 16

"Carrie?"

She thought Jerry Jackson had given up.

"How've you been? What have you been doing?"

"Oh, I've been terribly busy on my book, polishing. I'm planning on applying for a fellowship."

"Why don't you take a break so we can get together again?"

"I'm sorry, Jerry, but I don't have time to see anyone."

"I'm not *anyone.*"

"Well, I'm still busy."

"Surely you have an hour here or there."

An hour here or there, Carrie thought impatiently.

"I have very pleasant memories of our moments together," he said. "I'd like to see you. My male vanity is such that I'd like to be more important to you. I'd like you to make the time to see me."

"I can't."

"I must say I feel rather hurt you don't want to see me."

"I'm sorry, it's impossible. I have my life to attend to."

"You're rejecting me. You're hurting my ego by refusing to see me. I have a great capacity for love and affection and you don't recognize me."

A pressure threatened to boil over. "A man has to have

something to offer a woman besides the eternal glory of a prick," Carrie said. "What are you offering besides that?"

No, she thought angrily, no, I will not loan out pieces of myself to be used for an hour here and there. Then she went back to her desk to continue polishing the book and to gather together some chapters to send Roger Flournoy.

* * *

Larry Porter, tightly clutching Dolores' arm, grinned as they stepped off the plane at the Las Vegas airport. The sound of slot machines, humming air conditioners, phones ringing, and loudspeakers blaring reached their ears.

"Caesar's Palace," Dolores told the cabdriver.

They were whisked down the Strip with its garish neons flashing, flaming, spiraling, revolving in mammoth leviathan shapes of missiles, parabolas, hyperbolas, and cantilevered elliptical towers. Larry said, "This is the most thrilling moment of my entire life. I love you, Dolores."

"I love you too, sweetheart," Dolores replied. "This is forever."

The lobby of Caesar's Palace was jumping with hookers and hoods, oily pimps and dark-suited dealers, old ladies in nylon print dresses, professional gamblers and hicks, all crowded around the roulette wheel, the craps table, 21, black jack, and the slots. Dolores and Larry registered as man and wife. Minutes later, they made it legal.

"I've had enough of this place," Dolores said after a dull copulation. "Let's go on to Florida."

They hopped the National Airlines DC 8 Star Stream Jet service first-class afternoon flight for Miami, and registered at the Fontainebleau, where Dolores did some more shopping and got Larry to open his safety deposit box and show her the documents pinpointing Nathan Winston as his father.

"Hi, there, this is National Airlines," the syrupy voice at the other end of the phone said. "Our lines *are* busy. Will you please wait a moment so that we can discuss your travel plans with you?" An instant later Dolores had made her reservation for New York. Six hours after that her taxi pulled up in front of Nathan Winston's posh digs at the swank River House.

Oswald, the butler, showed her into the hallway past Nathan's collection of Breughels, into the study which housed his collection of Sumerian figures with knoblike shaven heads, as well as his collection of Mycenaean goddesses holding snakes. Sitting on a citron-yellow sofa, Nathan Winston waited.

He had changed little. Still the tall burly figure with the wild mane of white hair, the tightly clenched fists, the unsmiling mouth, the corners of which nevertheless drooped more now than they had previously. The Roman nose, so like Larry's profile, now had become even more inflamed and swollen from catarrh.

Dolores presented him with a packet of photostatted documents. "These are the Xeroxes," she said. "The originals are in my possession in a vault at the Morgan Guarantee. Half a million in negotiable bonds buys the originals."

"I see you haven't changed any," Nathan observed. "Still the biggest ball-breaker in town."

"This town or any town, and you better believe it." She gave a lusty snigger.

He peered at her with cold expressionless eyes. "Suppose I refuse?"

She shrugged. "It's your funeral. I'm not the ace who's running for election. So make up your mind, Nathan, is it worth your political career, your future, or is your life just about over anyhow? You decide. I always said you were finished, way back when. Remember?"

"I remember," he glared.

"But you seem to be hardier than I gave you credit for. You may be a bad ball, Nathan, but you sort of cling to life. So if you figure on hanging on awhile more yet, if you think the recognition and fame of a politico is important, to say nothing of your whisky company, then you're going to have to pay up, and that's that."

He was red and shaken. "What you did to my son—you *whoore*—"

"If anybody hasn't got the right to talk self-righteously about their son it's you, you smug son of a bitch—old fart, you—"

Nathan's legs shook like jelly. "I hear you've got a child," he hissed. "I pity the defenseless bastard who never asked to be given life in the first place, having a cunt like you for a mother. What did you do with the poor fucking son of a bitch, flush it down the toilet? Where do you hide the poor bastard?"

"For your information, I have a lovely and charming daughter," Dolores said archly. "And her nurse is watching her. Not that this has anything to do with the issue at hand, but I just thought I'd answer your question."

"Does Henry Haupt ever get to see his child? Or isn't he the father? Who is the father? Some fucking French gigolo?"

"Look, Nathan," Dolores' eyes narrowed. "I didn't come here for conversation, or to fill you in on my life. I came here for one thing. I've made my offer, you can take it or leave it. I'll give you forty-eight hours to make up your mind. You can either arrange things with the Morgan Guarantee, as I said—or you can leave yourself open to one helluva scandal. Take your pick."

Within forty-eight hours Nathan Winston had met her terms.

* * *

It felt as though life were beginning again after a long period of imprisonment. Hiring a part-time sitter for the baby, Eve now found herself busy most of the day with interviews and print work, grueling all-day catalog and stock stuff at Warsaw, Underwood and Underwood, Binder and Duffy, and Pagano. The work was exhausting but could net her between $200 and $250 a day, so she considered it a godsend, particularly since only one of her former commercials was still running. However, the agency planned to rectify that situation in short order.

Her social life was beginning again and she was besieged with more invitations than she could handle.

It was at a jet set cocktail party she met Bruce Forman, whose company, Forman-Warsham, produced "Take a Crack," the game show she had quit during her pregnancy. During the time she had worked the show, Bruce had been only an awesome name. Seeing him now she took note of the agreeable fact that he gripped her hand firmly and looked straight into her eyes upon greeting her, and that his shaving lotion exuded a strong enticing odor.

She was delighted when he suggested she come to his office the next day. "I have something that may be of interest to you," he said.

* * *

Bruce Forman's office had the expensive look of a sportsman, with row upon row of horse prints decorating the pine-paneled walls. In a white leather chair opposite his desk, Eve now sat expectantly, while he looked through her book.

"These pictures are beautiful," Bruce said. "You photograph just great."

"Thank you. I see you like horses."

"Thoroughbreds are my hobby," he replied, brightening. "I've just recently come from the yearling sales at Saratoga. I'm out at the tracks pretty regularly during season."

She noticed that when he spoke his mouth protruded a little and that in repose his lips formed an "O" that gave him a childlike pouting quality.

He said, "What I asked you to come in about is this: remember your old job on T.A.C.?"

"Sure."

"I caught you several times. You were marvelous on it."

"Thank you." His masculine yet smoothly deft and flowing hand movements fascinated her, and she appreciated the way he looked at her in a half-disarming manner which showed he was interested in what she had to say and gave thought to his own words as well.

Bruce paused, brought his hands together, rubbed his palms and said, "How would you like to go back on the show?"

"Are you serious?" Eve's eyes nearly popped out of her head. The steady income would be just what she needed.

He grinned. "The girl who replaced you is pregnant now. We've got a regular round-robin going here between you two." He leaned forward. "You have no more plans in that direction, have you?"

Eve blushed. "I—I'm divorced."

"Good. That's what I heard. Just checking. How would you like to start working next week?"

Would she!

"And how would you like to have dinner with me tomorrow night and celebrate?"

"I'd love to."

* * *

Charlene was happy Eve's future was beginning to take a positive turn. She said, "One sixty-five for one day's work a week isn't everything, but at least it's something steady to depend on."

"That's the way I look at it, too."

"From there you can get some new commercials going, and start making some real bread again."

Hearing the news about Bruce Forman's personal interest, Charlene frowned. "You're a woman now, Eve, a woman with a child. From now on it's important you play that part, or your whole life and the life of your son will go down the drain," she said. "Take my word for it, play it cool with Bruce Forman."

"What do you mean, Charlene?"

"You know very well what I mean."

"What?" Eve persisted.

"Look, Eve, there was a time when you could have had this whole town at your feet. You loused things up. You married a taxi driver. All right, there's still time, you're young yet. You've got another chance now, but you can't afford to make another mistake. There's only one youth. Just remember, Eve, of itself this business is nothing. If you use it as a springboard, it can be everything. Smart girls realize and make use of their opportunities."

"Meaning?"

"Meaning play your cards right with Bruce Forman."

"How?"

"I really have to draw pictures for you. Bruce Forman is eligible, he's loaded, he's got status, every girl in town would like to land him. It's obvious he's interested in you; he put you back on the show, he takes you out to dinner. How many times have you been out with him so far?"

"Three."

"All right, since I have to spell it out. You have a child, you need money, you need help. Let Bruce help you."

"He's already given me the show again."

"That's not enough."

"What else can he do?"

"Get him to keep you."

"Oh, Charlene, I couldn't, I'm not that sort of—"

"Grow up, Eve, it's done everywhere—all over town, all over the world, by the best ladies in the best circles—politics, society, show business—you'd be surprised. Half the girls in this agency are kept. It would be the best thing that could happen to you at this stage of the game. Certainly you don't want to get involved in another marriage—"

Eve broke in, "Yes, I *would* like to get involved in another marriage! I want a *better* husband next time. I want to be a wife, Charlene, not somebody's mistress."

"Well, one of the best ways to become somebody's wife is to let him keep you first."

"How would I know he'd marry me later?"

"Once a man starts investing in you, it's a short trip to the altar, if that's what you really want. Only speaking as a multi-married woman, I can't see the point of jumping quickly."

"I need security. I have a child to provide a home for."

"All the more reason to let Bruce pay your bills."

"I would hate to have him think I was using him."

"Honey, what you don't seem to realize is you're on a new level now. You're no longer the starry-eyed ingenue, you're a woman, and you have to act the part. Well, a real woman doesn't go with a rich man free. Not if she has any respect and evaluation of herself as a person. My point is you'd better make *sure* you're not just any other girl to him. And make sure *before* anything happens."

"How?"

"Put him to the test. Eve, if Bruce really cares for you, he'll do something. And if he doesn't care, you're better off writing him off without another minute's thought. You don't need another man in your life who makes no contribution. No, honey, it's not enough to simply get around socially. You get around, get seen too much, you're yesterday's newspaper. Even if you don't sleep around, it's the same as if you had; you get to be thought of as used and shopworn because you're going nowhere. To stay interesting and exciting, you have to marry, move around, divorce, be kept, change things, travel, be *creating* a life for yourself. You can't let men like

Bruce Forman avail themselves of your youth. Oh, Eve, do you have any idea of the turnover of girls in this town?" Charlene banged her fist on the table and Eve thought she looked in pain. "You can't afford to end up a casualty, Eve."

"But, Charlene, I—"

"All I'm saying is this: if you want to sleep with Bruce Forman be sure you're not just another lay, Eve—be special."

"But I know he likes me."

"Bullshit!"

"But the way he looks at me—"

"Bullshit!"

"Charlene—"

"Honey, take my word for it, I'm a lot older than you. When a man takes you to dinner and looks at you over the table in the candlelight, all aglow with wine, when he looks in your one good eye and says 'darling you're marvelous, you're thrilling, you're beautiful, you're what I've waited my whole life for,' look back at him with the other eye jaundiced—"

"Oh, Charlene—"

"Never let him know you're wise to him. But don't open one button till he gives you a damned good indication he thinks you're special—"

"Well, Charlene, you can't just sign a contract, I mean, you can't—"

"Use Andrew."

"What?"

"Andrew's a wonderful asset, Eve, he's a wedge. Do you realize how lucky you are to have this child? There's no better wedge in the world than a child. This is why most women have them in the first place."

"What do you mean?"

"Look, Eve, every time you go out of the house, you have to pay a sitter, right?"

"Right."

"And this adds up. On your salary, you can't afford this expense. Next time Bruce asks you out, tell him it's getting too costly and frantic for you to pay sitters day and night, and you need a nurse for Andrew. You need it for your peace of mind. Ask him for help—"

Eve considered.

"You really *do* need a nurse, Eve. You can't afford one on the salary Forman-Warsham pays you. If he wants you, Bruce *ought* to pay for a full-time nurse."

"Maybe if I were to say it was a loan?"

"Get into him for this one thing as a start. Then gradually other things will come up. It will be like a connecting chain. Once you get into a man for one thing, the rest comes naturally. Just let him begin an investment, and he wants to protect his interests."

"It sounds calculating, but maybe you're right," Eve conceded. "It's true, I *don't* want to be just like any other girl to Bruce. I do want him to know I'm different."

"A woman needs signs, she needs proofs. Words won't do. Words are cheap and meaningless. The sooner you learn the better. Don't feel it's wrong, Eve. This is done every day by any and every woman who has any self-respect. It's tough for a girl alone in the world today, and even more so if she has the added responsibility of a child. You make a lot of money in this business but most of it goes out in expenses."

"I know. Bills just never stop—"

"You're in no position to keep up the struggle and give yourself away for nothing to a man. The least he can do is show his appreciation. How do you think most of the girls in the agency get the money to maintain expensive apartments, where do you think they get their jewelry, furs, their clothes? A beautiful woman not only is entitled to all these things, she needs them. She needs them because *everyone else* has them. Should you be any different than the other beautiful women in the world? There's no reason why you shouldn't have a life full of all the things all beautiful girls have. Just don't let yourself go cheaply. Place a high value on yourself."

Eve nodded. "I guess that's how Dolores Haynes did it, isn't it?"

"You bet it is. Dolores and a million other women, myself included. Don't you be a sucker, Eve."

Eve pondered Charlene's words and knew them to be true. That night she straightened out the matter of Andrew's nurse with Bruce, and it was settled that he would be glad to assume the expense. I'm getting there, she said to herself. I'm getting to be a woman at last.

Dear Carrie,

I'm afraid I have to say no. I simply cannot even read your work, as my eyes have been bothering me these days, and I only have one hour a day in which to do all my reading anyway, and besides, it's hard on the eyes propped up in bed that way. Sorry. See you soon, I hope. . . .

Roger

Tears formed in Carrie's eyes. For a moment, she felt all her hopes drop, as if a dull weight falling from her chest to the pit of her stomach. Only moments later her ire was up and she fumed, he's just like all the rest of the men in this town. Only if there were something in it for him would he bother.

But regardless of anything, she would keep on. This book would be polished, finished, and published, NO MATTER WHAT. She believed in herself no matter what Roger Flournoy, the phony old bastard, might think.

Phooey! Carrie thought. *Roger Flournoy is a big dirty old fart!!!!*

Chapter 17

"Dolores, honey!"

Ginny's mouth drew into a wide aperture as Dolores came through the door of the stud service. Ginny strode toward her and planting a kiss on her cheek, enveloped her in a hearty abbraccio. "Welcome home, luv-luv!"

"Hi, angel. I'm not late, am I?"

"No, it's only a little after eleven. Say, let's have lunch, shall we? We've lots to catch up on." Ginny winked.

"Sure, right after my session. God, I'm horny today."

"Hey, it's Thursday. They're serving *bollito* at the Colony. Keep that in mind, luv."

"I will," Dolores promised.

"Have fun!"

"Thanks," Dolores waved, as she disappeared up the stairs of the sumptuous town house. An hour later she reappeared.

"Everything come out all right?"

"Best goddamn fuck I've had in a dog's age. Where'll we eat? I'm starved."

"I dunno. What do you say we stroll and go where we happen upon? There's lots of places in the neighborhood."

"Groovy. We're off."

Ginny pursed her lips into a large orifice in anticipation of the cigarette she was extracting. When she placed its cork tip in her mouth the orifice closed up like a Venus flytrap.

Dolores studying the menu said, "I always say the best followup for a good fuck is a good fondue."

"Unless, of course, you've got problems like I have," Ginny said. "My gall bladder's been kicking up shit lately."

"That's too bad."

"But one day of splurging shouldn't hurt. Jesus, this is a damned good martini. Hmmm. Lobster bisque looks good. Wouldn't want it if I ordered the thermidor though. Whee! roast woodcock—haven't had any of *that* in a while."

"Me either," Dolores said, giving Ginny a sly, snide, insinuating glance.

"Smart ass. Oh, *tournedos à la béarnaise*. That looks divine, too. And I adore ox tongue au gratin."

"It's really hard to decide."

"Say, did I hear correctly, you're divorced again?"

"Right. I'm a three-time loser now."

"Well, don't let it worry you."

"I won't."

"Oh, and, hey doll, didn't you used to know Nathan Winston?"

"Sure."

"I guess you saw in the morning papers how he died last night. Oh, goody, here's our hors d'oeuvres."

Dolores took a studied sip of Harvey's Bristol Cream on the rocks. "I haven't seen today's papers. What happened to Nathan?"

"Oh, the old bird kicked off outside a theater, waiting for his car. Well, the emergency squad rushed him to Bellevue but it was too late. Some model or actress or some ding-a-ling was with him."

"Figures," Dolores said.

"One of his ex-wives is one of our best customers. God, does that dame take them on. Screams her bloody lungs out, too, the boys tell me." Ginny yawned. "Lucky for me I've got good soundproofing in the place, huh? I'd hate to tell you what *that* cost." She picked up a stalk of celery and crunched.

Dolores said, "That new guy Bobby really gives a great workout."

Ginny took another audible sip of her martini, glanced at her escargots, and said, "You haven't tried Arthur yet."

"Arthur?"

"He's got a prick so long he'll tear your intrauterine device to shreds."

"Sounds interesting," Dolores considered. "Actually, I prefer thick pricks to long ones, but it's certainly worth giving the guy a tryout. What have I got to lose?"

"Listen, every bitch in town's signing up for a session with Arthur."

"He must have something."

"I told you, he does, and you can take it from me. I'm a hot cunt myself so I ought to know. I've got my Sun in Scorpio, and us Scorpios know a good screw when we get one."

"My ascendant's in Scorpio."

"We're sisters under the skin. Us Scorpio girls have the most talented twats in the zodiac, you know. We come equipped with snatches that spiral and swivel on the inside just like snakes." Sauce from the snails had dribbled onto her chin and Ginny wiped it away. "Most passionate pussies around. Take it from me as one Scorpio to another, Arthur's worth his price."

"Okay, put me down for the earliest opening—ahem."

"That'd be a week from Friday."

"Groovy."

"I'll have to let you know the time, I don't have my appointment book with me. You know, I think there's something wrong with my escargots. Too much garlic or something. Waiter. Oh, waiter! God, the service in this joint stinks."

Glancing upward between sips of lobster bisque, Dolores looked at Ginny appraisingly; large nose, oily at the corners, skin in need of powdering, could stand a treatment at Dr. Behrman's for removal of blackheads and small blemishes. The mascara had rubbed off from her lower lashes onto her skin. On her index finger she wore a large blue sapphire. Her head was crowned with a cluster of Little Orphan Annie curls. Dolores wondered how Ginny could keep up the hairdo and still lead an active sex life, until she realized Ginny was wearing a wig.

"Madame." The waiter was bowing over the table.

"Never mind, it's all right now," Ginny said, popping another escargot into her mouth.

Dolores said, "Hey, that waiter's pretty cute. I bet he'd make more money working for you at the house than here waiting on tables. Why don't you enlist him?"

"Uh uh. His prick's too small. I can size up a guy's dinkus by the slope of his shoulders and I'm never wrong. Could you pass me the bread?"

"Sure. Mmm. This soup's delicious. Have some croutons?"

"No, thanks. Seriously, you know, male tail, good male tail, that is, is sure as hell more and more at a premium with each passing year."

"Sure is."

"But our place deserves a gold star. I've personally trained every one of those boys at the house how to clamp in, hold out, and pump away."

"Congratulations, Ginny, you've done a great service to humanity."

"If I do say so myself, I've done what you might refer to as a bang-up job." When Ginny grinned her mouth twisted up to one side. "The reason I'm so sexually hip is I was a temple vestal in Egypt in a past life, and let me tell you, what I didn't learn about screwing from those high priests."

The waiter brought the main course and Ginny continued, "Our studs are wise to picking up a lady's rhythm, finding the position that really turns her on and holding it. You know how a fraction of an inch can spell all the difference in the world, and how so many guys are too damned egotistical to admit it." She bit into her *tournedos*. "It is sure a cinch the husbands aren't giving it the way the bitches want it. It's a rare husband who can do the job right."

"Tell me about it," Dolores said, cutting her meat. "I've had two impotent husbands. Two out of three."

"Can I have the pepper after you? Thanks. Like I say, our boys are specially trained to take their cues from the ladies. This is why we have the most prominent clientele in town. Everybody in politics, society, Who's Who. Jesus, what's a hot bitch to do when she's stuck with one of those weak-assed husbands or she's divorced and hasn't found a new bed partner yet? She knows damned well what she's going to do. Come to our place where she knows she can get it the way she requires it."

Dolores said, "Right you are, Ginny girl. Take me, for instance, as a good case in point. Now personally I know, as you yourself know, that men are pricks to begin with, that a woman's got to play her cards right and put on a hell of an act for them. And then the point is, we never get our own gratification because the idiots don't know how to satisfy a woman. Like you say, too damned much ego. Well, the thing about the stud house is I come here because I'm calling the shots. No arguments, no trouble. God, with other men, I just about start to get turned on, like I know I'd be ready to go off in another thirty seconds or a minute at the most, and damned if the bloody bastard doesn't *know* it and on purpose, he *moves*, he gets off like you say even a fraction of an inch, and my goddamned come is lost, I can't make it. That sure as hell never happens at the service, and that's why I come here."

"It's like the vagina has teeth," Ginny said, "and you have to clamp a guy's cock onto the right ones, kind of just into the right grooves at exactly the right angles. Well, the husbands, the pricks and the goddamn bastards of this world who have no idea what a woman's like, they come *off* the groove—on purpose. And you know why? Because they're *threatened*, that's why."

"Sure, sure they're threatened, the sons of bitches."

"They're threatened all of a sudden because their male supremacy is in danger. They're caught there, their cock is a prisoner being clamped by those vaginal teeth and they can't take the threat."

"That's right. That's exactly right."

"The whole trouble," Ginny said, "is that woman is supposed to be the leader. She's supposed to take the reins in accordance with the way nature intended. Only the average male is scared; he won't allow the woman to direct and he won't allow the current to pull and suck him in. He just can't give up that illusion of male supremacy; the idiot thinks he has to be *in control* till the bloody end. Shit. Like, I mean, it's just too goddamn grim. Want a taste of my *tournedos?* It's too much for one person."

"No thanks, I've got all this."

"Your broccoli looks divine."

"Bitchinest broccoli in town. How about a bite?"

"Well, just an eensy one. Mmmm. Yummy hollandaise. What were we talking about?"

"Fucking."

"Oh, yes, that's right. Well, as I was saying how it really pays a broad to be rich so she can come to our place. All the lady has to do is spread her legs and our boys'll pump it to her exactly the way her little cunt craves it. Most ladies come here on an average of two basic fucks a week, though some of them like to get it five times or more. I don't know, there are some who come every blasted day of the week." Ginny winked. "But no telling how many times they *really* come. Are you having dessert?"

"I think I'll break down. How about you?"

"I could be persuaded. Where's that tiny-weenie waiter? Waiter? Oh, waiter! I'm going to have some St. Emilion au chocolat. How about you, Dolores?"

"The melons with port looked awfully good to me."

Ginny lit an after-lunch smoke in her Venus flytrap fashion. Blowing rings thoughtfully, she said, "You've heard of Oedipus, of course."

"Of course."

"The reason I ask is this. Before going into the stud service training-and-management business, I was a classics major at Radcliffe. Nobody understands this whole sex thing. It's all been misconstrued. If you ever read *Oedipus at Colonnus* by Sophocles, you may remember the Erinyes, the 'awful goddesses.' Do you know about them?"

"Not offhand."

"Where Oedipus finds his last home in the grove, he implores these goddesses, calling them 'queens of dread aspect' and 'awful goddesses.' It's here in the grove of the 'awful' goddesses where Oedipus the wanderer at last comes to rest and finds his real home. He realizes his true strength lies in connection with the matriarchal goddesses. They're called 'awful' simply because, belonging to an ancient long-forgotten order of things, when women used to be the supreme deities and ruled with feminine wisdom and insight, they're now so far removed from the new Olympian culture that men view them suspiciously and with fear. But Oedipus realizes his strength lies in making his *peace* with them. This still applies today. In other words, men have made a joke out of women. Ergo, our women of today are in reaction against it."

Ginny played with her box of filter-tip cigarettes, turning it over and over on its side and on its end. She said, "The whole bloody trouble with the whole fucking world is *men* wearing the pants and trying to dominate. So what happens? Lousy sex lives, wars, racial problems, economic problems, everything."

"Shit," Dolores said, "the men of today just have no *chutzpah*, no balls, no *behtzeem*. Husbands are all prickless ball-less wonders, two out of three of them can't even get it up, for God's sake. Oh, waiter, I'm ready for my coffee now. How about you, Gin?" She swallowed her last bite of melon. "But in my opinion husbands weren't meant for anything more than security and a base of operation, a steady escort for social occasions."

"No, I say, as soon as men realize they've fucked the world up with their egotism, and let women assume their rightful role as leaders, sexually and otherwise, you'll see a different world. People will be walking around with smiles on their faces for a change 'cause there'll be peace and plenty. Plenty of peace and plenty of piece. I mean, sex will be sex again, for Christ's sake. Men'll be much happier, because it'll remove a burden they've never felt right about assuming in the first place. They'll be happier because they were never meant to take over the way they have. Jesus H. Christ. This whole power thing's gotten so out of hand it's ridiculous. The whole world's distorted and all because of sex."

357

"Too bad Jackie Kennedy never ran for President," Dolores said.

Ginny turned the restaurant matchbook over and said, "Red power, black power, green power, yellow power, flower power, it's all a fucking bore. The goddamned Democrats and the frigging Republicans, the whole world, for Christ's sake—like there's de Gaulle and his prostate problems. This whole power thing is nothing but a lot of impotent militants compensating for sexual frustration. Bunch of sick bastards. So the whole world suffers, and women like us don't get enough. But I should complain. My business is thriving because the world's in the shape it's in. I'm making money hand over fist."

Ginny took a final sip of her coffee. "Can you get the waiter's attention?"

"I'll try." Dolores kept one eye on Ginny and said, "Men. You know the more I see of them, the more I think we're *flattering* them by calling them pricks. That's too good a term for them."

"Right you are," Ginny agreed. "They ought to be called something really fitting—like—like—"

"Like what?"

"Like—*fleas!*"

"That's it! Perfect. I'd forgotten about that one, haven't heard it in years."

"Fleas that hop on and off."

"Oh, here's our waiter. Check, please, waiter."

"Fleas," Ginny repeated. "Fleas."

Chapter 18

It seemed she had wanted Bruce to take her to bed for ages, Eve thought, as the two of them sat close together under the fox-hunt prints in his library. Chang, the Chinese houseboy, had just been dismissed for the evening. Eve reflected that nothing ought to be standing in the way now; Bruce had not only sent flowers and agreed to pay for Andrew's nurse, he had just that day bought her a gold and ruby pin at Tiffany's. Everything Charlene had instructed her to make him do he had done gladly; certainly there could be no doubt remaining how he felt. Yet here they sat, distant with the strain of what they both knew would happen (tonight! tonight!) spreading over them.

Bruce lit a Schimmel Pennick, took a gulp of Scotch and smiled tautly. It was becoming increasingly apparent to Eve that he was as aware as she of the current of electricity between them, and of the gulf that needed to be breached. She would have wished for an occasion of romance and haphazardness, for the sense of being overcome after an evening of dancing, or of the chance happening of their being left alone after a party, slightly drunk, aroused, unable to control themselves. But she would have to be content with things as they were. Yes, tonight was the night, of that she was certain and decided. His body, close in physical distance, seemed so poignantly foreign and unknown.

Hands folded on her lap, she waited, thinking how stupid the whole situation was, hoping Bruce would have the expertise to bridge the gap quickly, painlessly. Anything she were to offer now in the line of chatter would sound hollow and superfluous, she knew. Her hands shaking, Eve lit a cigarette. Her body was trembling.

Then, before she even knew what was happening, Bruce turned to her, took her cigarette and snuffed it in an ash tray. He reached out, wrapping her in his arms, increasing the pressure of the embrace until she felt the full shock of his strength and let out a smothered cry. His hand moved inside the neckline of her dress and found her bare skin. With a rough jerk he pulled her closer yet, until finally under the strain and intensity of exploration, they fell back together, searching to reach the vitals of each other and to discard all burdensome inessentials of clothes, doubt, timidity, embarrassment, and incompletion.

In the effusion of feeling which ensued, it seemed she might explode, felled by so much rapture and inexhaustible thirst. And then, lying in the flickering shadows of candlelight, expended from their first desperate struggle, his breath was calm against her ear. The warmth it exuded, together with the comfort of his body in repose with her own, gave her a sense of thanksgiving. She wished she could find the words to tell him how she felt.

For some time they continued to hold each other, to stroke the newfound smoothness and plasticity of skin, at intervals reaching toward one another tenderly, touching each other's faces with parted, motionless lips. She loved the way he looked now, his hair ruffled, his face quiet, unstrained, serene.

"Are you happy?"

"Yes," she whispered, brushing his lips. "Couldn't you tell?"

"I'm glad it was good for you too. You're a wonderfully sweet girl, do you know that?" They kissed. "Can you stay the night?" his voice came huskily into her ear.

Her hands passed over the curve of his body. "As soon as Andrew's nurse is installed, I'll be able to stay as often as you like." They stared into each other's eyes, as the candles fluttered and cast soft patterns on the wall. *Thank you Charlene,* she thought, the way she used to thank St. Jude.

"At least we can have another go at it," Bruce whispered hoarsely. Then he lifted her up, carried her into the bedroom, and closed the door.

* * *

"I know my ideals have been too high," Carrie said. She and Eve were lunching at Le Gourmet. "I've been attracted to the wrong men but I've decided to compromise. You know, Eve, I've decided that maybe a dull, plain, ordinary man is the best kind of husband."

"Well," Eve said. "They seem to be the ones that get married the most."

"And maybe even dull men improve with marriage. Anyway, I've met somebody I'm going to try it on."

"Who?"

"His name is Jack Adams."

"Well, do you like him at all?"

"I don't know. We've had two dates and I've tried to get to know him. I keep asking myself what's behind that conventional exterior, you know, the short-cropped hair, the high-buttoned Madison Avenue suit with the paisley tie. He's kind of got a blond, washed-out face and a monotonous voice."

"He sounds awful."

"He's not the exciting type. But if it's the ordinary kind of man who is the best husband material, then I owe it to myself to make the best effort to be tolerant and to try, don't you think?"

"Well," Eve said, "I guess so."

Carrie sighed, "I'm going to do my best anyway, Eve. I do want a meaningful relationship with a man. I want that more than anything."

* * *

Staring at her reflection in the bedroom mirror, Dolores idly wondered what she would do this evening. November now; the social season was hardly under way and already she was frustrated. She considered it had been five years since she'd lost her contract and come to Manhattan. She looked around the apartment. She hadn't done badly, but she was thirty. How time had flown. What had happened? Why hadn't she achieved her goal? Self-doubt gnawed at her but she tried to push it aside. No, she would not give in. She would not!

She smoothed her hand over her skin, feeling its soft texture with an admiring caress. Here in the bedroom at her large dressing table with its triple mirrors, her beauty seemed heightened; the lighting offered just the right amount of mutedness, the rose tones from the bedspread and drapes reflected in the mirrors picking up and complementing her dark loveliness to perfection.

How different it was out in the world of the business, though, where one was constantly subjected to the strain of having one's appearance scrutinized carefully and there was the worry, are they seeing the crinkly lines, the tiny defects, the small, almost imperceptible blemishes she had spent a fortune trying to treat and cover and overcome.

Her fingers gently beginning to massage a masque into her skin, she recalled with fury some lines she had overheard at a cocktail party the evening before: "She was so beautiful in her day. Remember Charlene Davy? She used to be the toast of New York. Pity women have to age." She had turned and seen the deliverer of the remark to be a white-haired man in his seventies, a well-known roué who was never seen with a girl over twenty-five, and she'd filled with resentment. Why was it she still couldn't forget the antagonistic feeling it had roused in her? The self-doubts gnawed at her once more.

Shit, anyway, she thought, reaching for her modeling book, sifting through the pages slowly and appreciatively. The stunning photos greeted her. Enraptured with herself, she drank in the deep pools that were her eyes, the soft moue of her inviting provocative mouth, the gentle line of her breasts, the fluidity of her hair and body. Nothing to worry about, kid, she reassured herself, you've got a lot of mileage left on you yet. And what with modern techniques, what with Kounovsky and Benne and getting her quota at the stud service, she'd last longer than Charlene Davy had, so what the hell.

Last for what? That was the question. She wondered why it was she seemed to have become so bored with everything lately, why she couldn't seem to feel the same way about her social life as she once had. The thing was you had to keep it up; once you were launched in society you could never relax or you'd lose the image you'd fought so hard to attain.

But there ought to be something. *There ought to be something.* The refrain kept circulating in her mind. And days were as meaningless as nights. Where did the time go? Aside from interviews, Kounovsky's, Benne's, the hairdresser, lessons, there was shopping, of course, meeting people for lunch, appointments at the stud service. But something was missing, and she didn't know what. She was sick of it all with the too-rich diet of her cream-puff world; in fact, she was even getting fed up with the stud service.

Perhaps it was the work situation that was really bothering her. Now that she was a well-known figure in the fashion and society world, seen so frequently on the pages of magazines and in the gossip columns, it had become increasingly difficult to get jobs. The agency people were afraid the image of Dolores Haynes' *Vogue-Harpers' Bazaar-Women's Wear Daily-Town and Country* personality would detract from the image of the product. No further calls had come from Hollywood, and as for Broadway, she had spent time reading new properties, looking for a play to produce and star herself in, but as yet, nothing interesting had turned up.

While the masque was hardening, she wandered around the apartment surveying her treasures with a feeling of aimless disorientation: there were the Queen Anne and the French canape love seats, the boulle commode, the Louis XIV armoire, and the rococo desk; the palladian gilded settee, the group of medallion-backed chairs, the Carlin coffer decorated with Sèvres plaques, and the Bergère chairs, the *fauteuil* signed G. Jacob; there was her neoclassic tented Malmaison-style bed and so what? So what? So what? How often this way she would pace through the rooms feeling mean and restless, as though she were a caged animal needing to burst out at the seams, yet not knowing in which direction to go. Sometimes she would even kick the furniture and curse aloud.

She was obsessed with the thought, suppose I should lose all this, then what? And it seemed to her she was living in a house of cards. The maid, the doorman, everyone deferred to her—only because she could pay. Yet was this not precisely what she had striven all her life to attain?

Only now what? She would ask herself that over and over. *Now what?* She would idly thumb through her unread books and put them back on the shelves, rearrange her clothes, look in drawers, pace, call the maid in over some trifle, talk on the phone, look in the mirror, redo her makeup, read the gossip columns, and then ask herself over again *now what?* She'd wonder, what do I really want to do? And the answer would come, *I really don't know at all.* Let's see, what is there to want? Love? No, that's a farce, it doesn't exist. Beauty. I have that. Luxury—I have that too. Sex—sure I have all I want, whenever I want it. Adulation. Yes, I want that, being a focus of attention. This was what her publicist was working on, fine. But why didn't it happen, so she would *arrive,* be where she was meant to be?

Tina's nurse was leaving. She'd have to find someone else. Now the calls were coming in for appointments, in answer to the ad she had placed in the *Times,* but she didn't feel like taking any more calls. She was tired of all this nuisance, of her life being broken up into little pieces, her energy sapped in a hundred different directions.

United Parcel arrived with a new shipment of clothes from Allen and Cole. Dolores threw the packages on the bed.

Why was it everything was taking so long to resolve itself? So much was missing. The void in her life made her see her whole existence as the oversimplified, watered-down compositions in a child's book of piano classics, where the pieces contained the surface melody only. To a trained ear, the compositions were inadequately structured, whole chords missing, progressions seeming not to follow or emerge at all, the truth of the treble completely unapparent from the lack of bass support, the result sounding tinny and obtuse.

The masque was dry and she washed it off. It had done its work and tightened her skin. But she was dissatisfied with her appearance. Her hair needed another treatment. She called the beauty shop and made an appointment for later on in the afternoon.

* * *

Their eyes met in the mirror and held there. It was as if they were looking deep inside the other's being, as if they had known each other forever. Dolores caught her breath.

"Who is that?" she asked Jean-Claude, the homosexual hairdresser who was setting her hair.

"Fiona Barnes."

Fiona Barnes.

Roxie, the manicurist, said, "Have you seen the latest issue of *Vogue?* She's in it. Here, honey. Look with your free hand. Page seventy-six."

Dolores read:

Fiona Barnes, the exquisite soubrette, more glowing even than when spotlighted in the supper clubs, achieves her inimitable look here on these pages. It's a combination of today, the now, and her own uniqueness, with just the right dash of the Continental she borrowed when she was studying philosophy at the Sorbonne. The exciting provocative Fiona comes as the prismatic reflection in many mirrors, pouring herself out, ever radiant and childlike, yet at the same time able to display a hard-core toughness, an inward vulnerability when she sings. It's as if life had given her vision and understanding of the human condition. Indeed, gifted with natural clairvoyance, her eyes see deep into the truth, into the heart of things.

The essence of vitality and energy, Fiona shimmers like bits of shattered fireworks, bombilating, scattering magic; wherever she goes she radiates sizzling light. Tallow-haired and tragic, witty, intelligent, more often mirthful and sometimes jazzy, her moody songs alternate between the sad, the tuneful, the joyful; while Fiona herself reveals the woman underneath as knowing and needful, golden, free, abandoned, lovely.

Here over her intense and knotty body she wears a checked pants suit, boots, and a fleece coat.

Dolores continued reading the spread, looking at the photos of Fiona, at her perfect bone structure and smooth skin, at her enigmatic, smoldering, and compelling eyes. Then she looked up and found that Fiona was still smiling at her.

They both went under the dryer at the same time, emerged and had their comb-outs at the same time. And then they were in the cloakroom together, and she was standing next to the fascinating Fiona.

Hair all fresh and clean, zippy, perfumed, Fiona donned a cuir sauvage skirt, a jersey body shirt, and beige trench coat. The look was casual, easy, jaunty, sportif. Her style. Those eyes, those hurt eyes. Dolores met them again, those wise, yearning eyes, saying follow me, I want, I need, I can give. Yes, yes! It was as though all of Dolores' cells answered yes, yes! independent of her mind, as though her sensory makeup knew and understood here was the essence of all she had missed, that here, in this shining young woman, at last the void would be filled, the answer found.

On the street, Fiona's presence next to her sent shock waves through her body. Taxis flew past, whipping and slicing the wind, splashing her and blowing her hair, but it didn't matter; what mattered was only this, being next to this exciting person, feeling, being one with her, belonging.

*   *   *

They sat in a dark corner, talking, eating biscuits, and sipping sherry. Dolores met Fiona's soulful gaze and bathed in it, knowing release and harmony as she had never before experienced them. She lowered her eyes and found her reflection in the wineglass.

Fiona studied her intensely. She said, "I know you, I know you as if you were my sister. I know everything about you."

"Tell me what you know."

"I know you have a child. There've been many men. None of these things has brought you what you seek."

"True."

"You're not one of these women for whom a man or a child is everything, the justification for existence. Your life, what you are, is separate from all that."

Dolores nodded.

"You're a very complex woman."

"Yes."

"Complex and complicated. You're a great deal like me. We have so much in common." Fiona leaned closer. "You and I are going to be great friends."

Dolores said, "I don't make friends with women very easily, but this is different—I can tell."

The corners of Fiona's mouth turned up slightly in an inscrutable smile. "Yes," she said. "This *is* different."

Feeling herself unable to remove her eyes, Dolores wondered about the enigmatic, mysterious, compelling Fiona, and this attraction for her. What was it that was happening to her, in this feeling of being drawn in, of being sucked into a vortex, like a fly to honey. Somehow, it seemed to her that Fiona knew answers, that she knew—something, something she, Dolores, must learn also.

"Tell me more," Dolores said. "You were analyzing me."

Leaning back and with lids half-closed, Fiona said, "Your need is so great. Even you have no idea how great your need is. You have a tremendous need for everything—success, money, fame, love, admiration—everything."

Dolores nodded. "Go on."

But Fiona seemed to return from a reverie and, laughing like a child, clapped her hands together. "That's enough use of spiritual power for today." Looking Dolores directly in the eye once again, she said, "You know, you have a beautiful face. Fantastic. My hobby is photography, and I'd love to photograph you."

"Wonderful," Dolores agreed.

* * *

The antique shop was alive and shimmering, glowing and speckled with light and glass, replete with crystal and porcelain, jade and bronze statues, chains, clocks, figurines, hurricane lamps, and suspended from the ceiling, a plethora of chandeliers and jewel-like beads, all clarity, brilliance, and incandescent light.

Night was drawing on, and Dolores wanted to buy something for Fiona before the shades were drawn and the lights extinguished from the sparkling shop. All the while they browsed, she searched Fiona's face for further clues as to her magic, her hypnotic power. Fiona chose a porcelain figurine.

Outside once again, as they walked in the thickening mists of November, Dolores told Fiona about what she had been experiencing lately, about the vacuity of her life, and the fact that something was missing and she didn't know what. "I don't understand what I want next," she said as they rounded a corner, huddling close to the glass and brick of the walls. "I've always thought I knew exactly where I was going, and it's only just these past few weeks some crazy kind of doubt has started to creep in. I don't understand what it is. I've never felt like this before."

Fiona said, "Life is a constant progression of levels and shadows. There are always shadows of the self, each one contradicting the other, taking another direction, another convolution. You've progressed, that's all. You've been experiencing a period of transition, and soon you'll emerge knowing even more surely than you ever knew before exactly where you're going."

"You think so?"

"I know so. Didn't I tell you I knew all about you?" She exerted a magnetic pressure on Dolores' arm. "Another phase is beginning. From this day forward, life will be different, you'll see. A great change is beginning. This is epiphany for you."

They had reached another corner. Fiona looked deep into her eyes and said, "Here is where I must leave you, my dear sweet new friend, my lovely Dolores." She raised a gloved hand and touched Dolores' cheek lightly. "We'll be seeing a great deal more of one another," she said, and smiled and turned and walked away.

Chapter 19

"You look like the type of girl who prefers sculpture to spaghetti," Jack said at noon when Carrie met him outside Ratazzi's, where they were supposed to have lunch. With that they switched and walked over to the Modern Museum.

They'd settled down at a table, ordered food, discussed politics, music, and art, when Jack said, "You're a girl with a head on your shoulders. You're not like other women, you have a fine mind. You're very sensible. You're reasonable."

It was as though she were seeing beyond his words into an underlying attitude, reading the twinges of misogyny in him, and it made her cringe to feel he didn't want a woman to be a woman, but to be like a man.

It seemed they were so far apart. She kept thinking, Oh I long, how I long for someone to see me, to touch me—I mean, *really* see and touch, *inside,* to reach me and stir me and involve me. But then she reminded herself, this was what she had always looked for and where had it ever gotten her except in trouble.

After lunch they walked around. It was as if she could hear the chorus of humanity in the shapes and colors, in the paintings and in the crowds milling about the museum, all sending out their odors and noises, their silences, their perfumes, their tastes, their laughter, their shadows.

It struck her that life itself can be a work of art no less than a poem or a painting, that as the artist, in touch with higher forces, harnesses his vision, and the painting, the poem, the music, depend on his quality and scope, people's lives, too, bore witness to the totality of their truth and understanding.

She looked at Jack. What's wrong with me, she wondered. He's impeccable, kind, honest, diligent, intelligent—and dull.

Making love, would he be like that, calm and sensible, dull, like everything else about him?

Why? Why, Carrie asked herself, can't the substance of earth and sky and sea and laughter and love and joy exist in one human embodiment, that allows us to be complete? I want to be mature about all this, and maybe maturity is being content with less. Perhaps mature love is acceptance. And perhaps some hungers are too great to ever be appeased.

Jack's face was blank and expressionless. There was no current between them, nor was he captured by the paintings. I want someone to touch me, she thought, I want someone to touch me, and Jack never can.

* * *

The entire afternoon, Fiona had shot roll after roll of film on Dolores, heads, full-lengths, three-quarters, glamor shots, dramatic shots, color, and black and white. "You have the most fantastic face I've seen in ages," Fiona said, and Dolores basked in admiration. Now, tired from several hours' hard work, they sat close together in Fiona's apartment, partaking of the brandy and cakes Fiona offered.

Fiona asked, "Do you turn on?"

"Sure."

"So do I. We'll do that together sometime."

"How about now? Have you got any grass?"

"No rush. There's plenty of time. I want to get to know you." Her eyes bored meaningfully into Dolores.

"Blowing pot does wild things to me. Puts me way out there," Dolores said.

"Really? It makes me philosophical. I'm a natural philosopher to begin with, but pot makes me even more so." Fiona's laughter was sublime and tinkling. She leaned in. "Dolores, I feel I can say anything to you."

"You can. I feel that way too."

"You're so very beautiful. Is it perverse for me to admire your beauty so?"

The apartment was still. It felt as though time had ceased moving and that the two of them existed elsewhere, in another part of the universe. Fiona's eyes were immeasurably deep-seeing, as though they sucked in Dolores' whole existence.

"Do you have a sense of unreality?" Dolores asked.

369

Fiona's voice was hushed. "I know—they speak of the anti-world, and of the etheric double. That's in a sense how it is with us. I don't know, it's as though commonly we are merely reflections, appearances, shadows of shadows, the whole while knowing there is more, much, much more BEYOND somewhere— And here, now, with us, this is the most we have had, and it's a plenitude, this plenitude of shadows; you and I are recognizing each other's shadows after having searched an eternity."

Fiona's magnetism held Dolores riveted, transfixed. She drank in her mellifluous words as nectar as Fiona continued, "I think of us as rays from a prism, and yet the essence of us controls, dictates from very deep inside. This inner part of ourselves calls the rays forth, so to speak. And you and I have called each other to each other." She smiled knowingly, taking Dolores' hand in hers. "It's lovely outside at this hour. Shall we take a walk together?"

* * *

"I told you yesterday this is a time of epiphany for you, a time of personal revelation. Any revelation is just an indenture into something even deeper, more convoluted, more unfathomable, until you solve it, until you resolve it."

Darkness had gathered, the city was buzzing with traffic snarls and rushing crowds. Her steps moving slowly in perfect rhythm and coordination with Fiona's, Dolores said, "The thing with me is, the thing I've been feeling lately is this anger, this fury inside."

Their arms were entwined, anchored, and buried into the other's pocket. When Fiona shuddered Dolores had an urge to shield her. "I once felt that way myself," Fiona said. "I almost killed myself once."

"Really?"

"Damned near. I'd even selected the spot. The Pan Am Building, because I like the symmetrical view it has of Park Avenue below. I wanted that for my final view of earth, you know, as though reassuring myself order existed. As I was going up in the elevator, you know, those silent push-button ones they have, I wondered if anyone around me suspected what I was going to do. All of a sudden it really struck me as positively uproarious that of course no one *could* know, and that it was utterly possible for me to execute something as final as suicide in the midst of all those people, not one who could know my secret or prevent me from carrying out my plan."

"What kept you from it?"

"A voice."

"A voice?"

"Yes, when you spoke of the inner fury—I thought of this voice which came to me and saved me. It said, 'Find the *fury*, seek it out. Measure it, guard it, keep it, then let it out, unleash it, know it, understand it, conquer it, energize it, galvanize it, give, turn it to *love*. Spread treasure, give out, pour truth, take, give, conquer, know, understand, *be*.' Those were the words. I didn't understand what they meant, I didn't understand how to go about obeying the voice or executing a program around what the voice had told me, but the quality of the experience was so strong, that it was enough to save my life."

"Do you understand now?"

"Better. Yes, I think I'm beginning to understand." Fiona smiled. "I think the *whole* is somewhere else, and perhaps when the whole, or the All, comes together, if it ever does, it will mean either annihilation or fulfillment."

"Interesting idea."

"So I think the trick of this life here is to seek the relative, not the absolute. I think that's all we can have here."

"If you can really bring yourself to look at it that way, I suppose it would change a lot of things," Dolores said, feeling suddenly chilled and shuddering.

Fiona was thoughtful a moment. Then she said, "Despite your marriages, your money, your social life, everything you've done—you've never been a happy woman. Have you ever wondered why? Have you ever had any idea what it was that could make you happy in this life?"

"Yes."

"Have you ever wondered why everything is so unsatisfactory with men?"

"Damned right."

"Why it seems your whole existence with a man is manipulating them and playing games?"

"Right."

Fiona nodded. "I thought so," she said.

"Do you know the answer?"

"Yes," Fiona smiled, "And you will know too. Very soon."

* * *

In the shadows formed by a low-hanging tree growing in the center of the floor, several other couples huddled over drinks. Jack Adams was in a munificent mood as they sat in the cocktail lounge of one of his favorite spots, the Alray Hotel, where schmaltzy ersatz violin music emanated from behind potted palms, and people hid in dark corners, and out-of-town customers threw coins into the rippling fountain that trickled down a rock garden into a fieldstone well, or crossed the medieval moat that stretched from the bar to the entrance to the toilets.

Carrie's mind felt relaxed after one cocktail, but her stomach and limbs were in a state of agitation and nerves, still suffering from the day's appointments; trudging from one interview to the next had exhausted her, yet her body would not give up its tension.

"Pretty soon I hope we can go skiing together," Jack was saying.

She looked at Jack, at his bland, lackluster face, seeming so out of place with the whole of life. She wondered underneath the armoring and stiffness what kind of person there might be.

They rode in silence to her apartment. Standing side by side in the elevator, there was an uneasiness between them. The time spent with Jack had been neither pleasant nor unpleasant. It was almost as though someone other than herself had experienced it. If only there was something tangible she could grasp at, some experience, something. She knew she and Jack had never communicated and never would. Never in a million years could she feel close to him. How could she have considered him husband material? The whole thing had been a terrible idea. Her entire being rebelled.

Yet something made her reluctant to say good night. They reached her door, and Jack said, "How about a cup of coffee?"

"I have to be in early tonight—"

"I understand perfectly. A beautiful girl in the modeling business has to get her beauty sleep."

"Especially when she has a nine A.M. go-see."

"I'll only stay twenty minutes. You'll still get to bed early."

Meeting his gaze, she was filled with a sense of futility. His eyes, dishwater gray and expressionless, seemed to blend in with the beige cast to his unformed face and the sandy unparted short hair which she imagined never needed combing. In his hand he held a gray fedora which he had told her his firm had requested he wear in order to look older and more dignified. Across the hall a baby was wailing, the only sound in an otherwise unpunctuated atmosphere. The cries stabbed into her as she turned the key in the lock.

"It's only Nescafé," she apologized, handing him a cup from a tray on which she had also placed cream and sugar.

He eyed the TV. "Let's see if we can get some news," he suggested.

Flipping the dials, she settled for a somber-faced newscaster informing of the latest developments of crises in Europe, the Middle East, the Orient, Africa and South America, commenting on a turn of events in Vietnam, then offering an analysis of the national scene: on Capitol Hill, one coalition was blocking another coalition's attempt to put through a bill, the President was preparing to receive a visiting head of state, and the First Lady was recovering from virus. Also on the national scene, race riots were being put under control in the South and a Senator from the West had died after a long career in the nation's service.

Jack wasn't really watching the set, she knew. Nor was he concerned with his coffee. She heard his breath close to her ear. And then his hands were moving across her back, finding the skin under her sweater. If she could only avoid the individuality of his presence, be free of demands, make him anonymous, anyone, an imaginary lover, not Jack Adams, dullard, who could not possibly understand her or feel with her. There had been no one in so long. If only she could blank her mind and not know that the man who was now unhooking her brassiere was someone for whom she had no feeling whatsoever. His breathing came in short gasps in her ear. His forehead was sweaty, the palms of his hands moist.

She tried all the harder to depersonalize him; and then her fingers were reaching at his back, gripping him under his jacket, tearing his shirt from under his belt, and grasping at his bare skin. At the same time his hands moved across her breasts. The flaccid passivity of his touch made her want to scream out a plea to meet her and give her in strength and power the reassurance of human contact. As she opened herself she thought, I'm defenseless, here I am, here I am, Jack, a mass of flesh and bones, nerves and tissues and blood, brain and heart, soul if you want it, make of me what you will. I exist only in what you will have of me and give to me and receive of me. There is nothing more than this, and it's all here for you now, willing and wanting and needing if you will only show me that you are able to welcome and accept.

But Jack remained soft, passionless and clinical, experiencing the movements which ensued as though he were trying to prove something to a crowd of spectators more than to fuse and discover what another human being could give. God, she thought, God, can't you see how soft and permeable I am, like a hunk of hot wax that can spread all over; how can you be content with so little, when I am aching to have so much more, to give all of me, the whole core of me? She couldn't be filled with his soft nothingness; no, what she needed was more, more, everything, the sky, explosion into nothingness, into all time, into a never-ending eternal orgasm riding on forever to the ends of the universe, to the foundations of it— a never-ending orgasm, ecstasy till the end of time, forever and ever, amen. Jack, Jack, oh, God, how could he be so *apart?*

Afterwards she had no desire to speak.

He lit a Montclair and said, "We missed the first act of the late movie," grinned and took a deep drag.

She rose, collected the cups in silence, and plopped them in the sink with a crash. When she returned to the living room Jack had redonned his jacket and was standing in front of the mirror adjusting his tie. His hair, as she had figured, never needed combing. Reaching out for her, he held her at arm's length. Looking into his eyes, she was amazed at their lack of depth. She strained to find some recognition in them of the intimacy that had been between them, but there was no message to be found. Carrie knew he could call ten times a day for the rest of her life and she would never see him again.

* * *

After lunching together at La Chamade, Dolores and Fiona spent the afternoon shopping, gallery hopping, enjoying each other's company. Now, as they sat close to each other in the library at Dolores', the current was electric between them.

"I know," Fiona exclaimed, reaching into her purse with childlike delight, "you and I are going to share a joint!" She giggled at her double-entendre and handed Dolores the cigarette to light. Seconds later, they had both settled into comfort and euphoria. Fiona allowed the silence engulfing them to fill meaningfully. At length she said, "You're so lovely, Dolores. And so strange. You are a very, very strange woman."

"Yes."

"Strange, like me." Fiona stretched out, red-stocking-encased toes curling and uncurling, warming her feet by the fire in front of them. She stared deep into the crackling flames. "Prometheus brought fire from heaven. How can we bring fire back to heaven, I wonder?"

"You mean, get back up there, wherever it is, if it is? Is that what you mean?"

"In a way. I suppose it is an unusual idea." She dragged again, drawing the smoke deep into her lungs and holding it there. "But I feel I can say anything at all to you and nothing sounds wrong. I told you I'm a natural philosopher. That's what I get for being born a Sagittarius." She took a sniff of brandy. "Carlos Primero. Your taste is impeccable."

"Would you like another?" Dolores rose.

"No. Come back, luv. I want to rest with you. To be close, to share. You can give me nothing, really, and yet you can give me everything, do you know that? We can be all this to each other." Leaning back on the satin pillows, she regarded Dolores in her oddly compelling, magnetic, drawing-in manner. "Is it desire I feel for you?" she said. "What is it precisely? I've asked myself this these past three days since our first meeting. Is it love? Admiration? A kindred feeling? Yes, it is all these, and a recognition, too, a recognition of myself in you, this I know. Yet this recognition of myself in you goes beyond narcissism. This harmony, what is it, Dolores, my darling, do I see the defenseless in me? The unarmored? The naked? The vulnerable? I feel desire as I have never known it before. I believe it's because I've never encountered such unsullied beauty before, and that I need to worship the divinity of your essence."

Dolores took a final inhalation on the number. Its tip was burning her fingers but she scarcely felt it. Her mind and body seemed two separate entities, disunited. She said, "I feel very relaxed—with you."

"Ah, that's good, luv. Let's blow another number, shall we?" Fiona reached once more into her bag. "This is the only kind of joint a girl really needs," she said, and laughed wickedly as she passed the lighted grass to Dolores.

There seemed no rush, no urgency, only the natural need to absorb and distill, to float, to slip into another dimension.

Staring into the heart of the fire, Fiona said, "It's all in fragments; creation is all in fragments scattered all over the entire universe. We're all pieces and we meet pieces. We assemble; we lose some pieces and find others; there are always some pieces coming together and others being lost, all different combinations resulting. The universe is changing and expanding forever and ever, did you know that, Dolores?"

"I guess that's right."

"I often wonder, where is the original combination, the original pieces that started out belonging to each other? And how did the world ever get so sidetracked? But then, seeing you, Dolores, there is the sense of finding a portion of the original—"

Closing her eyes briefly, Dolores saw weird color patterns before her vision.

Fiona continued, "It's more than you think. This is beyond desire, beyond sex, and yet it encompasses all that, because it must. It's that you're pure, Dolores, you're lovely and you are *all*. It's for this reason I want so to embrace you, to kiss you, to show you—devoid of sex, and yet being All-Sex, because the physical is the only means at our disposal to express and crystallize, to consummate and give concrete expression to those powerful feelings which lie within us. We're all prisoners of our bodies, but once in a great while, the bridge becomes possible, we are given the key to transcendence in the form of another. We can go beyond the physical, you and I together, my lovely Dolores, because your spiritual reality is so great and—I love you—I love you as a very dear sister. Tell me, have you ever loved a woman before?"

"No." Dolores opened her eyes once more to the transfixing power Fiona held. What was it Fiona had which rendered her so yielding, so eager? Or was it the marijuana? She couldn't tell any more. But there had been that compelling enigma in Fiona from the start—and yes, yes, she was attracted to Fiona, sexually, yes, she would like to—

"My polar opposite. Tell me, Dolores, do you cry often?"

"No."

"Nor I either. Tears left me years ago; love left me then too. And now—and now I'm like you. Hard and soft both. And ever so much in need of dissolution before the final one—the unavoidable one."

"What do you mean?"

"Death. Yes. At bottom with you there is that same dread. But we can help one another. We both have that need to dissolve utterly before the inevitable claims us. I told you I knew all about you, didn't I? I know the deep crying need in you has never been met by a man. I would know that about you even if you'd never confessed it to me."

"How would you know?"

"I told you I'm psychic. The terror in your eyes told me volumes. I found that terror lovable. I identified with it and wanted to console you, to give you hope, to hold your hand and feel the touch of understanding in our fingers and our nerves. Because I understand your terror and I can help you find release. Only a woman can fully sense another woman's needs. I know all about you sexually, without your saying anything. I know the exact rhythm and spacing of intervals, of sighs, of movements, of licks, of caresses, of sucking in and breathing out, of all the subtleties you need for your delicately constructed, infinitely complex being." Fiona's voice seemed to emerge out of another long-forgotten age. "I want to go down on you, Dolores, to taste you, to know the perfume and musk of your body, while fingering and playing upon your fine, tightly strung instrument. The kind of finger fucking and cunnilingus I do, you'll never be satisfied with anything else. How about it?"

They exchanged a long look. Drinking in Fiona's heady fragrance, her ineffable mysterious odor, the power of her being, seeing that faint curved smile play upon her lips, Dolores was filled with expectation. Only now, with Fiona here beside her, had she become aware that for a lifetime she had been operating with a false energy, an energy she had known how to harness and which worked for her to a degree, but which nevertheless was not the true energy of her being. Only now did her real essence become clear to her. It was impossible to remove her eyes from Fiona, so deep were the chords that were struck, so long had they been silent. Reaching her now, it was as though fire and wind had touched her for the first time. She was hungry for wine, knowing all else had been water. Nothing existed but Fiona and the marvel of her being.

Dolores heard her own voice sounding unfamiliar and distant, yet filled with eagerness. "I—want you too," she said, her voice trailing. "God—God I'm high. I am absolutely stoned."

"That's good. Now. Now, luv."

Then came the surprise and pleasure of Fiona's magnificent body warming hers, the thrill of their breasts rubbing, the intensity of their breath, arms encircling one another, hands beginning slow caresses of exploration, drawing out and drawing in. Devoid of any feelings she had with men, brimming with emotion of a quality heretofore unknown, Dolores wanted to feel with her hands, her body, her eyes, oh, she thought, let me devour and be devoured, consumed as never before, in voluptuousness, in quiet, in furor, in lassitude, in longing.

"Oh, yes, darling, touch me there!" Fiona cried. "Hold me, let me show you how. Yes, yes, darling, yes, like that." Her whispers came, thrilling Dolores to the marrow. She thought, let me unleash and explode with you, let me pour myself into you.

And she felt herself letting go, sinking, sucking in Fiona's strength, taking it all in and letting it all out, as they sought each other and felt the gentle suppleness of smooth and incredibly silken flesh. Each kiss, each sigh, each caress became an infinitude of fullness of subtlest and most rarefied nuances.

Her body trembled for several minutes in a continuous spasm of orgasms that transcended anything she had ever experienced and left her limp and spent. Now she understood. How different than with men. That fight, that sense of combat, all the artifice and deceit missing, and instead here was the presence of a deep, profound, floating harmony.

"I am the darkness and you are the light," Fiona said, not stirring. "And now, my love, my ex-virgin, what could we possibly wish for in excess of what we have just had but the full extinction of the present moment, which would seem both a dissolution and an absolution—and more—yes, a redemption, a lifting to higher planes. Did you enjoy your first lesbian experience?"

"It was sensational."

Fiona chuckled. "That's only a small taste of what we can have together. The fun's only just beginning."

"Man, that was wild." Dolores' head was still spinning, whether from the grass or too many climaxes, she didn't know.

"We fully understand each other now," Fiona said. "I am your spirit, you are mine. Truth is one. We know truth is each other. It's like a portion of *ylem*, as Aristotle calls it, a part of the original mass has flown to its counterpart, and that's what we've discovered in each other. All the garbage is gone, and we're clothed only in *ylem* now, existing only for each other."

Gradually her head settled. It was as if she had been building a lifetime toward this dizzy moment, this—what was the word Fiona had used when they had walked that first evening in the misty November night—epiphany! Yes. This moment of belonging to a whole other order of things, where again as Fiona had described, like a reverse Prometheus, the fire was brought back to heaven. That was how it had seemed. It was a perversity made possible by the ambivalence of their two highly complicated natures, made actual by their absolute corruption and utter beauty. There had always been something missing and she had never understood what. Now at last she knew what her life had been crying out for all this time.

Chapter 20

"Here's another thousand," Charlene said, handing Carrie her latest set of residuals. "Krinkle Dip Chips, Scotties, Nervine. Spend it wisely now."

"I could try. But Christmas is coming."

"Tell me about it. Rex has been on the Coast ten days now and I'm going crazy without him. He won't be back till just before the holidays, which leaves me in one helluva predicament. I want to fire that Martita and close the print section for good. We don't bill that much in print anyway; the agency has never been high fashion; the money's always been in commercials. Hey, don't you have an appointment this afternoon?"

"Yes, late. Five-thirty. When are you going to fire Martita?"

"Problems, problems, problems," Charlene sighed. "That witch is an abomination, only Rex doesn't know it. He adores her. I have to wait till he gets back and tell him it's either Martita or me, it's come to that."

She threw a couple of dog biscuits to Warren and Kurt, and then extracted her Jack Daniels, poured a shot into a paper cup and took a gulp.

Carrie said, "It won't be long now, Charlene, and my book will be ready for the publishers. In the meantime I sure hope my Dove and Lipton's Tea take off. Oh, if I could just get ahead financially and be able to leave this business."

To her surprise, Charlene agreed. "You're right, Carrie. You were never cut out for the business. You don't belong here. You don't want to make my mistake." Her voice was hushed. "I threw my whole life away for a dream."

Watching Charlene's eyes resting on her framed photographs on the wall, Carrie thought, how sad for a person to carry their dead corpses around with them like this.

"At first it all seems exciting, but it wears thin. The whole trouble is you can never give up, because you keep expecting the answer is here in this business, that this is where it's at, it will all happen the way your dreams want it to." Charlene's chest heaved. "Then one day you realize you've sold yourself down the river, and you know how bankrupt your life really is."

The years etched on Charlene's face spoke louder than any of the words she was uttering. She had become so bloated, Carrie reflected, that it was now nearly impossible to find any features she had in common with the young beauty of the photos on the walls.

"My marriages were a farce. To silly empty men." She stared at the paper cup. "Champagne bubble, my life was a champagne bubble. My whole life—" Her words trailed as she took another swill of bourbon. "This business is a trap. You can never get out of it, your ego won't let you. If nothing materializes that ego suffers and you have to stick around and try to prove something. It's those few moments of glory and near-glory that drive us on; our environment is what makes us keep going. For what?"

Carrie felt uncomfortable and unable to cope, unsure of what to say to Charlene.

"I wanted to be the Eternal Goddess. I saw myself basking in the glory of compliments and envy and admiration—" Charlene's eyes were glazed over with tears. "You're right, Carrie. Get out before it's too late. You don't want to ruin your chances to be something more. You can be something in life, Carrie, I mean really have something that counts. This emptiness doesn't mean shit. I'm all for your writing or traveling or doing anything you damn well want to do, anything you really believe in and care about. Don't stick around the business and let it break your heart. The older you get the quicker the years pass; nothing happens, then all of a sudden you're old and you're nowhere. You can't keep up the rat race, you can't perpetuate yourself forever. Beauty changes, and besides, what does it mean to base your whole life on the way you look? You should have seen me at your age."

Carrie nodded and followed Charlene's gaze up to the photos once more, wishing she knew how to console Charlene.

"You want something solid, and to find it you have to pave the way, you have to live life in such a way that you'll attract it to you. Live like I did, and you'll end up like me. You don't want that, Carrie, let me tell you, you don't want that. Part of it is finding a man, but that doesn't guarantee happiness. Men, money, that's not it. The whole point is your core. Finding what's your real thing. That's what the *question* is," Charlene frowned, her eyes closed. "What's the *answer?*"

She returned to her bourbon, and Carrie thought that every time Charlene drank this way it was as though a point of contact between them were severed, Charlene becoming involved in her own interior world, communicating only with herself; no matter even if the conversation concerned advice, the center of the universe was still Charlene's own clouded mind. Whenever Charlene drank, it took her away from others.

Carrie asked, "What time is it?"

"Oh, honey, you'd better go now. You have that appointment. You'll be late."

"I hate to leave you like this, Charlene."

Charlene grumbled, "Oh, run along, I'm fine."

* * *

Kurt, stretched out on the floor, was whimpering softly, his legs moving involuntarily in a dream, as though he were trying to escape. Warren moved his cold snout on Charlene's lap, "Good fella." Charlene scratched behind his ears. She looked out the window at the streets. The city was a symbol of life going by at a clip, too fast, too fast.

Though Carrie had just left, it already seemed she'd been gone hours. How often time had that strange illusive quality of drifting into itself. Carrie. Why was she thinking of Carrie? Oh, yes, because Carrie was young and beautiful as she herself had once been. All of us are the same, Charlene thought. The years may pass but the beautiful girls falling into the trap are all the same, all the fresh-faced beauties piling into Manhattan every year, each one thinking she's different—all the same.

It was getting late. She hated slaving over the books till all hours in winter. Getting home was always a drag, being hit by all that coldness and wind and snow, the dogs keyed up and dawdling at every vertical along the way. She took another slug of the warming golden liquid, in order to set herself for the walk home; it tasted good and felt good, just what she needed.

She gulped some more Jack Daniels. God, her liver was shot. The Demerol she'd been taking lately to ease the pain helped, though; after a Demerol or two it was as if the organ didn't exist at all and she could forget the pain altogether, forget the ravages time had wrought to her body.

The silence was eerie. Suddenly Charlene thought, who am I? What have I done? Who is the real Charlene Davy? And the answer, so simple, through the clouded mist of alcohol came. The real Charlene Davy is the professional. Why have I been that way, Charlene wondered, giving advice trying to justify myself all the time? Life has been so long.

But the past was over and done with. Why did she always regret the past?

Well, the books were balanced. She could even do that half-crocked. The agency had billed $120,000 in November; it had been a damned good month. She shifted a pile of papers on the desk and came across her horoscope. She had forgotten to see what it said for the day and glanced at it now: "Beware of accidents." Pooh, she exclaimed under her breath.

She rose, donned her new purple coat with the fox collar, and her Russian cossack hat. Combined with her high black boots, the look was fetching. Taking the dogs' leashes from the hook on the wall, she called, "Come on, fellas," and was sick at hearing how hollow her own voice sounded in the stillness of the office.

Warren and Kurt were already standing, one step ahead of their mistress, as they always were. Poor dumb creatures, such sturdy, rugged, plucky animals they were. The three of them strode out of the office, leaving it dark behind them, Charlene reeling slightly on the way to the elevator while carrying on a running dialog with the dogs. She was telling them about the nice ten-block walk they were going to have home in all the snow when she thought she heard the lift move into place.

Yes, Charlene reflected again, it was the booze that had kept her on top all these years. She opened the elevator door to step in, the two dogs obediently remaining seated on their

383

haunches, as they had been trained to do, waiting for their mistress to command them to enter. She never did.

After the piercing shriek which chillingly vibrated from strident loudness into eerie moribund nothingness, punctuated with a final thud on the concrete eight floors below, the two salukis were never to hear the voice of their beloved mistress again.

Chapter 21

Everybody was horrified by Charlene's tragic death. Rex had rushed back from the Coast, made the funeral arrangements, and, though not much of an animal lover, had taken the dogs himself, feeling he owed it to Charlene. Martita Strong took over some of the extra duties, though everyone agreed no one could replace Charlene. Within a week Martita had taken down Charlene's rogues' gallery and had the agency change its name to Ryan-Strong.

Warren and Kurt still came to the office every day, looking forlorn and lost. They refused to stay in Rex's office but insisted on lying on the floor by Martita's feet as they had done with Charlene, ears pricking up at every footstep and sound, as though they expected their dead mistress to be restored to them.

"Goddamn mutts," Martita complained constantly, angry at having them underfoot.

"I'm sorry, luv," Rex apologized, "but they just sort of *gravitate* there—you know, out of force of habit. I don't know what to do."

Finally Martita laid down the law to Rex: "It's either me or them, and if I go, you lose the best business partner you ever had. Charlene was a nice lady, but I've got her beat in spades as a businesswoman. So make up your mind, Rex." Her eyes narrowed. "You know what losing me would mean."

Rex knew all right. He did not like the solution Martita

proposed, but knew if he were to displease her all would be lost. Very soon now he would be worth half a million dollars, and later even more. No, he could not risk engendering Martita's displeasure or anger.

Rex did what he had to do. He phoned his current love, Rod Pruitt, a handsome young male model, and asked him to come down to the agency and pick up the dogs. Then he phoned the vet and made arrangements to have the animals chloroformed.

Warren and Kurt, your lives are up, Rex thought, looking at the animals lying peacefully asleep, oblivious to the fate that awaited them. When Rod arrived, Rex helped put the dogs' leashes on.

"It's all been arranged," Rex said. "All you have to do is leave the two of them there. That's all."

"What about their leashes and collars?" Rod asked.

"What about them?" Rex asked impatiently.

Warren and Kurt stood by excitedly, aware only they would be going outdoors, which they always looked forward to.

"Well, I mean, do you want to keep the collars and leashes?"

"What the hell for?" Rex snapped.

"I—I dunno," Rod said lamely. "I thought—for a keepsake, or something."

"Hell, they're not *my* dogs," Rex grumbled.

The last glimpse Rex had of the two salukis, their tongues were hanging out, their hindquarters swaying, their tails wagging. He looked away. Then he heard the elevator door close, and that was that.

* * *

"Honey?"

Eve lay on her side of the bed expectantly while Bruce, bathed in light beams from the reading lamp, sat up with a frown on his face buried in the *Morning Telegraph*.

"Ummm." He did not look up.

"Are you still figuring, honey?"

"Mmmm. That Dromedary's a great mudder. On the other hand, Holy Terror just might connect with his closing punch.

Besides which, he's overdue for a win. His drills look awful good."

Horses, horses, horses! That was all Bruce Forman ever thought about or talked about or even dreamed about. Nostalgically, Eve remembered how romantic he had once been, when they had begun going together before the racing season. If she had imagined Bruce to be eternally gallant and quixotic, she had had a rude awakening. Romance was merely Bruce's winter game. Now that the tracks had opened it was a different story. No longer did Bruce gaze in her eyes; instead he now peered at endless columns of figures in the *Telegraph, Turf*, the *Racing Form, Herman's Handicaps, Bob's Touts, Tommy's Tip Sheet*, the *Yellow Card*, the *Green Sheet*, and various other publications of the equine world. And instead of using words of tenderness and love, he now spoke only of parlays, favorites, standouts, longshots, doubles, odds, scratch sheets, starting prices, morning lines, dead heats, win spots, and photo finishes.

"Might as well bet the favorite in the fifth," Bruce said. "I'm not sure about the sixth, though. It's a six-furlong claiming race for three-year-old geldings. Penny Ante can handle the route. He's been getting closer and closer every trip, and he only missed by a nose in a similar spot at Hialeah. He just might collect."

"Honey, look at this cute dress in the paper tonight. They have it at Bendel's."

"Go and charge it to me. You know I told you to charge whatever you want."

"I know, but I wish—"

"What?" Bruce looked up impatiently.

"I just wish I could charge it to *Mrs.* Bruce Forman instead of *Mr.*, that's all."

Irritated, Bruce said, "You know perfectly well how I feel about marriage. We've been over this scene so many times—"

"I know. I only said I *wish*. That's all. You can't blame a girl for trying."

Bruce returned to his handicapping. He said, "Night Welcome's got a lot of early speed. Set a record at Churchill Downs. On the other hand, it was a hard track. I don't know about the Hillside Distance Series."

Eve thought to herself, if only she and Bruce had some

communication. If only he would discuss the things that were on her mind. Like marriage, for instance. Every time she brought the subject up, it was the same thing. Bruce got mad, said he wasn't cut out for marriage and, his face contorted from the heavy strain of decision-making, went back to his horses and his handicapping.

"Hmm. Wonder what the clocker picks? Maybe I'll go for a longshot in the seventh. Big Star looks like he might have the speed to score. Did pretty well in the mile-and-an-eighth at Santa Anita."

"Honey? Couldn't you finish that tomorrow and make love to me?"

"Not tonight. I've got to get this done now."

"But I want you."

"I have to call my bookmaker."

Bruce picked up the phone, a direct line to his bookie, and gave instructions while Eve lay patiently, not moving a muscle. How sad Bruce so seldom felt like making love during the racing season and how unfortunate the season was not a short one, lasting from May till November. There were only Sundays she could depend on, that blissful day when all the tracks were closed, praise be to God, and they could lounge in bed all day, making love in the morning, followed by Chang serving them a lusty brunch (kippered herrings and hominy grits, favorites of Bruce's), followed by more sex until late afternoon, after which they would venture forth to a restaurant and sleepily wend their way back to Bruce's flat armed with the next day's papers containing the morning lineups at the track.

The energy Bruce exerted on his racing activities was staggering. Each morning he was jumpy and uneasy until Chang brought him his copy of the *Telegraph*. For the next half hour he would look over the entries, then call his bookie and place bets at distant tracks. At noon Chang would drive him to the flats in the company car. Eve would go along if she were not working or had no interviews that afternoon. Somehow Bruce managed to juggle all the tout sheets and make his harried last-minute decisions, glancing feverishly back and forth between the big board and the track sheet to the endless arithmetic he did on his own, using his own personal system, "based on quarter times but too complicated to explain to anyone who isn't a real railbird."

After the flats Bruce would be ready for the trotters that night. They would have dinner in the Sky Room and watch the races, between more frantic handicapping and juggling of figures, last-minute dashes to the pari-mutuel windows, and standing up to watch stretch turns, neck-and-necks, and photo finishes.

On their way out of the track he would pick up his nightly copy of *Tomorrow's Trots* and Chang would drive them back to town.

Luckily for Bruce, his business was well staffed and practically ran itself. Inasmuch as a good deal of his business activity crossed the lines into his social life, he was able to use the boxes he held at all the major tracks to advantage in entertaining clients and their wives, who never failed to be impressed with his vast storehouse of inside information on the racing world, and the help he afforded in handicapping.

It was a drag, but before her death Charlene had assured Eve it was bliss compared to most people's lives and that she ought to appreciate her good fortune. "Bruce Forman's a live one," Charlene had said. "You can't afford to lose him, no matter *what*." She wished she could pick up a phone and call Charlene right now. She missed her so much. Nothing was the same since she'd died.

Eve sighed deeply. She wondered if she oughtn't to call Andrew's nurse again and see if everything were all right. Bruce lay buried in his figures once again, totally incommunicado. She turned over and began mentally planning the next week, thinking it probably wouldn't be any different from the week before. Or the week before that. Or the week before that.

"Honey?"

"I'm busy. I've got a great parlay going."

Eve buried her head in the pillow and brushed a tear off her cheek.

* * *

The book was finished. Carrie had given the manuscript to a literary agent who would submit it for publication. In the

388

meantime, she was busy with go-sees. That day she had had interviews for Fab, Birds' Eye, RCA, and Ty-D-Bowl.

Returning home, she wondered what messages could be awaiting on the service. The same old people, she supposed, Geoffrey Gripsholm and the likes. Maybe the U.N. diplomat from Africa who gave orgies and once organized a black mass in the basement of a department store. The town was filled with the most charming men.

That night she could neither face being home alone again, nor could she bring herself to go out with any of the men who had been calling. So she walked, savoring the softness of air, wonderful in the aftermath of rain. In the ceaseless march of humanity, each individual was returning to his own private little cubicle in Manhattan or else on his way to join someone in an evening on the town. She went on, feeling a keen lack in the half-empty summer streets. So often she dreaded facing the flower stalls on Lexington, seeing lovers hand in hand, everyone rushing off together. Her own loneliness seemed heightened. She was like an outsider looking in. When would her note blend with another and create a harmonious chord?

Alone in the darkening light, she walked through the narrow enclosure of a wooden covering built on the sidewalk for pedestrian traffic. Then from the opposite direction, a shabbily dressed amputee was hobbling toward her. There was an almost startling radiance to the man, an enormous pride of self. Seeing her, he drew his body over to the side of the wall and huddled there. "Can you get by? Can you get by all right?" His courtesy caused her pain and embarrassment and shame. She met his eyes and they smiled. Alone once more, she asked herself, "Why am I whole of body and that crippled man not? Why am I young and beautiful and he not? And why did that man have to stand aside in order that I might pass?" And suddenly it struck her that she had so much to be grateful for; for wholeness and health and youth and opportunities, for a life ahead, and for the knowledge that she had been given all it took to accomplish something worthwhile and to have a meaningful life. Yet she hadn't known, hadn't suspected to how great an extent she had forgotten simple gratitude.

Later, as she recalled the crippled man's eyes, she felt

sure that someday, somehow, they would meet again in some distant land, and that she would be able to thank him for that gesture and all it revealed to her.

Chapter 22

Meetings in the city had kept Bruce from getting out to the track. The cab now zoomed across town with his head buried in the early edition of the morning papers and the results of that afternoon at Aqueduct.

"What do you know? A filly beat Darktown Dancer in the eighth! Paid a good price, too."

Eve made no comment.

"Saturday's the Greentree Futurity. We don't want to be late for that!" he said vehemently. "The purse is a hundred and fifty thousand!"

When the cab halted in front of Eve's building he leaned over and gave her a peck. "Let me know in the morning if you're going to be off in the late afternoon, and we'll head out to the Big A. I haven't really had a chance to look over the entries, but at a glance the morning line looks pretty interesting. I'm going to find out where the smart money is."

"Okay," Eve said, returning the peck. It was amazing how antiseptic their kisses had become since the horse world had come between them.

If at least Bruce would say he loved her—but he wouldn't even give that little much. As day after day passed, it seemed as if she were there just for a convenience, for someone to stand or sit by his side and be seen with him while he devoted himself to his real and only love, the track. Even going to bed with him had become like connecting up with a stranger.

It was all a thorn in her side, but she could never let him know of her disillusion. It was thanks to him she had a nice apartment and all the extras it would have been impossible to buy herself, besides which, it meant something to be seen with him, it made her important. Without Bruce, without the status of being his girl, who was she? For her birthday and for Christmas he had given her some stock in his company, the dividends from which were something she could count on for life. There was nothing she asked for he wouldn't buy her. Maybe he did it out of guilt, aware he was neglecting her real self, but she still had far more than most girls, didn't she?

Tiptoeing so as not to disturb Andrew's nanny, Eve peeked in the nursery and bent to kiss her son good night. Then she stole silently back to her own quarters.

Another day over. Another typical day in the life of Eve Paradise: up at dawn, rush from interview to interview, errands, shopping, meeting Bruce for dinner (at least she'd been spared the track today, that was one blessing!) then meeting his clients for an after-dinner drink. God, what a bore. She hated Bruce's way of life. And yet, she'd been around town long enough to know Bruce Forman was just about the best deal to be found: handsome, rich, important, clever, intelligent, charming, sexy—he knew everybody and everybody knew him. (Of course, they didn't know him like *she* did. They didn't know how impossible he was with his horses, how boring it was to have to sit with him while he conducted business, they didn't know how seldom the sexy Bruce Forman made love, didn't know how frustrated she was from the lack of love and attention.)

Her face covered with cold cream, Eve switched off the overhead light in the bedroom and lit the small bedside lamp, preparing to read herself to sleep. Enticing pictures in a travel magazine caught her eye, and as she read the articles, she wished she were visiting every spot described: how she would love to see Bull's Island, South Carolina, with its sandy trails and pine forests, its moss-bearded oaks and jungle creeper, bamboo and sand dunes, its shipwrecks and its ruined fort from pirate days! She could envision its cool pools of water lilies. And imagine visiting the lobster pounds at Campobello and Deer Island, New Brunswick, the Great Whirlpools—and oh, yes, the old gardens at Biloxi, Mississippi, too. And wild and desolate Okracoke Island, North Carolina, and the pueblo village of Taos, New Mexico. There would be seafront bars and eating crayfish bisque at Grand Isle, Louisiana; the dogwood, the camelias, and jasmine and magnolia at Fairhope, Alabama; and the casino and beaches in Bayou La Batte across Mobile Bay—

What wouldn't she give to be able to go to all those places, to see the United States, to take a car and just tour the whole country. The world was so vast, but her own life thus far had been so limited—outside of the New York area, what did she know of how the rest of the world lived? If only she could just take off, take Andrew, be free and just see everything. Not feel a prisoner, tied to a situation she hated and a way of life she hated. But how could she? It didn't matter that she had eighteen thousand dollars saved. You never knew what the future would bring, and you had to be prepared for it: there was no telling when there might be another Bruce Forman in her life; it was as Charlene had said, she needed the protection and security of a man to maintain her position.

She wished Charlene were here to talk to. If only Charlene hadn't died. Sometimes she didn't know which way to turn, for the void Charlene's death had left in her life. She had been Charlene's creature, Eve Paradise, she was the girl who'd had her whole life manufactured by Charlene. Now she was a shapeless form, not knowing how to handle her problems.

Eve turned off the light. As she lay awake staring at the ceiling, she tried to reassure herself that something would happen to change things, that something good would turn up.

Then, suddenly, an old prayer, only slightly altered, repeated itself silently in her mind. "Blessed St. Jude, patron saint of desperate causes, hear my petition and grant me my request. Help me know the path to take. Please, please hear me and help me, St. Jude."

A wave of relief passed over her. It had been a long time since she had prayed to St. Jude. Now, after so long a silence, she felt that warm glow, as a presence, inside her. Funny, how the life she'd led in the business had seemed to point out the fact that Catholicism was antiquated and narrow, that it didn't fit into contemporary life; and yet there was something true, a core that hadn't deserted her. Perhaps she could never completely return to her old ways of thinking, but her friend St. Jude, nevertheless, would always be a part of her. Thank God for that.

Yes, she was convinced, something, something *would* happen soon. St. Jude would guide her, he would show her which way to turn.

Comforted, Eve turned over on her stomach and fell asleep.

* * *

When Carrie looked through the evening papers, an item on page three caught her attention:

BUCKETSHOP DISCOVERED
IN MODEL AGENCY

Martita Strong, 42, co-director of the Ryan-Strong Agency, top New York agents for television commercials, was booked today on five counts of fraud due to complaints of numerous private investors that Miss Strong was running an illegal stock operation.

Subsequent investigation by authorities has revealed Miss Strong, who only six months ago became co-director of the Ryan-Strong Agency, had been operating without a broker's license, and that she had been running a successful bucketshop netting herself and as-yet-unnamed associates in the vicinity of two million dollars over a three-year period.

Miss Strong's partner in the model agency, Rex Ryan, claims he was unaware of Miss Strong's employing the agency as a front, or that his partner, using the agency's offices at 150 E. 54th Street, organized and presided over several evening poker and crap games. Ryan, a witness for the prosecution, will be asked to testify at Miss Strong's trial, following her indictment July 16.

Ryan, claiming he knew nothing of Miss Strong's illegal activities, has filed a suit against her, charging her with having defrauded him of over one hundred thousand dollars.

"I guess we'll have to get a new agent," Dolores said over the phone to Carrie. "Rex's license has been revoked temporarily—but I don't think he'll ever go back into the business."

"Why not?"

"I'm sure he inherited so much money when that rich old fag died, he doesn't need to work any more. I think he'll probably go off to Acapulco and buy himself lots of young boys with marvelous anuses and mouths, and just live the decadent life of all spineless voluptuaries."

Poor Rex, Carrie thought. He might be a spineless voluptuary in private, as Dolores said, but he had nonetheless always treated them in the most professional and courteous manner and had always been kind and encouraging. She hated to think of him in all that trouble.

"Well, it won't be my problem for long," Dolores said. "I'm closing my New York apartment and moving to London. That's where the action is."

"When do you leave?"

"Just as soon as I can get everything tied up and taken care of."

When Carrie's phone rang once more, it brought the voice of her literary agent. "Where've you been? I've been trying to reach you all day."

"Out. Running all over on auditions."

"You can forget about those. Your book's got a publisher. We got you a ten-thousand-dollar advance."

For several seconds Carrie was stunned speechless.

"Repeat that, will you?" she asked, finding her voice weak and trembling. "I'm not sure I heard correctly."

When she hung up, numbed, happiness spreading itself over her entire being, she had the feeling she was at a great crossroads. Then the phone rang once more.

"Carrie?"

"Yes."

"This is Peter Talbott. Remember me?"

Chapter 23

"TWA Flight 704, nonstop to London, now boarding at Gate 32," the voice blared over the loudspeaker. Dolores turned to Fiona and embraced her.

"Take care, luv," Fiona said.

"I will. Hurry on over, darling. I'll be waiting for you." She started up the ramp as Fiona waved a last goodbye.

"A foggy day in London town, had me low and had me down." The song had been going through her mind for days now. Yes, she had made a wise decision. London was tailor-made for her. New York was passé, it was minor league. Its theater was controlled by businessmen; there was no future in it. But in London, with the right kind of pull, an American could really make it big, both in acting and socially as well. The city was a mecca for everyone who mattered in the world—she would be within a short distance of Rome and Paris, she would meet all the important European film producers, and they would love her; she had the type of beauty Europeans admired. With her money and flair as a hostess, she would not be competing on the level of starlet.

How wonderful it was going to be, very soon now, with all her goals finally at the point of materialization. Could she ever want more than what was soon to be hers? A film career, a lovely house in Mayfair; rich, worldly, important friends, chic European clothes, admiration, adulation. Yes, at last the horizon was coming to her. She could feel it in her pores, the close reality of it. She would start right in entertaining, and all London would be vying for invitations to her parties. In short order she would be established as a luminary.

Fiona, Tina, and Tina's nanny would be joining her soon. In the meantime, she wouldn't want for action. By chance she'd run into an old acquaintance at the Oak Room at the Plaza, Mel Shepherd of all people. Mel was living in London now, producing his films from there. He'd given her his office number and told her to be sure to call him when she arrived. One of Mel's pictures had been up for an Oscar the past spring; he was a valuable contact and in a position to be of great help to her. From the way he looked at her, there'd been no doubt what he had in mind; in fact, if he hadn't had to catch a plane she was sure he would have invited her for drinks in his suite on the spot. But things would happen on her terms; she knew how to handle men like Mel Shepherd.

"And suddenly I saw you standing there," the words sailed through her head, "And through foggy London town the sun was shining everywhere."

Then in a roar the plane taxied down the runway, built up its soaring jet power, and lifted its mighty tonnage into the cloudless air.

* * *

"I'm so thrilled for you!" Eve exclaimed. "Carrie, I just can't believe it!"

"I almost can't either." Carrie removed her bag for the waiter to place a steaming bowl of onion soup at her place.

"Now that you've sold the book and you're well on your way toward fame and riches, I suppose you'll be leaving the country to do something glamorous like being an ex-patriot."

"No. What my plans are may surprise you, coming out of the blue like this, but I'm volunteering for the Quaker Project on Community Conflict."

"What's that?"

"A Friends' group that resolves conflicts and crises using nonviolent means."

"Sounds interesting. What kind of things do you do? I mean, I don't know anything about it. Tell me."

"Well, there are all sorts of things involved in the program; for instance, action teams that help diffuse hostile and violent situations such as riots and near-riots; there are community action projects to moderate situations, neighborhood workshops in tension areas, there are forums, seminars, civil aid programs. I guess that gives you some idea of the type of thing involved."

"It sounds very worthwhile." Watching Carrie speak, seeing the sparkle of confidence and happiness about her, against her will Eve was filled with envy. "How did you get involved in all this?"

"You remember Peter Talbott—the doctor. He's back from Vietnam. Well, seeing him again, hearing about what he'd been doing for the Friends in Quan Ngai, it made me aware of a whole world out there that could use help from people who care enough. This business has a way of making you get involved with yourself, so that it's easy to forget that. All of a sudden, seeing Peter again, I was ashamed, ashamed at the triviality of my life. I wanted to change, to do something that counts."

Eve felt strangely guilty.

"I realized one important thing, Eve—"

"Yes?"

"We have to give back to life what life has given us."

Eve nodded silently.

"How was I doing that?" Carrie asked. "It wasn't enough to write a book; that was satisfying a creative urge in myself. I wanted to give to *people* too, on a personal level. Besides which, I believe the faith I was raised with is able to do a great deal toward helping in these times, with all the trouble that's going on around us."

"And what about Peter?" Eve asked. "Is there a chance for anything there?"

"Only time will tell. He's grown more mature. I always respected him and thought highly of him. It's a consoling thought to find someone real and solid."

"You sort of light up when you talk about him."

"He's a fine person. Lord knows, everything else has been a flimsy bubble of nothing—"

"It's this business," Eve said. "It's just almost impossible to meet a decent man in the business. You're lucky you can get out. I wish I could. The business is the trap of all time."

Carrie said, "Yes, it's sad. Each year brings a new crop of girls, and the same men go after them. They play on our dreams and needs, on the needs for love and security and self-respect and fulfillment and a dignified place in life."

"I know," Eve said, thinking of Bruce.

Catching Eve staring into space with a troubled expression, Carrie said, "Where are you off to?"

Eve snapped back with a smile. "I was just thinking about how things are—you know, how the men never expect anything more of us than that we dress right and make up right and wear the right hairstyle. You're only supposed to be a ding-a-ling." Her eyes grew wistful. "It makes you wonder what it would be like to be a real woman."

"Yes," Carrie said. "It does."

At least Carrie was lucky in that she had a whole bright future ahead of her with her writing and her Quaker mission work, Eve thought. But here she was, stuck in a situation with a man who didn't want to marry her who led a boring life anyway. It was as if she were caught in a web of her own making. She told Carrie her predicament.

"You'd think I would have learned my lesson with Marty. I was glad to get out of that whole phony scene. Then I got stars in my eyes all over again. The lure of glamor and playboys and all that stuff was too much to resist. Now here I am and I hate it. Yet every time Bruce tells me he won't marry me, it kills me, it just absolutely kills me."

Her eyes had filled with tears. Embarrassed, she bit her lip and looked away. Carrie said, "But if you don't love him and you don't like the life he leads—"

"You're right, Carrie, you're absolutely right." The tears let loose then and poured down Eve's cheeks. "Sometimes I think I can change Bruce—I don't know," she sobbed. "I wish I could just do something—if only I could get away—but I'm even afraid of taking a vacation for fear of missing a job—I don't know—I guess the whole problem is I just want *something*," her voice broke, "and I don't really know if it has a name or if it even exists—" She fumbled with a Kleenex.

"Eve, just before she died, Charlene said something. She said that the thing we all want and miss finding, is the core. Oh, we find facets, but not the thing itself. It's that thing, that core, we're all seeking. And it's all involved in respect, Eve, finding it in yourself, finding it from others. It's respect for yourself as a person, not just you as a model but you as a human being."

"I just wish I could start over—or go somewhere."

"You have worked awfully hard," Carrie said. "You've certainly got a vacation coming. You're entitled to that."

"I know—but money."

"How much money do you have saved in the bank, if you don't mind my asking?"

"I've got eighteen thousand now, but—"

"How much do you feel you'd need in order to feel secure and able to start a new life?"

"I don't know. It isn't that I'm looking for any set amount."

"That's just it. The point of security never comes in this business unless you decide to make it happen," Carrie said. "You know, Charlene always symbolized our destiny to me, were we to continue as she did. And the two dogs, they were like the dogs guarding the gates to hell. Charlene always used to say once you got in this business, you never got out. There was always something just around the corner, something you *had* to stick around for. It's true. You're a prisoner of the system. When things taper off you wonder why you're not doing better so you go out and spend more money for new pictures, buy new clothes, get new composites; you take more classes, all the while rationalizing, telling yourself it's going to pay off. You keep on because you've come to think of yourself as the beautiful ornament everyone has made you into. They're to blame, sure; but so are we for accepting it. So time just passes without our even realizing it. But I think there comes a point where you make up your mind you're going to do something about the situation."

"What can a person do?" Eve asked.

"I believe each one of us has to find our own way in life. You have to be self-directed rather than being the pawn that somebody else moves around. If you have to sit there just waiting for someone else to make up their mind what they're going to do with you, I mean, if your whole life depends on *that*—"

"That's exactly the story of *my* life," Eve broke in wryly. "Everybody making decisions for me based on what was good for *them*. My parents, the church, the agency, Rex and Charlene, especially Charlene—clients, Madison Avenue people, now Bruce—"

Carrie nodded. "It can go on. You can just drift comfort-

ably in that way of life, or you can change, and become somebody who stands on her own two feet. Only *you* can decide
which way it's to be, Eve. You've got to respect yourself
enough to make the decision, and then stick to it."

*　　*　　*

Eve was still turning the conversation with Carrie over in
her mind when she entered her apartment an hour later.

The phone rang. "Honey." It was Rex. "I want to send you
somewhere."

It was the same as it had always been, now that Rex had
been cleared and had his license back again. The same as the
day before and the one before that, year in and year out.
"Ten o'clock tomorrow. Have your hair freshly washed and
look sophisticated."

She was sick of having people tell her how to look. What
was she anyway, some kind of mechanical doll? Tell it to
walk, and the legs obeyed, four miles a day. Tell it to smile,
and the face lit up automatically. Tell it to look seductive, the
lips parted, the eyes closed, the body went languid. What was
she, a machine? Whoever cared about her beyond what was
on the surface? It was disgusting. She dreaded that in a
couple of hours Bruce would be calling her when he got
in from the track. And on she would go, being a slave, a
slave to the business, a slave to Bruce Forman, doing things
his way, being his ding-a-ling.

Carrie was changing her whole way of life. If only she
could too. Help, Eve thought silently, please someone help!
What Carrie had said about the core was right. Yes, she had
facets, but it was the core that was missing. How to find that
core.

And then suddenly, out of nowhere, her entire being was
flooded with light as a picture of St. Jude came to her, filling
her with a gentleness and warmth. In her mind's ear she heard
the words: "Say the word and my soul shall be healed." In a
split second's flash of illumination Eve knew that her prayers
to St. Jude had been answered. She knew in all certainty in
that swift moment's insight that she didn't have to stick with
Bruce Forman any more than she had to go on Rex's ap-

pointment the following day. The choice was hers. I *can* change my life, she thought, I *can* change my life.

She didn't *have* to be a slave to Bruce or the business. Besides, what had she ever wanted to marry Bruce for anyway? To live at the track? What kind of a marriage would it ever have been? What could she ever have been thinking of?

All the while she had thought everything would be perfect if only Bruce would marry her. Now, in seeing the mistake it would have been, it was as if a burden had been lifted from her shoulders and all at once she realized it hadn't been Bruce Forman or the business she had been a slave to, but her own fears.

What was there to be afraid of? Eve smiled at the vanished phantoms of her own departed fears. Life would point her the way clearly, she was certain. If she traveled with faith, her direction would always be given. No extraordinary accomplishments were necessary; it was enough that she be self-directed, that she act from within and express what and who she was; that her life be shaped by what she knew to be the truth of her being. She had only to discover and come to know what she was about, to allow her personal unfoldment to happen. And the important thing was, as Carrie had said, to act from her own convictions, not from someone else's.

What were her own convictions? What would she most like to do? She thought of the travel magazine. Yes, she would love to take a trip. Well, what was holding her? She could sublet the apartment, leave town for three months or however long she wanted.

Why not?

She phoned Rex to tell him she wouldn't be able to make the appointment, then went out and bought a new car. She took a cab over to the Triple A office where she registered for membership and picked up a stack of tour books. From a phone booth she called the *Times* and placed an ad to sublet the apartment. Home once again, she discharged Andrew's nurse, then decided to start looking over her belongings to set about organizing and sorting.

On top of one of the closets she came across several boxes piled one upon the other, containing $4,000 worth of wigs, wiglets, and falls. Had she really spent all that money on hairpieces? It was no wonder her overhead was so high. One of the first things she would have to do would be to make a wise assessment of her true needs and begin living within a reasonable budget.

*   *   *

She had sorted out a few cardboard boxes of odds and ends, thrown out several pounds of fashion magazines that had accumulated, and was looking over tax receipts and bills from the desk drawer when Bruce rang the bell.

"I almost won the double today," he announced, settling down on the sofa, placing his feet on the coffee table. "It was a real frustrating day. Dropped a couple of grand."

"I'm sorry to hear that."

"By the way, remind me to look over your wardrobe and choose something for you to wear next Tuesday."

"Tuesday?"

"Yes, I hope you remember we're having dinner with some clients from out of town. I want you to wear something special. If you don't have anything that's absolutely right, we'll have to buy you something." He lit a Schimmel Pennick. "And no early appointments the next day, you can tell that faggot Rex Ryan. I want you to be out discothequing till dawn."

Eve regarded him silently.

He noticed the disorder. "I see you're doing your spring housecleaning."

"Not exactly," she replied, deciding to drop her bomb. "I'm leaving town."

"Leaving town?" Bruce's face was incredulous. "What do you mean?"

"For a while. I'm subletting the apartment for three months."

He recovered the breath that had been knocked out of him. "And where are you going, may I ask?"

"I'm not sure. I'm thinking of traveling."

Bruce waited a long moment. "May I ask why?"

"Because I want to."

"Oh. Just because you *want* to—because you get some sort of whim—"

"No, the thing is, I want to get out of the rut I've been in."

"I see. Isn't this rather sudden?"

"No. I've been thinking about it for a long time."

"You mean you'd up and leave—just like that?"

"Yes."

"Then this means nothing to you."

"What?"

"*Us.*"

"We never had any plans that I knew about."

"Oh, oh, I see. *Now* I see!" He nodded knowingly. "Well, let me tell you, if you're trying to pull this to get me to marry you, you can save yourself the trouble. I told you that marriage and I don't mix well."

"Who ever said anything about marriage?" Eve asked. "I never said a word."

"Are you ready to leave for dinner? Let's go." When Bruce stood up his legs were trembling.

*　　*　　*

"Well, I'm shocked." His hand shook as he took his wine. "I think this is pretty *sneaky* of you."

"Not at all."

"Oh, *no,* not much!"

"I only decided today, and you're the first person I've told my plans to."

"Just like that, you decide on the spur of the moment, without giving the matter any thought at all or consulting me or considering my plans, or anything."

She could see his ego was suffering, but so what? He'd dished out plenty of nonsense to her, why should she feel sorry for him? She said, "What is there to stay for?"

"Thanks a lot!" Bruce retorted. "You're very flattering."

Eve felt anger surge in her. "Just what kind of a life do you think this is for me and for my son?" she demanded. "Well, let me tell you something, Bruce Forman. It's *nowhere.* This whole situation between us has been going on for too long and it's time I changed things while there's still time."

"What about us?"

"What about us?"

"That means nothing to you?"

She shrugged, "It's been nice, while it lasted."

Exasperated, trying to control himself, he said, "I see. I see."

"Bruce, you're a nice guy, but you know, I haven't got a clue who you are, and you haven't got a clue who I am. So how can you say we have anything? You see that wall over there? I haven't had a grain of respect since I've been in this business. I've been approached like that wall. My problem is, I'm not a wall, Bruce. I'm a human being only you don't know that, and that's why I've got to get away."

"You can just write the whole thing off that way, just like that?"

"I can't see what you're driving at, Bruce, what your whole point is."

"You know perfectly well—" he stammered, his face scarlet. "You know *goddamned* well—"

"Are you trying to say you love me? Is that what you mean, Bruce?"

He wrung his hands uncomfortably. She had never seen him look more sheepish. Finally, with great difficulty wrenching it out, he said, "Maybe you're right. Maybe I do love you." He grinned guiltily at the concession he had made. "I guess I must if I don't want you to go."

"You'll get over it."

Bruce brought his fist down on the table. "You enjoy this, you get a kick out of making me miserable."

"No, I just simply don't see we have very much in common, or worth preserving."

In a voice so low and mumbled she could scarcely hear the words, he said, "Look, honey, maybe I could try. I know you don't like my being out at the track so much, so I could cut down on the amount of trips I make to the flats, and—"

"It wouldn't work."

"I've never wanted to before now—but now I see this *does* mean something to me—so I could try—I—"

"No. It would never work, Bruce." Hearing the words coming from her own mouth, Eve was surprised at her conviction and at the sincerity and quiet dignity with which she spoke. "You're not the marrying kind, Bruce," she said, meaning every word from the deepest part of herself. "You belong to the parties and discotheques, the business and the fringes of the business, New York nightlife and being seen with pretty models—"

She knew! At last she really knew. Yes, she had found that core of herself, that essence of realness where the truth of her own being lay. In speaking spontaneously, she was discovering a person she had never dreamed existed, a person of strength and honesty and depth, one who stood on her own two feet and had faith and self-respect. No longer was she Bruce Forman's ding-a-ling, or anybody's trinket, she was a person in her own right.

In a voice which exuded a maturity that had been there all along, just waiting to be drawn upon, she said, "That's not the way I want to live. I just want to be on my own now, to be my own boss and have time to get to know myself."

Bruce was regarding her with new eyes, with a look of wonder and admiration and respect. "What—what did you have in mind doing with yourself?"

"I'm not sure. I have to have time to find out. For a couple of months I'm going to take a long overdue vacation. Maybe I'll find out then—we'll see. I'm not really sure what—how should I call it—path—I'll be taking next in life. But one thing I do know: I'll find my way."

She knew she had gone beyond Bruce Forman and the whole kind of life he represented, that there was no going back, but that ahead lay something fine and worthwhile.

*   *   *

"I'm begging you to reconsider, Eve."

He stood there on the pavement at six A.M. and there was no doubting that this was the worst, most devastating thing that had ever happened to Bruce Forman's ego.

The summer air hung moist and hot. The day would be another typical Manhattan scorcher. Eve was glad to be escaping the city before the heat of the day, even gladder there would be no more interviews and sweat-drenched dresses, aching feet and calloused toes, and gladdest of all that she was free, her own boss, answerable only to herself.

"Please." He stepped closer, leaning forward, an anxious expression on his perspiring face.

"I can't, Bruce. I'm sorry."

"Mommy! Mommy!"

Clutching his teddy bear to him, Andrew bounced excitedly in his seat.

Eve got into the car and leaned out the window. "Goodbye, Bruce," she said, "and thanks."

Bruce pulled out a handkerchief and wiped his brow. He bit his lip. "Maybe when you come back—" he said lamely.

Eve smiled and made no reply.

In the rearview mirror Manhattan's tall buildings were receding in the distance. The sky was streaked with rose and yellow and with the pale turquoise of early morning. Clouds banked over the George Washington Bridge cast reflections on the Hudson River.

Driving ahead, Eve thought about how far she had come and how much she had changed since that first time she had walked in and met Rex and Charlene. Today, this very day, how many new young hopefuls, she wondered, would be knocking on the doors of the model agencies, each girl with an unnamed dream in her heart and the oh-so-fervent desire to become somebody, each one eager for her beauty to carry her to fame and glory. What strange roads would the business take them upon? And how many would find what she had found: that the answer was not in being beautiful, but in being somebody.

Eve smiled, grateful her life had come this present route. The city lay behind her now. The odor of the Secaucus garbage dumps only a few minutes ahead would be like the scent of heaven, bringing her to the Jersey Turnpike and onward—to the unknown, the uncharted. Her heart sang, I'm free, I'm myself, and I have faith, the faith to believe in what lies ahead.

What was it Carrie said about the business—that it was a trap? A trap because you kept living and perpetuating the image others had of you, instead of becoming the person you yourself really were inside, that person who was not just a pretty façade but a whole core of realness and strength.

I'm out of the trap, Eve thought.

And now to the freedom ahead, of being herself and creating a life of value.

Enter... # THE
BEAUTY TRAP

CAST-THE-MOVIE
SWEEPSTAKES

Sponsored by POCKET & BOOKS
and AVCO EMBASSY PICTURES
AND

WIN

Your choice of a trip for two
to the "fun" cities of Hollywood
or New York worth $1,000—
or $1,000 in cash
Or one of over 500 other big prizes
Please turn for Prize List, Rules
and Entry Blank

Soon Joseph E. Levine
will present
the motion picture
production of

THE
BEAUTY TRAP

an AVCO EMBASSY FILM

Which stars would you pick
to play the leading roles in
this movie?

★ Notice the list of prizes

★ Read the rules

★ And enter today

★ No purchase required

HERE ARE
THE FABULOUS PRIZES
YOU CAN WIN:

1 GRAND PRIZE

Visit the city of the "Beautiful People"—
your choice of
New York or Hollywood, California—
trip for two
or $1,000 in cash

2 SECOND PRIZES

Contoured mink suit stoles

25 THIRD PRIZES

Sunbeam hair dryers
with beautifying mist

500 FOURTH PRIZES

Balenciaga perfume
presentation sets

THE BEAUTY TRAP

CAST-THE MOVIE SWEEPSTAKES

Here is my choice of film star for each of the following characters from THE BEAUTY TRAP:

DOLORES HAYNES (model)—hardheaded, beautiful and ambitious. **CARRIE RICHARDS** (model)—searching for love and self-realization. **EVE PARADISE** (model)—a young innocent, but not for long. **CHARLENE DAVY**—a beauty in her day, now head of the modeling agency. **REX RYAN**—Charlene's homosexual business partner. **GEOFFRY GRIPSHOLM**—pseudo-intellectual millionaire playboy.

DOLORES HAYNES ....

CARRIE RICHARDS ....

EVE PARADISE ....

CHARLENE DAVY ....

REX RYAN ....

GEOFFRY GRIPSHOLM ....

My name ....

Address ....

City...State.........................Zip Code.................

Mail to:
THE BEAUTY TRAP, P.O. Box 765, Rosemount, Minnesota 55068